The Lights of Cimarrón

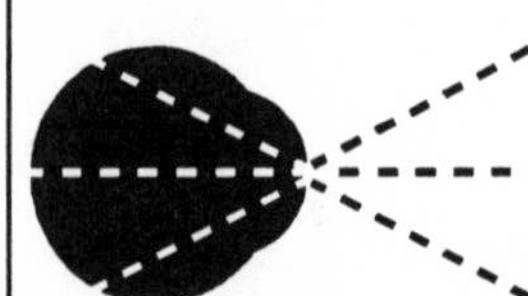

This Large Print Book carries the
Seal of Approval of N.A.V.H.

The Lights of Cimarrón

Jim Jones

WHEELER PUBLISHING
A part of Gale, a Cengage Company

Wheeler Publishing, a part of Gale, a Cengage Company.

Wheeler Publishing Large Print Western.
The text of this Large Print edition is unabridged.
Other aspects of the book may vary from the original edition.
Set in 16 pt. Plantin.

**LIBRARY OF CONGRESS CIP DATA ON FILE.
CATALOGUING IN PUBLICATION FOR THIS BOOK
IS AVAILABLE FROM THE LIBRARY OF CONGRESS**

ISBN-13: 978-1-4328-5121-7 (softcover alk. paper)

Published in 2019 by arrangement with Cherry Weiner Literary Agency

Printed in the United States of America
1 2 3 4 5 6 7 23 22 21 20 19

The Lights of Cimarrón

Chapter 1

The door to the sheriff's office flew open. I dang near jumped out of my boots, spilling my morning coffee all over my desk. Eva Armstrong, the wife of rancher Donald Armstrong, burst in sobbing uncontrollably. She clutched her eight-year-old daughter to her side as if the hounds of hell were hot on their trail. She was half out of her head with grief and it took me a while to get her in a chair and calm her down enough to tell me what had happened. Once she could talk, she painted a mighty grim picture.

"It was awful, Sheriff," she said, taking a deep breath. "Right before dawn, Donald stirred which woke me up. He said he'd heard some commotion out by the stables."

"What kind of commotion, Mrs. Armstrong?"

"The horses were making a ruckus, whinnying and kicking the stalls," she said. "I heard it myself once I got the cobwebs out of my brain. I heard men yelling and cussing, too."

Not the kind of noises I like to wake up to. I asked, "What happened then?"

"My husband pulled on his trousers and grabbed his rifle," she said. "He told me to take the children and hide in the barn. I tried to wake up Darcy," she said, pulling her daughter even closer to her side, "but it took a moment. She's a heavy sleeper."

I smiled at the little girl. She looked down. "Yes, ma'am. Then what?"

"Well, I finally got her moving but when I turned to tell my son, Jimmy, to come on along, I saw him run out the door after his daddy. He was carrying his .22 rifle." She shook her head. "It wasn't much good for anything but shooting squirrels."

As she told me of her son charging out into the face of danger with his little peashooter to come to the aid of his father, the woman was once again overcome with grief. I mustered as much patience as I could as I waited for her to regain her composure. I'm not much for people crying but I figured after what had happened, she'd earned the right to do a bit of it. She pulled herself together and continued her bleak tale.

"Me and Darcy made it to the barn without them seeing us," she said. She must have noticed a puzzled expression on my face. "Our barn is on the other side of the house from the stables, Sheriff. That's why they didn't see us."

I nodded my understanding and she continued. "There was yelling and shooting, it was a terrible noise. I swear, I thought my heart was going to stop. I shooed Darcy up the ladder to the loft and crawled up after her." She stared at the floor like she was ashamed. "We huddled like scared field mice over in the farthest corner of the loft."

"Well, there's no dishonor in that, Mrs. Armstrong," I said, trying to be as gentle as I could. "There was men intendin' to murder you and your daughter. You had to look after her."

She shot me a defiant glare. "Do you have children, Sheriff?"

"No, ma'am, I don't."

"Then you have no idea what it's like having to choose one over the other," she said in a soft voice. "I hid trembling in the barn while those monsters killed my little boy. I'll have to live with that every day for the rest of my life."

She looked down at the floor again but not before I saw the rivulets of tears running down her face. I knew firsthand those tears represented a pain that would never be erased. She had no way of knowing I'd had a similar experience as a boy when my ma and pa and sister were killed by Indians while I was away at a neighbor's ranch. I did have some idea about the guilt she felt but it didn't seem like a good time to mention it. For once, I kept my mouth shut and waited until she was ready to resume her account of the terrible events. In a moment, she continued.

"I don't rightly know how long the shooting went on," she said. "Time sort of gets away from you in the middle of something like that."

She was durn sure right about that. "Yes, ma'am, it does."

"I must have had my eyes closed," she said. "All of a sudden, it hit me that it was quiet." She shuddered. "Then I heard boots crunching in the dirt as someone walked toward the barn where we were."

I could only imagine her dread as she listened to that ominous sound, terrified that she and her daughter were about to die. I wanted to comfort her but like I said, I'm not much good at that sort of thing. I reached out and patted her on the leg. When I did, she flinched like she'd been burned by a hot poker. Reckon I won't do that again.

"Sorry, ma'am," I said, "I feel bad for you." I felt pretty lame saying that but I didn't know what else to say.

She went on as if I hadn't spoken. "Before they came in the barn, I whispered to Darcy to be still as a stone." Again, she hugged her daughter to her side. "I heard two voices but, at first, I couldn't make out what they were saying. When they got further into the barn, I could hear their words clearly."

"Did you recognize either of the voices, Mrs. Armstrong?" I was hoping she could give me a little hint about who had done this awful deed.

"No, sir," she said, "I did not recognize them."

No help there. "What happened next?"

"One of the men said there had to be a woman around somewhere because of the rancher's boy that they'd shot," she said. As she mentioned her son, her voice caught in her throat. "I hoped maybe they would have spared him, him being a boy and all." She sighed. "I was mistaken about that."

Me and Mollie didn't have any children but we'd talked about wanting some when the time was right. I tried to imagine what it would be like to hear the news that one of your children had been murdered. I'm pretty sure if I'd been in her place, I would have come screaming down from that loft like an avenging angel. I'd have killed those evil brutes or died trying, which would have done the other child no good at all. Lucky for young Darcy, her mama has better sense than I do.

Mrs. Armstrong continued her grisly description. "The other fella sounded like he was in charge. He said he didn't know if that was true or not but, in any case, they didn't have time to worry about it. He said they'd lost one man already and they had to gather the herd so they could move them to the ranch." She paused. When she spoke again, I could hear loathing in her voice. "That first man, he didn't sound like he just wanted to find me and Darcy to tie up loose ends. He sounded . . ." Her voice trailed off for a brief time. "I don't know, he sounded like he couldn't wait to have at us; like he really wanted to kill us and would enjoy it. I don't know, Sheriff, he just sounded evil."

I'd witnessed some evil up close since I'd taken up being a lawman. I wasn't eager to see it again but it sounded to me like I wasn't going to have a choice in the matter. I tried to set aside my personal feelings and get back to gathering information that might help me catch these monsters.

When she'd mentioned the man saying

they would take the herd to "the ranch," my ears had perked up. That made it sound like these were local boys, yet I knew all the ranchers in the area. There wasn't a one that I believed to be capable of this kind of violence against a neighbor. If I was right about that, then what did they mean by "the ranch"?

I asked her, "Are you sure you didn't recognize either of the voices?"

"I already told you, Sheriff," she said, her impatience becoming obvious. "They didn't sound familiar to me at all."

"Sorry," I said. "I'm tryin' to figure out what ranch they'd be talkin' about is all."

Eva Armstrong nodded and continued. "I heard them as they mounted up and rode off but I was afraid to move for the longest time. I feared they might have left someone behind to make sure there was no one else there. After a long wait, I worked up my nerve and crawled down the ladder."

Besides being afraid that one of the outlaws had stayed behind, I reckoned Mrs. Armstrong was every bit as afraid of what she would see when she walked out of the barn. I felt a knot grow tight in my stomach as I waited for her to tell me. She paused for a moment before continuing. As I watched, it seemed like every bit of emotion she had, every spark of life, drained out of her face. Maybe that was the only way she could describe the butchery she saw in that yard.

"Jimmy was lying over by the corral staring up at the sky. They'd shot him in the chest, maybe a couple of times. Donald was stretched out in the middle of the yard. He wasn't moving." She paused for a moment to take a breath, then continued. "I figured he was dead, too."

Somehow her lack of emotion was harder for me to endure than if she'd been crying. I felt chill bumps on my arms as she continued.

"Sheriff," she said in a voice that was eerily quiet, "whoever killed him didn't simply shoot him. They came to where his body lay and stabbed him in the chest over and over." She closed her eyes for a few seconds. "That's not even human. What would possess a man to do something like that?"

I could think of no reply that would be helpful. I sure didn't have an answer for her question. I motioned for her to go on.

Once again, she closed her eyes. This time she kept them closed as she continued this gruesome tale. "I got sick then," she said. "What I'd had to eat the night before just came on out of its own accord. For a time, I feared I would lose my mind along with my supper." She opened her eyes again and looked me in the eye. "Then I remembered I still had one child left alive. I could not surrender to madness, at least not right then."

I nodded. It's amazing how folks find the strength to do things that seem dang near impossible when they don't have any other choice. "You done better than most could have with what you witnessed," I said. "What happened then?"

"I heard my daughter crying; fact is, she was wailing like a banshee. She'd seen things that no child should ever have to see. I went to her, hugged her close, and covered her eyes." She continued to look me in the eye, ignoring the tears that ran down her face. "It seems like such a trifling thing to do. Seems like there should have been more I could have done but it was all I could think of at the time. I hugged her."

"You done the best you could," I said, knowing that was little consolation. I couldn't conjure up anything else to say. "What happened next?"

"I don't have a notion of how long we stayed that way. Might have been minutes but it could have been an hour. It finally came to me that I should report this to you." She gave me a challenging look. "You're the one's got to find those men and make them pay for what they done."

"That's my job, ma'am, and that's what I aim to do," I said with more conviction than I truly felt. I didn't want to tell her I had no idea who these renegades were.

"I was walking over to hitch the mule to the buggy when I saw the one of theirs that had been killed." She smiled a bitter smile. "I was glad he was dead. It wasn't much and it doesn't change my loss . . . but I was pleased he was dead."

Chapter 2

After Mrs. Armstrong finished telling me her heartbreaking story, I hurried over to the schoolhouse to get my wife, Mollie Stallings, to take care of this distraught woman and her child. I needed to hustle out to take a look at the bloodbath the woman had described and, anyway, Mollie is a whole lot better at helping and comforting others than I am. I can shoot folks if they need it but I'm not much good at consoling them. Once I'd fetched Mollie, filled her in on what had happened, and left Mrs. Armstrong and her daughter with her, I saddled up old Rusty and headed out for the ranch.

As I rode out toward the Armstrong place, I pondered this troubling turn of events. Would these things never end? It had only been a few months since we'd had to contend with Jake Flynt, one of the most vicious killers who'd ever run amok in the

New Mexico Territory. At the time, I was deputy sheriff; now I'm Acting Sheriff Tom Stallings. Flynt robbed banks and brutally murdered a whole passel of innocent folks before we were able to bring him to justice, or more accurately, to bring justice to him. To quote legendary former lawman Nathan Averill, "In the end, administering justice is the job of the Lord. It's up to us to arrange the meeting." When Flynt refused to surrender and drew down on him, Sheriff Tomás Marés shot him down like the mad dog he was. Meeting arranged.

Remembering that violent moment didn't ease my mind at all as I contemplated what I would find at the Armstrong ranch. Truth be told, I wasn't too sure I wanted to be sheriff of Colfax County, acting or otherwise. In addition to being an awful gol-darned dangerous job, there was also the little problem of the county seat having been moved to Springer a few years back. There was a lot of pressure from folks to move the sheriff's office to the new county seat, which actually made good sense. It was only because we'd solved the Jake Flynt trouble so neatly that we had a little breathing room with that problem. Sooner or later, it was bound to come to pass. If I was a betting man, I'd bet on sooner. When the time came, my wife would not be pleased. It was going to cause a huge old tempest at my house.

With all this running through my mind, I'd worked myself into a pretty foul mood by the time I arrived at the Armstrong place. As I'd feared, the upshot of the shoot-out was dreadful. I'd witnessed death in my twenty-one years, too much of it, in fact. It's not something I've grown accustomed to; I don't expect I ever will. Still, there was something especially appalling about the murder of a child. The Armstrong's thirteen-year-old boy had likely been performing the work of a full-grown man for a couple of years now but when you get right down to it, he was still a child. No, sir, it ain't right.

I looked down at the boy and confirmed what his mama had told me. He had several bullet wounds in his chest, any one of which probably could have killed him. The pool of blood she'd mentioned had soaked into the dirt where he lay but the dark outline was still visible in the dust. I took a deep breath and used my hat to shoo away the flies that had gathered over him. It took an almost physical effort to shoo away the horror and disgust that I was feeling. This was beyond awful but I couldn't dwell on that and still do my job.

From there, I walked over to where Donald Armstrong lay. My reluctance made my feet heavy, like I was slogging through mud. I hadn't known the man well; we were what you might call friendly acquaintances. While he and his family hadn't been in the area all that long, they'd shown every sign of being decent, upstanding folks. They surely didn't deserve this fate.

I knelt down beside him to study his wounds. As his wife had mentioned, I saw a number of stab wounds in addition to a couple of bullet holes. The only way I could make sense out of what I was looking at was that whoever had fired at him hadn't made a kill shot. The logical thing to do would have been to walk over to him and shoot him again. For somebody to take out their knife and stab him repeatedly suggested they'd been in the throes of a blood lust. A fella has got to be mighty brutal to commit a heinous act like that.

I'd inquired of Mrs. Armstrong if she wanted me to bring the bodies of her husband and son back to town to be tended to by the undertaker, Bill Wallace, who also happened to be the mayor. She insisted on their being buried right there close to the house. Since I knew I would have to dig some graves once I got there, I had asked Mrs. Armstrong where they kept their shovel. I walked over to the barn and sure enough, it was right where she said it would be. I picked it up and headed back out to find a spot that seemed suitable to bury her husband and son. There was a small grove of trees about twenty yards to the south of the house that looked like it might serve as a peaceful resting place. I started walking toward it, then stopped as I remembered there was a third body to be looked at.

I suppose we'll never know whether it was Armstrong or his boy who shot the man. I don't reckon it matters a great deal, anyway. The outlaw was sprawled on his back, his hat a few feet away from his body. I saw one bullet hole right in the middle of his forehead. A good shot or a lucky one? It was anybody's guess. Not so lucky for the bandit.

I wasn't about to bury this horse thief. I couldn't take him in myself today since I hadn't thought to bring my mule, Gentry, to haul him back on and the outlaws had stolen all the horses. Reckon I could send my deputy back to get the body, if I had a deputy. Since I don't, it meant another trip out here for me. If the undertaker wasn't the mayor, too, I might be able to order him to come out and fetch the corpse. I didn't think I'd have much luck on that with Bill Wallace.

I had an odd feeling the dead man looked familiar. Something most folks don't realize is a person doesn't look the same when they're dead. I've heard it explained that the muscles go slack, which alters the appearance. I think there's more to it. There's some kind of light we all possess that shows in the eyes and around the mouth. Once that light is extinguished, the appearance changes. This hombre's light was snuffed out, that was for darned sure. I stared at his face and noticed a scar running down the right cheek. Nope, it's his left cheek, only it's on my right as I stared down at him. I'd seen that face somewhere before.

I squinted and kind of looked at him sideways. At first, I wasn't sure, then it came to me. I'd observed this man's face on a wanted poster. I'd gotten a number of the things from the sheriff down in Las Vegas last week. I know this man's picture was on one of them. I'm pretty sure his last name was Chavez; I couldn't summon up the first name right off.

The thing I did remember clear as a mountain stream was the note the sheriff included in that bundle of wanted posters saying the men were believed to be members of a gang called the White Caps. I'd heard rumors about a group of outlaws operating down around Las Vegas. Word was they were not only brazen and vicious but well-organized and efficient as well. There was scuttlebutt that their leader was a saloon owner by the name of Felipe Alvarado. Some folks swore, however, that Alvarado was an upstanding member of the community, which muddied the water quite a bit. They claimed Indians were behind all this dirty dealing. What it amounted to was that nobody knew anything for sure but everybody had an opinion. That is not an unusual state of affairs.

At the time I'd read the note, I'd thought it sounded like a sticky problem but thankfully not one I would have to unravel. Now, I wasn't so sure. If this White Caps band had decided to expand their operation north, it was looking like I might have to get my hands dirty after all. *That's all I need right when I take over as sheriff. More murder and robbery.*

CHAPTER 3

"Who's your pard from Texas?"

I gaped at Tom Figgs. "What are you talkin' about, Tom?"

"Fella's been askin' about you all over town," Tom replied. "Says he's from Texas."

"That don't narrow it down by much," I snapped. I was still pretty raw from viewing the carnage out at the Armstrong place. "There's a whole passel of folks who reside in Texas."

"Maybe so," Tom said, sounding a bit smug, "but I reckon there ain't that many that's got a bushy red beard like this fella. I think he goes by Red."

I wracked my brain trying to think of anyone I'd known in the past in Texas who had a bushy red beard and went by Red. I came up empty. It left me feeling more than a little bit nervous to have a stranger in town asking about me when I didn't have a clue as to the nature of the inquiry.

"Did he seem friendly?" I was hoping Tom possessed more information about this whole deal than he'd let on up to this point.

Tom considered the question for a moment. "You know, I wouldn't say he was friendly or unfriendly. Kind of matter of fact is all." He grinned. "It was kinda hard to get a fix on his manner, though. I couldn't see much of his face 'cause of that danged beard." A puzzled look replaced his grin. "I told you his name was Red but that don't seem right after all. It was somethin' like that, though."

I shook my head and sighed. "Well, if you come across him again before I catch up with him, would it be too much trouble for you to ask him what his business with me might be? It makes me a might uneasy to have a fella askin' about me and for me not to know if he's friend or foe."

"Sure nuff, Sheriff," Tom said with a snicker. "Next time I see him, I'll ask him if he plans on shootin' you or shakin' your hand." Figgs waited for me to roll my eyes. Once I provided the reaction he was looking for, he headed for the door. "I'll catch up with you later. I got some horses to shoe."

I shook my head in mild annoyance as Tom Figgs strolled off to his blacksmith shop. It was hard for me to stay mad at Tom for any length of time, though. He was as good a friend as a man could have and he'd stood with me and my pards on a number of occasions against some of the most ferocious outlaws the New Mexico Territory had ever seen. I realized that the brutal attack at the Armstrong ranch along with my bewilderment about who might have committed the misdeed had me on edge.

I studied the wanted poster from Las Vegas and leaned back in my chair, resting my boots on the battered old desk that was a holdover from Nathan Averill's many years in the sheriff's office. Sure enough, the dead outlaw out at the Armstrong place was named Chavez. His first name was Gabriel, as it turned out. His picture emblazoned on the poster looked a bit different from the man I'd recently seen but he carried the tell-tale scar running down his left cheek. *What is an outlaw from Las Vegas doing way up here in Colfax County?*

In my mind, I tugged at the loose threads of the puzzle that was the murder of Donald Armstrong, trying to get a handle on who might have committed this wickedness. The process was jumbled, though, as the image of the Armstrong boy kept intruding on my thoughts. Try as I might, I couldn't eradicate the picture of the young man from my mind. I kept seein' those damned flies buzzin' around his face. *That ain't right.*

Mercifully, my unsettled reverie was interrupted by the door to the office opening. Bill Wallace, village mayor, undertaker, and owner of the mercantile, walked uncertainly into the domain of the acting sheriff of Colfax County. Have I mentioned that Bill was kind of jumpy while in my presence? He was painfully aware that I didn't think all that much of him, and he was worried that I might renege on the deal he'd made with Tomás Marés before he resigned as sheriff. While I had no intention of doing that, I didn't mind letting him lose sleep about it. Kept him humble.

"You busy, Sheriff?" He asked me in such a timid voice that I almost felt sorry for him. Almost.

"Well, I am busy, Bill," I told him, taking an irritated tone. "I'm considerin' a crime that was very recently committed." He shifted from one foot to the other. I let him sweat for a minute, then I continued. "I can spare a little time, though, if you got some business that needs attendin' to. How can I help you?"

"It's not that you can help me . . ." He stopped, considering that he might have offended me. "That's not what I meant to say, Sheriff. In fact, you've helped me quite a bit and I surely appreciate it, more than I can say. I wouldn't want you to get the idea that I didn't. Only I . . ." He trailed off, uncertain as to how to proceed.

Once again, I let him stew for a moment before riding to his rescue. "It's all right, Bill. What's on your mind?"

"Well, I only thought you might want to know that a fella's been asking for you around town."

That got my attention fast. "It wouldn't be a fella sportin' a bushy beard and red hair, would it?"

"Why, yes," Wallace said. "Have you already conversed with the gentleman?"

"Naw," I said, "I got word about it from Tom Figgs." I frowned. "You wouldn't happen to know what this fella wants with me, would you?"

"I didn't think it was my business to ask," Wallace said in a cautious tone. "He wanted to know where you were. Since I didn't know him, I was reluctant to give him much information regarding your whereabouts. I trust I did the right thing." He looked at me with a hopeful expression, sort of like our silly dog, Willie, does when he wants you to pet him. I was starting to feel bad for the man.

"You did fine, Bill," I said, doing my best to convey my approval, although I chose not to pet him. "Reckon I'd rather stumble on him than the other way around since I don't know why he's lookin' for me." Wallace stood there looking uncertain. "Was there anything else, Bill?" He was starting to make me jittery.

"Uh, no, I suppose not, Sheriff." He stood there for another moment, then he said, "I guess I'll be going." He waited for another couple of seconds as if waiting to be dismissed.

"All right, Bill, thanks for tellin' me about this fella." I was starting to worry that I might have to get up and escort him out of my office . . . or worse yet, give him a pat on the head. "If you see him again, I'd be grateful if you'd come and get me right quick." I nodded at Wallace, hoping that he would consider that an indication that he could get on out of my hair. Then a thought occurred to me. "Any chance you might make a run out to the Armstrong place and pick up the body of a dead outlaw? I'm gonna need to call on your skills as an undertaker."

Wallace drew himself up and said, "Much

as I'd like to accommodate you, Sheriff, I'm afraid my duties as mayor don't allow me time to do that sort of thing. If you'll have someone bring the body to me around back of the Mercantile, though, I can certainly take care of it for you." He eyeballed me with what appeared to me to be a mercenary glint and said, "I presume the county will reimburse me for my services."

I couldn't figure Bill Wallace out. One minute he's sucking up to me and the next, he's acting haughty because he's the mayor and finds the duties of an undertaker beneath him. I'm confused. "Well, Bill, the county pays what it pays and when it pays it. They don't get in any big hurry when it comes to lettin' loose of money. I'll tender a request once you get the job done."

Wallace continued to stand there as if I might produce the money right there on the spot. That wasn't going to happen.

"I'll see you later," I said, reinforcing the notion that he should leave. Wallace took the hint and walked out of my office.

Well this sure has the makings of a wreck. I have a murder to get to the bottom of, a body to fetch, and now I have a mysterious stranger inquiring about me for reasons unknown. In the past, I might have asked what else could go wrong. But, I've learned not to ask that question. There's always something else that can go wrong.

Chapter 4

Too many loose ends, too many questions I don't have answers for. I transported that outlaw's body to Wallace and had him take some pictures of it before he went to work carving on it or whatever it is that he does. I may have to make a trip down to Las Vegas to find out more about this Chavez hombre and the White Caps gang, if there really is any such thing. Todd Little is the sheriff down in San Miguel County and you could say we're friends. I took a prisoner down to him while I was still Deputy Stallings and he had me over for a nice meal with him and his wife. I figure he'll be willing to fill me in on whatever he might know about this mess.

I'm going to have to tell Mollie that I'll be away for several nights. She's never happy about that, which I understand. She has extra chores fall on her shoulders when I'm gone and besides, I think she kind of misses me. I'd like to think that, anyway. I walked over to the schoolhouse to tell her where I was going and why.

I tried to open the door quietly so I didn't disrupt the students too much. Some of those boys will use any excuse to get out of their lessons and I don't want to provide one for them if I can help it. I also don't want to get scolded by Miss Christy. She's pretty protective of her classroom when someone intrudes. To be clear, she isn't *Miss* Christy anymore since she's married to Sheriff Averill. Old habits die hard, though, and we've all called her that forever. She doesn't seem to mind and neither does Sheriff Averill.

I was so stealthy upon my entry that no one noticed me. I enjoyed a moment observing my wife working at what has become her passion . . . teaching young folks how to read. She was working with a girl who was probably nine or ten years old. I think she was the child of the gentleman who helped Bill Wallace out at the mercantile. She's a pretty little thing with a bow in her curly hair, which her mama had obviously fixed up that morning.

As I watched Mollie tutor the young girl, encouraging her when she stumbled over words, I could swear there's a glow around her head, almost like a halo. Maybe it's a trick of the sunlight coming through the window. Or maybe it's a reflection of how much she loves her job. Who am I to say?

Mollie looked up and saw me. I was pleased to see a smile brighten her face. She whispered something to the little girl and walked toward the back of the classroom where I stood.

"Let's step outside so we don't disrupt the class," she said softly.

"I know," I said conspiratorially. "I don't want to get in trouble and have to stay after school cleaning erasers."

"Silly," she said, "you're the sheriff now. You can't get in trouble with the schoolteacher."

I shook my head and chuckled. "Maybe you don't know Miss Christy as well as you think you do. She ain't above scoldin' me, I know that for a fact."

She wiggled her eyebrows and said, "You know, you're right, Tommy Stallings. Let's steal away while we can."

We walked out the door and I shut it with care. There's a big old cottonwood tree in the schoolyard that gives off a great bunch of shade. I clasped Mollie's hand and we strolled over to the shadows where it was cooler.

"Is something wrong?" An expression of fear flickered across her face.

"Naw, nothin' bad," I said. "I wanted to let you know that I am riding down to Las Vegas for a few days. I'm tryin' to figure out who the bloody renegades are that killed Donald Armstrong and his boy. Sheriff Little down there might have some information that could help me."

Mollie's face fell when she heard that I would be gone for several days. "I hate it when you have to go away."

I was touched. I took her hand and held it to my cheek. "I miss you, too, Mollie. I miss you somethin' fierce."

With exasperation in her voice, she said, "I didn't say I'll miss you, Tommy. It's only that I have to feed the horses, muck the stalls, and milk the cow when you're gone. It doubles me workload."

Her words cut me to the quick. Here I was thinking she was all torn up about missing me and it turns out she resents the extra work when I'm gone. My face must have fallen almost to my knees. In a pitiful voice, I said, "So all I am to you is a hired hand?"

She looked intently at me for a moment and then burst out laughing. "Tommy, you are so easy to tease, it almost doesn't seem fair. Of course I'll miss you." She grabbed me and gave me a ferocious hug. Stepping back and with a wicked gleam in her eye, she said, "Of course, I'm not pleased about the extra chores, either, especially mucking the stalls. Nasty work."

I shook my head. "I reckon this is what you call your Irish sense of humor, ain't it. I'm so glad I can provide you with amusement." I wondered if she noticed the sarcasm.

Mollie maintains that the Irish love to tease almost more than anything else in the world. She uses this as justification to have fun at my expense as often as she can. I suppose it's part of her charm, although, I don't find it all that charming.

"Don't pout, Tommy," she said, her tone brusque. "You're a grown man. If one of your cowboy pards was giving you a hard time, you'd think nothing of it."

Dang it. She had me there. I can either argue with her or accept that she's right. I contemplated it for a moment, then chuckled. "All right, you got me good."

She nodded with pride. "There, it didn't hurt all that much to admit it, did it?"

"It stings a little," I said, still chuckling, "but I'll get over it."

She turned serious. "When do you suppose you'll be back?"

I calculated how far it was to Las Vegas and what I was hoping to accomplish there. "It's Monday now, reckon I'll be back late Saturday afternoon."

Her eyes misted up a bit. The Irish can change moods in a heartbeat. "I will miss you, Tommy. You know that, don't you?"

"I do now," I said as I took her in my arms. We clung tightly to each other for a moment, then I stepped away. "I'll come back as quick as I can."

Chapter 5

The sun rose over the mountains and the rays woke me from a sound sleep. Nothing like a bed of pine needles and the scent of a fresh mountain breeze to allow a fella a good night's rest. The air was crisp and cold; I had to admit I wasn't all that eager to crawl out of my bedroll. I needed to get moving, though, if I hoped to make Las Vegas by midday. The quicker I get there, the sooner I can take care of business and then turn around to head back to my Mollie.

Old Rusty was grazing nearby. I removed his hobbles and brushed him down pretty good in order to get us both loose and ready to ride. He's a good red roan horse, not flashy or all that much to look at but he'll go until you're ready to stop or he drops in his tracks. He'll give you what you need. He's a good friend. He does have an annoying habit of trying to rub me off on whatever tree we might be passing by. I'd had to give him a couple of pretty good swift kicks on the ride down when we rode into those big old pine trees in order to convince him I didn't want to play his game. Once we achieved a meeting of the minds about that, things went a lot smoother. Anyway, his good points sure outweigh his bad.

It didn't take long for the day to warm up as we trotted along. The trail headed gently downhill and the country opened up as we put the pine trees behind us. I'd sent a telegram to Sheriff Little to be expecting me around noon on Wednesday but I didn't mention what I was coming to see him about. You never know who's gonna see those telegrams before they get to the person you intend them for, and I sure don't want people's gums flapping about the troubles we're dealing with up in Colfax County. For one thing, I don't want word getting out to anyone who might be involved in this God-awful murder. I want to leave them with the impression they've gotten away clean. Also, I don't much like gossip. What happens in Colfax County isn't really pertinent to the folks in San Miguel County as far as I'm concerned.

The sun was straight up when I rode into Las Vegas. I'd been there before and knew the sheriff's office was a block off the plaza so I trotted directly to it. I loose-tied Rusty to the hitching rail, loosened his cinch a bit, and walked over to the door, knocking noisily before entering. Todd Little was leaning back in the chair behind his desk munching on a tortilla filled with beans when I walked in. When he saw me, he put all four legs of the chair on the floor. He set his tortilla on the desk, wiped his hands on his pants as he got up, and walked over to greet me with his hand outstretched.

"Howdy, Sheriff Stallings," he said with a grin. "You got promoted since the last time I laid eyes on you."

"That's a fact," I said. "I ain't real sure if that's a good thing or a bad thing but it's a fact, nonetheless."

"Take a load off," he said, pointing to one of the chairs on the other side of his desk, "and tell me what brings you down our way."

He was being so sociable that I thought I should make some small talk, maybe ask him about his wife and young'uns. Considering the urgency of the matter I was there to discuss, I decided to omit the chitchat and get right down to business.

"We had some serious trouble the other day and I have a notion it may have come up from your part of the country."

He looked at me with a quizzical expression. "What sort of trouble and why do you think it comes from down here?"

I filled him in about the murder and rustling that happened at the Armstrong place. I included the details about the brutal stabbing of Donald Armstrong even though I wasn't any happier to talk about it than he was to hear about it. He winced as I told him what I'd seen.

"That clues me in on the trouble you've had," he said, "but it doesn't tell me much about how it's connected with San Miguel County."

"I'm gettin' to that," I said. I pulled out the wanted poster he had sent me a few weeks back. Leaning forward and turning the paper around, I pointed to one of the men on the poster. "You see that fella right there?"

"Yep," he said, "that's Gabriel Chavez. What about him?"

"He was gunned down during the dustup at the Armstrong place. I expect our undertaker, Bill Wallace, laid him in the ground sometime while I was travelin' down here."

"He's a firebrand all right," he said. "I don't know why he'd be making trouble up in your part of the territory, though."

"Neither do I," I replied. "That's why I'm payin' you a visit. I need to determine more about that bunch of thugs they call the White Caps. I got a bad feelin' they may be movin' up into Colfax County."

Todd Little gave a sharp whistle. "You'd sure better hope they aren't moving into your territory. Those are some bad hombres."

"After what I witnessed at the Armstrong place, I'd have to agree with you," I said. "What can you tell me about these scalawags?"

Little shook his head and grimaced. "Well, it's strange. I can't tell you all that much. Lots of folks around here don't believe they even exist. They say it's Indians been doing the foul deeds this bunch is accused of."

I shook my head. "That don't make sense," I said. "This Gabriel Chavez wasn't runnin' with a bunch of Indians. Armstrong's wife heard the voices of two of the other men in the gang that attacked them. She's sure they were white men."

"I'm not saying I agree with them that say such things," he said. "I'm telling you what people are saying."

"People say some pretty silly stuff," I said. "Just 'cause they say it don't make it true."

"Right enough," he replied. "I don't

believe it myself. I'm inclined to think there is a bunch of outlaws that call themselves the White Caps. I even believe I know who the leader of the gang is."

"Really," I said, my curiosity piqued. "And who might that be?"

"I suspect it's the man I think you know, Felipe Alvarado, who owns the Imperial Saloon."

"And you think this saloonkeeper is also the leader of a band of outlaws?" I must have sounded skeptical because Little kind of sparked up at me.

"That's the kind of thing folks say when I bring this up," he said in a frustrated voice. "They seem to think a man couldn't own a saloon and be an outlaw at the same time. Alvarado puts on an act like he's a model citizen. He has people bamboozled, thinking he's some kind of law-abiding citizen." He sat up straight in his chair. "I don't think that's the case."

"Easy there, Sheriff," I said. "I ain't arguin' with you, I'm just tryin' to get a handle on all this."

"Sorry," he said. "I'm just perturbed by how folks pay no heed to the facts and fabricate things that make no sense. Indians," he snorted. "That's just plum silly."

"Well, maybe it is and maybe it ain't," I

said. "The truth is that if there's evil in their midst, some people would rather pretend it ain't there than look it square in the face." I exhaled fully as I shook my head. "I've seen plenty of that up in my part of the territory, I promise you."

"You could be right," Little said. "Reckon I could use a little more patience in dealing with the good citizens of San Miguel County." He took a deep breath. "When people ignore menace that's right in front of their face, it isn't safe. It's kind of like pretending that rattlesnake in the trail ahead of you isn't there. You'll be fine until you step on him, then you'll wish you'd paid closer attention."

"Hard to argue with you when you put it like that," I said. I changed the subject. I don't like rattlesnakes. "Have you heard any talk about a secret hidey-hole . . . maybe something like a ranch where Alvarado or whoever's committing these deeds keeps the stock he steals?"

Little gave me a sharp look. "Funny you should say that. That's what I've been hearing. When these outlaws strike a rancher, they take the cattle and horses somewhere, yet no one has been able to find any trace. What makes you ask that question?"

"The widow Armstrong overheard the

outlaws mention takin' the stock they were stealin' to the ranch. She didn't recognize their voices. I don't think any of the ranchers from around there did this. Makes me think they got 'em a lair someplace."

"That sounds like our boys down here," Little said. "If they're spreading their operation up your way, I feel bad for you."

I felt bad for me, too. I'd be plenty happy to leave the likes of the White Caps gang to San Miguel County where it's Sheriff Todd Little's problem instead of mine. Course, when it comes to enforcing the law, I've noticed that things often don't go in a path that makes me happy. I was starting to think I might want to entertain a job change.

"After they get the stock to this ranch hideout, how do you reckon they dispose of it? It ain't like whoever is behind this is just buildin' up a herd like you would on a ranch that was on the up-and-up."

"Yeah, that wouldn't be logical," Little replied. He frowned as he considered the question. "I'd speculate they drive the cattle up the trail to those mining camps around Trinidad. That's the closest place to sell 'em quick and those boys are always desperate for beef. They'd probably buy 'em and not ask any questions."

That rung true to me. "You know what

I'd like to do, Todd," I said. "I'd like to make a pass through that Imperial Saloon, give old Felipe Alvarado the once-over."

"All right," Little said. He hesitated. "I can accommodate you if you'd like." He studied me cautiously. "You won't say anything to get him riled up, will you?"

His question caught me off guard. After a pause, I said, "I reckon not. Why do you ask?" Before he could answer, I asked, "And why would you care?"

He couldn't meet my eye. I could tell he was a bit ashamed of himself. "I probably shouldn't have said that," he said. "Alvarado is a pretty scary fella, though. You can get him whipped up and head on back up to Cimarrón. I live here. Me and my family got to see him every day." He shook his head and seemed to collect his courage. "You know, you ask him whatever you feel the need to ask. I'll handle whatever comes after that."

I whistled. "This Alvarado sounds like one bad hombre if he's got you spooked. You're as hard a lawman as I know, Todd."

Little appeared grateful. "I do my best, Tommy." He frowned. "I'm human, though, and I do have a family to think about. And yes, I believe Felipe Alvarado is a bad hombre." He paused. "A *very* bad hombre."

I stood up and clapped him on the shoulder. "Well, let's head on over and peruse this bad hombre," I said with an enthusiasm that I didn't really feel. I figured I'd better put on a brave face since Sheriff Little seemed to have developed feet of clay.

We walked in silence up the street to the Imperial Saloon. Above the entrance, there was a painting of a saloon girl with very few clothes on stretched out on a sofa. It's got some fancy name; Mollie would know what to call it but it plum eludes me right now.

"Nice painting," I said to Sheriff Little.

"Wait'll you see the real thing inside," he answered with a grin. "I'll tell you, if I wasn't a married man, I'd fritter away a lot more time in this place."

Being a married man myself, I understood. I face the same dilemma in Cimarrón with the Colfax Tavern. Knowing Mollie's outlook on such things, I find it pretty easy to walk the straight and narrow path. I believe she mentioned something along the lines of turning me into a steer.

"After you," I said to Little, urging him forward with a wave of my hand.

We entered through the swinging doors and I spotted Alvarado immediately. He was down at the other end of the ornate mahogany bar serving customers. He wasn't a big man, maybe a couple of inches shorter than me, but there was something in the way he carried himself that conveyed without any words that he was in charge. He looked well-turned-out with a fancy vest and his dark hair slicked down, yet there was nothing about his appearance that lent him the look of a dandy. I don't know if I can even put it into words except to say that there was something commanding about the man. Some folks are like that.

Alvarado saw us walk in and waved in acknowledgment. Little waved back and we sat down at a table a few feet away from the door. When Alvarado finished serving his customers, he walked over to where we were sitting.

"Good afternoon, Sheriff," he said in an affable manner. "What brings you into my establishment this fine afternoon?"

"I'm showing my friend Sheriff Tommy Stallings around town," Little said.

Alvarado turned his attention to me and I got the opportunity to look directly into his eyes. A person can lie with their mouth but the eyes usually show the truth. My first take was that he was indeed a mighty scary gentleman. His eyes reminded me of the bird they call paisano. It catches and kills rattlesnakes, grabbing the snake's head in its beak and beating it to death by slamming it on the ground. If you've ever seen one in action, you know that while they are killing the snake, they have no expression in their eyes. They're not bothered by the danger or the violence. They're only interested in killing their prey. That was what I observed in Felipe Alvarado's eyes.

After taking a moment to size me up, Alvarado asked in what seemed to me to be a brazen tone, "What brings you to our sleepy village, Sheriff?"

I didn't like his manner. I decided to ignore Sheriff Little's request that I not stir him up. "We had a little difficulty up in Colfax County, sir. From what I gather, it sounds like the same kind of difficulty folks have been having down here lately. I thought I'd head down this way and see if the two things might be connected." I smiled. "We had to shoot an outlaw. Maybe you know him. Gabriel Chavez."

Alvarado's eyes flashed briefly, then his face assumed a disinterested expression. "Why would you think I would be acquainted with this outlaw, Sheriff?"

"Aw, some rumors I've heard," I said in as casual a tone as I could muster. "That maybe things ain't exactly what they appear to be. I came down here to turn over a few rocks, see what I might find out."

"People talk," he said with a shrug. "That doesn't mean what they say is true." A cruel smile curled up the corners of his mouth. "Turning over rocks can be dangerous," he said. "You never know exactly what you'll find."

I reckon old Felipe was trying to scare me off. What he did instead was make me mad. I have no doubt that he's a scary fella but I've seen my share of scary fellas since I entered law enforcement. If he's trying to send me a message, I figure I'd do well to send him one right back.

"It's only dangerous if you ain't ready for what you find under the rock," I said. I tried to sound as confident as I could. "If you're ready for trouble, generally you can handle it."

Alvarado's eyes narrowed. "Maybe you never ran into any real trouble, Sheriff. The kind that can't be handled easily."

In Texas, where I'm from originally, I believe they would describe this as a "pissin' contest." It was my turn. "Whatever trouble you got down here, mister saloon-keeper, I reckon we've seen as bad or worse up in Colfax County."

He glared at me for a moment and then he chuckled. "Whatever you say, Sheriff. As you pointed out, I am only a humble saloonkeeper."

I think the contest was over. I couldn't tell if I'd won or not. I thought I'd throw out one more barb. "I'll be keepin' tabs on you, mister saloonkeeper."

"Feel free to do that, Sheriff," he replied. "You're not the only one who is doing so. You can usually find me right here tending bar." His grin looked brash to me. "Where else would I be?"

As he walked away, Todd Little said in a voice dripping with sarcasm, "Glad you didn't say anything to rile him up."

I was pretty hot. "That fella ain't a bartender, I promise you that," I growled. "I don't know if he's the man behind all your troubles down here but he's got the appearance of a stone-cold killer. I know that for a fact 'cause I've had me a couple of chances to stare in the eyes of some killers." I shrugged my shoulders to get rid of some of the tightness in my neck. That happens to me when I get mad. "He's damn sure one of the breed. He was tryin' pull a bluff on me. I ain't gonna let a son of a gun like that buffalo me."

Little gave me a curious glance. "You know," he said, "I think you've changed since I last saw you. You kinda got an edge to you now that you're sheriff."

That caught me off guard. Far as I can tell, I'm still the old Tommy Stallings. Well, okay, I'm trying to be Tom Stallings. Maybe I'm making headway.

"Don't know about any edge, Todd, but I do know you got to take a man like this serious. He carries himself like a gunslinger. If he thinks you're weak, he'll run right over you."

Little nodded. "You could be right. It's nothing we could prove in a court of law, though."

"That's true," I replied. "Reckon we both better keep searchin' for evidence to hang this bloody renegade with." I paused. "And I promise you, he's bloody all right." I glanced around the saloon at the customers, who seemed to be having a fine old time. If they were aware that there was an assassin in their midst, they didn't show any signs of it. "I've seen enough, Todd," I said. "I'll walk with you back to your office and then hit the trail back to Cimarrón."

"We could sit here and gaze at the ladies a little while longer," he said with an impish grin. "How much trouble could we get in just looking?"

"Don't know about you," I said, "but I could get in a heap o' trouble. It ain't worth takin' the chance."

He nodded, a little reluctantly I thought, then stood up. "You're probably right; we'll both get in a lot less hot water if we're somewhere other than here."

As we walked toward the batwing doors, I noticed that Alvarado was studiously ignoring us. As we walked out, I got a funny, prickly feeling along my spine. When I glanced back, I saw the saloon owner staring at me with a ferocious intensity that was chilling. *Yep, he's the one.*

We walked back to the sheriff's office without talking. When we arrived at the door, I declined Little's offer to stick around and have supper with him and his family. His wife was a good cook but I was plenty keen to get back home to my Mollie. I told him I'd keep him apprised if I uncovered any new information that might help him and he agreed to do the same for me. I ambled over, tightened old Rusty's cinch, and climbed into the saddle. It's a long ride back to Cimarrón and it won't get any shorter if I wait around.

Chapter 6

As I walked toward my office, I saw Tom Figgs walking rapidly in my direction, apparently intent on intercepting me. He looked agitated. "My Lord," Tom sputtered as he followed me through the door. "I didn't think you were ever gonna make it back. What took you so goldarn long?"

I was about to make a smart remark about not knowing I needed to report to him when I noticed the desperate look in his eye. Something was bad wrong and it was no time for joshing around.

"What happened?"

He shook his head to clear it and said, "I'll tell you while we head over to the mercantile."

He started for the door and I followed him. "Why are we goin' to the mercantile? Did somethin' dreadful happen to Bill Wallace?" I was only half joking.

He waited for me to catch up and said,

"No, but somethin' awful happened to Robert Woodrum, that young man that clerks for him." I could hear the distress in his voice. "Two nights ago, he was countin' the money after he closed up. Wallace usually leaves that chore to him while he goes home early. Woodrum takes the money home with him and makes a deposit at the bank the next day."

I was trying to place Woodrum. After a minute, it came to me and hit me hard. He was the father of that little girl I'd seen Mollie working with right before I left for Las Vegas. I had a sense of dread about what Tom was getting ready to tell me.

"Did somebody rob the place?" I asked. When I glanced over at Figgs, I saw that his face was ashen. Not a good sign.

"Somebody didn't only rob the place," he said in a voice taut with strain. "They murdered Woodrum. Gutted him like a hog."

"What?" I wasn't sure I'd heard him right. "What do you mean?"

"What part of 'gutted him like a hog' did you not understand?" Figgs was clearly sickened by what happened and frustrated that I hadn't been around at the time it occurred.

"Tom," I said with as much patience as I

could gather, "tell me what happened so I'll know what to do about it. I'm sorry I wasn't here but I was taking care of business down in Las Vegas. I rode back as quick as I was able."

Figgs took a deep breath. "You're right, I'm sorry to take it out on you. This is a catastrophe and there wasn't anybody with authority here to take care of it."

Not having any deputies currently was a problem. "Did you talk with Tomás?"

Figgs made a sour face. "I tried. He wouldn't discuss it with me. Said he wasn't the sheriff, anymore. Said I'd have to wait until you got back."

During the shoot-out with Jake Flynt, Tomás's father, Miguel, was critically wounded and later died. Right after that, Tomás resigned as sheriff. Said he no longer had the stomach for the job. Sounds like he's sticking to his guns on that.

"He's right, I reckon. It ain't his job anymore." I didn't want to talk about why Tomás had walked away or why I didn't have any deputies. I wanted to get to the bottom of this robbery and murder. "So back up and tell me what you know about what happened."

"Near as I can tell, somebody entered the mercantile after dark. The sign in the door was turned around to show that it was closed but I guess Woodrum didn't think about locking it. It looks like whoever it was attacked him with a knife. There's no bullet holes in him but he's cut up somethin' awful." Figgs paused and looked like he might lose his lunch. "I wasn't kiddin' when I said he'd been gutted like a hog. Bill Wallace liked to passed out when he came in late that night and found him."

"What was Wallace doin' there late at night?"

"When Woodrum didn't come home for dinner, his wife got scared and went to Wallace's house to find out if something was wrong." Figgs made a wry face. "She told me that at first, he refused to go check on her husband. His wife whispered somethin' in his ear and whatever she said changed his mind. Anyway, he had the good sense to tell Mrs. Woodrum to wait at his house with his wife while he checked the store. At least she was spared seein' her husband in that way."

"What did Bill do after he found Woodrum?" Wallace isn't one of my favorite folks but I do feel bad about him having to deal with this. "He knew I was down in Las Vegas. Who did he tell about what happened?"

"He came to my place," Figgs said. "I told him I wasn't sheriff and there wasn't nothin' I could do about it but he insisted that I come down and take a look at what had happened." Figgs closed his eyes for a moment as if that would take away the appalling images he'd witnessed. "I went, mostly so he'd quit squawkin' at me. I ain't gonna forget what I saw for quite awhile."

"Sorry you had to see that, Tom." I feel bad for Tom Figgs. I've seen some pretty dreadful things myself and they sure stick with you. It's what I signed up for when I agreed to be sheriff. It's not Tom's responsibility.

"Me, too," he said.

I wasn't going to solve this crime by dwelling on the gruesome details. "Did anyone see anything?"

"I don't rightly know," he replied. "Nobody came forward and said they did. I didn't go around and ask questions, though. It ain't my job."

"You're right," I said. "It's my job. When we get to the mercantile, why don't you show me where Wallace found Woodrum's body and I'll take it from there." I reached out and patted him on the shoulder. "You've done way more than you were obliged to. I thank you for that."

Figgs gave me a grateful look. "Thanks Tommy. You're right, it ain't my job but there wasn't nobody else around to do it. I'll be glad to turn it over to you now, though, that's for sure."

When we walked down to the mercantile, there was a sign on the door that said it was closed. I could see Bill Wallace inside and, after knocking, we walked in. I hadn't taken two steps before he stalked over and got right in my face.

"What I want to know, Sheriff Stallings," he said, putting a hint of contempt on my name as it rolled off his tongue, "is what you are going to do about this? It could have been me who got killed."

Where did that suck-up Wallace go, the one who wants my approval? The fact that his main concern was not for the death of his employee but that he might have been the victim went all over me.

"I'm sure Mr. Woodrum's wife and young daughter appreciate your concern for his well-being." He heard the sarcasm in my voice for dang sure. "They probably understand this is all about you, anyway. Their loss ain't that important."

Wallace took a step back as if I'd slapped him. I could see him struggling with whether to be mad at me or ashamed of himself. The man can act like a complete ass at times but he has his good moments, too. I was curious about which version would present itself.

After taking a deep breath, he said, "Sheriff, I'm sorry. You're right. It did scare the pants off me, though. If you'll recall, I also have a wife and young daughter. It could have been me; then they'd have been left without support."

Not being quite ready to let him off the hook, I asked, "Speaking of bein' left without support, what are you gonna do for Mrs. Woodrum and her daughter?"

"I hadn't thought that far ahead yet, Sheriff," he replied. "My wife is over at their place trying to provide as much comfort as she can to Cynthia . . . not that there's much she can do to ease the pain."

Dang Bill Wallace, every time I decide I don't like him, he'll do something decent and I have to step back and take a second look. "Bill, I'm sorry for flashin' back at you like I did. Somethin' like this could throw anyone. You got every right to be worried and scared for yourself and your family."

Wallace nodded gratefully. "Well, I am, Sheriff, I can't help it. That doesn't mean I'm not concerned about Cynthia and little Loretta." He straightened up and said, "And

I do want to know what you're going to do about this."

I shook my head. "Bill, I'll give it my dead level best to hunt down whoever did this and bring 'em to justice. You got my word on that. I got to inspect the place for clues first thing and then talk to folks to see if anybody saw anything."

"Of course, Sheriff, I understand you have to look into this and see if there's tracks that lead to the killers."

It sure would be nice if I had some help trying to figure out who the monster was that did this. Most sheriffs have deputies. Not me. I know Tomás Marés isn't about to change his mind and come back to help me. He's knee-deep in running the café and planning his wedding to Maria, which leaves no time for tracking down outlaws even if he was inclined to do so . . . which he ain't.

"I'll do the best I can, Bill, but I'm only one man. Unless whoever committed this brutal act is a citizen of our little village, which I highly doubt, it's likely they lit out for the hills with the money."

Tom Figgs remained silent throughout this exchange. He's not overly fond of Bill Wallace, either.

"I think you're most likely right about it not bein' someone from here, Tommy," he said. "We got a few hotheads who might get in a scuffle after they've had a few drinks but this is somethin' more." He shook his head in revulsion. "I don't know what kind of beast would take a knife to a man like that. It ain't right."

When he used that word, beast, it made me stop and think. Donald Armstrong had been viciously murdered as well, with the killer using a knife to finish him off. That happened out on their ranch and this happened in town but there was some similarity to the brutality of it. It makes me wonder if the same person committed both acts.

"It ain't right, Tom," I said. "You captured the truth about that." I glanced around the store and turned to Wallace. "If you could show me right where this happened, I'd like to take a look around."

"Sure, Sheriff," Wallace said, "I can show you. I don't know what you can learn from it, though. Robert was sitting at the desk behind the counter. That's where we keep the cash bag and where we tally up the day's receipts."

I walked over behind the counter to take a look. Both Wallace and Figgs followed me. They were getting on my nerves. I know I complained about not having any help, but I don't really want folks looking over my shoulder while I'm trying to think.

"You know, boys, I think I can take it from here. I'll probably have some more questions for you later but right now you don't need to hang around. If y'all got somethin' else to do, feel free to go ahead and do it."

Wallace and Figgs looked at me and then at each other. Neither seemed inclined to move. Maybe I wasn't clear enough.

"What I'm tryin' to say in a polite way," I said in a little louder voice, "is I would like both of you to skedaddle. You're in my way. I'm tryin' to think."

"Oh," said Wallace, sounding slightly indignant.

Figgs chuckled. "I can take a hint," he said. "Let me know if you need me for anything." He walked out.

Wallace lingered for another moment as if he had more to say. "Sheriff, I'm not a stupid man. I know you don't like me and I know that's my fault. I don't claim to be perfect but I am trying to be a better man and a better citizen."

There he goes again acting decent. "I know it, Bill, and you're right. I ain't in no position to judge anybody else. I'm far from perfect myself. I'll do my best to let whatever happened in the past stay in the past. You deserve that."

I could see the gratitude on his face. "Thank you, Sheriff; that means a great deal to me." He lingered for another moment, then said, "Well, I suppose I'll leave you to do your job. Please lock the door when you leave." He had a rueful look on his face. "Not that there's any money left for anyone to steal."

After he departed, I turned back to where Robert Woodrum had been sitting when he was murdered. I tried to see in my mind's eye what had happened. He would have been intent on counting the day's receipts and might not have heard someone enter. Sometimes people have a bell on the door so they can tell when customers come in. I walked over to see if there was something like that and sure enough, there wasn't. The killer could have snuck in without Woodrum taking notice of him.

Articles had been knocked off the desk and the chair was lying on its side. Tom must have had the sense to tell Wallace not to move anything around. There was a great deal of dried blood on the floor and some on the chair as well. We all think of blood as being red but once it hits the ground and dries up, it turns a kind of brown color. I tried to envision what it had been like for Woodrum when the intruder surprised him.

Did he have time to ask him who he was or what he wanted? Did he realize the man was there to rob him? Did the worthless swine who killed him say anything or did he attack him with a knife right away? Did Woodrum have time to feel the terror that must engulf a person as they watch their lifeblood run out? If the answers were in front of me, I sure couldn't see them.

Chapter 7

I hate to admit it but I'm stumped. I'm thinking that this murder and robbery is connected to the one out at the Armstrong place because of the vicious way the two men were killed. I'd like to think both acts were committed by the same man because I'd hate to think we had two brutal killers on the loose in Colfax County. Other than the knife work, though, they aren't all that similar. Those bloody scoundrels out at Armstrong's place stole cattle and horses. Whoever did the deed at the mercantile here in town got away with cash. Most of the time outlaws tend to specialize, either rustling cattle and horses or robbing banks but not both. Looks like we might have us a jack-of-all-trades here. That's not good news.

As I walked toward my office, I saw Father Antonio Baca strolling my way. I have a great deal of respect for Father Antonio, both as a man of God as well as a political firebrand. He and Tomás Marés's fiancée, Maria, have been printing out handbills describing the grubby deeds of those yellow dog politicians in Santa Fe for a couple of years now. They've been bullied and threatened but they've never backed down. Unfortunately, most of the good citizens of the New Mexico Territory resemble sheep in their general approach to life. They're more than willing to let someone else challenge the bad guys but they don't want any part of it themselves.

"Mornin', Father," I said as he got within hailing distance. "How is your day goin'?"

We both stopped and he sighed. "Not well thus far, Tommy, but thanks for asking."

"What's goin' on?" Father Antonio is usually about as optimistic a person as you could ever hope to meet. If he's feeling discouraged, it must be something bad.

"Ay, those Santa Fe Ring *cabrónes* . . ." He looked up to the sky and crossed himself. "Sorry, Father," he said. "Those criminals in our territorial capital have once again used the courts to steal land from a poor family over near Taos. That lawyer Thomas Catron was up to his old tricks, pretending to defend the family, only to take most of their land in payment when he won the case." He shook his head with disgust. "Those poor people could not read. They had no idea that his fee would involve their surrendering their land to him."

I felt my temper rising. Those filthy crooks have gotten rich off the backs of small landowners in the Territory of New Mexico. They've stolen land that has been in families for several hundred years. It appears that being a politician confers upon an individual a license to steal.

"Don't reckon I can say out loud what I think about this, Father, since I don't want to offend, you bein' a man of God and all. I am grateful for what you and Maria are tryin' to do about it, though. I wish more folks had the gumption you two have."

"Thank you, Tommy," he said. "I do not know if our efforts are doing any good. I cannot remain silent."

"I admire your courage," I said. "I hate to rush off but I'm tryin' to catch a killer and I ain't makin' any progress standin' here."

"I understand," he said. "Thank you for your kind words."

I nodded in acknowledgment and began walking toward my office.

"Señor Tommy," he called out. "I almost forgot to ask you. Did the gentleman from Texas with the bushy beard . . . I believe his name is Red . . . find you?"

A chill crawled up my spine. "No, he didn't, Father, but you ain't the first person to mention that he's been askin' after me. He didn't happen to say what he wanted, did he?"

"No, he did not. I told him where your office is located and suggested that he look for you there, although I know you are often out wandering around the countryside searching for outlaws."

This is getting irksome. I don't know who this rogue is but he's getting on my nerves. That wasn't Father Antonio's problem, though. "Thanks for letting me know, Father. I'll watch for him." You better bet I will.

I'm not sure how to move ahead with hunting for this murdering bunch if, in truth, it's the same men committing the crimes. I'd be well-served to do what Father Antonio mentioned, which is ramble around the countryside searching for these outlaws. At the same time, it appears that they aren't afraid to come into town and perpetrate their vile deeds as well. There is only one of me and I can't be in two places at once. I need help.

When Tomás Marés was sheriff, he would

have stayed in town protecting the citizens while sending his deputy . . . that would have been me . . . out to scour the outlying parts of the county to try to get a bead on these villains. My problem is that I don't have a deputy. I really need the help. It also seems to me that it would be nice to have someone to give orders to. Now that I'm the sheriff, even if I'm only the acting sheriff, I'm officially in charge. Problem is, I ain't got anybody to be in charge of. That's not nearly as major a problem as finding these killers but it does kind of rankle.

I know Tomás isn't going to help me and Tom Figgs has contributed more than I could reasonably expect of him already. As I ponder where to turn for help, it occurs to me that I'm not the first Colfax County lawman to face this situation. For most of the time he was sheriff, Nathan Averill had operated alone. Of course, the difference between him and me was that he could stand tall alone and get the job done. Me, I need all the help I can get. I figure it might not hurt to seek his advice. With my mind made up, I went looking for former Sheriff Averill. Unlike these murdering outlaws I was searching for, I knew right where to find him.

When I walked into the lobby of the St.

James Hotel, I glanced over to the comfortable chairs they had arranged in a circle in the lobby. Sure enough, there was Sheriff Averill sitting there sipping on a cup of coffee. I walked over to him with my hat in my hand. I can't think of anybody I have more respect for than Nathan Averill. "Mornin', Sheriff Averill," I said. "How's your day goin'?"

He looked up at me and nodded, saying, "It's goin' fine, Tommy. Have a seat and let's visit for a spell." He chuckled as I sat down. "You know, you're the sheriff now. It ain't necessary to address me as sheriff."

That caught me a bit off guard. Nathan Averill is one of the greatest lawmen who ever served out here in the West. Unlike some of the more famous ones you read about in the dime novels, he really did all those brave and dangerous deeds people give him credit for. I call him "Sheriff" out of respect for everything he accomplished over the years, for all the violent criminals he faced and brought down. I also call him that because to tell you the truth, he sort of scares me. I tend to feel like an awkward, tenderfoot kid around him. If I don't call him Sheriff Averill, I don't know what I will call him.

"Right, Sheriff," I said. "I'll try to work

on that."

He chuckled again and took a sip of his coffee. "Well, what's on your mind, Sheriff? I know you got your hands full with some pretty serious lawbreakin'. You probably didn't stop by just to socialize with me."

"You're right on all counts, Sheriff. We got us some more evil men preyin' on the good citizens of Colfax County. I need some help." I blew out through my lips, unconsciously imitating that sound old Rusty makes when he gets impatient for me to dish him up his ration of hay. That's how I was feeling . . . impatient.

Nathan looked steadily in my eyes. "What kind of help are you lookin' for?"

As I stared back at him, I perceived wisdom and patience in his gaze. In the past, I was more afraid I would see judgment there and that he would find me lacking. It occurred to me that even if I felt a bit like a greenhorn around him, he might consider me to be a fellow lawman, a member of the same tribe. Not necessarily an equal because there are darned few who are his equal but at least someone else who's in the same business he'd been in. He'd probably be willing to not treat me like some wet-behind-the-ears kid if I act like I at least halfway know what I'm doing.

"Seems like too many different kinds of help to count," I said. "You know yourself how much territory I got to patrol and I ain't got deputy one. That ain't your problem to solve, I know." I flicked a speck of dirt off my hat. Don't know how it got there but my wife gave me this pretty new Stetson. I want to keep it looking sharp as long as I can. "What I could use from you is some advice on how I should tackle this situation. There's so many different things I should do that I can't even figure out where to start."

"Don't be too hasty cuttin' me out of helpin' you unravel your deputy problem," he said. He noticed my eyes widen at that and waved his hand in a dismissive gesture. "We'll return to that in a minute. Why don't you start at the beginning? Tell me everything that's transpired and what you've done about it so far. If I have ideas or suggestions, I'll stop you and toss 'em out."

I didn't realize it until right then but ever since the trouble at the Armstrong place happened, I'd felt like I was lying flat on my back with a boulder on my chest. Knowing I had someone who was willing to listen to me and tell me if I was going up the wrong trail took a lot of that weight off. I felt like I could breathe again.

"That's exactly the kind of help I was hopin' you'd offer, Sheriff."

I spent the next twenty minutes filling Sheriff Averill in on everything that had happened. From time to time, he stopped me and pressed me for more details. When I told him about waving the flies off the Armstrong boy, his eyes narrowed. I could feel him tensing up, almost like a rattler that's coiled and ready to strike. It made me uneasy. When I mentioned my encounter with Felipe Alvarado down in San Miguel County, I could almost see his ears prick up, kind of like Rusty's do when he spies something ahead on the trail that makes him curious. I finally recounted all there was to tell right up to the present time and the tragedy that took place at Bill Wallace's mercantile. I sat back and tried to catch my breath.

Averill wore a pensive air. He didn't speak for a spell. I sat there and waited. I'd said my piece and I wanted to hear what he had to say about it. Finally, he began to speak.

"I know you're wonderin' if it's the same killer. My hunch is that it is, even though one crime happened in town and one out on the Armstrong place outside of town. You got a thief and a murderer both places. Stealin' livestock and stealin' money from the mercantile ain't exactly the same but thievin' is thievin' when you get right down to it. And the odds of havin' two sadistic killers in Colfax County at the same time who use a knife so cruelly are pretty slim." He shook his head. "Thank goodness for that."

I'd been thinking the same thing but it was reassuring to have someone with his experience see it the same way. "That helps, Sheriff, but it still doesn't provide me with much of a notion about where to start lookin' for these murderin' butchers. All I know is that Mrs. Armstrong heard them speak about a ranch. Where in hell's half acre that ranch might be is somethin' I've yet to figure out."

"The Armstrong place is located northwest of town, am I right?" Averill's brow was wrinkled, giving him that look you get when you're thinking hard.

"Yes, sir, it is," I said.

"You know, there's quite a number of canyons up that way. If I was gonna set me up a hidin' place for stock I was stealin', I'd be inclined to do it there. Might be worth your while to ride up there and check it out."

"Sounds logical to me, Sheriff," I said. "With this killer showin' he ain't afraid to come right into town and murder innocent citizens, though, I don't feel good about leavin' the town unprotected."

"That goes back to your deputy problem, don't it," he said. "I got a notion about how to crack that one."

"Beats me how you'd do that but, if you got ideas, I'm listenin'."

"Well," he said in a casual way, "it so happens that I've got a little bit of spare time on my hands, bein' retired and all. My wife hates to see me idle and keeps comin' up with chores to fill up my days. If I'm gonna do somethin' other than sit around the lobby of the St. James and drink coffee, reckon I'd rather do somethin' I enjoyed."

It took a second for me to realize that my jaw had dropped and my mouth was hanging open. I could have sworn Nathan Averill had just offered to be my deputy.

"Are you sayin' you'd be willin' to help me out by workin' as . . . ?" I can't bring myself to say the words "my deputy" but I don't know what else to call it. I wound up letting the words hang there in the air.

"I'm sayin' that if you'd be willin' to deputize me, I'd be willin' to lend you a hand." He raised his right index finger in the air to make a point. "My plan would be that I'd kind of oversee what's happenin' in town while you go out lookin' for these damned renegades. I ain't keen to go out roamin' around horseback all over creation and wind up gettin' shot again."

I could barely contain my excitement. "Well, of course not. Knowin' you were back here in Cimarrón lookin' after things would give me the freedom to search for this ranch up north."

"That's what I'm thinkin'," he said. "What do you say?"

I've faced some difficult decisions in my fairly short time as a lawman. This wasn't one of them. "Well, yeah," I said with a good deal of enthusiasm. "We'll get you sworn in as soon as I can get the village council to approve your pay."

Nathan chuckled and shook his head. "Let's ride right on past that one and get me deputized. I don't want any money for this. If I start gettin' paid, I might get to where I'm countin' on the money. That'd make it harder to quit whenever I'm a mind to."

I wasn't sure I understood his point but I wasn't about to argue. The sooner I can avail myself of the services of the finest lawman the New Mexico Territory ever saw, the better.

"Whatever you say is fine with me, Sheriff," I said.

He grinned at me and said, "And now that I'm gonna be your deputy, you really should stop callin' me Sheriff. That could get downright confusin'."

He has a point but I know it isn't going to matter. I'll continue to call him Sheriff and let folks figure it out in their own good time.

I was pretty excited about my new deputy and couldn't wait for Mollie to get home so I could tell her the news. I made my rounds and headed for the house right about the time she usually gets home from teaching school. I was sitting at the table in the kitchen when she walked in. I immediately jumped up.

"You're never gonna guess what happened today," I said.

"Nathan Averill volunteered to be your deputy," she said in a matter-of-fact voice as she set her books on the table.

Well, dang. That sure took all the enjoyment out of my surprise. In the past, I would have pouted for a while. Maybe I've acquired a bit of wisdom during the time I've been married to Mollie. One thing I've learned is that not much happens in my life that she doesn't know about almost immediately. Second, she rarely misses an opportunity to tease me about things. And third, she mostly does it for fun and doesn't intend to be mean to me. I decided to laugh it off.

"Didn't take you long to find that out, did it?" I shook my head and grinned at her. "Darlin', you're amazin'."

I think she was a little surprised that I didn't react the way she expected. That took a little bit of the sting out of her spoiling my surprise. She grinned back at me. "Nathan came over to the school right after the two of you talked this morning," she said. "He told Miss Christy. After he left, she told me."

"No secrets in this town," I said. I was pleased that Nathan was excited enough about this deal that he went right over to tell his wife. I was so excited I was almost bouncing up and down. "I can't believe my good luck, Mollie. I'll be gettin' counsel and guidance from one of the best lawmen that ever pinned on a badge."

Mollie frowned. "Miss Christy ain't quite as enthusiastic about it as you and Nathan are."

"What do you mean?"

"She made a little joke about it at first," Mollie said. "Said she must have made his list of chores too long. I could tell something was bothering her, though."

"Did she say what it was?" I wasn't sure I knew what Mollie was talking about.

Mollie gave me a withering look. "She almost lost her husband when he was sheriff, you eejit. She figured those days were behind her once he retired. Now he's back on the job." She shook her head. "You think it's easy for the wife to sit helpless at home while her husband goes off tracking dangerous criminals?"

She had a point, although I wish she hadn't called me an eejit. That's Irish for idiot. I don't think she meant it in an affectionate way, at least not this particular time.

"I hadn't thought about it that way, Mollie," I said. "I'm so happy to be gettin' the help, it didn't cross my mind to consider it from her side."

"Sure and it is a fine thing for you, Tommy," Mollie said. "It makes me feel a little better about the job you're doing to know you've got a famous lawman standin' by you." She glanced down. "Makes me feel almost guilty to be happy about it, though, knowin' that it doesn't set well with Miss Christy."

"Now that you mention it," I said, "reckon I feel the same. It's good for me, no question, but I hate to see her feelin' down about it."

Mollie's eyes flashed. "It would be mighty damned fine if someone else in this town had the gumption to step up and do the job of sheriff. Most of these folks are more than happy for you or Nathan or Jared Delaney to assume all the risks."

I can't argue with her. It's been that way for years in Cimarrón. I started to bring up that things might change once the sheriff's office moved over to Springer, then I reconsidered. Like I said, I don't want to argue with her and that move looming on the horizon is a mighty sore subject.

"You're right," I said. Better to keep it simple and steer clear of the storm as long as I can.

Chapter 8

"Nathan, there's a cluster of canyons out to the north of us. They could be hidin' out in any of 'em." It felt pretty awkward calling him Nathan but I sure wasn't going to call him Deputy.

"That's a fact," he said. "My best guess is that they wouldn't hide out in one of the first few canyons you come to, which is Dean, Templeton, and Chase." He paused and pondered what he'd just said. "Well, maybe Chase. If I was a bettin' man, I'd go with Compos Canyon." He grinned. "Of course, if you get shot in Chase Canyon, I'd lose my bet."

I was about to climb on old Rusty and head out to look for this mysterious ranch where the outlaws might be hiding. Nathan would stay in town and make his presence felt. That will make the citizens of Cimarrón feel a whole lot safer. It makes me feel better about leaving. He might be getting along in years but if any fighting needed to be done, there weren't many better than Nathan Averill, even now.

"I sure wouldn't want you to lose your bet," I said with a grin of my own. "I'll do my best to not get shot."

The journey out to the canyons was mighty pretty. With fall coming on, the aspens were turning and it looked like the mountains were covered with gold. The sun shone down on my back, keeping me warm, but there was a bit of a nip in the air. Winter wasn't too far off. By early November, we could count on getting a couple of feet of snow, which would make the traveling a lot more difficult. For now, you couldn't ask for nicer scenery. I would have enjoyed it if I wasn't so concerned with the prospect of getting shot.

In the area where I was looking, there was a series of interconnecting canyons. Some were named for the people who had first explored them and some weren't. If you weren't familiar with the lay of the land, you'd have some trouble figuring out where one canyon stopped and the next one started.

I knew the area well from gathering cattle for Jared Delaney. Those dang cows love to hide out up in those canyons. If they'd stay down in the bottom of the canyon, it wouldn't be a problem to chouse them out. Of course, that's not what they do. They climb up the slopes on either side of the canyon so you and your horse have to risk breaking your leg or your neck to fetch them down. I swear, those animals must be part mountain goat.

Like I said, I was pretty uneasy about the possibility of getting shot so I was looking right and left, up and down, as I rode along. Even though Nathan is probably right that these outlaws wouldn't set up a camp in the first one, Dean Canyon, I'm not taking any chances.

I made it through Dean and Templeton canyons and would likely make my way into Chase Canyon by early afternoon. I'd seen cattle tracks but I wasn't sure that meant anything. It could mean someone had pushed some stolen steers up through the canyons but it could just as easily be the tracks of some of those wayward bovine I'd mentioned earlier. I dismounted to stretch my legs and give Rusty a break. He grazed a bit while I chewed on some beef jerky that Mollie had packed for me in my saddlebags.

I was looking up the canyon to the northwest when the first shot came. I was already moving to grab Rusty's reins and head for the trees on the northeast side of the canyon as it registered in my mind that the shot came from the west. Did I say shot? There were a bunch of shots and from the sound of it, they were coming from a rifle. If I ever moved faster in my life, I don't know when it was. Bullets were whizzing around my feet. My heart was pounding so rapidly I thought it might burst.

Either I'm as swift as those antelope I see from time to time or the fella operating that rifle isn't a great shot. Rusty and I made it up into the trees and rocks without getting killed. Once I had some cover, I grabbed my Winchester and looked to see if I could spot the shooter. I wasn't having any luck with that and the shooting had stopped. It occurred to me that if this fella was part of the gang I was looking for, he might have departed to get some of his compadres to lend him a hand in the chore of finishing me off.

I wasn't eager to wait around for that to happen. From what the widow Armstrong had told me, there were at least four or five men in the gang that murdered her husband and son. I could either stay where I was and face them alone, or turn tail and run for help. I thought about it for maybe a half a second, then I hopped on Rusty and lit out for Cimarrón.

It took me a lot less time to get back to town than it did to get out to Chase Canyon. I had Rusty going at a full gallop for a good ways to obtain a sizable head start on anyone who might chase us. He couldn't gallop all the way back to town so I eased him into a lope once I had enough distance between me and those back-shootin' devils. As it was, he was pretty well used up by the time I arrived back in Cimarrón.

It was just about dusk when I pulled up on the hill to the northwest of the village. I could see the lights of Cimarrón shimmering as people lit lanterns in their houses to ward off the darkness. I walked Rusty down the hill into town and up to my office. I loose-tied him to the hitching rail. I needed to brush him down and feed and water him but it was imperative that I talk with Nathan first. I didn't know if he would still be in the office but I could see the dim light of the lantern through the window.

When I opened the door, I saw that the lantern was on a table in the far corner opposite my desk. There was a figure sitting in the chair behind the desk with his feet propped up. My first thought was that it was pretty brazen of Nathan to do that but since it was his desk in the first place, I couldn't really say much. As my eyes adjusted to the dim light, I realized that the man behind the desk wasn't Nathan Averill. I put my hand on the butt of my Colt.

"I don't know who you are, stranger, and what you're doin' sittin' behind my desk," I said. My jaw was clamped down and I was gritting my teeth as I spoke. I'd had more than enough surprises for one day. "You better talk fast and make damn good sense when you tell me why you're here."

The man chuckled. As my eyes adjusted, I saw that he sported a bushy beard. It wasn't light enough for me to tell if it was red but I had a pretty good notion that it was. Here was the mysterious stranger who'd been asking for me. His hat was pulled down low. I couldn't make out his eyes or any facial features. I wrapped my fingers around the butt of my pistol. I was somewhere between real scared and real mad.

"Stranger," I said, my voice trembling with tension, "put your hands up and identify yourself pronto." The man laughed again. Slowly, he raised his hands up above his shoulders. As he did, I eased my gun out of the holster.

"All right, Sheriff, I'll do as you say," he

said. "That ain't much of a way to greet family, though."

Family? I had no idea what he was talking about. "Keep your hands up," I said as I edged over to where the lantern sat. I picked it up with my left hand, not taking my eyes off the stranger, and stepped carefully back over in the vicinity of the desk.

"If I keep my hands up and move real slow," the stranger said, "do you mind if I push my hat back a bit?"

I wasn't sure what his game was but I figured I had him covered pretty well. "Do it," I said, "but mighty slow."

Once again, he chuckled. Very slowly, he used his right hand to push his hat back on his head. My jaw dropped.

"Rusty?" I was dumbfounded. "Rusty Stallings?" I'll be danged. Sitting there in front of me was my long-lost cousin.

Chapter 9

"Looks like he took off, Manuel," Pat Maes said. "How in the hell did you miss him, riding up the canyon like that right into your sights?"

Manuel Maldonado didn't like Maes's tone. Maybe the Boss had made him the leader of this little band for now but that didn't mean Manuel had to endure his insults.

"If you think you are a better shot, maybe you should have been the one to take it." Manuel spit on the ground. "Once I missed the first time, he moved fast, like a paisano, up into the rocks and trees. That is when I figured I should come back and get the rest of you."

"That gave him the chance to slip away," Maes said in a contemptuous manner. "Did you lose your nerve?"

"You want to test my nerve, *cabrón,* you keep talking. I show you my nerve." Maldonado's right hand crept over to hover above his pistol, which was holstered on his left side, butt forward.

Pony Dolan shook his head as the two men bickered. An old hand from the Clanton gang over in Tombstone, he didn't have a great deal of respect for these two. It was only because he was getting paid well by the Boss that he was willing to tolerate it. For now.

"We ain't got time for your fussin'," Pony said. "We need to decide if we're gonna follow that son of a bitch or get these cattle out of here before he comes back with a posse."

Maes and Maldonado glared at each other for a moment longer. Maes looked away first.

"Pony is right," Maes said. He looked at Dolan and the other two men in their little band, John Dorsey and Rafael Espinosa, as he contemplated the best course of action. "I think the smart move is to take the herd on up to Trinidad. That way, we get paid. If that *pendejo* comes looking for us with a posse, he will not find nothing."

Maldonado muttered something under his breath.

"Do you have something you want to say, *amigo*?" The way Maes stressed the word "amigo" made it clear he meant anything but that.

Maldonado stared at him for another brief moment, then shook his head. "Not right now, *amigo.*" He smiled at Maes but the smile didn't extend up to his eyes. They remained cold. "Later I will say more but now, we need to get these cattle moving."

Chapter 10

"You sure are a fine cook, Mrs. Stallings," Rusty said as he served himself more fried potatoes. "Tommy is a lucky fella."

"Sure and I tell him that every day," Mollie replied. "You can call me Mollie, by the way, you bein' family and all."

I thought about telling Rusty that I go by Tom now but decided it wasn't worth the effort. No one else seemed to pay attention to me when I brought it up; I don't know why my cousin would. Maybe it's not that big a deal.

"I appreciate that," Rusty said. "I don't know how much Tommy has told you but we do go back a ways."

"He's told me quite a bit," Mollie said. "I know your family had the neighboring ranch." She hesitated, then she continued. "I know he was working at your place the day his family was killed by the Comanche."

I sat quietly and listened as my wife and

cousin dredged up those awful memories. I still carry guilt about not being there to defend my family, even though I was just a boy and would have been wiped out with them. There was a time when I wished that had happened. Now that I have Mollie, I don't feel that way most of the time.

"That was a terrible day," Rusty said. "Tommy lost his family. My daddy lost his little brother. It leaves a mark on your soul."

"Tommy lived with you after that, didn't he?" Mollie seemed pleased to meet one of my family members in the flesh. Even though I'd told her all this information, she seemed to want to hear it from someone else as well.

"He did," Rusty said. "He was with us for several years." He turned to me. "Up until you turned sixteen, right?"

"That's right," I said. I didn't want to go into the painful details. After my family was killed, I was pretty prickly to live with. I was angry at the world and I took it out on Rusty and his family. I'm not proud of it but it's the truth.

"It was a rough patch for my cousin here," Rusty said, nodding in my direction. "There was times he was pretty hard to get along with but we tried to be understandin'."

I was getting tired of the two of them digging through the bones of my past. I decided to change the subject. "Rusty's gonna stick around here for a while and be my deputy, Mollie. What do you think about that?"

"My goodness," she exclaimed. "Just the other day, you had no help at all. Now you have yourself two deputies. Some folks might call that an embarrassment of riches."

That hit me kind of wrong. "Well," I said testily, "since I'm allowed three and up to now, I ain't had any, I reckon I ain't that embarrassed."

"Oh, I'm just teasin' you, Tommy," she said. "I know how hard it's been on you." She stood up and grabbed Rusty's plate. "Here now, I'll clear the table and wash the dishes. You boys go relax on the porch and catch up."

I was more than happy to stop reliving my past. I didn't mind not doing the dishes, either. "We better get movin' before she changes her mind," I said to Rusty. "You go on out and pick you a rockin' chair, I got a surprise for you."

He grinned as he got up from the table. "Mollie, that was a fine meal. I sure appreciate your hospitality and thanks for takin' care of them dishes. If you was to choose to invite me back for another meal, I'd be happy to take on the dishwashin' chore next time."

"I'm glad you enjoyed yourself, Mr. Rusty Stallings." Mollie beamed at his compliment. "And I'll have none of your washin' dishes when you're at my table. That's a job I don't mind at all."

Well, that fried me just a little bit. She didn't seem to have any problem letting me help out with the dishwashing chores. Still, she was happy and I didn't want to spoil her mood. I did permit her to clear my plate from the table. As long as she was inclined to do the dishes, I figured I'd take full advantage of it.

I went over to the cabinet where we stored our silverware and good plates, along with a few other important items. Mollie calls it her China cabinet and she's awful proud of it. It's made out of polished oak with some nice designs carved in the doors. I have to agree that it's mighty pretty. It was in the house when we moved in. I think Nathan Averill bought it years ago to spruce up the little two-room place the county provides the sheriff to live in. He lives with Miss Christy now and we get to reap the rewards of his reckless spending. I don't think we have anything from China in it but I don't say anything to Mollie about that, seeing as how much she likes it.

I reached in and pulled out a bottle of whiskey with the seal still intact. Not rotgut stuff but prime sipping whiskey. I'd spent far too much money on it several months ago at the Colfax Tavern and had been saving it for a special occasion. I reckon seeing my long-lost cousin counts as a special occasion. I poured three fingers of the good stuff in two glasses. When I walked out to the portal, Rusty was seated in one of our rockers looking to the west. He rocked gently as he gazed at the pale rose-colored glow behind the mountains.

"This is pretty country you're settled into, cousin. We got nice sunsets in Texas but not many mountains to look at."

"I can't complain about that part of it, cousin," I said.

"You can't complain too much about that pretty wife of yours, neither," he said. "She's easy to look at, she cooks good, and she's got spunk. I can tell from the spark in her eyes."

When he laid it all out like that, I felt kind of bad for being irritated with her. I know she was being hospitable with that thing about the dishes and she was only teasing me about the deputies. I really was a lucky fella.

"I did notice that you didn't say anything about gettin' shot at today," Rusty said.

"There was no need to upset her," I said. "She worries enough as it is."

"You also failed to mention our agreement," Rusty said.

"Now that ain't fair, Rusty," I said. "I did tell her the part about you helpin' me out by bein' my deputy for a while."

Rusty rolled his eyes. "Yeah, Tommy, but you left out the part where you said you'd come home with me to Texas to help us stand up to them rustlers that've been plaguin' us. You're not gonna try to welsh on our deal, are you?"

"No, I ain't welshin' on anything," I said. "That'll be down the road a piece, though. I didn't see the need for explainin' something that ain't gonna happen for quite some time. Like I said, she worries plenty as it is. I didn't see any call to give her more to worry about."

He took a sip of his whiskey. "Right."

I'd seen that mocking look before. I knew my cousin wasn't done with rattling my reins about telling Mollie of our agreement. I don't think he grasps how important timing is with these things.

"You've just seen the cheerful side of Mollie," I said. "She's got a bit of a dark side, as well. You don't want to be around when she flashes that part, I promise you."

Rusty laughed. "I'll take your word for that, Tommy. Just give me some warnin' when the thunderclouds start to gather."

"I'm afraid they may start gathering pretty soon," I said. "There's been talk for months about moving the sheriff's office over to Springer, seein' as how it's the county seat." I shuddered. "That ain't gonna set well with Mollie. She's got a good job here and friends. She has no interest in bein' uprooted."

Rusty could see I was serious. "Reckon that makes sense. If you got a good thing goin', why would you want to up and leave it?"

Since I'd been putting off discussing this move with Mollie, I couldn't see any reason to talk about it with Rusty. It would happen soon enough. I decided to change the subject.

"So," I said in as serious a tone as I could conjure up, "I got an important question for you."

Rusty looked concerned. "What is it?"

I stared at him long enough to make him uncomfortable before I spoke. "What's with all that fur on your face?" I could see I'd caught him off guard, which amused me no end.

He shook his head and then laughed. "Ah, the beard. There's no real story behind it. We were out with the wagon for quite a spell last spring and it just grew." He grinned at me. "When I got home, Mama near had a fit about it. Said she liked the looks of my face and couldn't see it when it was all covered up."

My cousin Rusty loves to tease people almost as much as he likes to eat. I could just see my aunt puttering around, clucking and making disapproving remarks about his beard. Along with that image, I could see Rusty throwing back his head and laughing at her.

"You know," I said, "if she'd react different, it wouldn't be so much fun for you. I reckon you'd shave that thing off if it didn't matter so much to her."

"You know how she is, though," he said. "She can't let nothin' alone. And you're right, it wouldn't be any fun at all if she didn't respond the way she does." I could see him getting that look of merriment that usually appeared right before he gave someone a hard time. "Seems I recall someone else who's like that."

I knew he was talking about me. Heck,

Mollie had made that point to me on more than one occasion. She probably thinks I didn't listen to her. I figured I'd show her and Rusty both. "I don't know who you're talkin' about." I swiftly changed the focus of the conversation. "You know, you caused quite a stir bein' a stranger in town with your beard. Why didn't you just come straight to my office and say howdy?"

"Tommy, you know I always liked messin' with you a bit. I figured it'd get you steamed up to know some stranger was askin' about you. That ain't all of it, though." He took another sip of his whiskey. "I didn't know how you'd act, seein' me again after all these years. We didn't part on the best of terms."

Looked like we were getting down to it. I left my aunt and uncle's place in a flood of harsh words. I accused them of taking advantage of me, making me work for free and favoring Rusty over me. None of it was true. They treated me like family. We all had chores to do and everybody did them without complaining except for me. I couldn't change what I'd done in the past but I could own up to it.

"No, we didn't," I said, "and that was my fault. You and your folks took me in. You gave me food and a bed, and you taught me a trade. I wouldn't be half the cowboy I am today if it wasn't for Uncle Joe."

"They tried the best they could," Rusty said. I could see the earnest look in his eyes. "I think it hurt Mama most of all to part on such rough terms." There was a catch in his voice and he paused before continuing. "She did care about you, Tommy. Still does."

I felt like someone had stabbed me in the heart with a hunting knife. It occurred to me that I deserved to feel that pain. "I know it, Rusty. I know it now and I knew it then. I just couldn't bring myself to admit it. I'll do anything I can to make amends."

"I appreciate that, Tommy. Mama and Pa would, too." He took yet another sip of his whiskey. He was getting ahead of me so I took a gulp as well. "That's the main part of why I'm askin' you to come back to Texas and lend us a hand. We could use the help and I figure it'd give you a chance to smooth things out and have a new beginnin'."

He was right and I knew it. When the time came, it would be hard to explain it to Mollie but I had to make her understand. Family ties are everything. I couldn't say no to my cousin. We had quite a bit of work to do before any of this came to pass, however.

"When the time comes," I said, "I'll be there. Count on it."

Rusty tossed off the rest of his whiskey and said, "Enough of this somber talk." He grabbed the bottle and refilled both our glasses. "Remember when you got on that old gray outlaw right after breakfast. You said you could ride any horse we had on the ranch." He laughed. "You sure couldn't ride that one."

As I recall, the old snorty gray tossed me off in a couple of seconds. I'd landed in some prickly pear cactus and spent most of the rest of the day picking out spines. The wound to my pride was as deep as the wounds to my hide.

"Well, I bet I could ride that nag now," I said. "If Uncle Joe still has him, I'll scale that hurricane deck when I come to Texas."

Rusty threw back his head and guffawed. We spent the next couple of hours swapping tales from our past. I was surprised at how many good memories Rusty had. Maybe it hadn't been as bad as I recalled. We finally called it a night. Rusty went out back to bed down in the stable and I crawled into bed with Mollie. I'd had a bit too much whiskey and was hoping she might be delighted to see me. It didn't turn out that way. She stirred briefly but didn't wake up. Oh, well.

Chapter 11

Mollie whipped up a fine breakfast with fresh eggs from the chicken coop, a nice slab of bacon, and some more fried potatoes. Rusty raved on and on about her cooking again. She acts like he's ten feet tall and she kind of ignores me. I'm not all that pleased about it but she washed the dishes without my help again so it wasn't a dead loss. When she was done, Mollie headed off to school and we walked down to my office.

As we sauntered down the boardwalk, I noticed I was about as tall as Rusty. When I'd left the ranch at the age of sixteen, he'd been a couple of inches taller. Of course, that made sense because he was two years older than me. He could whip me in a fist-fight back then and did so on a number of occasions. That might not be the case now though I had no interest in finding out. I planned to treat my cousin a lot better than I did back when I was a snot-nosed kid with a chip on my shoulder.

"Tell me about your deputy, Tommy," Rusty said. "You make him sound like he could whip a grizzly bear."

"I can't get used to callin' Sheriff Averill my 'deputy,' but I do look forward to you meetin' him, Rusty," I said. "I don't know if he could whip a grizzly but he faced down some of the toughest outlaws this territory has ever seen and he always came out on top." I tipped my hat as we passed Tom Figgs's wife, Annie. "Mornin' Mrs. Figgs, how are you today?"

She smiled and said, "I'm just fine, Sheriff. Headed over to the mercantile." Her smile faded. "Terrible thing, what happened to Mr. Woodrum."

"Yes, ma'am, it was terrible," I said.

"I've checked in on Cynthia," she said, a concerned look on her face. "I'm afraid she's not doing well."

"Don't see how she could be, with what happened," I said.

She nodded. There wasn't much more either of us could say so we continued on our way.

"Why did Averill get out of the sheriff trade? If he's so good, sounds like he ought to be the sheriff still." Rusty coughed. "No offense, cousin, but you describe him like he's the king of the hill."

I laughed. "None taken, Rusty. I'd be pleased as could be if he was still the sheriff. The thing is, as he's gotten older, he's slowed down a bit. That and he got bushwhacked a few years ago." I briefly went back in my mind to the time we thought Nathan Averill had been killed. "He was hurt pretty bad but, in the end, he walked away and them two fellas who shot him didn't."

"I reckon we all slow down sooner or later," Rusty said. "Pa's movin' a bit more deliberate than he used to these days. If you need cows worked, he can still get it done. He may not move as fast as he used to but he works smart. That makes up for a lot."

"That's Sheriff Averill to a *T,* Rusty," I said. "There may be faster men around but he's forgotten more about bein' sheriff than the rest of us will ever know. I'm glad to have him on my side."

We arrived at the office. I went in first. Not that I figured that Nathan would shoot Rusty and then ask questions but the times were a bit tense. Having just reunited with my cousin after too many years apart, I didn't want to lose him by being careless. He followed me in.

"Mornin', Sheriff . . . I mean, Nathan," I

said. Averill was over by the wall looking at wanted posters that I had tacked up. "I'd like to introduce you to my cousin, Rusty Stallings, from Texas."

The two men eyed each other. Physically, they couldn't have been more different. Rusty was a young man a shade under six feet tall. He had a stocky build, freckles, and dark orange hair. As I recall from our childhood spent together, he had a sunny disposition most of the time but he had that redheaded temper if you pushed him too far. He was the kind of outgoing fella who would start up a conversation with a stranger . . . or a fence post.

In contrast, Nathan Averill was clearly older, although "old" was not the word I would use to describe him. Maybe "weathered." He stood a couple of inches over six feet and while he was slim, he moved with the grace and strength of a mountain lion. He didn't act in a threatening manner and yet, somehow, he seemed dangerous. He was more prone to listen than to talk. You got the feeling that he could size you up and figure you out pretty quickly. I was hoping they would get along.

Rusty made the first move. "Sheriff Averill, it's a genuine pleasure to meet you," he said as he stepped forward with his arm outstretched. "I'd be honored to shake the hand of the man my cousin Tommy says is the finest lawman to ever serve in the New Mexico Territory."

Nathan reached out and took Rusty Stallings's hand firmly. "He said that, did he?"

"That or some words to that effect." Rusty grinned.

"I think he flatters me so he doesn't have to pay me," Nathan said, grinning back at my cousin.

I was happy they were getting along even if I was getting ragged on a bit. I joined right in. "It seems to be workin' pretty well."

"Yep, and you're gettin' exactly what you're payin' for." Nathan chuckled. "So far I haven't done anything."

It was time to get serious. I wish we had the option of sitting around swapping stories for a while but the man or men who took a shot at me out in Chase Canyon pose a real threat to the people of Colfax County. We needed to come up with a plan.

"I think that's about to change, Nathan. I better fill you in on what happened yesterday."

He could tell from the look in my eye that we were done fooling around. He immediately switched over to a no-nonsense approach. "Let's hear it."

I recounted what had happened as I was about to enter Chase Canyon. When I told him about being shot at, his eyes narrowed a bit but otherwise, he listened without expression. I hope he doesn't think it was cowardly of me to turn tail and run. If he does, there's nothing I can do about it now. At the time, it made the most sense to me.

He asked, "What do you intend to do?" If he thought poorly of me for my actions, I couldn't tell.

"I'm plannin' for me and Rusty to head back out to the canyons and see if I can figure out what those yellow cowards did after I left." I would have liked to have done that yesterday afternoon but by the time I got back to town, dark was coming on. "I figure they either decided to move their headquarters further up into Compos Canyon or else they took the herd they been hidin' there and headed north for Colorado."

"If I was a bettin' man, I'd say they took the herd and skedaddled," Nathan said. "They're bound to know that you'd come back with help. They wouldn't want to risk gettin' caught or losin' the herd." He looked over at Rusty. "You gonna be joinin' up with us?"

"If you don't have any objection, I thought

I would." Rusty said, "Tommy's my family. He needs help. Seems pretty clear to me what I ought to do."

Nathan nodded. "All right, I'll keep an eye on things here in town. We won't know what our next step should be until we find out what they did."

"That's the way I see it," I said. I walked over and took two Winchesters from the gun cabinet. I handed one to Rusty, then walked over to my desk and took two boxes of cartridges from the top drawer. "If they're still there, I'll take a count of how many of 'em there are and decide whether or not Rusty and I can take 'em. If there's too many, we may come back and fetch you. You all right with that?"

Nathan grinned. "To tell you the truth, I been gettin' bored walkin' up and down these streets. I wouldn't mind takin' a little ride out in the country, maybe have a bit of a dustup with these fellas."

"If we need you, we'll dang sure come get you," I said. "You can count on it."

"All right," he replied. "You boys be careful. Don't go ridin' in whoopin' and hollerin'. Stealth is the name of the game."

"What did you think of my deputy?" I was eager to hear Rusty's opinion.

"You know, Tommy, I didn't think all that much of him at first." He noticed that my face fell and he smiled. "That changed when you were tellin' him about your little trek up the canyons. I swear, the look on his face when you told him you'd been shot at scared me." He shuddered. "It was just there for a second but he had the look of a killer. I'm glad he's on our side."

I chuckled. "That's the thing about Nathan Averill. He acts friendly, which puts you off your guard, then quick as a snake, he's got the drop on you. He's braced many a bad hombre over the years. No one ever took him head to head."

"Let's hope that streak continues if we catch up with these boys we're chasin'," Rusty said.

"Yeah, well first we got to find 'em," I said. We were approaching the entrance of Templeton Canyon. "I think Nathan's probably right that they took off but just in case, why don't we spread out so we don't make an easy target. You head over to the edge of the trees there on the east side. I'll go left."

Rusty did as I had directed and we crept along carefully. I was paying close attention to the sights, sounds, and smells of the canyon. Even if you can't see the enemy, sometimes you can tell they're there when the birds quit singing. Sometimes a fool gets careless and rolls himself a smoke while he's waiting to ambush you. I've even known folks to keep their campfire going to get that extra cup of coffee and wind up giving themselves away. You never know.

We were coming up to the spot at the entrance to Chase Canyon where that fella started using me for target practice. The muscles around my stomach tightened as if an icy hand was gripping them. I stopped old Rusty . . . my horse Rusty, that is . . . and scanned the tree line. Nothing. I listened close and heard the birds chirping. Good sign. I sniffed the air and got the scent of fresh pine but no telltale smoke. I urged Rusty forward.

As we pushed on up Chase Canyon, I got a strong feeling that the gang had taken off with the cattle. There were a lot of tracks, both going into and coming out of the canyon. A good tracker could probably tell which ones were the freshest and determine if they had moved them out yesterday. I've never been accused of being a good tracker. I couldn't tell. Me thinking they had taken off was just a gut feeling.

The canyon curved around to the west. Up ahead, I saw what appeared to be a makeshift corral. I searched around for signs of life and saw none. There were remains of a fire that looked like it had been cold for some time and a deserted lean-to. I got down off Rusty and led him over to the edge of the camp, keeping him between me and anyone who might have been left behind to ambush us. I don't think Rusty understood that I was using him for cover; otherwise he might not have been so cooperative.

"Rusty," I hollered to the two-legged Rusty. "Check from that side to make sure there ain't nobody there. I'll meet you in the middle."

He dismounted and began searching cautiously around the corral. I examined the lean-to and found it used fairly recently but empty now. The more I looked, the less I saw, which relaxed me a bit. I stopped to listen one more time and, again, I heard the birds singing away at full force. If there was anyone up in the woods gunning for us, they'd had their chance to take us out. That icy hand loosened its grip on my stomach.

"Looks to me like they cleared out," I said. "If I had to guess, I'd say it was yesterday right after they took those shots at me."

"That's how I see it, too," Rusty said. "Got any idea where they headed?"

I took off my hat and scratched my head. "I'd say they took whatever herd they'd stolen and drove 'em up through Raton Pass to some mining camp up by Trinidad. That's the only course of action that makes much sense to me."

"How far you think they might've got?"

I'd been pondering that question. "If they took off right after they shot at me yesterday and drove hard until sometime after dark, they could have made it pretty close to the south end of Raton Pass. With an early start this mornin', they could be through the pass and fairly close to one of the mining camps by late this afternoon."

Rusty contemplated what I'd said. "You told me that sheriff down in San Miguel County thought that's what they were doin' with 'em, didn't you? Can you think of any reason why they'd take 'em down around Las Vegas first?"

"That wouldn't make a lick of sense," I said. "I been thinkin' that the main reason this outfit decided to move in on this territory is that it's closer to where they make their money. They can steal cattle here and cut two days off the trip to Trinidad. If that's the case, I can't see any reason they'd take 'em back to Las Vegas now." I shook my head. "Naw, I'd say it's a safe bet they skinned out of here and headed north towards Raton Pass."

"Sounds right to me," Rusty said. "What now? Do we go after 'em?"

I'd been giving this some thought, too. Rusty was plenty rough but he'd never been a lawman before. Holding your own in a fistfight is not the same thing as surviving a gunfight with hard men. We needed help.

"I don't know that we could catch up with 'em if we left right now," I said. "Chances are if we see 'em at all, it'll be when they're on their way back." I paused for a moment, thinking about the possibilities. "You know, if we time it right, we might be able to set up an ambush for them on the south end of Raton Pass. After those back-shootin' devils tried to waylay me, I kinda like the idea of returnin' the favor."

"Revenge is sweet, right, cousin?" Rusty grinned. "Do we head out right now?"

I didn't want to express my doubts about Rusty's abilities to handle a gunfight, but I needed to make a decision. "I believe we'd be better off goin' back to Cimarrón and gettin' Nathan to join us. I'd rather have too many guns than not enough."

Rusty glanced at me sideways like he was suspicious of my motives but he didn't question my decision. "Whatever you say," he said. "Let's get movin'."

We set off at a steady trot back towards

town. We rode for several miles in silence, then Rusty edged his horse over a little closer to me.

"So, cousin, I'm a little curious about something."

I had no idea what he might be getting at. "If you got a question, spit it out," I said.

"You named your horse Rusty," he said.

I thought I could see where this was headed. I tried to keep a straight face. "Yep, I did."

"Did you name him after me?"

I smiled at him. "Sure did."

He seemed puzzled. Pleased but puzzled. "Why'd you go and do that?"

"Well, take a good look at him," I said. "What kind of horse do you see?"

Rusty, the cousin, surveyed Rusty, the horse. I could see an expression of understanding cross his face. "He's a red roan." He laughed. "I get it. We got the same color coat."

I gazed at him for a long moment. "Naw," I said. "I named him Rusty because he's stubborn. He likes to play tricks on me, like ridin' close to a tree and tryin' to rub me off. He's hard to get along with and you got to watch him every second."

Rusty, the cousin's, face fell. Rusty, the horse, didn't seem to mind at all. I held out as long as I could, then I burst out laughing.

"Of course I named him Rusty 'cause he's a red roan." I laughed again at my cousin's discomfort. "Just goes to show you that even though it's been quite a spell since we've seen each other, I didn't forget about you."

Gradually my words seemed to sink in. His air of disappointment changed to one of pride. "Oh," he said. "Well, all right then."

Maes and the other outlaws were about a three-hour push from the mining camp southwest of Trinidad, Colorado. It was nearly sundown and time to decide whether to bed down and bring the cattle in first thing in the morning or try to take them all the way in the dark.

"I say we go all the way tonight and get this over with," Manuel Maldonado said. "You know that lawman was gonna get help and come after us."

Pat Maes was tired and irritable. Up to this point, he'd been undecided about whether to stop for the night or push on. Maldonado seemed to bring out his contrary side. As soon as he stated his opinion, Maes made his decision.

"Naw, we're all tired and so are the cows.

Bad things could happen if we try to drive them in after dark."

Maldonado threw up his hands. "And if that *pendejo* sheriff catches up with us while we're sleeping tonight, you think that's not a bad thing?"

Maes was tired of Maldonado questioning every decision he made. "I'm looking at the odds, *cabrón.* I think there's more of a chance that something will go wrong if we push on. If you don't like, tough."

Maldonado turned to his compadres. "What do you think? Pony? Rafael? Dorsey?"

Maes had had enough from Maldonado. He thought he might need to pistol-whip the impertinence out of him. He had the size advantage on the man. He was only a short distance away from him. If Maes edged his horse one step to the left as he drew his gun, he figured he could knock him out of the saddle before he knew what was coming. Once he was down, he could beat him bloody. Before he could implement his plan, Pony Dolan spoke up.

"You two need to stop bickerin'." He glared at Maldonado. "Pat says we stop. The Boss says Pat's in charge . . . so we stop. End of story."

John Dorsey and Rafael Espinosa hadn't

said a word during this exchange. Now Dorsey spoke up. "I'm worn out, Pat. Stoppin' is fine with me."

Espinosa nodded in agreement. "Me, too. I say we take turns on guard in case that lawman tries to sneak up on us. I'd rather take my chances with him than risk ridin' into some arroyo in the dark."

Maldonado shook his head in disgust and muttered under his breath. Maes thought he might have heard him say the words "yellow dog," but he wasn't sure. He chose to ignore him and postpone the confrontation that he was planning.

"All right, boys, let's get these cows movin' and find a good place to bed down."

Chapter 12

We tied our horses to the hitching post, loosened their cinches, and walked into my office. I was startled to find Bill Wallace sitting at my desk. He had his hat in his hands and he looked nervous.

"Hey, Bill, how long you been sittin' there?" I tried to keep the irritation out of my voice at the fact that he was sitting in my chair. "Did you need to talk with me about somethin'?"

He cleared his throat. "I've been here a couple of hours, Sheriff. I knew you'd have to come back sooner or later. I hope you don't mind me waiting in your office this long but I do need to talk with you about something extremely important." He paused, searching for the best way to proceed.

"Did you intend to tell me what it is?" I didn't bother to keep the irritation out of my voice this time around, "or do you want me to guess?"

"I'll tell you, Sheriff," he said. "It's bad news, though, and I know you're not going to be happy about it."

"It ain't gonna get any better with you dilly-dallyin' around, Bill," I said. "Come on, spit it out."

"The mayor and two councilmen from Springer paid me a visit this morning," he said. "They were carrying a letter from the territorial governor directing you to move your office to the county seat of Colfax County immediately."

This was about as close as possible to the worst possible news I could get without somebody dying. We'd known this was coming but it was still hard to swallow. I knew my wife was going to be the one who had the most difficulty swallowing it.

"Ain't there nothin' you can do to push it down the trail a bit, Bill?" I didn't like the pleading tone in my voice but I couldn't help it.

I saw the regret in Bill Wallace's eyes. "You know I can't, Tommy. The village council was able to put it off before but I'm afraid we've done all we can do." He shook his head. "They got the goldarn territorial governor on their side."

"They really said immediately?" I was

hoping we could still find some room to wiggle here. "Does that mean like sometime in the next few months?"

Wallace seemed remorseful about being the bearer of these bad tidings. "No, Sheriff, they were very clear about it. When they say immediately, they mean they want you to start packing today. They expect you to show up there in Springer tomorrow morning."

"Well, Bill, how in the hell am I supposed to do that?" I exploded at Wallace even though I knew this wasn't his fault. "For one thing, I live in Cimarrón and it's a full day's ride from Springer. For another thing, I'm right in the middle of tryin' to track down a bunch of desperados. If I stop what I'm doin', they'll get clean away."

"I'm very sorry, Tommy," he said.

I started to spark back at him for not calling me by my official title of sheriff, but I realized that he was trying to be sympathetic. No point in taking out my anger on him. I opened my mouth a couple of times to say something but nothing came out. I didn't know what to say.

"I've done everything I know to do, Sheriff," he said. "I think we put this off as long as we could but now we've got to do it."

I wanted to hit someone but there was no

one there who deserved hitting. I looked down and noticed that my fists were clenched. Since I wasn't going to hit anyone, I slowly unclenched them. "What do I tell Mollie?"

"I don't know," Wallace said. He turned his hands over in a gesture of helplessness. "I don't know." He stood there for another moment, looking like he wanted to say something more. Apparently, he couldn't think of anything else to say, either. He shrugged and walked out the door.

Rusty had been standing by while all this transpired. Now he spoke. "I know I'm late gettin' to the party but I don't understand all that was just said."

I felt like I'd been punched in the gut. Like I said, we'd all known this was coming. I guess I'd been fooling myself that it wasn't going to happen.

"The territorial legislature changed the Colfax County seat from Cimarrón to Springer back a year or so ago," I said. "The sheriff, bein' the lawman for the entire county, generally has his office in the county seat. We been stallin' this move for quite a while and the folks in Springer have been pushin' for it all along. Looks like they got the governor on their side now. With me trying to track down this White Caps gang, this couldn't have come at a worse time."

"What if you just say you ain't goin'?" Rusty posed the question I'd been asking myself ever since this subject was first raised.

"I don't know for sure," I answered, "but my best guess is they'd say, 'fine, you're fired.' Then they'd appoint somebody from Springer and that'd be that."

"Would that be a bad thing?"

"Only if you consider not havin' a place to live and any money to buy supplies a bad thing," I said. "We don't need a lot of money, Rusty, but we need more than Mollie brings in from helpin' out at the school. And the house we live in comes with the job. I'd bet a dollar they're plannin' on movin' that to Springer, too."

Rusty grinned at me. "Better not bet," he said. "If they fire you, you ain't gonna have a dollar to spare."

I was in no mood for jokes. "Rusty, I don't think you understand. Mollie has a good job here. She's learnin' to be a teacher and gettin' paid for it. There ain't no job like that for her in Springer."

"Would it be so bad if she had to take a different job for a spell?" I'll give my cousin credit; he was pitching in to try to work out the problem. "Sometimes we all have to do things we'd rather not do to get by."

"Think about it, Rusty," I said. "What are the jobs you see women doin'? If she ain't a teacher, what do you reckon she'd do?"

"Well, she could . . ." He didn't know what to say. "I see what you're gettin' at. If she ain't a teacher, there ain't all that many jobs left over for ladies, leastwise respectable jobs."

"I think you're gettin' the point now, Rusty." I took a deep breath, dreading what I had to do. "I better try to catch up with Mollie before she hears about this from somebody else."

As I led Rusty, the horse, up the street toward the house, I dreaded the thought of the conversation I was about to have with my wife. I know how important her work is to her and I hate the idea of her having to give it up. I reckon a wife's place is with her husband, though. I'm hoping we can have this talk without all the explosions and tears and yelling that sometimes goes along with our "talks."

"Mollie, are you home?" I knew she was. School had been out for several hours and I figured she was bustling about, cleaning and straightening like she does. I didn't know how to begin the discussion, though, and asking if she was home seemed like as good an opening as anything else I could come up with.

"I'm out back pullin' some weeds from the flower bed. Come on back, you can help me."

Mollie had planted some pretty flowers in back to make the house seem more like it was ours and didn't belong to Colfax County. I experienced a new pang of sadness as I thought about all the things she would be giving up. I walked out back.

"Where's your redheaded cousin? I've kind of taken a likin' to that boy."

I'd decided this conversation should be a private one between me and my wife. Rusty had no problem with that. "He's over at the office conversin' with Nathan," I said.

Mollie looked up and read my expression. "What's the matter, Tommy? You look like the world is comin' to an end." For once, she hadn't heard the news before I had a chance to talk with her about it.

"I don't know about comin' to an end," I said, "but the world is sure nuff about to change for us."

"What do you mean?" From the look on her face, I suspected that she had an idea about what was coming.

"I got the news from Bill Wallace when me and Rusty got back to town a little while ago." I paused, grasping for the right words. There weren't any right words. "Some town officials from Springer strutted into his office this mornin' with a letter from the territorial governor sayin' that I had to move the sheriff's office to Springer right away. Right in the middle of these murders I'm tryin' to figure out. Said I had to drop everything and do it."

I felt my stomach flop over as I waited for her to explode. Unlike some other times when I thought her reactions were unreasonable, I figured she probably had every right to explode at this news. That didn't mean I enjoyed it. Her response was entirely different than what I expected and caught me totally off guard.

"I've been expectin' this," she said in a calm and measured tone. "I've been givin' it serious consideration for some time now."

I felt a surge of relief. Maybe there wouldn't be an explosion. "Have you been thinkin' about what kind of job you might be able to find in Springer? They're bound to have a school over there, don't you think? Maybe they could use some extra help."

"No," she said in the same calm voice, "I've been thinkin' that I might not go."

I felt the blood drain from my face. I couldn't believe what I'd just heard. "Did you just say you were thinkin' you might not go?" I'd heard people described as being dumbfounded. I'd never known for sure what that meant until now.

"That's what I said." She looked down for a moment and then looked me in the eye. "I haven't made up me mind for certain but I need to tell you it's what I'm considerin'."

Apparently dumbfounded can last a while. I was still having trouble making sense out of the words she was saying. "How can you say that, Mollie?" I have to confess I raised my voice. Turned out there was an explosion after all, it just didn't come from the party I'd expected. "You're my wife. You go where I go. I thought that was understood." The more I mulled over what she'd said, the more agitated I became. "Where in the hell do you think you'd live, anyway?"

"Could you lower your voice and not curse at me, Tommy?" She looked sad and serious. "We've got to try to talk this through in a reasonable manner. Cursin' at me ain't gonna help."

She's got a lot of nerve saying that after all the times she's raised her voice to me. I almost pointed that out but stopped the words from coming out of my mouth. This was a lot more important than a contest of who was the more reasonable one.

"You're right," I said. "I'll try to calm myself but I'm havin' trouble makin' sense out of what you're sayin'. Why in the world would you not want to be with your husband?"

Mollie frowned and shook her head. "I never said I didn't want to be with you, Tommy, but it's a lot more complicated than that."

Maybe so but I didn't see it. "How is it complicated, Mollie? You're my wife, you go where I go. I've got to go to Springer, you go with me. What's complicated about that?"

"Are you really askin' me that question or are you just sayin' it to prove your point?"

Since it hadn't occurred to me that she might have a good answer, I suppose I was only trying to make my point. I was trying to be reasonable, so I figured I'd have to let her come up with her answer before I told her it didn't make any sense.

"Go ahead," I said in an injured tone. "Let's hear your answer to how complicated this all is."

She responded in the same calm tone that was starting to get on my nerves. I can't believe that I'm missing the Mollie who cries and rants and raves but I am.

"Let's say I move with you to Springer."

Good, we were finally getting somewhere. "I can't find a job at the school so we scrape by on the pittance the county pays you for bein' sheriff."

"It might be tough, Mollie," I said earnestly, "but we'd find a way to get by. Maybe you could take in laundry, have a vegetable garden. There's ways."

"Sure," she said. "It ain't what I want to be doin' but we could figure it out and get by."

Maybe this wasn't going to be as hard as it had looked like. "There, you see," I said in my most reassuring voice. "It ain't that complicated. We just got it figured out."

Mollie shook her head. "And what if one of these times when you're out lookin' for these outlaws that you chase, one of them shoots you dead?"

She sure was looking at the negative side of things. "I reckon that could happen, Mollie, but it could happen while we're livin' in Cimarrón, too." I wondered if she'd heard about me getting shot at up in Chase Canyon the other day.

"It most certainly could, Tommy Stallings," she said. "I worry about that every day. The difference is that if it happened while we're living here, I would have a job that didn't involve me lyin' on me back and

I'd have good friends to help me through me grievin'."

Her words cut me deep even though the same fear had run through my mind. "What do you mean, a job lyin' on your back? Are you sayin' that if I got killed, you'd turn to whorin'?"

"I'm sayin' that if we lived in Springer, I'd have to survive." She sniffed. "Look around you, Tommy. Take a walk down to the Colfax Tavern. You think all them ladies there are engaged in that business because they like it?"

I hadn't given it a lot of thought but I could see her point. Probably most of the soiled doves at the Colfax Tavern and, for that matter, every other lowdown, cheap tavern or dive in the territory, weren't doing what they did because they enjoyed it. They were doing it because they had no other choice.

"I see what you're sayin'," I said, doing my best to keep my voice down. "But Springer ain't that far from Cimarrón. You could come on back here and get your job, couldn't you?"

With a laugh lacking in mirth, Mollie said, "Miss Christy needs help every day. You think she's gonna hold my job open on the off chance that you'll get killed and I'll have to come back to Cimarrón? You think there's not one or two ladies over at the Colfax Tavern who wouldn't jump at the chance to change their life the way I was able to do? What would I do then?"

Dang. She was right, it was complicated. I wasn't sure what to say. "Mollie, I hadn't thought through any of this. It's all brand-new to me. I can see what you're sayin' but it don't change the fact that you're my wife, I love you and I want you by my side."

The only other time in my life I'd felt this low was when I came home to find my family slaughtered by Comanches. Mollie was my family now and my life. I couldn't imagine living without her.

In a voice choked with emotion, Mollie said, "I feel the same way about you, Tommy. That's what makes this so all-fired complicated. I don't know what to do."

Neither did I. I felt like my heart was going to burst right out of my chest. "Mollie, I don't know what else to say." I had to get away. "I'm gonna go back to my office and start packin' things up. Reckon we've both got a lot of serious thinkin' to do."

On my way to my office, I stopped in the telegraph office to send a message to the mayor in Springer to let him know there was no way I could make it there by the next morning. That was a true statement but I intended to embellish a bit by saying I couldn't possibly be there for three days. I didn't know if they'd buy it but I figured it was worth a try. I'm going to require some time to work things out with Mollie and there was also a little matter of that bunch of thieving, murdering outlaws on the loose.

"Ben," I said, "I want to send a telegram to the mayor of Springer."

"Good afternoon to you, too, Sheriff Stallings, I'm fine. Thanks for askin'." Ben Martinez, the telegraph operator, was something of a smart aleck. Of course, he had a point. It was rude of me not to at least say hello before I started throwing orders at him.

"Sorry, Ben," I said. "I've got a lot on my mind, which you'll see as soon as I tell you the message I want sent." That also meant that within fifteen minutes of sending the message, Ben would make sure the whole town was aware of the news. Ben was a bit of a busybody and gossip as well as a smart aleck.

Ben rubbed his hands together vigorously, either to warm them up before he started tapping on his telegraph key or in anticipation of the juicy gossip he was soon to be spreading. It was hard to tell.

I found a pencil and a pad on the counter and wrote down my message to the mayor of Springer. I'd heard his name before but I couldn't recall it at the moment. I kept it brief, telling him that I was following his orders and moving my office over but that it would take me three days to finish the job. I handed the message to Ben and he looked it over. He whistled.

"I heard this was coming," he said, "but I didn't know it was happening now." He shook his head and whistled again. "This is some kind of change, Sheriff. The sheriff's office has always been in Cimarrón, as long as I can remember. When is the missus going to join you in Springer?"

Well, he'd cut right to the heart of my distress. There was a long list of questions I couldn't answer about this move and this one was right at the top of the list. I didn't appreciate him asking me such a tough question, particularly since I didn't see that it was any of his business. I needed him to send the telegram, though, so I considered it wise not to say the first rude thing that popped into my head . . . something along the lines of "mind your own business, you nosy varmint."

"Ben, I don't have time to converse about

this, I got to get my things together. Could you please just send the dang telegram?"

He looked a little wounded but probably not as much as he would have if I'd called him a nosy varmint. "Well, aren't we touchy today?" He harrumphed a couple of times, then set about sending the telegram. "Do you know the name of the mayor?"

"Naw, I can't call it to mind right now," I said, trying to keep the edginess out of my voice. "Don't you reckon if you just start out sayin' 'to the mayor,' the fella on the other end can figure out who to give it to?"

"That'd probably work," he said. He set to tapping on his key and in a very short period of time, he looked up and said, "Done. Anything else you need?"

I thought about it for a moment and decided I ought to let Todd Little down in Las Vegas know I was moving. Since we were both trying to track down this White Caps gang, if there really was such a thing, it'd probably be good for him to know in case he needed to send me a telegram or mail me some wanted posters.

"Yeah, Ben, why don't you send a message to Sheriff Little down in San Miguel County. Tell him I had to move my office to Springer. If he needs to contact me, he should do it through the telegraph office there."

He tapped away for a few seconds and then looked up. "All done. Is that it?"

I knew he was going to start spreading the news as soon as I stepped out the door and to tell you the truth, I wasn't too upset about it. Word would leak out pretty quick, no matter what, and he, at least, possessed the straight information, seeing as how he'd sent the telegram. I figured the sooner word got out, the better. I decided to take steps to speed up the delivery of the news.

"I don't need anything else right now, Ben," I said. "If you get a reply from the mayor, though, could you come find me and let me know what it says? I'll be down at my office. Maybe they'll tell me to take all the time I need." You bet that would happen. I started to walk out, then stopped as if I'd remembered something at the last minute. "You know, Ben, I'd kind of appreciate it if you'd keep this under your hat for now. There's some loose ends I should tie up. I'd like to get 'em taken care of before word gets out."

I swear it looked to me like he was quivering with excitement. "Oh, sure, Sheriff," he said, nodding so hard I thought his head might fall off, "it'll just be between you and me."

Yeah, right. "Thanks, Ben, I appreciate it." I turned and walked out the door. I considered stepping to the side so I didn't get trampled as he ran out to spread the news. I wonder what the telegraph operator is like in Springer.

CHAPTER 13

It was late morning of the fourth day since the gang had delivered several hundred steers and a nice remuda of horses to the mining camp in Morley. They'd spent the next two days laying low in the foothills immediately north of Raton Pass, keeping a sharp lookout in case they'd been followed by Sheriff Stallings. Now, Pat Maes and his gang were at the top of a hill looking down at the ranch house below.

"Feast your eyes, fellas," Maes said. "That's a fine bunch of horses in that corral down there. I heard they need horses at Cokedale. What do you think? Should we take 'em?"

The gang was on their way back from Trinidad. They had intended to head back south to Las Vegas to get further instructions from the Boss but this opportunity looked too good to pass up.

"This is a bigger spread than that last one

we hit," Pony Dolan said, "but I reckon most of the hands are out workin' cattle at this time of day. I wouldn't think there'd be too many folks hangin' around the house." He smiled. "I say we do it."

Manuel Maldonado had been about to say that he thought they should follow their original plan and continue on to Las Vegas. When Pony spoke up, he changed his mind about weighing in. It was one thing to disagree with Maes. Manuel was not afraid of Pat Maes and looked forward to the time when he would settle his score with the man. Pony Dolan was another matter entirely. The man had ridden with the Clanton bunch in Arizona and was a good hand with a gun. Maldonado had also seen the vicious streak he possessed. When he'd come back from his short trip into Cimarrón to rob the mercantile, Dolan had been covered in blood. That had opened Maldonado's eyes. He kept his mouth shut.

Maes turned to Dorsey and Espinosa. "John, Raffy, what do you think?" He intentionally left Maldonado out, knowing it would further antagonize the man. He didn't care. He flat out didn't like him.

Espinosa shrugged. Dorsey said, "Might as well, Pat. They're right there for the takin'. I doubt we'll get a better chance anytime soon." He grinned, showing yellow teeth. "More horses, more money for us."

Maes nodded. Only then did he turn to Manuel Maldonado and ask, "What do you think, amigo?"

I ain't your amigo. Maldonado kept that to himself. There would come a time when he would take care of his business with Patricio Maes but now was not that time. "Sounds good to me."

Maes was surprised at Maldonado's compliance. A flicker of suspicion crossed his mind. *What is this cabrón up to?* The thought passed quickly, however. He was eager to get on with the business of stealing these horses.

"All right, then," he said. "We go in loud, hard, and mean. We kill everyone who is there. And like the Boss says, we give them something to remember." He looked at Pony Dolan. "You savvy, amigo?"

Dolan just smiled.

In the back room that served as his office, the man they referred to as "the Boss" rubbed his hands together and smiled. *I love a small town. No matter what happens, you are bound to hear about it sooner or later.* Sheriff Little received a telegram from that surly sheriff from Cimarrón yesterday. The telegraph operator went home and told his wife, who told a friend, who told the clerk at the mercantile. At that very moment, one of his bartenders was in the mercantile picking up some supplies and overheard the news. He came back and told the Boss. Now the Boss was contemplating his next move to undermine the efforts of Stallings. He smiled as he put together the small package that would accomplish the task. *Only one person in Springer knows my nephew, Ramon, the son of my dead sister. That man is my primo. Ramon can slip in and deliver the gift without anyone noticing, then hide in the shadows until it is discovered. I wish I could be there to see the look on Stallings's face.*

Chapter 14

The events of the past two days are a blur. After I left the telegraph office, I went down to start packing up my things. Rusty was already there. He could tell from looking at my face that something was wrong. I explained curtly that we were moving the office to Springer. When he asked for more details, I told him I didn't want to talk about it. He'd known me long enough to know I meant what I'd said. He just shut his mouth and went to collecting items to pack.

I intended to borrow a wagon from the livery so I could load up the desk, chairs, and guns and such. There were about fifty pounds of paper . . . everything from wanted posters to arrest warrants to letters from other lawmen around the territory . . . and I didn't know how to get it all together so it wouldn't blow away while I was traveling to Springer. I considered burning it but since most of it was official business, I decided against it.

As I was puzzling out how to load everything in the wagon that I didn't have yet, Ben Martinez came in with a telegram from the mayor of Springer, whose name, as it turned out, was Manuel Salazar. The honorable Mayor Salazar had instructed me in no uncertain terms that I was to report for duty in Springer the following day. I told Ben to send a telegram back saying that I would be there in two days and not to bother me anymore in case the good mayor replied. I would get there when I got there. Might as well set the right tone from the start.

I didn't go home that night until late. I had way more to do than I could manage but the real reason was that I didn't want to talk to Mollie. I still didn't know what to say to make her see things my way and I didn't want to have a fight. She had every right to be upset about the situation but the way I saw it, she was my wife and she belonged with me. I didn't understand why she couldn't see that.

My thoughts were jumbled. Mollie had to know that she couldn't stay in our house in Cimarrón for very long with me working in Springer. Where did she think she would live if she stayed here? A much bigger problem that I would have liked to ignore was the question of what in the world would she do in Springer when I left with Rusty for Texas. I couldn't ask her to move and then mention afterwards that, by the way, I would be running off to try to fix a family problem for some folks she'd never met. I couldn't seem to see my way clear to figure this whole mess out.

When I got home, she was already asleep. In fact, I suspect she might have been pretending to be asleep. Likely she wasn't any more eager to talk to me right then than I was to talk to her. The next morning, we tiptoed around each other. I told her what Mayor Salazar had said and what my plans were. She just nodded. I waited, hoping she might say that she'd thought everything through and would be joining me soon in Springer. She didn't say anything.

We stood there feeling awkward, like two shy youngsters at a church social. When I realized she wasn't going to say anything more right then, I cleared my throat and said, "Well, I'm goin' on down to my office to finish loadin' up." I gave her another moment, then said, "Reckon I'll be headin' over once I get everything in the wagon." I waited. She said nothing. "Guess that's that."

As I turned to go, she cried out, "Tommy, wait."

I turned back quickly, hoping she would come to me and hug me and tell me she'd had a change of heart. She didn't.

"I don't know what I'm goin' to do. I love you and I want to be with you." Was she giving in? "You've got to understand that I need to look after meself, though." I started to protest but she waved her hand to silence me. "I know you're goin' to say that you'll look after me but what do I do if somethin' happens to you? What if you're not there to take care of me?" She choked back a sob. "I'll not become a whore, Tommy Stallings, I won't! I went a ways down that path before we met, I'll not go there again."

"Nothin's gonna happen to me, Mollie," I said. "We'll be together and I'll take care of you." As soon as the words sprang from my mouth, I realized how empty they were. I'd been shot once before and shot at more times than I wanted to remember. I was pretty good at being a lawman but mostly, I was alive because I was lucky. Here I was asking the woman I loved to gamble her future on my luck holding out. I could see that, yet I still wanted her to get in the wagon with me and make the trek to Springer. With me planning to go with

Rusty to Texas, I know it's wrong of me to want that and yet I'm so desperate to have her with me, I can't bear the thought of her not being in Springer when I come home.

She smiled but it was the most heartbreaking smile I'd ever seen. "Tommy, you know that's not true. I can see it in your eyes."

Like I said before, the eyes give you away. "So, what do we do, Mollie?"

She shook her head. "I don't know, Tommy. I'm not sayin' I won't come to you but I need more time to think about all this." I thought I saw a flash of resentment in her eyes. "When I'm helpin' these youngsters with their readin', I feel strong and fine. I feel like I'm givin' them somethin' that will change their lives. The boys don't have to be ranch hands because that's what their daddies do and it's all they know. They can choose to be a lawyer or a banker if they want. And the girls, Lord, maybe they won't have to depend on a man to take care of 'em 'cause they don't know how to do anything worthwhile for themselves." She stamped her foot impatiently. "Can't you see what that means to me?"

I sighed. "I do see it, Mollie. I just never thought you'd have to choose between doin' what you loved and bein' with me."

"I never thought it, either, Tommy," she

said. "Like I said, I need time."

I didn't have the words to change her mind. She said she needed time and as far as I knew, I had that to give her. It's not like I have a good alternative, anyhow. "If you need time, Mollie, take it. I'll talk to Bill Wallace about lettin' you stay in the house for the time bein'. It ain't like anybody else will be movin' in right away." I smiled at her even though I was as sad as I'd ever been. "We'll figure somethin' out." Then I walked out the door and made ready to leave for Springer.

Chapter 15

Well, here I am in the town of Springer in the Territory of New Mexico. Cimarrón is a pretty little village nestled between the mountains and the plains. Springer is just plain ugly. It's right on the edge of that old Big Empty where the land rolls and flows forever without anything interesting to look at and the wind always blows. I don't know a soul in town except for my cousin Rusty and I miss my Mollie something fierce. Being away from her is bad enough but the manner in which we parted makes it so much worse.

We got in late last night, a day later than Mayor Salazar had insisted upon. I didn't much care. We'd hitched up my spare horses, an old bay and a paint, to the wagon and trailed Rusty, the horse; Gentry, my mule; and the other horse, the one my cousin, Rusty, rode, behind the wagon. By the time we got to town, we were worn out and, of course, there was no one at the livery to help us with the horses and Gentry. We got them some hay from the stables and watered them at the trough out front. Not knowing what else to do, we hobbled them and Rusty and I threw our bedrolls under the wagon.

The sun was barely up when I heard a voice saying, "Señor. Wake up, señor."

I sat up fast, almost bumping my head on the underside of the wagon. I could see boots and the bottom half of a man's legs beside the wagon. Rusty had managed to sleep through the noise so far.

"I'm awake," I said, although I sounded groggy even to myself. "Let me get my boots on and I'll roll out and talk with you." It occurred to me that I might want to clarify who I was talking to before proceeding any further with this discussion. "Are you the fella who runs the livery?"

"Sí," said the voice coming from just above the boots I could see. "I am Arturo Garcia. Who are you?"

"I'm Tom Stallings," I said, trying to infuse an official-sounding tone in my voice. Mostly, it sounded like I'd swallowed some sand. "Sheriff Tom Stallings. We just got here from Cimarrón late last night. We didn't have any place to stay so we pitched our bedrolls here under the wagon." I cleared my throat to get the sandy sound out. "We took some of your hay for our horses and mule. I'll be glad to pay you for that."

"*Muchas gracias,* señor," Arturo Garcia said. "There is no need, though. If you are the sheriff, the county pays for the feed for your animals. You just have to fill out those papers and they give me the money."

Great. More paperwork. Just what I need. "Thanks, Señor Garcia. I'll attend to that as soon as I decipher where my office is."

By this time, I had gotten my boots on and rolled out from under the wagon. When I stood up, I was looking down on Arturo Garcia. Way down. The man couldn't have been five feet tall with his boots on. I had no idea how old he was because he was wrinkled up like an old grape. He grinned up at me.

"I can tell you where your office is," he said, still grinning. "It is the only empty building on the street."

Great. I don't have an office. That fit with what we had heard months ago when Tomás Marés was still sheriff. I had hoped they might have made a little progress in getting the office ready since that time. Like a lot of things I hope for, it sounded like this was not to be.

Still grinning, Arturo said, "Pardon me, señor, but if you do not mind, I would like to give you some advice."

Arturo seemed friendly enough and since I didn't have a clue about how to carry on, I figured it couldn't hurt to get his advice. "I don't mind at all, Arturo. Is it all right if I call you Arturo?"

"Sí, señor Sheriff," he said in an agreeable manner. "After all, that is my name."

"Well, pleased to meet you, Arturo," I said as I extended my hand. "You can call me Sheriff Stallings. No need to add on señor or anything fancy like that." I felt like maybe we were making some headway. "So, what was that advice you have for me?"

"I would advise you to go right over to Mayor Salazar's office and be waiting for him when he comes in." He shook his head, an expression of concern on his face. "He is not happy with you."

I wondered how the man who owned the livery would know that the mayor was displeased with his new sheriff. "I just got here, Arturo. I ain't had time to do anything to rile him up yet, as far as I know. Do you know what's botherin' him?"

"Sí," he said. Apparently, he recognized the look on my face as one of confusion and surmised that I was baffled by the lines of communication between the mayor and the liveryman. "Mayor Salazar is married to Lupé, my sister, señor. Last night as we were eating tortillas and beans, he mentioned that he had been expecting you the day before." His concerned look deepened. "He was very displeased when he said this, señor. He said some other things as well but I do not think I will tell you what they were because I do not know you that well yet."

Great. I just got to town and I've already made my boss mad. I was about to explain to Arturo that I'd sent the mayor a telegram informing him I would be coming a day later when it occurred to me that it would probably be better take it up directly with my new boss.

"It's all right to spare me the details, Arturo," I said. "I think I get the drift."

I got directions to the mayor's office from Arturo and left Rusty to take care of the animals and wagon. Sure enough, when I got to the office, there was no one there. There was a hitching rail in front of the boardwalk so I leaned against it and waited. I hadn't been there very long before I saw a man walking up the street in my direction. Walking is probably not the best word to describe what he was doing. Strutting fits better. He looked a bit like a rooster as he made his way toward me. I assumed it was Mayor Salazar.

As the man got closer, I took in the details of his appearance. Like Arturo, he was short, although he, at least, came up to my shoulders. Arturo barely came up to my waist. Like some other short men I'd known, he exuded a quarrelsome manner. The closer he got, the more I was aware of his chin sticking out as if he couldn't wait to light into me. I suspected my initial meeting with the mayor of Springer was going to have some bumpy spots. I figured I'd do my best to be agreeable and try to smooth over those bumps if I could. On the other hand, I wasn't going to lick his boots. As far as I was concerned, if he fired me, I could go back, hitch up my wagon, and head home to my Mollie.

"Good mornin', sir," I said in as friendly a manner as I could muster. "I'm bettin' you're Mayor Salazar, aren't you. I'm Sheriff Stallings. Pleased to meet you."

He didn't appear nearly as pleased to meet me as I was to meet him. He ignored my outstretched hand, walked past me without a glance, and unlocked the door to his office. Without glancing back at me, he growled, "Follow me," and walked in. Not a great beginning to our first conversation. I followed him in and waited while he took off his coat and went around behind his desk. Once he was seated, he looked up at me.

"Sit," he said in the same growl, pointing at a chair in front of his desk. I sat. I wasn't sure exactly what to say and for once, had the good judgment not to say anything.

He stared at me for an uncomfortable length of time. It seemed like he was taking my measure. It was clear from his expression that he found me lacking. "You are late."

Mayor Salazar was proving to be a man of few words. Sometimes that's a good thing. In this case, at least so far, his words had either been gruff orders or criticism. That's not a good thing in my opinion, although I was beginning to suspect he wasn't all that interested in my opinion. If I was going to work for him, we'd have to make some adjustments to that pretty quick.

"Did you get the telegram I sent you?" I kept my voice neutral. "I sent a message that it would take me a day longer to take care of business in Cimarrón. I got here as fast as I could."

He glared at me. "Sheriff Stallings, when

I give you an order, I expect for you to follow it. I do not expect for you to defy me."

Although I had referred to him as my "boss," technically he wasn't since I was hired by the county. In many ways, that was just a formality, however. My office was in Springer and he was the mayor of Springer. As a result, he was pretty sure he was my boss. I didn't figure it was the best time to split hairs with him about the lines of authority between a mayor and a county sheriff.

"Mayor," I said, doing my best to maintain my composure, "it was not my intention to defy you. Surely you understand that getting everything in my office together and loaded up took some time. And that doesn't even take into account that I had to say goodbye to my wife and figure out how to try to keep the village of Cimarrón, which, by the way, is a part of Colfax County, for which I am sheriff, safe from the outlaws that have robbed and murdered a number of people in the past few weeks." I realized I had made a speech. I had more I could say but figured I'd shut up again.

If I thought he had glared at me before, this time it looked like sparks were flying from his eyes. "You are in Springer now, Sheriff. You will do things my way or you will not be the sheriff for very long. Do you understand?"

You know, I couldn't say that I did understand. This wasn't the way it was supposed to be, but I didn't know enough about the situation to know how to deal with it. I've worked hard to learn to control my temper. My efforts were certainly being tested at this moment. I took a deep breath to steady myself before I responded.

"Mayor, I hope you'll forgive me for not bein' familiar with the way y'all do things here. I want to do a good job of keepin' Springer . . ." I hesitated, then added, ". . . and the rest of the county safe." Although I was doing my best to be cooperative, I figured I should be clear about what my job was all about. "If I've gotten off on the wrong foot with you, I apologize." I was proud of myself for not gagging when I said that.

It appeared to me that the mayor was trying to decide whether to respond to my apology or address my impertinence for suggesting I owed allegiance to the entire county rather than just the town of Springer. Apparently, he decided he'd made his point clear that he was the big dog here and could ignore my comment about serving the entire county.

"I will overlook it this time, Sheriff," he said, "but if you defy my orders again, I will not be so lenient."

What a nice fella. As I continued to struggle mightily with my urge to gag, I said, "I surely appreciate that, Mayor. Is there anything else? I need to get busy moving my things into the office so I can get on with the job of keeping Springer safe." I smiled.

Apparently, I had groveled sufficiently to satisfy him for the time being. "No," he said, "there is nothing else at the moment." With a dismissive wave of his hand, he said, "Get to work."

He took some papers off his desk and began reading them as if I had already left. I couldn't see that my saying anything more would improve my first heart to heart talk with Mayor Salazar. There was certainly the potential that it could go downhill fast if I said what was really on my mind. I figured that leaving was the best option. I walked out, carefully shutting the door behind me rather than slamming it. See there. I am making progress in controlling my temper. Once I got outside, though, I did gag once.

I walked back down to where my new office was located and found Rusty there hard at work moving things in. He'd hauled in the chairs, boxes of papers, and most of the guns but had waited for me to carry in the desk and the gun cabinet.

"How'd your meetin' with the mayor go?" He glanced over at me as he toted a Winchester and a shotgun in.

"I'd say the only way it could've gone worse is if he had fired me outright," I said. "Come to think of it, that might've been an improvement."

"That don't sound all that promisin'," he said. "What did you do, smart off to him?"

I was wounded. "I beg your pardon, Mr. Rusty Stallings. I was quite civil to the man, which I can tell you, was no easy task. Think about it like you was tryin' to be friendly with the biggest rooster struttin' around in the barnyard. That's about how it went."

"That bad, huh." He grinned at me. "You sure you didn't punch him or say somethin' insultin'?"

"I was as polite as a preacher at a church social, although my tongue is probably bleedin'."

"What was he upset about?"

"Well, he seems to think Springer is a kingdom and he's the king," I said. "Sounds like he's used to folks dancin' to whatever tune he plays. He told me to get here in one day and I didn't do it. He wasn't the least bit interested in my explanation of why that wasn't possible."

"This don't sound real encouragin', cousin." Rusty paused, a frown on his face. "What did he say about me bein' your deputy?"

"I didn't have much of an opportunity to bring that up," I said. "I also didn't think the time was right to explain to him that my other deputy, Sheriff Averill, was stayin' in Cimarrón."

"Why would he have a problem with that? He don't pay you or your deputies, the county does." Rusty snorted. "Surely, he can see that with these murderin' bastards runnin' around, you got to have somebody in Cimarrón lookin' out for those folks, too."

"I get the feelin' Mayor Salazar doesn't care a lick about the rest of Colfax County," I said. "I think he wants me right here in Springer under his thumb."

Rusty chuckled. "I reckon you understand, cousin, that this job ain't likely to go well for you. You ain't one to keep your mouth shut when somebody gets on your nerves."

He was right, this wasn't going to work. As a matter of fact, I didn't even really want it to work since it was likely to wreck my marriage. I had two problems, though. One was that I needed some sort of a job so I got paid regular. The other was that I felt an obligation to figure out who was killing the citizens of Colfax County and bring them to justice. I believe I owe that to the widow Armstrong. She lost a husband and a son to those monsters. It's the least I can do for her.

"We're gonna have to figure out how to make it work, at least for a little while." I had no idea how to do that but it sounded right to me. "Now let's unload that desk and get things situated. When we get that done, we'll go find us some food."

Chapter 16

"Sheriff, we need your help quick. Somethin' terrible happened."

Startled, Nathan Averill glanced up at the cowboy who had burst into the former sheriff's office in Cimarrón. Nathan hadn't bothered to take the sign out front down and had brought in a couple of chairs. He was using it as his headquarters so that anyone looking for him might be able to locate him. He had just been contemplating whether to get a bite to eat at the Marés Café or the St. James Hotel when this young man rushed in.

"I ain't the sheriff, son, I'm the deputy," Nathan said. "Slow down and tell me what happened."

"It's awful, Sheriff," the cowboy said, ignoring what Nathan said. "Somebody killed 'em all."

That grabbed Nathan's attention. He stood up quickly. "Who got killed?"

"You know the Elliott place northeast of town?" The cowboy was so agitated he was hopping from one foot to the other.

"Yeah, I know it," Nathan said, trying to mask his impatience. "Can you get on with tellin' me what happened?"

"Yes, sir, I can," the cowboy said. "Me and the boys were doin' some brandin', we'd been out with the wagon for a couple of days. We got in this mornin' and found 'em dead." The cowboy's face was pale and he looked like he was going to be sick. "They hadn't just been shot, Sheriff, they'd been cut up pretty good."

That sounded to Nathan like the same bunch that had killed the Armstrong fella and Bill Wallace's clerk. He knew he was going to need to summon Tommy and his deputy back here from Springer to look into it but he wanted to gather as much information as he could before he sent a telegram to Springer.

"How many people were killed, son? Can you tell me their names?"

"Oh, yes, sir, sorry. It was Bobby Elliott, his wife, Nancy. They had one boy, Billy." The young cowboy choked up and couldn't continue for a moment. When he recovered, he said, "Billy was just a couple of years younger than me. We was friends. I don't know why anyone would do 'em that way, Sheriff." He turned away from Nathan and wiped at his eyes. Turning back, he said, "Billy didn't come with us 'cause he was fixin' the fence in the corral. I'd been breakin' a colt in there a few days before and he got all snorty, buckin' and such. He knocked down part of the fence." The cowboy stared down at the ground. "If that hadn't happened, Billy would have been with us."

Nathan could see the young man was wracked with guilt. "It ain't your fault, son, it's just bad luck. Be sad for your friend but don't blame yourself."

The cowboy wiped his sleeve across his face. "Maybe you're right, Sheriff. I sure feel awful, though."

"Well, of course you do, boy," Nathan said in a surprisingly gentle voice. "Of course you do." He didn't want to be unfeeling but it was necessary to collect more information so he continued with his questions. "You got any idea when this happened?"

"Reckon it happened yesterday, Sheriff. We left in the afternoon day before yesterday and got back this mornin'. It must've happened sometime yesterday."

"Did these killers take anything?" If they'd followed their previous pattern, they would have made off with the stock.

"They took some fine horses, Sheriff. We had some good young colts we were startin'. Every dang one of 'em was gone."

Sounded like the same bunch to Nathan. "All right, son. Here's what I want you to do. Ride back out to the ranch and have the hands watch over the herd. We don't want those damn yellow dogs comin' back and stealin' the cattle." Nathan didn't think there was any likelihood of that happening but he wanted the hands engaged in a job so they wouldn't go traipsing off after the outlaws themselves. "I'll get a message to the sheriff in Springer, then I'll ride out and take a look at things."

The cowboy appeared puzzled. "You ain't the sheriff?"

Nathan shook his head. "I know it's confusin'. I used to be the sheriff, now I'm the deputy."

"Why's the sheriff in Springer?"

"It's complicated," Nathan said. "I don't want to waste any more time explainin' it to you. Just do what I said, I'll be along directly."

Nathan took the young man by the arm and escorted him to the door. The cowboy continued to seem dazed. Nathan patted him on the back and then gently shoved him out the door. The cowboy looked back at him and waved, then walked over to where he had tied his horse to the hitching rail and climbed aboard. As he rode north out of town, Nathan headed south down Main Street to the telegraph office.

We didn't know where to eat in Springer but I figured if the Brown Hotel was anything like the St. James in Cimarrón, we could probably get filled up without being poisoned. It wasn't hard to locate the hotel since it was three stories tall and set right on the main street. I didn't think it was nearly as impressive as the St. James from the outside. Once we walked in, I didn't see anything to make me change my mind. I found it to be pretty drab. To be fair, I was downright determined not to like anything about Springer. Maybe another person might've liked it fine. Me, well, I missed my friends and most of all, I missed my wife. I wanted to be in Cimarrón.

Sure enough, the hotel had an eatery located off the lobby. Rusty and I took off our hats and walked in. It was around midday but there were only a few other folks in there. A fella came over and made a fuss over us, pulling out our chairs and such. I was not used to being fawned over and found the whole thing pretty doggone irritating. Rusty didn't seem to mind so much.

"Pretty fancy place, don't you think," he said.

"Humph," I responded. "It's all right, I suppose. Don't match up to the St. James, though, if you ask me."

Rusty laughed at me. "If I was to guess, I'd say there ain't much about Springer that'll match up to Cimarrón in your opinion."

I started to argue with him but he was right. I laughed. "Ask me again in a year, maybe I'll see it different by then."

They had a beef stew going in the kitchen. We got large bowls full along with a plate of fried potatoes each and all the coffee we could drink. If I was honest, I'd have to say it wasn't bad. Of course, I wouldn't say it out loud. We were just finishing up our noon meal with a big slab of apple pie each when Mayor Salazar strutted in, accompanied by another fella that I didn't recognize.

"There you are, Sheriff," the mayor said in what sounded to me like a disapproving tone. Was I not supposed to stop to eat? "I have been looking for you." He made it sound like I'd been hiding from him.

"Well, we got done movin' things in the

office and figured we could take a short break to fill our bellies," I said, trying not to sound argumentative. "We were fixin' to head back and start gettin' everything organized." Since Rusty was sitting right there in plain sight, I figured this was as good a time as any to break the news to the mayor that I had a deputy. "Mayor Salazar, this is my deputy, Rusty," I said, waving my hand in his direction. I decided not to share his last name. I didn't know if they had a law against hiring your cousin or some such, although that was hard to imagine since dang near everybody up in these parts is related. You just never know.

Salazar nodded perfunctorily. He gestured to the gentleman who accompanied him and said, "This is Señor Jesus Abreu. He is president of the bank and a member of the town council. He wanted to meet you."

I thought that was interesting. Last summer, Mr. Abreu's bank was robbed not once but twice by the outlaw Jake Flynt and his gang. Since we had tracked Flynt down and killed him, I hoped Abreu might view me in a favorable light. Of course, since Flynt robbed his bank twice in the space of a couple of weeks and killed some folks while doing it, he might have some hard feelings about that.

"Pleased to meet you, Mr. Abreu," I said, standing up and reaching out to shake his hand. He took my hand and shook it warmly. Maybe that was a good sign.

"It is my pleasure, Sheriff Stallings," he said. "I know you had a great deal to do with tracking down that murderer, Flynt, last summer. I wanted to meet you and say muchas gracias."

"You're welcome," I said. "We were doing our jobs, is all." I started to say I was sorry about the people getting killed but I figured there was no need to bring up unpleasantness. If he had hard feelings about that, I'd find out soon enough.

Salazar was watching this interaction carefully. Apparently, we'd spent enough time on pleasantries as he broke in abruptly. "I will not detain you from your duties any longer, Sheriff. I only wanted you to meet Señor Abreu, who, as a member of the town council, is also one of your superiors."

I figured at some point we would need to come to a new understanding of who exactly it was I worked for if this job was going to work out. Now didn't seem like the best time, though. I chose not to respond. Mayor Salazar and Councilman Abreu took their leave. Abreu nodded a cordial goodbye. Mayor Salazar ignored us and strutted out.

"Friendly fella."

"Which one?" Sometimes I can't tell whether Rusty is joshing me or being serious.

"Why, the one who was bein' friendly," Rusty said with a snicker. "The bank president fella. That other goober could pass for a peacock if he had some long tail feathers."

"Don't say it too loud," I replied, "he thinks he's our boss."

"Yeah, I kinda got an inklin'." Rusty shook his head. "Cocky little devil, ain't he."

"He is that." I took the last couple of bites of my pie, which was decent but not of the caliber made by Anita Marés in Cimarrón. "Let's head back and finish straightenin' up our new digs."

"Say," Rusty said. "Where exactly are we supposed to bunk?"

I had given this a bit of thought. "You know as well as I do that once we've run down these outlaws that are killin' and robbin' folks, I intend to head back to Texas with you. I reckon we can throw our bedrolls on the floor in that poor excuse for an office or on the bunks in the cell."

"That works for me," Rusty replied. "I've slept in worse places."

We walked back at a fairly leisurely pace due to the fullness of our bellies. We were a half a block from the office when I noticed a man standing right outside the door. He was pacing in a short circle and gave off the clear impression that he was waiting impatiently for us to arrive back. He looked up as we got a few steps closer and began walking briskly in our direction.

"Are you the new sheriff?" He held a piece of paper in his hand. As he got to within a few feet of us, I could see that it was a telegram.

"I'm the sheriff," I said, "and I reckon I'm new to Springer. Who might you be?"

"Oh, sorry," he said. "I'm the telegraph operator. My name is Jim White."

He had the decency to stick out his hand so I figured I could be decent, too. I shook his hand and said, "I'm Sheriff Tom Stallings." Beside me, Rusty smothered a chuckle. He can't seem to get over calling me Tommy. Mildly irritated by his lack of respect, I jerked a nod his direction and said, "This fella is my deputy. He don't have a name, we just call him 'deputy.' "

White was momentarily confused by the exchange but chose to ignore it. "Sheriff, I have an urgent telegram for you from that other sheriff fella over in Cimarrón." Noticing my confused expression, he said, "That would be Sheriff Averill. In the telegram, he says he's your deputy but I know he used to be the sheriff. I don't understand all that but it ain't as important as what he said in the telegram."

He handed the paper to me and I quickly read it. I handed it to Rusty and felt my meal begin to churn in my stomach. The telegram briefly detailed the robbery and murders at the Elliott ranch and urged me to return to Cimarrón right away.

I took the telegram back from Rusty and turned to Jim White. "Thanks for getting this to me so quick. I appreciate that, Mr. White." I pondered it for a minute, then said, "Mr. White, would you please send Deputy Averill a telegram back and notify him we're goin' directly to the Elliott place. Tell him I'd like him to remain in town and keep an eye on things." Looking back at Rusty, I said, "If we hurry, we might get there in time to pick up their trail. I think we'd be better off not wastin' time goin' to Cimarrón. This is gettin' out of control."

Nathan hated to miss the action but he figured Tommy was right to go straight to the Elliott place. If there was a chance to catch up to the rustlers, and he suspected it might already be too late for that, bypassing Cimarrón and going directly after them was the way to go. He also figured his staying back in town made sense. This bunch was not only murderous, they seemed to be pretty cagey as well. He wouldn't put it past them to try a sneak attack if they thought Cimarrón was unprotected.

Of course, Springer was unprotected but Nathan didn't much care about that. He'd always headquartered in Cimarrón and the safety of the citizens of the village was his main concern. He appreciated that times had changed and wondered if this might be a problem for Tommy. *It's not my problem.* Nathan chuckled. *I think I could get used to this deputy business. Not as many politicians breathin' down your neck.*

He walked over to Ben Martinez's office and told the telegraph operator to send a brief message to Springer saying he'd gotten Sheriff Stallings's instructions and was following them. As an afterthought, he told Ben to add the words, "Good hunting, keep me posted" at the end. With that task done, he took a stroll around town, occasionally stopping to visit with folks to see if they'd noticed anything or anyone who appeared suspicious. Nobody had seen anything out of the ordinary.

Chapter 17

I was worried about Rusty's lack of experience in gunfights, but I figured if he was going to be my deputy, he'd have to get his feet wet sooner or later. The way things had been in Colfax County for the past few years, sooner was more likely than later.

"We'll take a look at things at the Elliott place and see which way the tracks lead. They may take the stock to that hidden ranch or they may take off north to sell 'em right away. Either way, we're chasin' these fellas. I'm tired of playin' catch-up." I reached down and patted the Winchester tucked into the saddle scabbard. We'd taken the time to get as much firepower and ammunition as we could carry before we left Springer.

"You reckon some of those cowboys at the Elliott place might want to join up with us and chase these nasty varmints?" Rusty sounded a little nervous.

"Rusty, I know those boys at Elliott's. They're pretty fair hands but they're awful young. They don't have any know-how about chasin' outlaws. I'm afraid they'd be more of a hindrance than a help."

Rusty kind of flared up at that. "Sounds like you're sayin' you already got your hands full wet-nursin' me and don't need any more tenderfoots to look after."

"I wasn't sayin' nothin' about you," I said with as much patience as I could find. "I was talkin' about those cowboys at Elliott's. Since you brought it up, though, I'll tell you exactly what my thoughts are on the subject."

"Well, I would sure appreciate it if you would," Rusty said. He sounded mad but also maybe a bit hurt as well.

"Rusty, I know you got grit, you're as tough as they come. I don't doubt that for a second."

"Well, thanks for that, at least," he said.

I tried to think about the best way to put into words what I needed to say next. "The thing is, bein' in a fistfight, standin' up to a bully, that ain't the same as havin' somebody shootin' at you. It takes some gettin' used to." I chuckled although the situation wasn't all that funny. "The only way to get used to it is to do it. To get good at it, like Nathan

Averill, you got to survive it . . . and that ain't easy."

"I didn't reckon it would be easy," he said, "but I sure intend to survive it."

"Of course you do," I said. "So do I and so does everyone who ever finds themselves in a situation like that. Bein' tough, knowin' how to shoot, that's important. The thing is, sometimes it comes down to dumb luck." I shook my head. "You can't plan for luck."

Rusty's eyes had gotten a little bigger as I talked. Maybe he hadn't thought this whole deputy thing through before now. Like I said, though, he's tough. He squared his shoulders and said, "Tommy, as far as me and Mama and Pa go, you're still part of the family. I know you're my cousin but really, you're like my brother. I came out here to find you and tell you that. I don't plan to deliver that message and then get killed." He grinned. "That'd pretty much make a mess of everything."

"That would put a damper on the family reunion, wouldn't it," I said, going along with the joke. It's a hard thing for cowboys to say how much we mean to one another. We don't generally do it. I knew what he was getting at, though. "We'll get through this; I got a good feelin' about that. Just don't think it's gonna be a church picnic.

These are some vicious outlaws we're trackin'. They'd kill and gut us both without thinkin' twice about it." I nodded at him, doing my best to convey in that simple gesture both the seriousness of the situation as well as how much I appreciated his standing beside me.

With a sigh, he said, "Glad we got straight on that." He paused for a heartbeat, then said, "Hey, Tommy, if you get killed, can I marry Mollie?"

When it comes to cowboys hoorahing each other, nothing is sacred.

Pat Maes and his boys were plenty tired. Two days of bad weather made the trek up to Trinidad with those young horses a nightmare. The damn dinks kept spooking at every bolt of lightning and then they'd have to slog through the mud to chase them down. They'd started out with twenty colts and got to Colorado with eighteen. Pat figured he could live with that since they commanded a fair price. He was ready to head home to San Miguel County.

"Once we're through the pass, we'll swing a bit to the east before we head down to Las Vegas." The five outlaws had stopped on a rise about a mile north of Raton Pass. "I don't know if that lawman is gonna chase after us or not but I don't want to take any chances."

"Let's hope he ain't waitin' somewhere off the trail in the pass," Maldonado said. "I don't want you leadin' us into some ambush."

Maes had already thought about that possibility and was plenty concerned. The fact that it was Manuel Maldonado who brought it up irritated him mightily. "I tell you what, Manuel," he said, "I'd be happy to let you lead us if you'd like. Why don't you ride on out front there?"

The other men laughed. Maldonado said nothing in return, his jaw clinched in anger and his thoughts bitter. *Why, so you can shoot me in the back, cabrón? I'll show you.* He spurred his horse and set off at a fast lope towards the entrance of Raton Pass.

The other men looked at each other in amusement. They urged their horses forward, forgetting for the moment how tired they were. Rafael Espinosa kicked his horse into a gallop and overtook Maldonado as they came upon the opening leading into the pass. He took off his hat as he rode past Maldonado and swatted him with it. Angered by this affront, Manuel gave chase. The other three rode hard so they could have a good view of the horse race.

With no warning, a shot rang out. Espinosa tumbled from his saddle and rolled a good ten feet before coming to a stop against a large boulder. He didn't move.

"Good shot, cousin," I said. I just hoped the man my deputy had shot was one of the outlaws we were chasing. Since there wasn't much of an opportunity to stop and discuss it with them, I figured we'd forge ahead. "Let's try to take some others down before they find cover."

As I spoke, the four outlaws split off and raced for the cover of the trees and rocks up the slope of the canyon. Two went west, two went east. We fired at them but failed to hit anyone. We could see the men dismounting and grabbing rifles so they could return fire. It had been pure luck that we'd stepped down off our horses to look at tracks a moment before the outlaws came riding full tilt in our direction. I was impressed with how quickly Rusty reacted, yanking his Winchester out of the scabbard and pulling off a shot.

"Find some cover pronto," I barked. "They're fixin' to start shootin' back." As I spoke, I spotted a group of boulders, led my horse over, and quickly slid in behind them. I'd barely made it behind the rocks when the gang unleashed a firestorm of bullets in our direction. I hadn't seen whether Rusty had made it to cover or not. At the moment, I didn't dare look.

After a harrowing couple of minutes, there was a brief lull in the shooting as the rustlers reloaded. In one quick motion, I stuck my head up over the biggest rock and looked around for my cousin. Rusty was about twenty yards away, crouched down behind some boulders of his own. Satisfied that he was safe for the moment, I returned fire. I emptied my rifle and then slid back down behind my cover to reload.

I had a full ammunition belt and there were two additional boxes of bullets in my saddlebags if I could only reach them without getting shot. Rusty, my horse, had exercised good judgment by bolting up into the trees. That would probably keep him safe but it would make it more difficult for me to get more ammo if I needed it. As far as I knew, Rusty, my cousin, might be in the same situation. If we remained locked in a standoff with the outlaws, sooner or later, we'd come out on the short end because we were outnumbered. I pondered my options. *Reckon we'll let this play out a bit and see what happens. It might be necessary to make a break for it.*

■ ■ ■ ■

Maes and Pony Dolan were up in the rocks on the west side of the canyon entrance. Maldonado and Dorsey had made it to the east side. Pat could see Rafael Espinosa lying in the same spot where he had rolled to a stop. He hadn't moved and Maes figured he was probably dead.

"What do you think, Pony?" Maes had been in some gunfights but he knew Dolan had a lot more experience with this sort of situation. He was willing to let him take the lead if he had a plan.

"One of us should head up into the trees, see if we can ease on behind 'em. I'll do that." Dolan took off his hat and wiped sweat from his forehead. Putting his hat back on, he said, "Looks to me like there's only two of 'em. See if you can get Dorsey to do the same thing as me on the other side. Once we get 'em in a crossfire, they'll be ours for the takin'."

Maes contemplated the idea briefly and then said, "All right, go."

As Pony Dolan slipped away up the slope to the west, Maes whistled to get Dorsey's and Maldonado's attention. When they looked over, he pointed to where Pony was moving carefully up the side of the canyon and then motioned with his finger that one of them should do the same on their side. It took a moment for them to understand what he was trying to communicate, then he saw Dorsey nod. They appeared to have a brief squabble about who would go. Dorsey must have won the argument because he started winding his way through the boulders up to the east side of the canyon. *This should be over soon enough.* He smiled.

There was a break in the shooting as the outlaws began to execute their plan. I took the opportunity to yell at Rusty. "They're tryin' to get behind us. If they do, we're dead men."

Rusty didn't say anything but I could see that his eyes were as wide as a couple of dinner plates. I craned my neck to see where his horse was and observed that the animal had done the same thing my horse had . . . headed up the hill to safety. Smart critters. Maybe they knew what they were doing.

"Rusty, when I say the word, run for your horse like your tail's on fire. We got to get out of here." I saw him nod. I took a deep breath, got into a crouch so I could get a good jump, and then hollered, "Go!"

It took the outlaws a second to realize what we were doing, which probably saved our lives. I made it to Rusty's side and swung into the saddle as they started firing at us. Thanks to my horse's good judgment, the trees shielded us. I didn't squander a second. I spurred him down the slope and headed south at a full gallop. I didn't look for my cousin because my full attention was focused on staying in the saddle but out of the corner of my eye, I saw him pull up even with me. From there, it was a horse race.

Maes and Maldonado saw the lawmen sprint up opposite sides of the canyon. They blazed away at them but the men and their horses were moving too fast. The pass made a gradual curve to the west and they were very quickly out of sight. Dolan and Dorsey heard the gunfire and saw what had transpired. Unfortunately, they were both up in the trees and couldn't get a clear shot at the escaping men.

Maldonado ran for his horse. He glanced back at Maes and realized he was standing still. "Come on, *cabrón,* they're getting away."

"Hold up," Maes barked at him. "Wait until Pony and John get here."

"Are you loco?" Maldonado was livid.

"They're getting away."

Maes ignored Maldonado and waited as Dolan and Dorsey quickly made their way down to where he was standing. They were puffing a bit from the run and waited for Maes to speak. Maldonado grudgingly made his way over to the group.

"Yeah, we could go barrelin' after them, John," Pat was saying as Maldonado stepped up beside Pony Dolan. "We might catch 'em, you're right. They also might go a mile into the pass and pick a nice spot to ambush us as we ride after 'em."

Dorsey thought about what Maes was saying. After a moment, he nodded. "You got a point. So, if we don't chase 'em, what do we do?"

"Well, there ain't no good way to get down to Las Vegas other than through the pass. We have to go that way but we can damn sure be careful about it. I say we get up in the trees, two to a side. We take our time and keep on the lookout. If we catch up to 'em, we'll finish 'em off. If not, we'll ride back home and see what the Boss wants us to do."

"Cobarde." Manuel Maldonado muttered the Spanish word for coward under his breath.

Pat Maes's head whipped around. "What

did you say?" he demanded.

"Nothing, amigo. I just said it was a cautious plan." Maldonado smiled at him. "I would not expect for you to come up with a bold plan."

"I've had enough of your mouth, *cabrón,*" Maes snarled. "Let's settle this here and now."

Maldonado took a step in Maes's direction but Pony Dolan stepped in between them. "You boys need to put a lid on this. We got more important business to take care of than your little feud. I don't think the Boss would be too happy to hear that we let those damn lawmen get away 'cause you were fightin' with each other."

The two men glared at each other. Without taking his eyes off Maldonado, Maes said, "You're right, Pony, we got business to take care of." Through clenched teeth, he said, "Don't think I will forget about this, *hijo de puta.* A time will come . . ." He left the rest unsaid.

Manuel Maldonado smiled back at him. "I look forward to it."

I was pretty sure one of us was going to suffer a broken neck. Things can always go wrong when your horse gallops on level ground. When you're going full out through a rocky canyon, the odds of having a wreck are a whole lot higher. I could tell that Rusty was getting winded and knew we'd have to pull up pretty soon. I reined him in to a lope and waited for my cousin to catch up with me.

"Why in the hell are you slowin' down?" Rusty asked in an alarmed voice. "We need to get out of here."

"Slow down, Rusty," I shouted at him. "If our horses give out or we get throwed, we ain't gettin' out of nothin'." He reluctantly slowed down and pulled alongside of me.

"All right, now what?"

"We strike a lope for a bit," I said. "If we find some flat stretches, we can push the horses a little but we got to save their strength. We got a pretty good start on those back-shootin' outlaws. They can't gallop the whole way, neither."

"What do you think about pullin' off the trail and waitin' for 'em?"

I had considered that but had rejected the notion. "That's a great idea as long as it works. The trouble is they'll prob'ly be expectin' it. If so, we could wind up right back in the spot we were in before. I don't think we can take the chance." Rusty looked relieved.

"Well, if you think that's best, all right, then."

"I do. I think our best bet is to ride back to Cimarrón for some help. We could use Nathan's gun in this tussle." I chuckled. "We could use his experience, too. He's done this kind of thing a whole lot more than you and me. He might come up with a plan that'd work."

"Sounds good to me," Rusty said as he looked back over his shoulder. "Damn," he said, "I got this prickly feelin' runnin' down the middle of my back. I kept waitin' for a bullet to hit me."

"Welcome to the law enforcement business, cousin," I said. "I'd like to tell you that you get used to the feelin' but I'd be lyin' if I did."

"Well, that's just great," he said.

We picked up our pace a bit and continued south. As worried as I was about the outlaws on our trail, I still found my mind straying to the possibility of seeing my wife when we got to Cimarrón. In the short time I'd been in Springer, I'd gone back and forth between missing her something fierce and being furious with her. I was doing the best I could to understand why she hadn't just packed up and followed me but I have to confess that I didn't quite comprehend it. I had no idea how we would work this out and the uncertainty was wreaking havoc with my nerves. I had a nagging suspicion in the back of my mind that my expectations of my wife were mighty unreasonable given that I intended to head to Texas when this business was done. I did my best to ignore it but it was there nonetheless.

As if he was reading my mind, Rusty asked, "You plannin' on seein' Mollie while you're in town?"

"Don't know if I'll have the time," I snapped. "I can't hardly stop in the middle of chasin' outlaws to visit with my wife now, can I?"

"Ain't you the prickly one," Rusty responded. "I was just askin'. No need for you to get all over me 'cause you're frustrated about somethin' else."

He was right, of course, but I wasn't willing to acknowledge it. Even though my own mind had been wandering into this territory, I lit into him. "We got some killers on our trail, cousin. Now ain't the time to be worryin' about the condition of my marriage."

He didn't say anything back at me but I could see from the look on his face that I'd stung him a bit. He was just showing his concern for me. I should have apologized to him straight away but I wasn't ready to let it go. Along with everything else, I think my pride was wounded by Mollie's not moving with me to Springer. It was tough to swallow.

We rode along in silence, keeping a steady lope when the terrain allowed for it. We were near the south end of Raton Pass when I said, "There's a stream up ahead. I think we're all right to stop and water the horses. You do that while I keep an eye on our backs."

Rusty didn't say anything in response. I could tell he still had his long johns in a tangle. I reckon he had a right to be upset with me. He was just asking a simple question and I'd taken out my aggravation on him. It wasn't his fault me and my wife were having troubles.

"Look," I said as we pulled up at the edge of the stream, "I know you was only askin' a simple question back there. It just happened to be one that I got no good answer to and it's causin' me a ton of grief." I swallowed a chunk of pride and said, "I'm sorry for flarin' at you. You didn't deserve it."

"I know I didn't deserve it," he said. "I also know it's a matter that's been eatin' at you. I probably shouldn't have brought it up but I'm worried about the both of you."

He stepped down out of the saddle and took the reins in his left hand. "You're family and in the short time I've known your wife, I've come to think a lot of her. I want you to be happy."

I dismounted and handed him the reins to Rusty, then took my Winchester from the scabbard. "I know you do and I appreciate that. It's a tough deal we're goin' through. The worst part is I got no idea how it's all gonna turn out." I turned to the north to keep an eye out for the outlaws on our trail.

He led the horses over to the stream. "I wish I had some answers for you, cousin. Sometimes it just requires the passin' of time for things to shake out. Right now, you're both stuck. Somethin's bound to change sooner or later. When it does, y'all will get back together. I believe that."

"Thanks, Rusty, I appreciate it. I sure do hope you're right." Of course, he had no way of knowing that for a fact but it still made me feel better. I chuckled. "Who knows, if we survive today, maybe things'll start lookin' up." I couldn't have been more wrong.

"You were too timid, amigo," Manuel Maldonado said with a sneer. "Oh, did I say timid? Maybe it would sound better if I said you were too careful. Those *cabrónes* didn't slow down until they hit Springer. Now we got to watch our backs all the way to Las Vegas."

The outlaws had dismounted and were looking at tracks in a wet spot on the trail. The hoof prints were deep and it was clear that the riders had been going fast and hard. Pat Maes knew that if they had kept up such a pace, they would be too far ahead of the gang for them to catch them in the pass.

"Sí, amigo," Maes retorted, "and if we had blundered ahead like you wanted to do, they could have ambushed us and wiped us out. Would that have satisfied you?"

Maldonado shook his head in disgust but didn't respond. Dorsey walked off a little distance, apparently looking to separate himself from the ongoing conflict between Maes and Maldonado. Pony Dolan, on the other hand, had put up with as much bickering as he could tolerate.

"You two better knock it off or I'm gonna shoot both you sons of bitches," he said in a matter-of-fact tone. Both men gave him an inquisitive look, unsure as to whether or not he was serious. He could see the uncertainty in their faces and smiled at them. "You don't want to find out if I'm joking or not. Let's keep moving."

He was right, neither man wanted to take a chance at calling out Pony Dolan. Although Pat Maes was the designated man in charge, Pony was the de facto boss because he was the roughest hombre amongst them. Maes clearly understood that and wanted to keep him as an ally.

"Pony's right, amigo," he said. "We're wasting time. When we come out of the pass, we need to swing to the east of Raton. Those *pendejo* lawmen will most likely head due south to Springer. We can swing back to the southwest towards Las Vegas once we get past Clayton. They ain't gonna set up an ambush that far off their trail."

Maldonado's anger simmered but, like Maes, he was scared of Pony Dolan. He could tell that Maes was kissing up to Dolan so that he would be on his side if it came down to a fight. He didn't know how successful this effort was, but he didn't want to take a chance that might involve his confronting Dolan directly. He would put off dealing with Pat Maes until it was just the two of them.

"Fine by me, amigo," he said. "Let's quit jawing and ride."

Chapter 18

We pushed hard for twenty miles or so and then camped south of Raton Pass. We struck an early start the next morning and arrived in Cimarrón in the early afternoon. I desperately wanted to see my wife but I knew it was more important to find Nathan first and fill him in on what had happened. I figured between the two of us, we could come up with a plan for tracking these outlaws. I wish I could be more confident that between me and Mollie, we could come up with a plan for ourselves.

We rode into town and went straight to the former sheriff's office. Sure enough, the door was open. When we walked in, Nathan was sitting in a chair, tilted back on two legs against the wall, drinking a cup of coffee. As soon as he saw us, he jumped up.

"No need to get up, Nathan," I said, "we'd be happy to have a seat and visit."

He reached into his vest pocket and pulled

out what appeared to be a telegram. "I don't reckon you're gonna want to sit and visit once you read this, Sheriff Stallings."

His formal tone threw me off and it took a second for it to register that when he said "Sheriff Stallings," he was talking to me. That realization was immediately followed by the thought that this must be pretty grave business. Even before I read the telegram, I had a pretty good idea who it would be from. My new friend, Mayor Salazar, seemed determined to stay on top of me like I was his personal lackey. Apparently, he hasn't received the news that I'm employed by the county of Colfax rather than the town of Springer. Either that or he just doesn't care.

"Let me guess," I said, making no effort to keep the sarcastic tone out of my voice, "it's from the honorable mayor of Springer."

"It is," Nathan said. "I took the liberty of reading it." The look of apprehension on his face stopped me from making any more smart-aleck remarks.

I unfolded the telegram and read through it quickly. Yet again, I felt like I'd been punched in the stomach. It was a feeling I was experiencing too often these days. I read it again more slowly but the reaction of shock and dread remained. The note said

I was to return to Springer immediately or face legal action. I had no idea what this referred to or what legal action I might be faced with but it sure sounded grim. I wracked my brain trying to think of what might have spurred the mayor to send such a message. I could think of nothing.

I pondered the situation for a moment, then spoke. "You got any hunches as to what this is about, Nathan?"

Nathan did his own pondering before responding. He shook his head. "I ain't clear on what he's referrin' to about you facin' legal action. I knew Manuel Salazar before he was mayor. He's always been full of himself, even when he was a youngster. I ain't surprised that he ordered you to come back pronto, that fits his style. It's the 'legal action' part that's got me worried."

"Got me worried, too," I said. I was sorely disappointed with this latest communication from the good mayor. I had hoped to spend a bit of time with Mollie. I didn't know what I would say to her but it didn't matter. I needed to see her. Now it sounded like, much as I hated it, I'd have to put that off. "Reckon I'd better burn up the trail over to Springer and check this out."

Rusty had been quiet up to now. He asked, "Do you want me to come with you or head out again to track those outlaws?"

I didn't want Rusty out on the trail of those killers by himself but I didn't want to say it out loud. "I want you to accompany me. Until we find out what this is all about, we don't know how to move ahead with tryin' to find those murderin' thieves. Once we know what Mayor Salazar is up to, we can figure out our plan." Turning towards Nathan, I asked, "Does that sound right to you?"

"Makes sense to me," he said. "I know you hate all this startin' and stoppin' with tryin' to track these murderin' thieves down." With a trace of a grin, he said, "Makes you wonder how many criminals we'd catch if we didn't have all this meddlin' from the politicians."

I shook my head and rolled my eyes. "What it really makes me wonder is what in the world I was thinkin' when I took this job. I don't know how you stood it all those years."

"Well," he said, "it takes some time but you figure out how to handle the different politicians. Some of 'em you have to sweet-talk and some you have to get in their face." His eyes narrowed. "I'll tell you this, it ain't gonna help anything for you to get in Manuel's face. No matter what he throws at you, keep a level head."

Since I wasn't exactly known for keeping a level head, I figured I had my work cut out for me. I respected Nathan's judgment, though. If he said I needed to do a little smiling and groveling, I'd do my best.

"I'll be so level-headed, you won't even recognize me, Nathan." I thought for a minute, then said, "If you'll keep an eye on things here, I'd feel a whole lot more settled. I'd also appreciate it if you'd send a message back to the mayor tellin' him I'm on my way. Make sure you tell him I won't get there until tomorrow. We're gettin' too late a start to get there today. We'll have to camp tonight. Tell him I reckon we'll get in around noon." I turned to Rusty. "We ought to change horses, these critters need a rest."

I hated not having my horse Rusty with me. He's my amigo and there's just something calming about having him around. He'd been ridden hard, though, and given me the best he had. I wanted to return the favor and give him a little break.

"I'd like to be there to see you bein' level-headed." Nathan smiled. "Send me a telegram once you get this mess figured out."

We got fresh horses and lit out towards Springer. For the first few miles, we talked about what that "legal action" thing might mean. It soon became clear that we could talk about it all day and still not figure it out so we let it drop. We spent some time recollecting adventures we'd had when I lived with Rusty and his family. Like usual when cowboys get to talking about wrecks they've been in, the memories were a lot more amusing than the actual events had been at the time.

As dusk settled in, we found us a spot close to a stream. We watered the horses, got them hobbled, and built a small fire to heat up some coffee. We made do with jerky and cold biscuits and turned in pretty quick once we choked it down. I wanted to get an early start in the morning and we ought not to stay up swapping lies around the campfire.

I was up before dawn the next day. I got Rusty rolled out and, to his dismay, I refused to take the time to heat up a pot of coffee. I didn't want to arrive later than the mayor expected and if at all possible, I wanted to be early. We did little talking as we rode briskly towards Springer in the east. We got there a good hour before noon.

As we rode into town, Rusty asked, "Do you want to stop by your office first?"

"I don't see any point in that," I said. "I'd

just as soon find out what this is all about and get it over with as quick as I can."

We eased the horses up the street and tied them off at the rail in front of the mayor's office. The door was closed so I knocked. A gruff voice told me to come in. When I walked in, I saw the mayor seated behind his desk. He immediately hopped up and pointed to a chair in front of that desk.

"Sit," he commanded.

It sounded like he was talking to me as he would to a dog, which I didn't particularly appreciate. However, since I was being level-headed, I sat. Rusty looked at me in confusion, unsure of what he should do. I nodded to the other chair in front of the desk and he sat down. Mayor Salazar ignored him as he glared at me.

"You are in serious trouble, Sheriff Stallings," he snapped.

I waited as he glared at me some more, hesitant as to how I should respond. When he didn't say anything else, I spoke up. "I got that impression from the telegram you sent, sir. I'm baffled as to what I'm in trouble for, though. Me and my deputy here have been out chasin' some dangerous criminals who have robbed and murdered citizens of Colfax County. I have no idea how I could have got myself in trouble while

I was doin' that."

Another long glare, then he took something off his desk and held it out to me. "Maybe this will shed light on what you are in trouble for, Sheriff." He held out a piece of paper and a small leather pouch.

I frowned in bewilderment and took the items from him. There was something with some weight to it in the pouch and there was writing on the paper. I decided to read the note first before opening the pouch. As I read the words, I was stunned. In disbelief, I read the note again. The words on the paper were the same thing the second time around. The note said, *"Here is another payment for you. There is more to come if you back off."*

It took me a moment to find my voice. When I did, I said, "Mayor Salazar, I have no idea what this means. Where did you get this?"

"Look in the pouch, Sheriff," he said in a harsh voice. "Tell me what you see."

I opened the pouch and poured out the contents. They clanked and jingled musically as they settled on the surface of the desk. I looked closely and saw that there were five twenty-dollar gold pieces in front of me. Gradually, it dawned on me. I was being framed.

Reminding myself I shouldn't rile the mayor any more than he already was, I spoke in an even voice. "Mayor, I have no idea what this is or where it came from. Why do you think it has anything to do with me?"

He slammed his hand down on his desk, causing both me and Rusty to jump. "Because Jim White found it on your desk when he came to deliver a telegram to your office. I think the meaning is very clear. My only question for you is, who is paying you off?"

I could feel the anger rising and struggled to keep myself under control. "Mayor, I don't know anything about any telegram. If Mr. White brought it to my office, he sure didn't leave it anywhere that I could see it. And more importantly, no one is payin' me off."

"Why would they leave this money and note for you then?" He looked at me with scorn. "I was warned about you, that you would be insubordinate. I didn't think you would be dishonest as well."

The question briefly crossed my mind as to who might have warned him about me but I had more important issues to deal with first. "Mayor, I don't know who's settin' me up but that ain't my money and I ain't done nothin' wrong."

"We will see about that," he said. "We will

have an investigation and get to the bottom of this."

I strove mightily to keep that level head I'd discussed with Nathan. Though I knew I hadn't done anything wrong, the situation looked bad. As Salazar took the note and pouch back from me, I turned to Rusty and whispered, "Get over to the telegraph office and send a message to Nathan. Tell him I'm in deep trouble. Ask him to get over here as fast as he can." Rusty got up and headed for the door.

"Where are you going, deputy?" Mayor Salazar demanded of Rusty.

Thinking quickly, Rusty said, "It looks to me like the two of you may be here a while. I'd better take care of the horses." In a deferential tone that must have nearly caused him to choke, Rusty said, "I hope that's all right with you, sir."

Salazar apparently didn't see any harm in it. Clearly, his business was with me rather than with my deputy. "All right, deputy, go take care of the horses. Be quick about it, though. I want you to get back to the constable's office to guard the prisoner."

It took a moment for me to understand his meaning. "What do you mean, Mayor?"

"What I mean, Sheriff, is that until this matter is cleared up, you will be in the cell in the constable's office."

I exploded. "You're plum loco, Salazar. Someone's settin' me up. In the meantime, we got outlaws killin' people. I need to be out there tryin' to apprehend 'em." So much for being level-headed.

If I thought he had glared at me before, this time around it looked like he might burn a hole in me. "It is *Mayor* Salazar to you, Sheriff. If someone is setting you up, we will get to the bottom of it. In the meantime, you are suspected of accepting a bribe. Until I say different, you will be locked in a cell."

It didn't seem like the time to point out to him that his third-rate constable's office cell didn't even have a lock that worked. I didn't know what to do other than go along with what he said and hope that Nathan got the message and got over here as fast as possible. This had turned into a real mess.

I took a deep breath to compose myself and said, "I apologize, Mayor Salazar, if I sounded disrespectful. I do understand you can't ignore somethin' like this. The thing is, I know I'm innocent. While you look into it, the men who are terrorizin' the county are gettin' away. I ain't happy about that."

Only partially mollified by my apology, Mayor Salazar said, "Your happiness is not my concern, Sheriff. I will *not* have corruption in my town."

Another deep breath. This being level-headed was hard work. "I understand, sir. Would you like for me to go on over to the constable's office and get in the cell?" Under different circumstances, I might have found it amusing that, in effect, I would be arresting myself.

Salazar seemed momentarily confused but he recovered quickly. "Yes, that would be acceptable. When your deputy returns from taking care of your horses, tell him to stop in to see me for further instructions."

"Yes, sir, I'll do that."

I got up, took myself into custody, and escorted myself down the street to the constable's office, feeling pretty foolish as I did so. There wasn't much else I could do at this point except wait for Nathan to arrive and hope that he had some sway with Salazar.

In the shadows, a young man leaned up against a window. Furtively, he listened to the conversation, thinking how pleased his uncle would be at the developments.

Christy enfolded Mollie Stallings in her arms, doing her best to soothe her as she sobbed. She had just finished imparting the information that her husband, Deputy Sheriff Averill, had shared with her before he left in a rush for Springer. She gently patted Mollie on the shoulder and waited for the sobs to subside. It took several minutes before Mollie was able to collect herself.

"I don't know what to do," Mollie said as she choked back her tears. "I never should have let him go to Springer without me. I don't know what I was thinkin'."

"That's nonsense, Mollie," Christy said. "You had good reason to be hesitant about leaving Cimarrón. We don't even know for sure what Tommy's troubles are all about but I can promise you, you couldn't have prevented it by moving to Springer."

"Maybe so, but I still don't feel good about it," Mollie said. "Tommy was right. A wife's place is with her husband." Another sob escaped her lips. "He must feel so alone."

"You know it's more complicated than that," Christy said. "Your husband does, too, even if he's had a hard time saying so. It may take a while for the two of you to figure it out. Whatever this other thing is, it's completely separate."

"I just feel so helpless," Mollie said. "I wish I could do somethin' to help him. Here

I am miles away when he needs me by his side." She stamped her foot. "I must see him, Miss Christy."

"He knows you love him, Mollie, whether you're by his side or not. We don't know what kind of mess he's in yet. You can't rush headlong into what might be a dangerous situation. We have to trust Nathan to manage whatever the trouble is." She smiled at Mollie. "You know, don't you, that when it comes to handling trouble, there's no one better."

Chapter 19

Felipe Alvarado couldn't stop smiling. Ramon had just filled him in on the situation in Springer involving that bothersome Sheriff Stallings. After Ramon planted the fake bribery evidence, Alvarado sent a message for the sheriff to the telegraph office in Springer. In it, he had stated that it was important and asked that the telegraph operator, Jim White, hand deliver the message to the sheriff. Jesus Abreu had assured him that White was a busybody of the highest order and he was counting on his curiosity leading him to explore the package there in plain sight in the office. Apparently, White had fallen for the trick, looked at the package, and immediately reported it to Mayor Salazar, who now had the sheriff installed in a cell in the old constable's office. Alvarado had hoped to sew the seeds of doubt in the mayor's mind to perhaps complicate the sheriff's investigation. He hadn't anticipated that the ruse would be so completely successful. The image of that cocky lawman stewing in a cell brought yet another smile to his face.

He rubbed his hands together as he considered his next move. He figured that even if Stallings was able to convince the mayor this was all an attempt to frame him, it would likely take several days. In the meantime, there were more cattle and horses to steal up north of Cimarrón. He would give Pat Maes the order to take his men and ride out immediately.

He wondered briefly if he should send his nephew with them to take the place of the man they had lost. He decided against it, figuring it was better to keep him around to run his errands. His job as a teller at the bank had allowed him to be quite useful so far. Alvarado figured it was a good thing the owner of the bank was frightened of him. That made it easier for the bank owner to grant Ramon the flexibility to take time from his job to do his uncle's bidding. Maes would just have to deal with being a man down.

He frowned as he thought about Maes. He was aware that Maes and Maldonado hated each other and he wondered if he'd made a mistake putting Maes in charge.

Perhaps it would have been better to declare Pony Dolan the leader. Dissension in the ranks could lead to men turning on one another. Sooner or later, that might come back to haunt him. He would have to reflect more on the question.

I couldn't sit still as I waited for Nathan to arrive. Soon after I'd situated myself in the unlocked cell, Rusty arrived from the telegraph office and told me the message had been sent. I knew that Nathan would come as quickly as he could. In the meantime, there was nothing to do but wait and fret.

I passed a mostly sleepless night on the lumpy bunk in the cell. Rusty had moved his bunk out of the cell so no one would be confused about who the prisoner was. In the morning, Rusty had brought a meager breakfast to me from the restaurant at the Brown Hotel where we had eaten before.

"Who do you reckon would do this?" Rusty had pulled up a chair next to the opening of the cell.

"I got a pretty good idea *who* did it," I said. "I'm havin' trouble figurin' out *how* he did it." I took a few bites of the cold tortilla and beans that Rusty had brought and washed it down with a swallow of lukewarm coffee. "I'd lay odds it's that Alvarado fella down in Las Vegas. I know he's the brains behind this whole deal." I shook my head. "I just can't prove anything yet."

Rusty chuckled.

"What's so damn funny?" I snarled at him. I wasn't seeing much humor in the situation.

"Well, the whole state of affairs is kinda funny if you think about it." He paused to snigger some more. I was still not amused. "The notion of you walkin' down here and puttin' yourself in jail . . . you gotta admit that's pretty funny."

"I believe the word my schoolteacher wife would use is *absurd,*" I said. In spite of myself, I did feel a smile begin to twitch at my lips. "Can you believe that banty rooster mayor? He's so cocksure of himself he just ordered me to arrest myself." Now I did smile. "And of course, I did what he said." I laughed out loud. "Dang it, cousin, you're right. It *is* funny."

The door to the constable's office opened and village councilman Jesus Abreu walked in. "*Hola,* Sheriff," Abreu said as he walked over to the cell. "How are you doing?"

"Not all that well, sir," I said. "I'm stuck in here while some dangerous criminals are runnin' loose in Colfax County. That's got me a might upset."

"I heard about it from Mayor Salazar," Abreu said. "It does not look promising for you."

"I know it don't look good, sir, but the fact is, I'm bein' framed. I was gettin' too close to those murderin' rustlers. I think someone wanted me off their trail." I threw up my hands. "Sir, you know about me. You know I helped bring that devil Jake Flynt to justice after he robbed and murdered folks here in your own town. Why would I start takin' bribes all of a sudden?"

Abreu stood with his hands on his hips for a moment. He looked at Rusty and then back at me. "Sheriff, I do not think you would take a bribe. I agree that someone is probably setting you up."

"Well, if it ain't too much trouble," I said, "would you mind tellin' that to the mayor?"

Abreu chuckled. "I already did."

"And what did he have to say?"

He chuckled again. "In case you hadn't noticed, Sheriff, our mayor is quite impressed with his own importance. He does not like to hear from others all that much. He told me we would see what the investigation showed."

I snorted. "And what does that mean?"

"It means that he heard what I said and at some point, he will present it as his own idea. As soon as he sees some indication you did not take a bribe, he will come to the same conclusion that I've already come to . . . that you are innocent."

"Who's gonna be in charge of this investigation the mayor is waitin' on?" I didn't know how the politicians in Springer operated other than I figured they'd give a lot of speeches and not pay much attention to what anyone else has to say.

"Oh, I thought you knew," Abreu said with a smile. "Mayor Salazar sent a telegram to former Sheriff Averill over in Cimarrón asking him to come to Springer immediately."

Rusty and I looked at each other in astonishment. "He sent for Nathan?"

"Certainly," Abreu said. "The mayor and Sheriff Averill go back a long way."

Well, son of a gun. That had to be the best news I'd heard in a long while.

"Sheriff Averill, how nice to see you," Mayor Salazar said. As Nathan walked through the door to his office and over to his desk, Salazar immediately jumped up and walked around to the front of the desk with his hand out to greet the old lawman. "It has been too long."

"Yes, it has been, Manuel. Far too long."

Nathan smiled. "And it's Deputy Sheriff Averill now."

"A formality," Salazar said with a dismissive wave of his hand. "You will always be Sheriff Averill to me."

Nathan nodded his appreciation. "So, what's the story on Sheriff Stallings? There weren't a lot of details in your telegram but it sounds to me like he's bein' framed." Nathan chose not to mention that he had also received a telegram from the other deputy, Rusty Stallings, urging him to come to Springer immediately.

"I do not know, Sheriff," Salazar said, a note of uncertainty creeping into his voice. "We have evidence in the form of a note and five twenty-dollar gold pieces that suggest otherwise."

"Evidence can be falsified, Manuel," Nathan said. "Your evidence means that someone is up to no good. I seriously doubt it's Sheriff Stallings."

Salazar nodded his agreement. "I understand that, Sheriff. This is why I asked you to come immediately. I would like for you to investigate this matter while the sheriff spends some time in our jail cell."

"That's one of the things I want to discuss with you, Manuel." Nathan pointed to the desk and said, "Do you mind if we sit down?

At my advanced age, I'd rather sit than stand any time."

"Certainly, amigo," Salazar replied. They walked over and Nathan took the chair in front of the desk.

"Looks like you've done mighty fine for yourself, Manuel," Nathan said as he looked around the room. "It would appear that bein' elected mayor of Springer worked out well for you." He grinned. "Reckon politics agrees with you."

If he detected any sarcasm in Nathan's voice, Salazar chose to ignore it. "I believe it is important for us to serve our community. Between the two of us, I am considering setting my sights even higher. In the next few years, I am thinking of making a run for governor of the territory." He puffed out his chest with pride. "What do you think of that, my friend?"

Nathan chose to remain focused on his mission rather than share his personal opinion of politics and politicians with the mayor. "Why I think that's just outstanding, Manuel. I think the territory needs someone like you."

Salazar beamed. "Gracias, amigo. That means a lot coming from someone who knew me before I was doing well."

"We do go back a ways," Nathan said.

"Much as I'd like to talk about old times, I reckon we ought to address the business at hand."

"Certainly, Sheriff," Salazar said. "What are your thoughts?"

"Well, the thing is, I want to take Stallings into custody. If he's guilty, I want to be able to keep a close eye on him. If he's not, I want to put him to work helpin' me figure out who's behind all this."

Salazar took a deep breath. "If anyone else but you was proposing this to me, I would say definitely not. I am not as convinced as you of Stallings's innocence." He shrugged. "However, if that is what you wish to do, I will agree to it."

"Well, all right," Nathan said, standing up. "We got that settled. I hope you don't mind if we take care of this pretty quick. These outlaws have been committin' some heinous acts. I got a feelin' they ain't gonna quit until someone stops 'em." Salazar rose and Nathan led the way to the door. He glanced back over his shoulder and said, "Let's go retrieve our young lawman."

When they walked into the constable's office, they found Tommy and Rusty engaged in a game of checkers. The cell door was open and Rusty had pulled a chair up to the entrance.

"What is the meaning of this, Deputy?" Salazar stalked over to the entrance of the cell. "Why is this cell open?"

Rusty glanced uncomfortably at Tommy and Nathan before responding. "Well, sir, the lock's broken. It didn't seem to matter much whether the door was closed or not." He cleared his throat. "Tommy wasn't goin' anyplace without your permission, I promise you."

Nathan stepped in quickly. "Sheriff Stallings, Mayor Salazar has asked me to look into the accusation that you took a bribe." With a stern look, he said, "I was shocked when I heard what they're claimin' you did."

I felt like I'd been slapped. Did Nathan really believe there was anything to this frame-up? For a moment, I stared at the ground, feeling as ashamed as I ever had in my life. When I looked up, I noticed that the mayor was several steps behind Nathan and couldn't see his face. Nathan winked at me and flashed a swift grin. I caught on to his game.

"I was framed, Deputy," I said with as much dignity as I could gather. "Once this whole thing is investigated, the facts will show I'm innocent."

"Well, I intend to get to the bottom of it, that's for dang sure," Nathan said in a stern voice. "I told the mayor I wanted to take you into my personal custody so I could keep an eye on you. He's generously agreed to let me do that." He glared at me. "You understand what kind of trouble you're in, don't you?"

Out of the corner of my eye, I could see that Rusty was baffled by the proceedings. He had been expecting Nathan to come in and assert my innocence. Instead, it sounded like the old lawman was more suspicious of me than the mayor. I was kind of getting a kick out of this.

"I know it looks bad, Deputy," I said, "but I'm sure once you do get to the bottom of it, you'll see I didn't take any bribes or do anything else wrong, either, for that matter."

"We will see, won't we?" Giving me another firm look, he then turned to the mayor. "Manuel, if you don't mind, I'd like to take Sheriff Stallings . . ." He paused and glanced at Rusty. "Oh, and I reckon I'll take this deputy, too, and get movin'. We got some outlaws to track down and I've got to establish if this lawman is one of them or not."

All of this seemed to be happening a little too fast for the mayor. He had a confused look on his face and seemed ready to question his decision at the last minute. With a quick and subtle nod of his head in the direction of the door, Nathan indicated that we should get on out of there before the mayor changed his mind.

"Manuel, we need to make time to get together when we don't have other pressin' business so I can hear all about your plans to become the governor of this fine territory." He moved us rapidly toward the door as he spoke. I grabbed up my gun belt, which I had removed before placing myself under arrest. "Great seein' you after all this time."

For a tense second, I thought the mayor was going to object. Then he seemed to give in to the inevitable. "A pleasure as always, Sheriff. I agree, we must get together. Perhaps you can help me with my campaign."

Nathan smiled and waved as we walked swiftly out the door.

"Where are your horses?" Nathan directed the question to Rusty.

"The livery," Rusty replied. He seemed as if he wanted to ask questions but wasn't sure where to start.

"Help him with his campaign? He's gonna be governor? And you're takin' me into your own personal custody?"

Nathan grinned. "I'll explain it once we're on the trail. Let's get movin' before he changes his mind."

Back in his office, Mayor Salazar was reviewing his conversation with Nathan Averill in his mind and trying to decide if he'd made the right decision. Based on his history with the old sheriff, he trusted the man unconditionally and yet there was something slightly off about what had transpired. The door opened and Councilman Abreu walked in.

"Manuel, did I just see Sheriff Stallings riding off with Nathan Averill?"

The mayor felt a flicker of exasperation at the man's judgmental tone. Abreu frequently questioned his decisions and yet he depended on him a great deal to help him run the town. The man was his political advisor and the first person to have suggested that he run for higher office. He sensed that he was about to receive a lecture.

"Jesus, why do you question every single thing I do?" Salazar didn't like the whiny tone he had assumed but he couldn't seem to help himself. "Can you not ever just tell me that I am right?"

Abreu shook his head. "Manuel, every

decision you make will come back to you when you make your run for governor. Some will drive you toward your goal and some will haunt you. Each has to be looked at very carefully."

"I know, you are right." Salazar sighed. "And yes, Sheriff Averill took Stallings into custody. He said he would keep an eye on him. If it is true that he is being framed, he can use his help in getting to the bottom of the situation."

"I have never had as much faith in that old sheriff as you have, Manuel," Abreu said. "I am not sure he has your best interests at heart."

"I do not know how you can say that," Salazar said indignantly. "You know very well that he turned my life around when I was a young man. He could have put me in jail. Instead, he lent me a hand."

"Yes, yes," Abreu said, waving his hand in an indifferent manner. "I have heard the story more than once. Just because he helped you out before does not mean he is truly your friend." Abreu arched an eyebrow at Salazar. "If he is going to take a side, it will always be the side of his compadre, the young sheriff. He cares nothing about what would happen to your political ambitions if word got out that you released a corrupt lawman back into the community."

With a stubborn set to his jaw, Salazar said, "I do not believe that Nathan Averill would try to trick me into releasing a guilty man."

"Have it your way," Abreu shrugged. "I only hope I do not have to come back and say I told you so." Abreu prepared to leave. "I must go back to the bank and tend to some business. I will come back to chat about this further with you later this afternoon."

As Abreu left, Salazar fidgeted at his desk, rearranging the papers that were in front of him. There were so many factors to reflect on when one had political aspirations and there was seldom a clear path. He glanced at Abreu's back as he walked out the door. From that angle, he could not see the sly grin on the man's face. As a result, he wasn't aware that Abreu was up to something and that it had little to do with the mayor's political ambitions.

Chapter 20

We maintained a pretty good lope for the first few miles in order to put some distance between us and Mayor Salazar. The pace was not conducive to conversation so I didn't have a chance to ask Nathan anything for over an hour. When he slowed down, I reined my horse over beside him. He looked at me and grinned.

"Reckon you got some questions," he said with a chuckle. "Where would you like to begin?"

I had to laugh along with him. "I ain't even sure where to start." I noticed that Rusty was frowning in Nathan's direction. "Maybe you could start by explainin' to my cousin why you made that crack about bein' shocked. I think he's still a little hot about that."

"I don't blame you, Rusty," Averill said as my cousin edged his horse a little closer so he could hear the exchange. "If I'd meant it, it would have been a lowdown thing to say."

"What do you mean, if you'd meant it?" Rusty asked. "If you didn't mean it, why did you say it?"

Nathan looked over at me. "You want to tell him?"

"Sure," I said. "Rusty, if Nathan had come in actin' sympathetic to me, it would have looked to the mayor like he was takin' my side against him. That would have showed him up. He wouldn't stand for that."

"Tommy's right," Nathan said. "Manuel has a pretty high opinion of himself. Even though I was pretty sure he'd go along with what I wanted him to do, I needed him to believe I was takin' what he'd done serious. If he thought I was sayin' he'd made a mistake puttin' Tommy in jail, he'd have been offended. I wanted to get you boys out of there."

"I get it now." Rusty nodded slowly. "You were pretty convincin'. It's only because you got the mayor to let Tommy out that prevented me from callin' you out on it."

"I'm glad you kept your mouth clamped tight, Rusty," Nathan said with a sly grin. "If you'd called me on it, Manuel might have changed his mind . . . and you might have hurt me, too."

I couldn't help myself, I snorted out a laugh. Rusty shrugged, looking sheepish. "I ain't sayin' I could have taken you, Sheriff Averill, I'm just sayin' I'd have tried."

"Oh, I know, son," Nathan said. "I'm just havin' a little fun with you. I set great store by folks who stand up for their own. It would've been the proper thing for you to do if I'd meant what I said."

I couldn't wait any longer to ask my next question. "What do you have on Salazar, Nathan? I wouldn't have been surprised if he'd have gotten down on his knees and licked your boots."

"That's a debt of gratitude that goes back quite a few years," Nathan replied. "Back when Manuel was young and a bit on the wild side, he got caught with a neighbor's horse he had no business havin'. He tried to say he'd found it wanderin' loose and that he'd intended to return it." The old sheriff grinned. "The fact it'd been gone for a couple of weeks and folks had seen him ridin' it for most of that time kinda poked a hole in his story. I arrested him and the horse's owners wanted him to go to trial for horse thievin'."

"That's a hangin' offense in Texas," Rusty said.

"Same here in the New Mexico Territory,

Rusty," Nathan said.

"So, I take it you came up with another answer to the problem," I said, "since Salazar is not only walkin' around a free man, he's the mayor of Springer."

"I did indeed," Averill said. "While he was in the jail cell, I spent some time gettin' to know him. In spite of how cocky he is, he's not a bad fella at heart. It seemed to me he'd made a bad decision on the spur of the moment and then hadn't known how to back out of it."

"You can say that again about makin' a bad decision," Rusty exclaimed. "There's been many a neck stretched over horse thievin'."

"So how did you set this one straight, Nathan?" I was always interested in and impressed by the clever ways the old sheriff settled problems.

He grinned. "I had a long talk with the owners of the horse. I told 'em Manuel was a dumb, wild youngster but not a bad sort."

"That's all it took?"

"I said it was a *long* talk. They weren't convinced at first. I told 'em Manuel would do all their worst chores for a year if they'd drop the charges. The notion of not havin' to muck stalls, fix fence, clear brush and such was mighty appealin'. He smiled again.

"I also told 'em if he did anything shady, refused to work, or talked back, I'd come out and arrest him. I said they could press charges for stealin' their horse then if it came to it."

Rusty chimed in. "After watchin' the mayor operate the past few days, I'm havin' trouble seein' him out there muckin' stalls and takin' orders."

"The threat of a noose hangin' over your head can make a fella give serious consideration to what he's willin' to put up with." Nathan wiped sweat off his brow. "The funny thing is that these people and Manuel became friends. He worked his tail off for 'em. After a while, it was because he wanted their respect, not because he didn't want to hang."

"I'm with Rusty," I said. "I can't see the man I've been dealin' with actin' that way."

"That's because things ain't always the way they appear, fellas," Nathan said. "There's some people who rub you the wrong way but when it comes time to take a stand, they step right up. Others will say all the right things until you really need 'em beside you and then they're nowhere to be found."

Having rubbed some folks the wrong way myself on occasion yet standing firm when the time came, what he said had the ring of truth to me. I wasn't ready for me and Mayor Salazar to be best pals yet but after what Nathan said, I figured I'd take a second look.

"Speakin' of nowhere to be found," I said, "we do have this little problem of a gang of murderin' cutthroats spreadin' fear and terror throughout Colfax County."

"Not to mention the fact that you're accused of takin' a bribe to allow it to happen," Rusty said.

I glared at my cousin. "Yeah, there's that, too."

Nathan took off his hat and scratched his head. "I been puzzlin' on that one. Assumin' you're innocent . . ." he chuckled when he saw me start to protest. "I do assume you're innocent, Sheriff Stallings. I'm tryin' to figure out who planted the money and note in the office. At some point, we're gonna need to talk with folks around town to find out if anyone saw a stranger lurkin' around."

"You're right," I said. "Springer ain't that big of a place. A stranger would stick out like ears on a mule."

"The thing is," Nathan said, "somebody had to come up with the idea. Somebody with some brains is behind this outfit. Maybe more than one person."

"I told you about that Felipe Alvarado character down in San Miguel County," I said. "I couldn't prove anything yet but I'd swear he's the one behind all this."

"I don't doubt it, but you're right, we got to be able to prove it." Nathan frowned. "Somehow, I got a feelin' there's more than one fella behind the scenes." He shook his head. "Maybe I just run up against that darned Santa Fe Ring bunch once too often. It seems to me like there's more than one honcho pullin' the strings in this deal."

It was my turn to frown. "That makes me worry that even if we do catch up with these men who're robbin' and killin' folks, we might not get to the man, or men, behind it all."

"That worries me, too," Nathan said.

Rusty had been listening attentively. Now he spoke up. "I know what y'all are talkin' about and you're right. We need to get the honchos if we really want to stop this. In the meantime, though, people are gettin' robbed and killed. Where do we start?"

Even though I'm the sheriff, I instinctively looked to Nathan. "You did this for a lotta years and lived to tell about it. What do you think?"

The old lawman pondered the question. "Rusty makes a good point."

Rusty puffed up a bit. "Reckon I ain't as dumb as I look."

Without missing a beat, Nathan said in a matter-of-fact tone, "That's a relief." Rusty started to sputter and I started to laugh. Nathan held up his hand. "His point is we got at least three different slants we need to look at. We're gonna have to split this up."

"Makes good sense to me." I grinned. "If I can investigate myself, I bet I can clear me of all the accusations pretty quick."

Nathan laughed. "It's temptin' but I don't think we'd get away with it."

Rusty was still stinging from Nathan's quip and didn't seem to be enjoying our joshing as much as we were. "Y'all are real funny but we still don't have a plan."

Nathan chuckled once more and then said, "You're right, Rusty. Here's what I think we should do if it meets with your approval, Sheriff Stallings."

"Let's hear it." I appreciated that he paid me the respect of leaving the final say with me, although I didn't doubt for a minute that I'd go along with pretty much any plan he came up with.

"When we get to Cimarrón, I think Rusty should get a bath, a meal, a good night's sleep. In the morning, he'll get himself a fresh horse, and ride back to Springer." He addressed Rusty directly. "I'll send a telegram to Manuel tellin' him I want you to talk to the townsfolk and find out if they saw anything suspicious in the past few days. I'm pretty sure if I ask him, he'll back you up."

Rusty didn't look all that pleased about having to return to Springer so soon but he nodded his assent. I wondered what part Nathan wanted me to play and what part of the job he would handle.

"What do you want me to do?" I asked.

"Seems to me you were closin' in on the men who are committin' these crimes. I reckon it would be a good idea for you to continue to look for 'em, particularly up in those canyons where you went before."

"Yeah," I said, "up in those canyons where they took a couple of shots at me."

"That's right," he said. "Because of that, I think you should be mighty careful. Don't try to apprehend 'em by yourself or nothin'. Just see if you can establish where their hideout is."

"Works for me," I said. "What's your part?"

"I think I need to see if I can locate the head of this snake," he said. "I know folks all over the northern part of the territory; I'll start askin' questions and maybe call in some favors. I think we all need to get a good night's rest when we get back to Cimarrón. After that, we each need to go do our jobs. We should probably meet back up in town in about three days. That should give us time to either find out somethin' or run into dead ends." He looked at me and I could see concern in his eyes. "You probably need to spend some time with your wife, too. This ain't been easy on either one of you."

He got that right.

"Oh, Tommy, I've missed you so bad." As was her custom, my wife was practically choking me to death as she hugged me.

When she let off the pressure a bit, I was able to speak. "I've missed you, too, Mollie. I've thought about you every minute of every day I've been gone."

She shook her head. Tears were rolling down her cheeks but she had a smile as wide as Raton Pass on her face. "It's just so good to see you." The smile faded. "I was so worried when Nathan got the telegram sayin' you were in trouble in Springer. What on earth happened?"

I took a deep breath and recounted the story. "Someone tried to frame me. They planted a pouch full of money and a note sayin' I should keep cooperatin' with the outlaws." I snorted. "They made it look like I was in league with the gang."

Mollie's voice rose with indignation. "Who'd believe such folderol?"

"Apparently, the telegraph operator and the mayor of Springer believed it," I said. "I don't know if anyone else knows about it so I can't say who else might believe it."

Mollie turned away and walked to the window of our little house. She stared out the window for a moment before turning around. "This whole thing is such a tangled mess, Tommy. Movin' to Springer has been a calamity." When I started to protest, she waved her hand to silence me. "You don't need to explain to me again why you did it. I know you were tryin' to do the right thing and catch these murderin' outlaws." A bitter laugh escaped her lips. "Seems like them that try to do the right thing are the ones who wind up with their lives turned topsy-turvy."

I opened my mouth to speak and then shut it. I thought about what she said. "I expect you're right, Mollie. The thing is, we can't let that prevent us from tryin' to do the right thing."

"Why not?" Mollie said, her voice choked with emotion. "Who says we can't?" She must have seen the shock on my face because she lowered her voice. "Who says we can't, Tommy Stallings?"

I could see she expected an answer to her question. "I wish I had some fancy way to explain it, Mollie." I took a moment to think. "The thing I learned from Jared Delaney and Nathan Averill is this. When I look in the mirror, I got to be able to look myself in the eye. If I can't respect myself, then I got nothin'."

She shook her head in disgust. "So, you're sayin' if the price you have to pay for bein' honorable is that your life is destroyed, so be it?"

"I don't think that's what I'm sayin', Mollie. I am sayin' that doin' the right thing can be awful hard. Sometimes you do pay a high price . . . maybe too high a price. But what price do we pay if we start turnin' our heads and lookin' the other way. Then these wicked men win." I reached out to take her hand. She let me. "The more power they get, the more likely they are to destroy our lives, anyway. Somebody's got to try to stop them."

Mollie let go of my hand and went over to sit down on the little love seat. "It just makes me tired, Tommy," she said in a subdued voice. "Maybe you're right but where does that leave us? Where does that leave me and you?"

I gave her the only answer I had. "I love you, Mollie. I don't have answers about what we're gonna do or how to stand up to these evil individuals or even how I'm gonna stay out of jail. I just know I love you. I know that for a fact."

She looked at me, a sad smile on her lips. To my amazement, that old familiar sparkle she got in her eyes when she was about to tease me appeared. "I was hopin' you had some of those other answers, too."

I had to laugh. "Ain't you Irish the most irreverent folks on the face of the earth?" I laughed harder. It was all I could do. Mollie joined in and we laughed together. It felt good. I walked over and sat down beside her on our love seat. "The only other answer I got besides tellin' you I love you is that I'll do my dead level best to catch these vicious scoundrels. When I've got that done, I'll come back to you. It won't matter whether I have to chase 'em to Springer or Raton Pass or hell, I'll come back to you."

She smiled at me. "When you're done, you ride back to me, Tommy Stallings. When you get to the rise north of town, you look down into this village and look for a light in this window. I promise you the light will be there and so will I."

Chapter 21

As Rusty approached Springer from the northwest, he stretched in the saddle. He was stiff from the night he'd spent on the ground but he figured a hardy breakfast and about seven cups of coffee at that restaurant where he and Tommy had eaten before would fix him up. He fully intended to get filled up before he went to talk with that banty rooster of a mayor. Although Nathan had sent the mayor a telegram outlining what assistance he was requesting, Rusty wasn't totally confident he would cooperate.

When he'd agreed to serve as his cousin's deputy, Rusty hadn't really thought it through. For him, it was simple. Tommy was family. When family asked you to help, you helped. He'd never had a lot to do with any lawmen before and didn't have much of an idea what it was they did. He had a vague notion about chasing outlaws but that was about it. *If I'd known I'd have to spend my time askin' folks questions and puttin' up with swaggerin' politicians, I might have said no.* He smiled. *Naw, family is family.*

Rusty dismounted in front of the Brown Hotel and tied his horse to the rail. He was loosening the cinch when he heard a voice call out behind him.

"Deputy, what are you doing? Come to my office immediately."

Dang, this is the kind of thing I was afraid would happen. He turned and mustered up his best smile as the mayor stalked up to him. "I was hopin' to grab a bite to eat before I got started, if that's all right with you."

"No, it is not all right with me," the mayor said emphatically. "I expect this investigation to come to pass as swiftly as possible. I do not want anyone to be able to say we did not pursue the truth in as thorough a manner as possible."

Rusty was thinking that the truth probably wasn't going to change all that much in the time it took him to down some coffee, eggs, and bacon. He decided to keep that thought to himself. "If that's what you want, Mayor."

"Come to my office. I will give you a personal note that authorizes you to question the citizens of Springer." He beamed.

"Anyone who sees this note will give you their full cooperation, I guarantee."

I reckon most people agreed with the mayor just to get him out of their face. Again, he kept this to himself. "Whatever you say, Mayor."

As they walked down the street toward his office, the mayor seemed a little friendlier. "Did Sheriff Averill tell you about our past?"

Rusty was unsure of what to say. He cautiously replied, "Only that he'd known you for a long time."

The mayor chuckled. "I was headed down the outlaw trail, young and wild with no common sense. I took a horse that was not mine. If he had wanted, Sheriff Averill could have had me hung."

Clearing his throat, Rusty said, "He may have mentioned a little somethin' about that."

"I will bet he did." This time, the mayor laughed out loud. "The good sheriff pointed me down the right path. He showed me that if I worked hard and made good choices, I could be a success." He shook his head. "He also made it clear that if I did not, the future was grim."

Not knowing what else to say, Rusty replied, "He does have a way about him, don't he?"

"If not for Sheriff Averill, I would be dead." Salazar was no longer smiling. "Instead, I am the mayor of this town." He seemed to get a faraway look in his eyes. "This is not the end for me, either. I will do even bigger things before I am through."

All this personal information was making Rusty uneasy. He didn't want to be friends with the mayor, he just wanted to get this over with and ride back to Cimarrón. As they walked toward the office, Rusty figured he might as well start his investigation at the top of the heap.

"I hadn't had a chance to ask you this yet, Mayor. I've been hearin' there was a young stranger in town . . . any chance you saw him?"

Salazar said, "In fact, I did see a young man recently but he is not a stranger. He is the nephew of Jesus Abreu's cousin, Felipe Alvarado, from Las Vegas. I was surprised that he was in town. Jesus has no contact with his cousin anymore. Some people in Las Vegas believe he is some sort of outlaw."

Rusty chewed on this new information for a moment. "You didn't happen to see what direction he headed when he left town, did you?"

"I have more important things to do than follow a young man around town to see which way he goes when he leaves, Deputy Stallings."

The mayor's tone left no doubt in Rusty's mind what he thought of his question. "Well, sure, Mayor, I can understand that, I was just askin'."

If it was the mayor's intention to make him feel like an imbecile, he had succeeded. Rusty decided he didn't like this investigation business much at all. He wasn't sure what to say next. Fortunately, they arrived at the office. When they went inside, the mayor took a piece of paper off his desk and handed it to him.

"As I said, show this to all the people with whom you speak. They will cooperate fully." He walked around behind his desk, took off his jacket, and sat down. "If I were you, I would start with Jim White at the telegraph office. Even if he did not see anything, he hears all the gossip in town. He may know something."

"Thank you, sir, that's what I'll do." Rusty felt like he should salute or something. Instead, he nodded to the mayor and walked out.

When he left the mayor's office, he went directly to meet with White. Sure enough, the man had heard rumors from a number of people that they had seen a stranger in town for several days prior to his finding the note and money at Tommy's office. White gave Rusty the names of several individuals and told him where to find them. It turned out that Salazar was right. As soon as he showed them the note authorizing his asking questions, everyone was very cooperative. Some of them even said nice things about Mayor Salazar. *Go figure.*

The stories were all similar. People had seen a young man who was not from Springer. No one had gotten a good look at him and he apparently didn't interact with anyone. After several hours, Rusty concluded that there had been a stranger in town. There was nothing he heard that would help him identify the man and no one actually saw him enter the sheriff's office. He was standing on the boardwalk by the office trying to figure out his next moves when Jesus Abreu approached him.

"Deputy Stallings," the man said in an affable manner. "Good to see you. What brings you here today?"

Rusty remembered that the bank owner had seemed sympathetic to Tommy's plight, unlike the mayor. "I'm here investigatin' to find out who framed the sheriff," he said. He kind of liked the idea of his being involved in an investigation. It sounded important. *Maybe bein' a deputy ain't as bad as I thought.*

"How is your investigation coming along?" Abreu smiled at him and seemed very interested.

"Hard to say yet," Rusty replied. "There's some who claim to have seen a young stranger in town about the time the money and note got planted. Nobody can tell me much about what he looked like, though, and they didn't see him go into the office."

Abreu looked pensive. "You know, I believe I saw a young stranger around that time as well." He squinted as he pondered. "I did not see him go in the office, either. I did see him ride out of town, though."

"Really?" Rusty thought maybe he was getting somewhere. "Did you happen to see which direction he headed?"

Abreu appeared to think some more. "It seems to me that he rode north out of town. Maybe headed for Raton, maybe Clayton. *¿Quien sabé?*"

Rusty frowned. He would have expected Abreu to say the man rode south. Nathan and Tommy both figured the man behind all this was Felipe Alvarado. He lived in San Miguel County, which was in the opposite direction. This didn't fit.

"North, you say?"

"Sí," Abreu responded. "I remember it clearly now. When I saw him get on his horse, I wondered to myself who he was. I watched as he rode out of town."

"Hmm," Rusty grunted. "That don't exactly make sense but if that's what you saw, I reckon that's what happened." He stood there uncomfortably for a moment. "I don't know who else to talk to or what to ask. You got any suggestions?"

Abreu smiled and clapped him on the shoulder. "I think you have done a fine job, Deputy. Maybe it is time for you to report in to your sheriff."

Rusty took a deep breath. "Reckon you're right, sir." He felt indecisive and tentative about his next course of action. Abreu seemed friendly and obliging. He couldn't think of anything else to do so he decided to take the man's counsel. "I'll ride on back to Cimarrón, I guess . . . after I get me somethin' to eat over at the Brown Hotel."

"That sounds like a good plan to me, Deputy," Abreu said. He smiled and stuck out his hand. "I would join you but I have business to attend to at the bank."

Not knowing what else to do, Rusty shook the grinning man's hand. He turned to walk away and did not see the crafty look in Abreu's eyes as he continued to smile.

■ ■ ■ ■

Rusty sat in a chair opposite Deputy Sheriff Nathan Averill in what had been the sheriff's office prior to the move to Springer. He was still a bit in awe of the old lawman but he'd grown more comfortable with him after he came to get Tommy out of jail. In a funny way, because the old man gave him a hard time in the manner in which cowboys typically do, it made him feel a lot more relaxed. Your cowboy pards don't generally make fun of you unless they like you.

Rusty looked around the office. "You reckon Cimarrón is gonna get a constable?"

"I'd say it was pretty likely," Nathan replied. "Why do you ask?"

"Just curious. They had one in Springer and now we're usin' the old constable's office for the sheriff's office. I just thought maybe they'd swap things around and let Cimarrón have a constable."

"Well, it ain't actually up to the same people, Rusty," Nathan said. "The county makes the decisions about the sheriff; the towns are the ones that pay for havin' a constable." He chuckled. "I know old Bill Wallace is still smartin' from havin' the sheriff taken away from him. He used to lord it over Mayor Salazar that the sheriff was headquartered in his town. Now the boot's on the other foot."

Rusty joined Nathan in chuckling about the political comeuppance of Mayor Wallace. "I can't say as I know Mr. Wallace, but I reckon Mayor Salazar is gonna pay him back and then some if he gave him a hard time about that."

"I think you can count on it," Nathan said. "So, what did Manuel say when you told him what you'd found out about this mysterious stranger?"

"He didn't seem too impressed one way or the other," Rusty said. "He said that even if there was a stranger in town, it didn't mean he'd planted the evidence against Tommy. I couldn't argue with him about that." Rusty shrugged. "You know, I was a little surprised when that banker, Abreu, told me he'd seen the man ride out of town to the north." He pursed his lips as he contemplated the information. "That don't fit with Tommy's notion of him bein' connected with that Alvarado fella down in San Miguel County. He was headin' in the wrong direction."

"That he was," Nathan said. "Of course, things can appear to be one thing and turn out to be somethin' entirely different. In the same way that it's true what Manuel said about a stranger bein' in town not meanin' he'd tried to frame Tommy, that he rode out to the north don't mean he couldn't circle around and head south." Averill leaned back in his chair and looked at the ceiling for a moment. "It don't even mean that what Abreu said was the truth."

Rusty looked startled. "What, you think he was lyin'?"

"It's not impossible."

"I reckon not," Rusty replied. "He's been downright friendly and helpful to Tommy durin' all this trouble, though. Why would he make somethin' up like that?"

"That's a question we need to answer." Nathan set all four legs of his chair on the floor. "Remember me sayin' things ain't always what they seem?"

"Well, sure, I remember that, you just said it."

Nathan nodded. "While you were in Springer, I did some checkin' in with old friends. The word I got is that Jesus Abreu has got his hooks into quite a few different schemes, one of 'em bein' Manuel Salazar's plans to be governor."

"Why would that have anything to do with him lyin' to me about what direction this mystery fella lit out of town?"

"Well, another piece of information I got about Señor Abreu is that he comes from San Miguel County. He grew up down there with Alvarado." Nathan shrugged. "It could be a happenstance."

"Dang," Rusty said. "This is gettin' more complicated all the time." He stood up and walked to the window of the office. "You heard anything from Tommy?"

"He ain't back from his trip out to the canyons yet," Nathan replied. "I expect him sometime today." A worried look crossed his face. "If he ain't back by suppertime, I might start becomin' a little worried."

"Ah, he'll be back any time now," Rusty said with a conviction he didn't really feel. "Tommy can look out for himself."

"I don't doubt that at all," Nathan said. "But you can look out for yourself and still get ambushed." He rubbed his left shoulder. "Take it from me, I know a lot about that."

I'd been moving pretty slow through Dean Canyon and then Templeton Canyon, being as vigilant as I knew how to be. I kept to the side, close to the trees, so I wasn't right out in the middle where someone could blaze away at me. I'd been lucky the first time I rode out this way. Whoever had been shooting at me that time wasn't a particularly good shot. I didn't want to take any chances that they'd been practicing up since then.

There were plenty of tracks through the canyons, both horse and cattle, but best I could tell, they were at least a few days old. It didn't look to me like anybody had been through there lately. Still, I was on the alert as I rode along. When I came to the spot in Chase Canyon where they'd taken those shots at me, I got a prickling up my spine. I knew I'd been lucky that time. I also knew you can't count on luck. Better men than me had been killed in ambushes. Heck, Nathan Averill, one of the best lawmen around, had almost met his death in an ambush. Not for the first time, I wondered how much longer I wanted to do this job.

I rode along, my senses on high alert, listening for any sounds that might be out of place. Everything sounded the way it was supposed to . . . birds singing, wind rustling through the pine needles. I got through Chase Canyon and made the turn north into Compos Canyon. If I was going to find anyone, it would be there.

Unlike Chase, Compos Canyon zigzagged back and forth. The further I rode, the more jumpy I got. Every time I came to a turn, I got a little closer to the trees so I could make it to cover as quickly as possible if the shooting started.

When I was about halfway through the canyon, I came to a spot where it turned back to the north. I stopped behind a big old pine tree that gave me cover as I stared ahead. The canyon spread out a bit and sure enough, I saw some primitive corrals. I looked around the area but saw no signs of man nor beast. If this was where they kept their stolen stock, they'd moved them all out.

I waited a few minutes before leaving my cover. I listened intently but heard nothing that made me suspicious. It didn't sound like anyone was there and it didn't feel like it, either. I decided to ride over to inspect the corrals. Even though I was pretty sure the place was deserted, I pulled my pistol. I figured it would be easier to put it back in my holster once it became evident I didn't need it than to have to pull it out if someone started shooting at me. I'm not the fastest draw around and that extra second or two it would take for me to get my gun in my hand could make the difference between living and dying.

As I rode over to the corrals, I hunched over in the saddle, making myself as small a target as possible. I'd heard the Indians did that and I figured if it was good enough for them, it was good enough for me. Turned out I didn't need to bother. There was nobody there. Even though I'm not the world's best tracker, I can generally tell a fresh track from an older one. It was clear that it had been several days since anyone had made tracks there.

I have to admit I was relieved there was nobody there to shoot at me but disappointed I hadn't located the gang. Sooner or later, we've got to find them if we're going to catch them. The good news is I'd found the hidden ranch that Eva Armstrong had heard them talking about when they killed her husband and boy.

The corrals turned out not to be as primitive as I'd first thought. Whoever put 'em together had done a pretty fair job. They weren't fancy but they were sturdy. That made me think it was likely they'd be back at some point. It wouldn't make a lot of sense to go to the nuisance of building these pens if they didn't plan to use them more than once. The trick would be figuring out when they would be back so we could meet up with them when they returned.

I'd seen about all there was to see here. It was time to get back to town, check in with my deputies, and come up with a plan. I had to laugh as that thought crossed my mind. One of my deputies knew more about being a lawman than I ever would and on top of that, he was investigating me for taking a bribe. My other deputy was my cousin who'd never been a lawman in his life until I roped him into it. The good news was at least one of us had an idea about what he was doing.

I turned old Rusty around and brought him to a lope back toward Cimarrón. I felt more hopeful than I had in many a day. Now we knew where these dirty scoundrels took their stolen stock. We just had to be here to catch them the next time they came back.

CHAPTER 22

As I rode out of the canyons, I let down my guard a bit and enjoyed the beauty of the northern New Mexico Territory in the fall. The aspens were turning and everywhere I looked, it was a brilliant gold, like those Spanish doubloons I'd heard about. There was a gentle breeze. It sounded like someone was whispering tenderly in my ear. I couldn't help but imagine it was my Mollie, saying sweet things to me in her lilting Irish accent. That made my heart ache. I'm not sure what I'm going to do to make a living once we get this White Caps gang put away, but I know it'll be something that allows me and my wife to be together. No more of this living apart. Of course, there was that little matter of me going to Texas, which would involve living apart for a while longer. I still didn't know how to break that news to Mollie.

I could feel the tug as old Rusty and I

entered Cimarrón from the north end of town. It was all I could do not to nudge him into the schoolyard and go sweep my wife up in my arms. I forced myself to ride on toward my former office. The sooner we get this outlaw predicament taken care of, the sooner I can spend all my time with my bride. Well, maybe not *all* my time. She tends to become impatient with me when we've been together too long, says I get on her nerves. I'll settle for spending a lot of my time with her.

As I rode down the street, I noticed folks looking at me funny, kind of sideways out of the corners of their eyes. Looks like word of my fall from grace had made it to Cimarrón. Funny how fast news travels from one little town to the next.

I didn't know if Rusty was back from Springer yet but I figured Nathan would be at the office. I was eager to share the news that I'd found the outlaws' hideaway and find out what Nathan had discovered. When I opened the door, it took a moment for my eyes to adjust from the bright sunlight to the dim light of the office. I could just make out the shapes of four men.

"Howdy, boys," I said in a lighthearted way. "Am I missin' a meetin'?"

No one said anything in response to my

attempt at humor. That, in itself, was not remarkable since they didn't find me nearly as amusing as I did. As my eyes got use to the faint light, I could see that Nathan was seated at the desk and Rusty was across the room leaning against the wall. Something seemed off about the way he was standing. I peered closer and could see his jaw was clamped tight, his fists were clenched, and he had that squint in his eyes that I recognized as his "I'm gettin' ready to fight somebody" look. The other two men in the office were Mayor Bill Wallace and Tom Figgs.

I gazed around the room again and could see something was going on. Nathan looked angry and Bill Wallace appeared indignant. Tom Figgs wouldn't meet my eye.

"Reckon I am missin' a meetin'," I said, all the humor gone from my voice. "Y'all want to tell me what's goin' on?"

"We've been discussin' the accusations against you," Nathan said quietly. "There's some divergence about what to do about it."

I stared at Bill Wallace and Tom Figgs. "You boys got anything to say, I'm right here. You can say it to my face." Wallace's face turned bright red. Tom still wouldn't look me in the eye.

"Well, you've got to admit it seems pretty bad, Sheriff." Bill Wallace's voice was pitched a little higher than usual, like his collar was too tight.

"Really," I said, sarcasm dripping from my words. "You think it looks bad? I hadn't noticed."

"Now there's no need to be discourteous, Sheriff," Wallace replied. He was beginning to get that expression of indignation on his pudgy face, the one I'd seen quite a few times before when someone called him on his nonsense.

I turned to Tom Figgs. "What about you, Tom?"

Without glancing up, he said, "It don't look good, Tommy."

Bill Wallace's righteous indignation and willingness to turn on me was not a surprise. We'd caught him cold with his hand in the till in the past and now it was his time for payback. Sure, it made me mad but it was not unexpected. The fact that Tom Figgs, a man I considered a friend, wouldn't stand up for me . . . wouldn't even meet my eye . . . that was different. That stung.

"That's sort of the point in framin' somebody, ain't it, Tom?" Figgs still wouldn't meet my gaze. "Look at me," I roared. "Damn it, look me in the eye."

"Tommy," Nathan barked, his voice full of command. "Knock it off." He saw movement out of the corner of his eye and turned his authority on my cousin, who was starting forward with his clenched fists coming up. "Rusty, you knock it off, too. Right now!"

Rusty turned his gaze to me. I nodded. He stepped back and leaned against the wall once more.

Nathan stood up. "Right now, I'm the actin' sheriff. The accusations against Sheriff Stallings were made in Springer. Mayor Salazar asked me to investigate it and that's what I'm doin'." He cast his steely eyes around the room. "That means I call the shots on how this goes. I will keep Sheriff Stallings in my personal custody. I will be responsible for him." With disgust written all over his face, he glared at Wallace first and then Figgs. "I have no doubt that once I get to the bottom of this, he will be cleared of all charges."

Both Wallace and Figgs were looking down now. They seemed to shrink in their chairs. Neither responded to the old lawman.

"Gentlemen, this meeting is over," he said. Both men sat there, unsure about what to do. "That means get the hell out of this office," he said. We were all a bit shocked. Nathan rarely used profanity. "Now!"

Bill Wallace got up quickly, turned, and walked out of the office. Tom Figgs rose hesitantly and for the first time, looked me in the eye. "I'm sorry, Tommy," he said. "It just sounded very bad is all."

I expect the time will come when I understand. Today was not that time. I looked away from him. He waited for a moment, then he shrugged and walked out. We stood there in silence for a moment, none of us sure what to say or do. I made up my mind first. I walked toward the door.

"Tommy," Nathan said, "we need to talk about this."

I looked back over my shoulder at him. "No, we don't, Nathan. Not right now."

He must have heard the flint in my voice. He let me go.

I wasn't sure where I was going when I left the office; I just knew I had to get away. My problem was that what I needed to get away from was me. All the old resentments about how unjust life is, left over from when my family was massacred by Comanches, came bubbling right to the top of the cauldron that was my temper. I hadn't done anything wrong and yet a man I'd considered a friend didn't have enough faith in me to believe I was innocent. That hurt.

I left Rusty hitched to the rail and headed up the street in the direction I had come in to town. I didn't have any thoughts about a destination, I only needed to keep moving. My first impulse was to say to hell with everyone. I could talk to Mollie and try to persuade her to come away with me. We could go with Rusty to Texas and make a new start. Of course, that would mean I would have to walk away from the best friends I had ever known. There was also the strong possibility Mollie wouldn't agree to chuck it all and leave with me. And finally, I would have to figure out how to live with the knowledge that when things got rough, I'd cut and run.

All right, maybe this wasn't such a good plan. I didn't have a better one, though. It had been quite a while since I was this confused. I walked doggedly on past the schoolhouse and continued beyond where our little house sat on the north end of town. I was slowing down when I realized I was almost to the graveyard that sat on a hill on the outskirts of the village.

The grave markers were surrounded by a wobbly picket fence that needed some upkeep. I opened the sagging gate and walked in. I wasn't really sure why I was there but it felt right. I didn't feel like being around another living person at the moment. Maybe the dead had some wisdom they could share with me. Or maybe there was some comfort in knowing that unlike them, I was still above ground.

The newer graves were located toward the back of the graveyard. Even if you didn't know the people who were buried there, you could probably figure out they were the most recent additions to the cemetery because there were fresh flowers on those plots. I reckon at some point, family and friends move on and no longer honor their lost with decorations.

I walked over to the newest grave and looked at the marker. I knew it belonged to Miguel Marés, father of Tomás, Estévan, and Esperanza, husband to Anita, and owner of the Marés Café. He was my friend and one of the bravest men I ever knew. He fed the people of the village and made them feel welcome in his establishment. That by itself would have been enough to make him memorable to me. More than that, though, every time his home, family, and community were threatened, he quietly joined the ranks of the men and women who stood up to the evil and powerful who sought to exploit them. Every single time. This last time, he had fallen in the process.

Right next to Miguel's grave was that of Juan Suazo. Juan was the husband of Maria and had been business partner to Jared Delaney. Beyond that, he was my mentor and one of the best cowboys I've ever known. Like Miguel, he stood up to the wicked men who ran roughshod over the common folk. Like Miguel, he had fallen in the fray.

These men were my friends; men I respected; men I wanted to be like. When there was trouble, they hadn't left or cowered in the shadows like many of the citizens of Cimarrón. They had paid the ultimate price as they defended all that was good about this place that had become my home. If I tucked my tail and ran now, how could I explain it to them or to the loved ones they died protecting? How would I explain it to my friend, Jared Delaney, who had risked his life over and over as he stood against the powerful, predatory men who exploited the weak? And how would I explain it to Nathan Averill, who had made a career of taking on crime and corruption in this New Mexico Territory?

I didn't have good answers to these questions. Unfortunately, I didn't have any answers at all as to how I was going to get out of this predicament I was in. I realized that if I ran, it would confirm people's suspicion that I'd taken a bribe to look the other way while this current crop of outlaws ran roughshod over the good people of Colfax County. My good name meant a great deal to me, maybe more than most folks understood. Sure, I was kind of happy-go-lucky and one of the first to make a joke. It didn't mean that doing the right thing wasn't important to me. I'd stood with honorable men before; reckon I'd have to find a way to do it again.

The shadows of the grave markers were getting longer. I'd spent enough time with the dead. I knew what Miguel and Juan would say to me if they could speak. They would say *go to your wife, tell her you love her, and then get back to work.* I didn't have all the answers I needed but I did have a direction. There were bad men doing evil deeds in Colfax County and I was the sheriff. I had a job to do.

I was walking toward our little house with my head down when I heard a voice up ahead of me calling my name. "Tommy, hold up."

I looked up and saw Eleanor Delaney in a buckboard with her two children. She had a load of supplies in the back, which explained her presence in town. From the direction she was headed, I assumed she was about to make the return trip to the ranch she and her children shared with her husband, Jared Delaney.

"Howdy, Mrs. Delaney," I said, trying to inject a cheerful note into my voice. "How are you and the children today?"

"Tommy, you know you can call me by my given name, Eleanor," she said crisply. Eleanor Delaney spoke with authority just about any time she opened her mouth. "And, as a matter of fact, I'm madder than I've been in a long time."

This made me uncomfortable. "I hope you ain't mad at me, Eleanor."

"No, Tommy, I'm mad on your behalf." She set the brake on the buckboard as she pulled up beside me. "I just heard about those false charges against you. That is complete hogwash. I can't believe silly Mayor Salazar for a moment considered that it might be true."

"Best I can tell, he's still considerin' it might be true," I said ruefully. "Reckon that means he's givin' it serious contemplation for a lot longer than a moment."

"Well, I know you, Tommy Stallings," she said in a tone of righteous anger. "As soon as I heard it from Christy, I knew it wasn't true." She shook her head. "I'm half glad Jared is still up in Colorado on the cattle drive. I don't know what he would do if he heard about this. I suspect Mayor Salazar would get a piece of his mind."

I couldn't begin to express the gratitude I felt to Eleanor Delaney and her husband for their unwavering support. I realized I'd been shaken both by the accusation as well as having a man I thought was my friend express doubts about my honesty.

"I think it'll turn out all right in the long run, Eleanor," I said. "Nathan is workin' on it. You know he has a way of gettin' things straightened out when he puts his mind to it." I took off my hat and stepped a little closer to the buckboard. I had to clear my throat before I could speak. "It means a great deal to me that you and Jared believe in me. I don't know anyone in the world that I think more of than the two of you."

She reached out her hand and patted me on the shoulder. "You know Jared and I feel the same about you and Mollie. I'm sorry Jared can't be here to help you with all these awful raids on the ranches."

I shook my head. "Your husband has done his share and that of about ten more people when it comes to dealin' with this sort of thing. I'm glad he's concentratin' on the ranch for y'all."

"Well, be that as it may, I know he'll want to talk with you as soon as he gets back," she said. "In the meantime, if there's anything I can do, please let me know."

I smiled at her. "You've already done a great deal . . . more than you even realize."

She stared into my eyes for a moment with that penetrating gaze of hers, then said, "I'm glad, Tommy. Very glad." She let off the brake and clicked the horse into a trot.

As I watched her and the children head off to the north of Cimarrón, I said a little prayer of thanks for friends like Jared and Eleanor Delaney.

Chapter 23

As Jesus Abreu rode up to the run-down line shack, he thought back to more contented times when he was a boy. He and his cousin would come to this spot and use it as a base as they trapped anything with fur . . . beaver, coyotes, bobcats. They sold the pelts for a tidy sum to dealers in Las Vegas, who then garnered a much greater sum when they sold the furs to hatmakers back east, who then made the largest profit when they sold their hats to the people clamoring for the latest styles.

He smiled as he reflected on the different lessons he and his cousin had incorporated from the experience. He had decided he would much rather be on the end of the chain where the most money was made. He was happy to let someone else do the dirty work. He would then figure out strategies allowing him to cash in on that effort. His cousin, on the other hand, enjoyed the dirty work. More specifically, he enjoyed killing.

Felipe Alvarado stepped out of the cabin and waved to his cousin. "Chuy, glad you could make it. We have much to discuss."

Abreu hated it when his cousin referred to him by that nickname for Jesus. He was pretty sure that was the reason Alvarado did it. Of course, he had his own nickname for Alvarado. He called him "paisano." He had those soulless killer eyes.

"I presume this is important since you had Ramon send me a telegram." Alvarado's nephew, Ramon, worked as a teller in the bank in Las Vegas and as part of his job, he regularly communicated with other banks by telegraph. When he and Alvarado needed to get in touch, they used Ramon as the intermediary. They figured communications between banks would look less suspicious than the two of them having direct contact should anyone decide to scrutinize their activities.

"It is important. I wanted to talk with you about expanding my activities up north now that we have that *pendejo* sheriff out of our way."

"I have news about our *pendejo* sheriff," Abreu said. "It is not good."

"What do you mean," Alvarado demanded. "Salazar locked him up when he discovered the bribe money and note."

"He did," Abreu responded. "Unfortunately, that old sheriff from Cimarrón rode over and got him out."

Alvarado exploded. "How did this happen? How could Salazar let that old man waltz in and take him?"

"Averill has some sort of hold on Manuel," Abreu explained. As always, his quiet tone contrasted with the strident tone his cousin typically adopted. "He told Manuel he would investigate the crime and keep an eye on Stallings."

"And Salazar let him have the man?" Alvarado shook his head. "Why did you not stop him?"

"Because I was not there, Felipe." Although he found his cousin's outbursts annoying, he'd learned through many years of experience that it paid to be patient with him. Responding in kind to Alvarado tended to result in his escalating to violence. Abreu had learned that the hard way when the two were young. His cousin had administered more than one beating when he'd dared challenge him directly.

"And where were you?" Alvarado's tone was accusatory. "You are supposed to be . . ." he paused. "I believe the term you use is 'handling' him."

"I also have a bank to run, Felipe. I cannot hold Manuel's hand every waking moment."

Alvarado stewed for a moment. He smacked his fist into his other hand. "This complicates things for me." He took a deep breath in an effort to calm himself. "I have two ranches up north of Cimarrón that I want the boys to hit. They will pay off big. The last thing I need is to have that *cabrón* Stallings lurking around."

Abreu knew he needed to proceed cautiously. "I am worried that the lawmen will be especially vigilant in the vicinity of Cimarrón right now. Perhaps it would be prudent to delay your plans a bit. That would give me some time to work on Manuel. I might be able to persuade him to change his mind and take Stallings back into custody if Averill doesn't come up with something that clears him pretty soon. If Stallings goes back to jail, that would stretch them extremely thin."

Alvarado shot his cousin a sly look. "I could have the boys hit that place just north of Springer. If Stallings is with Averill in Cimarrón, they could be halfway to Trinidad before he even heard about it."

"No!" Abreu shouted the word and immediately regretted it when Alvarado's eyes flashed. He quickly lowered his voice. "What I mean, Felipe, is that you know our agreement. You keep your men out of the immediate area around Springer. I want Manuel to become territorial governor. If he cannot keep outlaws and cattle rustlers away from his town, it will look like he is weak. He needs to appear strong."

"We are very different, you and I. I take what I want. If anyone gets in the way, it is their misfortune." Alvarado shook his head. "You like to play games and trick people into doing what you want."

"Not everyone can be as bold and strong as you, Felipe." Abreu figured it wouldn't hurt to flatter his cousin. "Your methods would not work for me. You have to admit that I, too, am rather clever when it comes to getting what I want."

Alvarado smiled. "I do admit it, Chuy. I do not understand it fully but I see that you achieve results."

"Those *cabrónes* in the Santa Fe Ring are making a fortune from grabbing land," Abreu said. "If I can arrange for Manuel to obtain the governor's job, I will be in position to take a large portion of that fortune." He nodded respectfully at his cousin. "You know I will be glad to incorporate you in my plans and share the rewards. There are less risky ways to get what you want."

Alvarado laughed. "You truly do not understand, Chuy. I like it my way. You use the power of others to achieve your goals. I prefer to use my own power."

It occurred to Abreu that his cousin often had others do his dirty work, which wasn't all that different from his own approach. However, he also knew that Felipe was more than capable of engaging in violent behavior to get what he wanted. He was aware that from time to time, Felipe committed horrendous acts of violence purely because he enjoyed it. He worried that this proclivity might spin out of control and ultimately lead to his downfall.

"We each must follow our own paths," Abreu said. "That does not mean we cannot both benefit from the other's labors. I only ask that for just a brief period, you refrain from raids around Cimarrón as well. This will take the heat off and buy me time. Once I put Stallings back behind bars, the path will be much clearer." He laughed. "Of course, we need to install a lock on the cell in Springer so we can keep him there. Otherwise, we will have to find a different place to stick him."

Alvarado looked at his cousin with a thoughtful expression. "I will try to give you some time, Chuy," he said, "but I may not be able to pass the word to the boys before they raid around Cimarrón. If you do not lock Stallings up soon, I will take matters into my own hands." He smiled. The effect was chilling. "When I do, you will not have to worry about where to lock him up. The question will be where to bury him."

"How do you like workin' for the Pinkertons, Charlie?" Nathan Averill had made a special trip to Santa Fe to meet with his old friend, Charlie Carter. Carter had been a deputy in San Miguel County when he was younger and they'd worked together tracking down cattle rustlers on a number of occasions. His old friend had recently joined up with the famous Pinkerton Detective Agency.

"They keep me pretty busy, Nathan," Carter replied before leaning over to spit tobacco juice into the spittoon beside his desk. "I'm roaming all over the country." He grimaced. "That isn't making my new bride all too contented, I have to tell you." Carter had recently married a Santa Fe girl who, by all accounts, was stunningly beautiful.

"I can see that," Nathan said. "You know, though, there's somethin' to be said for stayin' away an adequate amount of time so that they miss you. When you're around constantly, your ways can start to wear a bit thin." Nathan chuckled. "I'll bet your new wife ain't all that fond of your chewin' and spittin', is she?"

Carter laughed out loud. "That's a fact. It's funny how they say they married you because they love you and then they set about to change every danged thing about you." He cocked his head at Nathan. "You got hitched here a while back, didn't you?"

"That I did," Nathan said. "Smartest thing I ever did in my life. Christy is the schoolteacher there in Cimarrón." He left out the detail that prior to that, she'd been the most desirable working girl at the Colfax Tavern. His wife was entitled to her privacy.

"Well, I'm pleased for you," Carter said. He had a puzzled look on his face as he said, "I heard you'd given up law enforcement. When I got your telegram saying you were coming to visit, you said you were looking into a crime. Are you back in the game?"

Nathan nodded. "Just sorta helpin' out a young friend, you might say. Tommy Stallings . . . he was Tomás Marés's deputy if you recall . . . inherited the job unexpectedly when Tomás up and quit."

"I heard about that," Carter said. "His father was killed when they were chasing Jake Flynt." Carter shook his head. "I suppose that could make you lose your stomach for chasing outlaws."

"I reckon Tomás decided he'd done his share and then some for the citizens of Cimarrón," Nathan said. "He lost his father and both he and his brother have come pretty close to losin' their own lives. He figures it's about time other folks make some sacrifices. I can't say I blame him." Nathan smiled. "He's gettin' married soon, too. Maria Suazo, a young widow. They're runnin' the family café and doin' fine."

"Well, good for him. Like you say, he put in his time behind a badge. Let some other poor fool take over." Carter raised his hands in a quizzical gesture. "I know you didn't come here to chitchat about who got married. What was it you wanted to talk with me about?"

"The older I get, the more I enjoy gossipin', Charlie." Nathan sniggered. "You're right, though; I had more on my mind than just catchin' up with who married who."

"So, what's going on?" Carter leaned back in his chair and crossed his arms.

"You spent a good bit of time down in

San Miguel County," Nathan said. "What can you tell me about an hombre named Felipe Alvarado?"

Carter's eyes narrowed and the muscles in his jaws tightened noticeably. "I can tell you he's a dangerous man. A lot more so than many folks around those parts realize."

"What's his story?" Nathan leaned forward in his chair.

"Alvarado owns the Imperial Saloon. Compared to a lot of joints I've seen, it's a pretty respectable establishment." Carter shrugged. "Not many fights, the girls are lookers, and they run an honest game. Even the churchgoing folks there in Las Vegas don't have a big problem with the place."

"Based on what you said about Alvarado, that's not what I would have expected to hear," Nathan said.

"I think that's part of his scheme. On the surface, he looks like he's on the up-and-up." Carter frowned. "Beneath all that, I think the man is filthy. He runs a gang called the White Caps. They steal stock, they rob honest folks, and they appear to enjoy killing. What I hear is that, mostly, Alvarado plans the operations and his men carry out the dirty work. Sometimes, though, word is that he likes to get his hands bloody."

Nathan shook his head wearily. After all

his years in law enforcement, he was not surprised at the number of brutal men in the world. He was, however, tired of dealing with them. Briefly, he wondered if his decision to help out young Stallings had been a huge mistake.

"It looks like Señor Alvarado has expanded his illegal activities to the north. We've had stock stolen, people killed. Someone even came into town and robbed the mercantile. Whoever did it was brazen . . . and very brutal." Nathan frowned. "Gutted the clerk like a hog."

"That all sounds like Alvarado and his boys," Carter said.

"There's a couple of things that strike me as curious, though," Nathan said. "Whoever's doin' this seems to have a good feel for the lay of the land. They've picked out ranchers that were pretty isolated and they seem to know when to hit 'em when they got the most stock and the fewest people around to protect their places." He scratched his head. "The other thing that seems odd to me is even though there's a number of ranches just to the north of Springer, none of them have been hit. Same with the businesses in town. It's almost like they've singled out Cimarrón and are leavin' Springer alone." Nathan cocked his head at

Carter. "Any ideas about why they might do that?"

Carter scrunched up his face as he contemplated the question. Nathan waited patiently for him to assemble his thoughts. Finally, he said, "Only one possibility I can think of and it's a bit of a stretch."

"What's that?"

"Alvarado's cousin lives in Springer. He's the banker there . . . name's Jesus Abreu as best I can recall. He might have the connections to know what ranches were the best targets." Carter shook his head. "I never heard anything about him being involved in anything shady, though. Maybe Alvarado is staying away from his town because he's family."

Nathan wrinkled his brow as he contemplated what his friend was telling him. "That's a pretty thin connection between Alvarado and Abreu." He laughed. "Best I can tell, near 'bout everybody is cousin to everybody else up here in the northern part of the state. I'd need more information before I got too suspicious of Abreu."

He shrugged. "I wish I had more I could tell you. All I know is that if Felipe Alvarado is doing business in your neck of the woods, you got big trouble."

Chapter 24

After my heart to heart with the spirits in the graveyard, I went down to the school and waited for Mollie to conclude her day. There's an enormous cottonwood tree in the yard and it's the perfect spot for killing time. I sat in the shade with my back against that old trunk and for some reason, I was more at peace than I'd been in months. I didn't know how long that tree had been there but I figured it'd seen a lot of the troubles folks had been through over the years. Somehow, it was still standing. I took comfort in that.

I heard the school bell ring and I stood up quickly so I could avoid getting trampled by the students as they made their burst for freedom. After the stampede cleared out, Mollie and Miss Christy walked out the door. I was gratified to see Mollie bust into a wide grin when she laid eyes on me. Christy waved at me and walked back inside. Mollie sprinted over to where I stood and as she is inclined to do, grabbed me in a bear hug.

I'm of two minds when it comes to Mollie's hugs. I appreciate them because I know they are a physical expression of how much she loves me, which, judging from the strength of the hug, is considerable. On the other hand, they tend to go on for a good while and at some point, I need to breathe. When I started feeling a little light-headed, I disentangled myself from her.

"I'm sure glad you're happy to see me, Mollie," I said with a grin, "although sometimes I'm afraid you're gonna do bodily harm to me while you're lettin' me know."

"Don't be such a pansy," she said. "Just because me name is Mollie doesn't mean I'm about to mollycoddle you."

All I could do was laugh. When it came to teasing me, Mollie could keep up with any of my cowboy friends. "You're right; reckon I need to toughen up."

Her response was to throw her arms around me again and squeeze me some more. I had caught a deep breath before she got ahold of me and was able to endure it until she was done.

"That's more like it," she said. She stepped back and looked me up and down.

Her expression changed from merry to troubled. "What are they doin' to you, Tommy Stallings? Sayin' you took a bribe, after all you've done for this place. What a bunch of eejits."

"It does sting a bit," I said, "though, to be fair, those folks over in Springer don't know me that well. Whoever is settin' me up did a superior job. If I didn't know what a fine, honest fella I was, I might be suspicious, too."

"Eejits!" Mollie sniffed in indignation.

"You could be right," I said. I didn't want to let on how concerned I was about how this would play out. "With Nathan in charge of investigatin' me, though, I figure the truth will come out."

Mollie seemed reassured by this. "I expect you're right. Sheriff Averill is as fine a man as ever pinned on a badge."

"He is indeed," I said agreeably. With a sweep of my hand, I said, "Enough about all this work folderol. I've been missin' you somethin' fierce. I don't want to spoil our time talkin' about nasty goings-on."

She stepped back and gave me a prim look. "Sure and you wouldn't be makin' advances towards me now, would you?" Her prim look transformed into a lascivious smile. She wiggled her eyebrows at me.

We're married but it still made me blush.

"I will admit somethin' along those lines had crossed my mind," I said. "Before we take that under consideration, I thought we might sneak down to the Marés Café. I haven't seen Tomás and Maria in quite a spell. I figured we'd get 'em to cook us up some frijoles and a steak and talk about their wedding plans." I shook my head. "I'm so tired of chasin' outlaws and such, I want to talk about somethin' cheerful for a change."

A broad smile crossed Mollie's face. "I do like the sound of that, Tommy Stallings." She arched her eyebrows at me and said, "You think you're so exceptional that they'll open up just for you?" Typically, the Marés family café shut down in the afternoon for siesta time.

"Hey," I said with mock indignation, "Tomás better open up for me. He owes me. After all, if he hadn't walked away from the sheriff's job, I wouldn't be in this mess."

"Maybe so, but walkin' away was the smartest thing he ever did." A look of concern crossed Mollie's face. She gave me a stern look and said, "Might be smart for someone else to give walkin' away some consideration."

"You could be right but I ain't got time to

think about that right now," I said, even though I'd been thinking about it a lot. "We got to capture these outlaws and clear my name. Once that's done, it'll be time to think about what comes next." I stamped my foot in mock frustration. "Hey, I said I wanted to talk about cheerful things. Let's go get us some grub."

I offered her my arm and we walked down the street to the Marés Café. When we got there, the door and windows were closed as they usually were after the noon meal. I banged on the door and cried out, "Open up, it's the law."

A moment went by, and then the door opened a crack. I saw Maria Suazo's face and in the background, I heard Tomás call out, "Who is it, Maria?"

Maria opened the door wide and grinned at us. She shouted back over her shoulder, "He says he is the law. He just looks like Tommy Stallings to me."

She stepped out and grabbed me in a firm embrace. I'm glad some folks still like me but I'm starting to get a little tender from all this hugging. Mercifully, she let go of me pretty quickly and turned her attentions to Mollie. In the meantime, Tomás strolled out from the kitchen where he had been cleaning up after the rush of the noon meal.

"Hey, amigo," he said, "it is good to see you." He stuck out his hand. I took it and surprising both him and myself, pulled him into a brotherly hug. I guess all this hugging is catching. Tomás is no more of a hugger than I usually am so he quickly extricated himself. He laughed and said, "It is not *that* good to see you." Stepping back, he waved us in. "Come, let us visit."

Maria took charge immediately. "Tomás, get dishes. I'll cook up some frijoles." She turned to me. "You want a steak?" She laughed. "Don't bother to answer; I already know you are hungry. You are always hungry."

She knew me well. "I wouldn't want to offend you by saying no, Maria. I'll do my best to choke down whatever you fix."

She glared at me and poked me in the shoulder with her fist. It hurt. She's not a big woman but she's sure enough strong. Then she turned to Mollie and said, "Come with me, let us leave these cowboys to prattle while we take care of important business." They hurried off to the kitchen.

A few minutes later, Tomás returned from the kitchen with two plates laden with beans and tortillas. "This should hold you until Maria gets the steaks cooked," he said. He went back to the kitchen and quickly came back with two steaming mugs of coffee.

"Muchas gracias, amigo," I said. Tomás winced as he usually does at my appalling Spanish accent.

"De nada," he replied. With a grin, he said, "That mean's 'it is nothing,' in case you did not know."

We both laughed. If ever there was a prime example of Texans mangling the Spanish language and creating new words, it was me. Still, I think he appreciated that I at least tried to speak his first language. He sat down and took a sip of his coffee, looking at me over the rim of the mug. The merriment faded from his eyes. He set his mug down and scrutinized me closely.

"Things have taken a nasty turn, *qué no*?" He frowned. "It is bad enough that you risk your life chasing these evil *cabrónes,* now you have to suffer being falsely accused of something that you would never do."

I couldn't begin to say how much it meant to me that he expressed unequivocal support for me. It didn't take all the sting out of what had happened but it helped. Not that I would have expected any less from him but after my experience with Tom Figgs, I had begun to question who my true friends were.

"It has complicated things, no doubt," I

said. "It's a good thing Nathan is tight with old Mayor Salazar. If Salazar didn't trust him, I'd probably still be sittin' in that unlocked jail cell over in Springer."

"I did not know Salazar was in Nathan's debt until I heard what had happened. They go back a long way, before my time most certainly."

I was more interested in Tomás's time, particularly when he was deputy sheriff and then sheriff. "You know, I admire you for gettin' out right before they made us move our headquarters over there. That was pretty good timin'." He just grinned back at me. "What I'm wonderin' is how much time you spent around the mayor and what your take on him was."

Tomás scrunched his face up as he contemplated the question. Finally, he said, "I did not spend much time around him but what time I did spend, I found him to be a decent man down deep." He grinned. "Of course, one had to overlook that he could at times strut around like a rooster. I think he puts on a show for people when he first meets them. He wants them to know he is important."

"I got that second part in spades about him wantin' you to know he's important," I said. "He sure put me in my place right away. It's interestin' to me that both you and Nathan think he's a good man. I confess I haven't seen that side of him yet."

"The two of you did not start off on the right foot," Tomás said, "so it does not surprise me that you have not seen his better side yet. He does not know you and one of the first things that happens is he gets information that says you are taking bribes." He arched an eyebrow at me and said, "Also, you sometimes have an annoying way of speaking to those who have authority over you. Not everyone is as patient as I am."

I choked on the mouthful of hot coffee I was in the process of swallowing. I coughed for a moment before I could catch my breath and respond. "I beg your pardon, Tomás Marés, but I've been nothin' but respectful to that little banty rooster. And I think you got problems with your memory 'cause I don't recollect you bein' all that patient."

Tomás laughed with mucho gusto. It's strange but I don't remember him having this good a sense of humor when he was my boss, either. When he could speak, he said, "Tommy, you have no idea how you tested my patience. A less tolerant man would probably have shot you."

"Humph," I grunted. He was probably

right. "Well, I didn't come here just to reminisce about the good old days. I'm tryin' to get a handle on what's goin' on and who's behind it all. It sounds to me like you're sayin' Mayor Salazar is one of the good guys."

"I believe that," Tomás said with conviction. He paused. "You know who I had doubts about?"

"No," I said with just a hint of frustration in my voice, "but I'm hopin' you'll tell me sometime today."

He ignored me. He'd had a lot of practice doing that when he was sheriff and I was his deputy. Apparently, he hadn't lost his touch. "That banker, what was his name?"

"Abreu." I was surprised. "Jesus Abreu is his name. You think he's a bad guy?"

"I do not know for sure," he said, "but I got a bad feeling from him."

I shook my head. "That's funny. He's been a lot friendlier to me than Salazar. It seemed like he was interested in helpin' out, even after they locked me up." I snorted, disgusted. "Well, after I put myself in the cell. There ain't no lock."

Tomás nodded. "He always acted like he wanted to be helpful to me as well. For some reason, I had a feeling that this is what it was . . . an act."

"That's interestin'," I said. "Nothin' we can use in a court of law but maybe it gives us another rock to turn over."

"What makes you think that someone in Springer may be involved in the trouble with these outlaws?"

"Reckon I'm kinda like you," I said. "It's just a feelin'. I got a strong hunch this Alvarado hombre from down in Las Vegas is the man behind all this. The thing is, his gang seems to know an awful lot about what goes on up here . . . who has stock for the takin', who's a long way from help. That sort of thing." I frowned once more. "It also strikes me as a little suspicious that none of the outfits around Springer have been hit. Why would that be?"

"It is a good question," Tomás replied. "One for which I have no answer."

The door from the kitchen burst open. Maria and Mollie swept out in a flurry of giggles and chatter, carrying plates. Maria stopped in mid-stride, taking in our solemn expressions.

"Oh, no," she exclaimed. "We will not discuss business. We will talk about wedding plans and joyful things. My Tomás is all done with wearing badges and getting shot at."

As usual, she sounded determined. Tomás

looked at me and shrugged. "She is right," he said, smiling at his fiancée. "We will be happy."

I must confess I felt a stab of envy and maybe even a little bitterness. More than once since he'd handed in his badge, I had wondered how Tomás could just walk away, especially since he'd left me with my tail in a pretty good crack. Now, as I saw how he and Maria looked at each other, I realized it *was* possible to let it all go. Lord knows Tomás had given his all defending the people of Colfax County and he'd lost his father in the bargain. A man has a right to determine when he's given enough. I wasn't sure how you measured how much was enough. I was determined to figure it out, though.

"Bein' happy sounds mighty fine to me," I said. Turning to Maria, I said, "I reckon you been tellin' Mollie all about the plans for the weddin'. If you don't mind repeatin' it, I'd sure like to hear myself."

Turned out Maria was more than happy to repeat herself. A couple of hours slipped away as we talked about their plans and dreams for the future. None of this solved my problems but it felt great to step away from them for a while.

CHAPTER 25

"You boys need to quit squabbling or I'm gonna shoot you both." Pony Dolan's voice was low and menacing. Pat Maes and Manuel Maldonado had been arguing about the best way to steal the horses from a little spread over by Ute Park, west of Cimarrón. As usual, Maldonado had waited to hear what Maes had to say and then immediately began to challenge him.

"I don't want you to shoot me, Pony," Maes said, his frustration boiling over, "but if it means you'll shoot this *hijo de puta,* too, it might be worth it." He glared at Maldonado. "If I say it's daytime, he says it's night. I'm up to my gills with him questionin' everything I say."

Maldonado hawked and spit on the ground. He grinned insolently at Maes. "Maybe it's 'cause near everything you say is just plain stupid, Pat."

Maes uttered a growl and started to reach

for his pistol. Before he could clear leather, Pony Dolan had his gun out and was training it on him.

"Take your hand off your gun, Pat," he said very calmly. "I'd rather not shoot either one of you. We need you both if we're gonna get this job done. I'm fed up with your bickerin', though."

Maldonado snickered. Pony turned his gun in his direction. "That goes for you, too, Manuel. You need to wipe that grin off your face, you bloody fool, and keep your mouth shut. We got a job to do. Truth is, we got a couple of jobs to do and we need to get 'em done pronto. You don't want me tellin' the Boss we didn't do his biddin' 'cause you and Pat kept squabblin' like a couple of schoolgirls, do you?"

Apparently, Maldonado decided that unlike Pat Maes, Pony Dolan would not tolerate being prodded and provoked. Clearly, he was not willing to be challenged.

"As you say, Pony, we got a job to do. I only want to make sure we get it done proper and live to collect our pay." He avoided looking at Pat Maes, who was so mad he was quivering.

"I tell you what, Manuel," Dolan said. "Why don't you let me worry about the plan, along with Pat. You keep your mouth shut and do your job, you might live to collect your pay. You clear on that?"

Maldonado looked for a moment like he wanted to face up to Pony Dolan for his threatening tone . . . but only for a moment. "Sure Pony, whatever you say. I trust *you,*" he said, making sure Maes could tell from his tone that the same thing did not hold true in his case.

"Good, I hope we got that settled," Dolan said. He was all business now. "Here's the problem I see, Pat. We ain't sure how many horses they got at this place we're hittin' in Ute Park. Once we get 'em, we got to run 'em up to the corrals in Compos Canyon. We're gonna be passin' pretty close to Cimarrón when we do that, ain't no other way to get there." He frowned. "The more horses we steal, the more that can go off the rails and call attention to us. If some ignorant bastard happens to be out for a little ride and sees us, he might scoot on back to town and tell the law."

Pat Maes avoided looking at Manuel Maldonado. He looked like he was working hard to control his anger as he responded to Pony Dolan. "I ain't arguin' with you, Pony, but that's the job the Boss gave us. Hit this place in Ute Park, take the horses to the canyon, and then do that other job to the northeast. I'd appreciate any ideas you have on how to cut down on the risk."

"I do have an idea, Pat," Dolan said. "It's got some risk with it, too, but it's a different kind."

"Let's hear it," Maes said. He still looked like he'd eaten something disgusting and was choking on it as he tried to swallow.

"I say we charge in just ahead of sundown. We kill everybody, round up the herd, and head up for Compos Canyon when it gets dark." Dolan slapped his leg for emphasis. "That way, we'll be ridin' past the town when folks ain't likely to be out and about."

Maes frowned as he considered the idea. "Well, you're right about nobody bein' out at that time of night. It sure ups the chances of one of us havin' a wreck, though, drivin' those horses in the dark."

"We got a full moon, Pat," Dolan said. "Besides, I thought you boys was all *muy bueno vaqueros.* A little darkness shouldn't be a hitch for the likes of you, right?"

Maes could see how Dolan had suckered him in. He couldn't object without looking like a tinhorn and he couldn't ask Dorsey's opinion without having to listen to Maldonado's views, too. He didn't like it but he didn't figure he had much say in the matter at this point. Without any formal discussion, it appeared that Pony Dolan had taken over as the honcho of their little gang. He shrugged.

"The way I see it, there's some risk no matter how or when we do it. I got no problem doin' it your way." He hesitated, then added, "This time."

Dolan fixed him with a cold stare. "Yeah, sure, Pat," he said meaningfully. "This time."

"I talked with Tomás about this White Caps gang." I was having coffee with Nathan at the St. James Hotel. It was nice to be back in a place I felt at ease. The Brown Hotel in Springer was all right but for my money, you couldn't beat the St. James.

"I'm a little surprised he would talk with you about it," Nathan said with a chuckle. "Maria must not have been around."

I laughed. "She and Mollie were in the kitchen talkin'. I promise you, when they came out, she put an end to the discussion pronto."

"So, what did Tomás have to say?"

"I mentioned to him it seemed a little strange that this bunch wasn't botherin' the ranches over near Springer. I asked if he had any ideas about that." I nodded at Nathan. "You probably won't be surprised that he had the same take on old Mayor Salazar as you. He said once you get past the cocky rooster bit, he ain't a bad guy." I chuckled. "I can't wait to get past that part."

Nathan grinned at me. "Reckon you still got a ways to go."

"I'm afraid you're right," I said. "You know who Tomás was a bit mistrustful of? That banker, Jesus Abreu." I took a sip of my coffee and pondered this. "That's funny to me because he's the one that's been the friendliest to me. Seems like all he's wanted to do is help out."

When I mentioned Abreu, Nathan had sat forward in his chair. Now he nodded thoughtfully. "That's interestin'. When I talked with Charlie Carter over in Santa Fe, he mentioned Abreu, too." He looked down at his coffee mug and saw that it was empty. He motioned to Juanita over behind the desk and she brought him a refill.

"Hmmm," I said. "It's curious that both of 'em would bring up Abreu."

"You know what's even more curious is that Abreu is Felipe Alvarado's cousin. Did you know that?"

"No, I didn't know that." I sat up, my interest increasing. "Don't know what it means, if anything, but it puts a little different shine on things."

"It might not mean anything. Dang near everybody's cousins in this part of the world. Still, it's worth lookin' into," Nathan said. "Maybe we could have Rusty ask around over in Springer, see if anyone knows about Abreu and Alvarado bein' in communication with each other lately."

Rusty would be less than thrilled about making another trip over to Springer. His enthusiasm for being a lawman seemed to have waned a bit once he discovered that the work involves long hours of boredom when you're trying to get information from folks mixed with moments of terror when some bloody scoundrel is shooting at you. Still, he signed on to be part of this outfit. You don't always get to pick your chores, whether you're herding cattle or chasing outlaws.

"Good idea," I said. "Why don't you tell him?"

Nathan grinned. "I look forward to it."

We both had a good chuckle as we anticipated Rusty's reaction to his next assignment. I was getting a kick out of Nathan's ribbing my cousin. In our upside-down cowboy world, how much you like someone is generally measured by how hard a time you give them. I was glad to have Rusty back in my life and it made me feel good that a man I respected a great deal had taken a shine to him. Having pards you can count on means the world.

As that thought crossed my mind, my good spirits flew out the window. I would have sworn I could have counted on Tom Figgs to back me up without question. Turns out I'd been wide of the mark.

"Nathan," I said, "I'd like to get your view on a bit of a touchy subject."

He laughed. "If you're gonna ask me for advice on how to talk to your wife, don't bother. I spend most of my time confused about what's goin' on between me and Christy. I don't reckon I could help you much with Mollie."

I shook my head. "It ain't about my marriage, it's about Tom Figgs."

Nathan's expression turned serious. "That stuck in your craw the other day, didn't it?"

"You can say that again. I thought he was my friend. It's kinda like somebody snuck up on my blind side and sucker punched me." I shook my head again and frowned. "I wasn't surprised that Bill Wallace acted the way he did. We ain't never been amigos. I know he was glad to see me be the one who got caught lookin' like he was a crook. I didn't expect it out of Tom, though."

"I ain't gonna defend him," Nathan said,

" 'cause I think he was wrong not to take your side. I will say a couple of things in his behalf, though." He paused and took a long pull on his coffee. "Bill had been workin' on him pretty hard before you got back to town, whisperin' in his ear that you were a part of this whole mess. Tom was pretty disturbed from seein' that young Woodrum fella all cut up when the mercantile got robbed. I think all that maybe clouded his judgment a bit."

"I know that hit him hard," I said. I was trying to be fair rather than fly off the handle like I've done more than once in the past. "Sometimes I have to remind myself he ain't a lawman, he's a farrier. You know better than me that we see some gory things as we go about tryin' to catch these vicious men who live outside the law." I shrugged. "That don't mean I feel good about it, though."

"No reason for you to feel good," Nathan replied. "I expect with a little time, Tom'll come around." He smiled. "He ain't perfect like you and me but he's a decent man. He'll see his blunder sooner rather than later."

I laughed, mostly at myself. "Yeah, well maybe you're perfect but now that you mention it, I know I've blundered more than once in the past and came to regret it. I'll try to keep that in mind and cut him some slack."

"Not a bad idea," Nathan said. "Don't forget, he's stood by you more than once in the past." He laughed. "As for me bein' perfect, I know that's the case but my wife would have you believe different."

That surprised me. I assumed that like the rest of us, Christy thought Nathan Averill walked on water. To hear otherwise was a bit of a shock. Everyone who knew the two of them considered it providence that they'd found each other so late in Nathan's life.

"Well, I hope y'all ain't havin' . . ." I searched for the right word. This was unfamiliar and mighty uncomfortable territory for a cowboy to be in. Finally, I settled on a word. ". . . troubles."

Nathan laughed even louder. "Naw, we're fine. It just ain't all that easy for a proper lady like my wife to put up with the appallin' habits I developed from bein' a lifelong bachelor." He grinned. "See, I had no idea about things such as how you're supposed to spread the bed covers every mornin' and put a bunch of pillows on the bed. It's been enlightenin' for me, to say the least."

"I never knew other husbands landed in

the doghouse for that sort of thing," I said. "I thought it was just me. That's a comfort."

"Well, it can't be smooth sailin' all the time." He got a look of mischief on his lined face. "Sometimes it's worth havin' a little trouble just so you can make up."

I found myself blushing. That was way more information than I wanted to have about one of my heroes. Still, it was good to know I wasn't alone when it came to landing in disfavor with my wife.

"Reckon it ain't a bad thing I'm gone as much as I am," I said. "Gives Mollie time to forget about the things I do that get on her nerves."

That thought reminded me of my current state of affairs of living in a different town than my wife. Being back in Cimarrón, even temporarily, had pushed that to the back of my mind. The pleasant time we'd spent with Tomás and Maria had made it almost seem like things were fine. The reality hit me square in the face. I needed to get this situation with the White Caps gang resolved and then make some decisions.

"Nathan," I said, "I don't know how you did it all those years. I don't know how much more of this I can abide. Bein' separated from my wife, havin' people question my honesty. It ain't what I signed up for."

He stared at me for a moment, then spoke quietly. "Yes, it is, Tommy. It's exactly what you signed up for. Nobody said this job was easy or that folks would be fair with you. As long as you're doin' a decent job and they feel safe, they take you for granted. As soon as there's problems, they start pointin' fingers and blamin' you for it."

"That's exactly right," I said vehemently. "That's what I'm sayin'. How did you put up with that for so long? It seemed like it never bothered you much at all."

He shrugged. "Of course it bothered me some, though over the years I kinda grew a thick skin. The thing is, you can't let it get to you. People will be people. Sometimes they don't conduct themselves as well as we'd like 'em to. You still got a job to do."

"I reckon you're right," I said. "Still, I have trouble overlookin' it when people stab me in the back."

Nathan nodded. "I understand. You got to keep in mind what's most important about your job, though."

"And that would be?"

"Takin' a stand against evil," he said in a quiet yet firm voice. "You know what I'm talkin' about, you've stood up to those men yourself. You draw a line in the dirt and say, 'no more.' If you don't do it, nobody else will and they'll take over. Then evil wins."

"I know you're right but that don't make it easy." I heaved a sigh. "Sometimes I just want to go somewhere else where none of this exists."

He chuckled. "When you find that place, let me know. I want to go there, too."

"All right, I get it," I said. "There ain't no such place. I either need to stick it out here or turn tail and run." I have to admit I felt pretty disheartened. "I just don't know if I can do it."

"You don't have to do it alone, Sheriff," he said. "You got me backin' you up and you got your cousin, Rusty. A man could do worse when it comes to havin' help."

As if on cue, Rusty walked in the door. He looked back and forth between the two of us. Sensing that things were a bit on edge, he asked, "What's goin' on?"

"Ah, nothin'," I said, "we was just talkin'." I grinned at Nathan. "Deputy Averill has somethin' to tell you, though."

Nathan informed Rusty of the plan for him to return again to Springer to see if he could find out more about the connection between Alvarado and Abreu. As we'd suspected, he was not pleased.

"Why do I have to be the one?" Rusty sounded like a whiny child.

Nathan slowly stood up and stared at Rusty for an uncomfortable moment. "If you wanna be a big dog, son, you gotta get out from under the porch."

Rusty quit whining.

Chapter 26

"Aiee!" Pat Maes howled as the branch sprang back and slapped him in the face. "You stupid *pendejo*!" He was positive that Maldonado had done it on purpose.

"Sorry," Maldonado said, sounding not the least bit remorseful. "Don't follow me so close."

"You two shut up," Pony Dolan said, a dangerous edge to his voice. "I've had all I'm going to take of your bickering. We got to get these horses to the corrals and get some rest. We got another job to do and it needs to be done straight away."

Things had not gone well. When they arrived at the ranch where the horses were, the rancher, his wife, and two hands mounted a spirited resistance. It appeared that word had spread about their raids and as a result, folks were more alert to the threat. In the end, they'd killed them all but not before John Dorsey took a bullet in the leg. It was painful but not lethal and he could still ride for now. Dolan was concerned that either blood loss or infection would render him useless by the time they made their next raid, though. With the loss of Rafael Espinosa and the ranchers becoming more vigilant, they would require every man to be at full strength.

Dolan had begun to question his decision to push the horses past town at night. Although he felt his reasoning was sound about avoiding detection, they'd already lost one of the horses. It stepped off the narrow trail and went down with a broken leg. They couldn't risk shooting it so close to town so he had cut its throat. Now he was seriously considering doing the same to Pat Maes and Manuel Maldonado.

They were nearly through Chase Canyon and should arrive at their hideout in Compos Canyon by daybreak. Once they herded the horses into the corrals, he intended to have some beans and bacon and then take a long siesta. The last thing he wanted was to have Maes and Maldonado jabbering at one another when he was trying to sleep. As appealing as it was for him to kill them both, he knew he couldn't do that until they'd finished the next job. Once that was done, he was seriously considering shooting them both and telling the Boss they'd been ambushed by that lawman from Cimarrón. He doubted if Dorsey would care one way or another. He figured he was tired of the constant sniping as well.

It seemed that Maes and Maldonado had heeded his threats. They were quiet for now at least and he had time to reflect as they rode along under the full moon. Pony Dolan wasn't sure how much longer he wanted to continue his association with this outfit. He'd been paid some good money for his work so far and if he chose to stick around, he planned on hitting the Boss up for a raise. He ought to be in charge of the gang officially since, for all practical purposes, they did what he said, anyway. He smiled grimly. There would likely be an opening for a new boss of this gang in the near future. He would make sure of it.

He couldn't figure the Boss out and that troubled him. He was a dangerous man, there was no doubt about that. From time to time, he'd accompanied them on raids and Pony had been impressed with his ferocity. He had a strong stomach but some of the things he'd seen the Boss do to his victims made him a bit queasy. What Dolan couldn't work out was why, when the Boss decided to expand his operation to the north of San Miguel County, he'd chosen to ignore the territory around the town of Springer. He'd been very clear in his instructions to avoid that area and focus on the ranches to the north and west of Cimarrón.

A noise distracted him from his ponderings. Once he'd identified it as the hoot of an owl on the hunt, he went back to thinking about the situation. The decision to avoid Springer made him think the Boss had a pact with someone there. In general, the Boss didn't strike him as a man inclined to have a partner but his behavior suggested otherwise. Pony didn't like being in the dark about such things. He wanted to know who he was working for and how the decisions were made. Things could go south in a heartbeat. In his experience, when that happened, those at the top usually began giving up their underlings. If the Boss had a partner who had a say in the plans, Pony wanted to know who he was so he could be wary of him if everything fell apart. He was still considering this question as the sun peeked over the mountains and they arrived at their hideout.

Chapter 27

"Deputy Stallings, how is the investigation of the sheriff proceeding?"

It was interesting, Rusty thought, that there was no howdy, no how've you been or any other pleasantries from Mayor Salazar. Well, at least you pretty much knew what to expect from the man.

"Deputy Averill is still studyin' it, Mayor, but he's pretty sure somebody set Tommy . . . I mean Sheriff Stallings . . . up. They been goin' at it pretty hard tryin' to nab those thievin' outlaws who been killin' folks around Cimarrón." He paused, wondering how far he should go in questioning the mayor. He figured what the hell. "Mayor, we need some help tryin' to solve this riddle. Would you be willin' to help me think about some of the notions Deputy Sheriff Averill has about who might be behind all this?"

"I am not a lawman, Deputy Stallings,"

the mayor said. "Still, I do know people all over the northern part of the territory. Maybe I could be of some assistance." They had been standing on the boardwalk outside Salazar's office. Now the mayor said, "Please come in and have a seat."

Rusty felt a little nervous about the mayor's newfound attitude of cooperation. He'd intentionally attributed the idea of who was behind the attacks on the ranchers as belonging to Nathan Averill. He figured that would set better with Salazar than his mentioning the opinion actually belonged to his cousin. He decided not to risk upsetting this new partnership by telling the truth at this point. He sat in the chair across the desk from the mayor and leaned forward.

"Mayor, Nathan has a suspicion these boys that are goin' around stealin' and murderin' are part of a gang called the White Caps from San Miguel County." He leaned back. "Do you know anything about that bunch?"

"Most certainly I do, Deputy," Salazar said. "I know of them but I am surprised that they might be working in this part of the territory now. In the past, they have confined their law-breaking to the area around Las Vegas. If it is true that they have expanded their base of operations, it would not be good news."

"Well, the Sheriff . . . I mean Deputy Averill, of course . . ." Rusty said, catching himself, "talked with a Pinkerton fella over in Santa Fe. He says the way these renegades are goin' about their business up in these parts is mighty similar to what they've done down in Las Vegas."

"As I said," Salazar replied, "if this is true, it is dire news." He took a deep breath and stroked his moustache. "It would mean that Felipe Alvarado is attempting to expand his criminal activities."

"So you know about Alvarado?"

"Oh, most certainly," Salazar said. "He is Jesus Abreu's cousin."

Rusty was surprised, to say the least. He had planned on mentioning Alvarado's name to the mayor to see if he knew anything about him but he hadn't intended to bring up the connection to Abreu. He wasn't sure exactly how to proceed. This part of being a lawman, what Tommy referred to as the investigation, was unfamiliar terrain for him.

"So, you know about the connection between Abreu and Alvarado?" He said this in as neutral a tone as he could manage.

"Oh, yes," Salazar said. "It is common knowledge, although I would not say they are connected. Jesus cut off contact with Felipe years ago because of his illegal activities."

Rusty stepped cautiously in his next question. "You don't think there's any chance that maybe they might have been in touch recently then?"

"Of course not," Salazar replied. "Jesus has political ambitions. I do not think he would put them at risk by getting involved in illegal activities."

From what he'd heard from his cousin, Rusty was pretty sure one of the most effective ways to advance your political ambitions in the New Mexico Territory was to get involved with illegal activities. He kept that thought to himself.

"So, as far as you know, Abreu hasn't been in communication with his cousin any time recently?"

"Not to my knowledge," Salazar replied. He paused. "It is curious, though. I did see Felipe's nephew, Ramon, in town not long ago. I do not know why he would be here. I know it was him because Jesus introduced me one time."

"Did anyone see this nephew talkin' with Señor Abreu?" Rusty felt a fluttering in his stomach. It reminded him of the feeling he got when he was hunting deer and saw movement in the brush that suggested his prey was hiding close by. Maybe he was on to something.

"I have no idea, Deputy. You could ask around, though. Jim White, our telegraph operator, seems to know almost everything that happens in town. What he does not know about, Arturo down at the livery would know." He cocked his head and looked at Rusty with skepticism. "Surely you do not think that Jesus would be involved in this robbery and murder."

Rusty figured he'd pushed his luck as far as he dared with the mayor. "Oh, I don't think so. I'm just tryin' to pull all the pieces of the puzzle together." He laughed. "They don't pay me to think. I just gather information and bring it to my boss. I'll let him figure it out."

Salazar nodded and smiled at him. "I understand, Deputy. You are just doing your job." He looked down at a stack of papers on his desk. Looking back up, he said, "If there is nothing else you wish to discuss, I have some important matters to attend to."

Rusty nodded back respectfully and stood up. "No, sir, that was about all I had. If you don't mind, I might have short conversations with the telegraph fella, White, and Arturo over at the livery before I head on back to Cimarrón."

"That is fine, Deputy," the mayor replied. He then looked down at the papers on his desk, completely ignoring Rusty. Apparently, their meeting was over.

Rusty let himself out and contemplated whether to speak with White or Arturo first. He was closer to the telegraph office so he headed up the street to see if White was in. The bank was across the street from the mayor's office but Rusty was not aware of the eyes that observed him as he walked away from his meeting with Salazar. Shortly after he made his way to visit with Jim White, Jesus Abreu walked across the street and entered the mayor's office without knocking.

Salazar looked up, impatience etched on his face. Apparently, he thought Deputy Stallings had returned to ask more questions. When he saw it was Abreu, the impatience vanished, replaced by a smile.

"Jesus, it is good to see you," he said. "What can I help you with today?"

The thought that flashed through Abreu's mind was that he did a lot more to help the mayor than Salazar did to help him. In this instance, he hoped it would be different.

"I saw the deputy leave your office, Manuel," he said casually. "It made me curious about how this investigation of our wayward sheriff is going."

Salazar laughed. "I am starting to think that perhaps Sheriff Stallings was telling the truth when he said he was framed. That appears to be what Sheriff Averill thinks." The mayor nodded thoughtfully. "I do not know this young man well but if Nathan Averill believes in him, that makes me inclined to believe in him as well."

Abreu was concerned this scheme he was involved in with his cousin was not progressing as well as he'd hoped. When they came up with the plan for the White Caps gang to move into the territory in Colfax County, they were counting on the sheriff being short-handed. Seemingly out of nowhere, he had produced not one but two deputies. Worse yet, one of them was one of the most respected lawmen in the New Mexico Territory.

"I suppose you could be right," Abreu said, "although I am not convinced."

Abreu sat down in the chair across from Salazar, which was still warm from Deputy Stallings's recent visit. He hoped to find out what these lawmen were thinking so he could help his cousin plan a strategy to elude discovery and capture. Alvarado had spent years cultivating his cover as a legitimate businessman in Las Vegas. He and Abreu had a master plan that would allow them to take over control of the northern part of the territory, both politically as well as economically. Those plans would be dashed if the scope of his cousin's illegal activities was uncovered.

Abreu crossed his legs and rested his hat on his knee. "If Averill does not think Stallings is a part of this, what are his thoughts about who might be behind it?"

Salazar frowned. "It is disturbing what he is thinking but I worry that he may be onto something." He tapped his chin as he thought about how to proceed. "He suspects that your cousin, Felipe, has dispatched men up to this part of the territory to rob and murder."

"I would know nothing about that," Abreu said. "You know I have not seen Felipe in years." Realizing that he had responded with greater vehemence than he'd intended, he smiled. "You know my cousin is the black sheep of our family. His own mother, mi *tia,* does not claim him."

"That is probably a sensible decision on all your parts," Salazar said. He chuckled. "Deputy Stallings appears to know you are connected by blood. He asked me if you had had any contact with him recently. I think they are only grasping for information, though." He smiled. "I told him that you were above suspicion. As always, mi amigo, I have your best interests at heart."

Abreu felt his pulse quicken when Salazar mentioned that the lawmen knew of his association with Alvarado. He tried to keep the look of shock off his face. To the best of his knowledge, they had no way of connecting him with his cousin other than by the accident of having been born into the same extended family. It would take more than that to expose his culpability in this matter.

"I know you do, Manuel," he said. "We look out for one another. That is what partners do." He smiled back at the mayor. "And I believe our association will take us both far." He rose to leave and as he did, he extended his hand to Salazar. "Here's to a fruitful partnership."

Salazar rose and grasped Abreu's hand, shaking it enthusiastically. "I agree completely, Jesus. Together, we will be a force."

Abreu turned to go. As he reached for the door, Salazar said, "Oh, before you leave, you might find this interesting."

Cautiously, Abreu turned around. "What is that, Manuel?"

"Recently, I saw Ramon in town. You remember, you introduced me one time. It struck me as odd but I had not given it much thought. Did he get in touch with you while he was here?"

Once again, Abreu felt his heart beat faster. He tried to remember if anyone had seen him visiting with Felipe's nephew. As far as he knew, their brief encounter had not been witnessed.

"No," he said, "I did not know that he had been in town. That does seem strange but I know nothing of it." He turned again to go.

"I did not think you had had any contact with him," Salazar said, "and certainly none with your cousin." He paused, recalling his conversation with the deputy. "He asked me what direction Ramon took when he left town. I think he was trying to make a connection between him and Alvarado, believing that if he rode south, he would be going to Las Vegas. Not that you would know anything about that." He smiled at Abreu. "I told Stallings I had no idea which direction he went when he left Springer."

Abreu felt light-headed as he walked out the door. This situation was spiraling out of control. Did someone see him meet with Ramon? He could not be sure. Although he could always deny it if someone reported this to Stallings, it still pointed a finger in his direction. He had also deliberately misled the deputy, telling him Ramon rode out to the north when he left town. If anyone else had seen him ride south and reported this, there would be further reason for suspicion. Although neither of these events were damning by themselves, they shone an unfavorable light on him when taken together. To compound his troubles, Felipe had no idea he had introduced Ramon to Salazar. Alvarado assumed that Jesus was the only person in Springer who knew Ramon's identity. He would not be pleased if he found out that this was not the case. Something had to be done to get this state of affairs under control.

If his cousin were here, Abreu knew what he would do. He would ambush the deputy and put an end to it quickly and ruthlessly. That was not Jesus Abreu's way. He had not even fired his rifle in quite some time. He was not sure he would succeed if he chose to risk going down this path. As he considered his options, he knew he needed to act fast. Making his decision, he returned to his office. He kept a loaded rifle there on a gun rack in the event that someone might attempt to rob the bank. He'd always been more comfortable with a long gun since the days of his youth when he hunted with his cousin. Now, it appeared he would need to hunt once more.

Taking the rifle off the rack, he exited through the private door at the rear of the building. He then hastened up the alley toward the livery. He was counting on the fact that Arturo Garcia would be down at the café enjoying his noon meal. With any luck, he could slip the horse he kept there out without Arturo's being aware of it. When he thought about shooting the deputy, his stomach felt as if it was turning inside out. No time to be squeamish, though. It looked as if he would need to get his hands bloody.

As Abreu snuck down the alley to the livery, Rusty Stallings walked into the telegraph office. The telegraph operator looked up and asked, "Can I help you?"

"Howdy, Mr. White," Rusty said. "I'm Deputy Stallings. We met the other day if you recall."

"Oh, yeah," White said. "I knew you looked familiar. I still got the same question, though. Can I help you?"

"Maybe so. I got a question for you. I was just talkin' with the mayor," Rusty said, dropping the mayor's name in hopes of greasing the wheels a bit. "He told me you know pert near everything that goes on in town."

White looked suspicious. "I try to keep my eyes open, Deputy. Ain't nothin' wrong with that, I reckon."

"Not at all," Rusty said in his friendliest manner. "I believe the mayor meant it as a compliment."

White relaxed when he heard this. "Well, I do my best to help out. What do you want to know?"

"A while back, I hear there was a young fella in town who wasn't from around here. Do you recall anyone like that?"

"I sure do," White said. "I saw him skulkin' around town for a day or two. Seems like I mentioned that to you before when we talked."

Taking note that White apparently saw the young man as being sneaky, Rusty asked, "I'm just followin' up, sir. Did you see him talkin' with anyone?"

White squinted as he thought back. Finally, he said, "Nope, I can't say that I did. I wondered what he was doin' here but I got better things to do than follow strangers around to find out what they're up to. That ain't my job."

It occurred to Rusty that as one of the town's busybodies, maybe it should be considered part of White's job. He decided not to mention that.

"So, you got no idea what his business here was." It sounded to Rusty like he wouldn't be getting any new information from the telegraph operator. Too bad.

"Nope, I don't." White replied. "I just saw him ride out to the south after he'd been here for the better part of two days."

"Well, thank you for your time, Mr. White," Rusty said, turning toward the door to take his leave. He stopped in his tracks and turned around. "Did you say he rode south out of town?"

"That's what I said, Deputy. He rode south. Why?"

Rusty's mind was racing. This contradicted Abreu's report of the man's riding north out of town.

"Oh, no reason," Rusty said. "I'm just tryin' to figure this whole thing out is all."

"Good luck with that, Deputy," White said. "If you don't have any other questions for me, I got some telegrams to send."

"No problem, sir. Thanks for your help."

Rusty walked quickly out of the telegraph office. He debated whether to head back to Cimarrón immediately or to take the time to question the liveryman. He wanted very much to get back but he figured Nathan would ask him why he hadn't followed through with the other witness. He didn't know if he would uncover any new information but he figured it would be better to be thorough. He also didn't want to let the old sheriff down.

When he got to the livery, there was no one there and one of the corrals was open. He wasn't sure what to make of that. As he went over to the open gate, Arturo Garcia walked up.

"Hey there, Deputy, why did you leave my gate open?" Although he spoke in a joking manner, there was a slight edge to his question.

"Oh, no," Rusty said quickly. "That wasn't me. It was open when I got here. I was just takin' a look at it when you walked up."

The old man looked at him suspiciously. "I do not know who would have left the gate to the corral open while I was gone." He strode by Rusty and went in the corral. When he came back out, he said, "It looks like Señor Abreu decided to take a ride."

Rusty's ears perked up. "Why do you say that, sir?"

"Oh," Garcia said, "His horse is gone. He does not take it out often. I suppose he did not think to close the gate." He took care of the chore of closing the gate himself and turned back to Rusty. "Can I do something for you, Deputy?"

"I had a question for you. Do you recall seeing a young man from out of town here a while back?"

Garcia didn't hesitate. "Of course," he said. "He was here for a couple of days. I wondered who he was."

"Did you see him talk with anyone while he was here?" Rusty held his breath and waited for the answer.

"It is funny that you ask," Garcia said.

"What's funny about it?"

"It is funny because we were just talking about Señor Abreu taking his horse out for a ride. It was Señor Abreu that the stranger talked to."

Rusty could hardly wait to start back to Cimarrón now. He just had one more question. "Did you happen to see which direction he went when he left town?"

Garcia thought about it for a moment. Nodding to himself, he replied, "I believe he headed south."

Rusty felt his heart beat faster. One time might be written off as a misunderstanding. The second time made it start to look as if Abreu was not telling the truth . . . about a number of things.

Chapter 28

As Jesus Abreu settled in behind the boulders off to the north side of the trail, he was painfully aware that he was out of his element. This was what his cousin, Felipe, would do or at least pay someone else to do. It wasn't Jesus's style. And yet here he was, lying in wait like he was hunting elk, which he'd done as a boy growing up in the northern New Mexico Territory. He was never especially good at it and as he grew into adulthood, he'd given up hunting for sport.

It occurred to him that he wasn't hunting for sport now, he was hunting for survival. He'd never pointed a gun at another human being, and as he waited for Rusty Stallings to ride up the trail, he felt unsure about how he would handle this task. Shooting an animal was one thing. Shooting a person with whom you had conversed and exchanged pleasantries was something else entirely. Jesus was desperate, though, and could think of no other way to deal with this.

It was public, although not widespread, knowledge that he was related to Felipe Alvarado. However, as far as anyone knew, he'd not had contact with his cousin for many years. The deputy had uncovered a clear and current connection however, one which could derail all of his political and financial aspirations. He'd invested far too much time, effort, and money into propping up Manuel Salazar, the marionette whose strings he intended to maneuver as he positioned himself to become one of the major players in the lucrative political climate in Santa Fe. He could not . . . would not . . . allow all his efforts to come to naught. The deputy had to die and there was no one else to get it done.

Abreu was so deep in thought that he almost missed his opportunity to take a shot at Rusty Stallings. He'd ridden up the side of the canyon about seventy yards so he could tie his horse to a tree out of sight. He hadn't planned particularly well. Too late, he realized that a rider would come around a bend in the trail and be in his line of sight for only a brief period before the trail took another turn. Stallings had already come around the bend and was quickly approaching the next turn. If he made it, Abreu would either have to pursue him and risk engaging in a pitched gun battle or give up and seek another avenue to deal with the problem.

Sweat ran down into his eyes as Jesus made his decision. His hands shook but he knew he had to take the shot. He tried to remember tips his cousin had given him when they hunted for elk . . . deep breaths, keep both eyes open, squeeze the trigger rather than jerking it. Stallings was nearly out of sight. All the advice from the past flew out the window. Jesus Abreu jerked the trigger of his Winchester repeatedly until the magazine was empty. He was firing blindly and did not see Rusty Stallings duck and simultaneously spur his horse into a gallop. When the gun was empty, he looked down at the trail, searching desperately for a body. There was none.

Rusty Stallings was confused. He was also tense, agitated, and scared, in no particular order. He was pretty sure he had solid information that could not only link Jesus Abreu to Felipe Alvarado but also demonstrate that he'd lied about the stranger in town, probably in an effort to throw off the investigation. He had seemed like a good fella to Rusty but it was beginning to look like that was all a sham.

That Abreu had unexpectedly taken a horse out for a ride had Rusty's mind racing. Although the man had never been threatening in their previous encounters, Rusty now realized that he'd badly misjudged his character. Clearly there was more to Señor Abreu than what appeared on the surface. Was it possible that along with being a conniving weasel, he might be an assassin as well? Rusty didn't know and he hoped he didn't find out.

All of this was on his mind as he came around a bend in the trail. Up ahead, he saw another turn about twenty yards further on. He was on edge as he scanned the landscape for any signs of an ambush. The forest came right up to the trail to his left and was so thick that Rusty didn't think it would make a good spot for an attempt to bushwhack someone. Still, he scrutinized the trees along the trail carefully. He saw nothing that set off any alarms in his mind.

He took a deep breath and looked around again. Just as he turned his attention over his right shoulder, everything went to hell. He caught the briefest image of sunlight glinting on metal followed by the unmistakable sound of a rifle firing repeatedly. He frantically urged his horse forward as the din echoed through the canyon. It was all he could do to hold on, particularly since he was hunkered down in the saddle trying to make himself as small a target as possible. His world narrowed to the twenty yards between himself and the bend in the trail ahead. He heard a high-pitched scream and wondered where it was coming from. It took a second for him to realize it was coming out of his own mouth.

Rusty had heard that time slows down when you're in danger. He'd even experienced it a time or two on a bad horse. That was nothing compared to the feeling of hearing bullets whine past his body. He was almost to the turn when it crossed his mind that if he got shot in the last few feet, he was really going to be angry. It was a good thing his butt cheeks were clinched so tight from the terror coursing through his mind and body; otherwise, he was pretty sure he would've lost control of his bowels.

He reached the safety of the bend in the trail but continued spurring his horse, galloping at breakneck speed. He pondered how odd it was that a part of him seemed to be outside of the action, observing what was happening, while the rest of him was caught up in the panic and shock. The observing part thought that this was the second time in a very short period where he'd found himself careening wildly through a canyon while trying to escape someone who was trying their best to kill him. *Maybe I'm not cut out for this job as a lawman.*

Rusty might've galloped all the way back to Cimarrón but his horse began to flag and slow down. His best chance of escape would be to pace his mount. With an effort of will, he overcame his fright and reined his horse in to a trot. All his senses were alert as he listened for any sound of pursuit. The only possible way the unseen shooter could catch up to him would be on horseback. He strained to hear the sound of hoofbeats. All he heard was silence. He relaxed but only a little. If he'd been eager before to get back to town to report to Tommy and Nathan, he was positively desperate now.

Jesus Abreu was in a quandary. The deputy hadn't fallen from his horse and had made it around the bend but he was hoping he might have hit him with one of his wild shots. He knew he should get his horse and give chase but the prospect of engaging in a running gun battle with the lawman made his stomach roil. Once again, he thought how poorly suited he was to this line of work. Then it occurred to him that Stallings might double back and try to ambush him. The churning in his stomach intensified. He decided the wisest or at least the safest course of action would be to head back to Springer as fast as his horse could take him.

Jesus knew he needed to get word to Felipe that the lawmen were aware of the connection between them. He dreaded telling his cousin about his failed attempt to shoot the deputy, knowing the scorn that would be directed his way. In his mind, he went back over his actions and realized he'd panicked when he saw that Stallings was almost out of range. *If I had another chance, I would do better. I know I would.*

Chapter 29

As he awoke, Pony Dolan felt like he was stumbling out of a fog. It took him a moment to orient himself and recognize he was in the cabin next to the gang's corral in Compos Canyon. He sat up, scratched his head, and looked around. It was late afternoon and he appeared to be the only one stirring. He heard a muffled roar from outside that turned out to be Manuel Maldonado's snoring. The man had tossed his bedroll under a tree and was sprawled out on his back. Over by the corral, Pony could see where Dorsey had bedded down. Pat Maes was not in sight.

Dolan's initial idea had been to rest up for a few hours and then head out to hit the other ranch they'd been ordered to attack. He could see now how unrealistic that plan had been. He was pretty tough but he was still worn out from the all-night ride through the canyons with the horses. He figured the other men were more exhausted than he was. The smart thing to do was to postpone the raid until the next day after they caught up on their rest.

Pony heard a noise from the stand of trees behind the corral and quickly drew his pistol. He put it away when he saw Pat Maes walking unsteadily in his direction. Apparently, he'd also just awakened and was coming over to talk about their plan. Dolan figured he would play along, letting Maes believe he was still in charge of the gang. Of course, they would still do exactly what he wanted them to do. He chuckled as Maes approached him. Sometimes this was too easy.

"Let's head over to the trail so we don't wake these boys," Pony said quietly. "I reckon they need the sleep."

The two men strolled in silence for about fifty yards. Dolan walked over to a cottonwood and leaned against the trunk. He took out his tobacco pouch and rolled a smoke for himself. He glanced up at Pat Maes.

"You want one?"

Maes seemed slightly taken aback by Pony's friendly manner. He hesitated for a moment and then said, "Sure, why not."

When Pony got the two smokes rolled, he straightened up and handed one to Maes.

He produced a match out of his vest and struck it on his chaps. Cupping the flame with his hand, he offered to light Pat's smoke. He then lit his own and took a puff, savoring the flavor. He blew out the smoke from his lungs and nodded at Maes.

"I don't know about you, Pat, but I'm thinkin' the boys need a bit more rest before we tackle that ranch. People get tired, they make mistakes. Mistakes get you killed." He grinned at Maes. "I'm just offerin' my opinion, you know. It's your call."

A look of uncertainty crossed Pat Maes's face and Pony wondered if he'd gone too far with his accommodating act. Then Maes stood up a little straighter and puffed out his chest. Dolan smiled inwardly. *I got him right where I want him.*

"I know it's my call, Pony," Maes said, "but I appreciate you tossin' in your counsel. I believe in this case, you're right. If we tried to ride this evenin', them boys wouldn't be worth a damn." He frowned. "I don't know how bad Dorsey's wounded, neither. I doubt it would hurt to give him another day to rest."

"I think you're most likely right, Pat," Pony said. "It ain't gonna matter if we get all this stock up to Trinidad a day later. They'll pay the same." He flashed a cruel smile. “Hey, that’ll give those third-rate ranchers an extra day to live, right. They’d probably appreciate that.”

Maes laughed uncomfortably. He’d seen Dolan’s brutality up close. He was no stranger to violence but the cruelty the man inflicted on his victims and the pleasure he seemed to derive from it was disturbing. In this way, Pony Dolan was not unlike the Boss. They both seemed to enjoy inflicting pain.

“Reckon you’re right about that, Pony. Who knows, maybe them folks won’t be at the bunkhouse when we hit ’em tomorrow,” he said hopefully. “That’d be their lucky day.”

“You just want to take all the fun out of it, don’t you, Pat?” Dolan stared at Maes for a moment. The man grew increasingly uncomfortable. Then Dolan laughed. “I’m just joshin’ you,” he said. “We’ll do whatever we need to do tomorrow to get the job done.”

Maes appeared to be unconvinced. “Sure, Pony, whatever you say.”

Dolan nodded. As he did, he thought, *that’s about right, ain’t it. What I say goes.* He kept the thought to himself. He puffed on his smoke for a moment, then said, “I got a question for you, Pat. You been runnin' this little outfit for a while now, I expect you know the ins and outs."

Maes frowned, unsure of where the conversation was leading. "That's true. You got some questions?"

"Matter of fact, I do," Dolan said. He kept his tone casual. "I been thinkin' about the Boss. I had the impression he ran things. Lately, I been wonderin' if he don't have some help in makin' decisions."

Maes looked befuddled. "I ain't sure what you're askin', Pony. What kind of help?"

"Like there's another boss whisperin' in his ear," Dolan said. "Like he's got a partner."

Maes shook his head as he considered the question. "If he does, I sure don't know nothin' about it. He's the only one ever talks to me or gives me orders." He frowned. "If there's someone else, I can't figure who it might be."

Dolan watched the man carefully as he responded. Maes seemed genuinely confused by the question and as far as Pony could see, he was telling the truth as he knew it. That didn't mean what he said was accurate, though. Pony had a strong hunch there was more going on behind the scenes than any of them knew about. That left too many loose ends in his opinion. He preferred to have as much control as possible and loose ends were out of his control. He would have to find some other way to get to the bottom of this.

Nathan and I sat quietly and listened as Rusty reported on his time in Springer. Rusty couldn't sit still as he recounted his escapade in the canyon on the way back. I was a bit concerned that with his pacing back and forth, he would wear a rut in the floor of my former sheriff's office. On the other hand, considering how I felt about my forced move to Springer, I figured good riddance.

"I'm gettin' pretty danged tired of people shootin' at me," Rusty said with considerable feeling.

"Don't blame you for that, Deputy Stallings," Nathan said. "I never much liked that part of the job myself. It *is* part of the job, though." He motioned to the third chair in the office. "Why don't you sit down and take a load off. You're makin' me dizzy."

Reluctantly, Rusty walked over and sat down in the chair. "Sorry, I just ain't calmed down yet. I come close to runnin' my horse into the ground ridin' back from Springer. Lucky he had the good sense to slow down on his own. I hope he don't wind up lame."

"I don't reckon we got a problem with you hotfootin' it back to Cimarrón since you didn't know if whoever took those shots was followin' you to finish the job," I said.

Rusty shuddered as he remembered what had transpired. "That was all I thought about that last bunch of miles, cousin. I felt this itch right in the middle of my back, like any second a bullet was gonna knock me right off my horse. I don't mind tellin' you I hunkered down in the saddle and made myself as small a target as I could."

"Don't blame you a bit," I said. "I'd have done the same thing. Could we go over what happened before you left Springer one more time, though? The best way to keep from gettin' shot at again is to get to the bottom of this muddle and arrest the back-shootin' yellow dogs who are behind it all."

"You're right." Rusty took a deep breath to calm himself. "What part do you want me to go over again?"

Nathan took over at this point. "Tell us what White and the liveryman said about which way the young stranger headed when he rode out of town."

"They both said south," Rusty said emphatically. "I know because I asked 'em twice. That's the exact opposite of what Mr. Abreu told us."

"Yes, it is," Nathan said in a reflective voice. He pursed his lips as he considered the information. "And the liveryman said he saw Abreu talking with the stranger?"

"He told me that, yes, sir," Rusty said. "He seemed a bit surprised by it."

"And you say the liveryman was positive it was Abreu who took the horse out for a ride or some such business?"

"That's what he said," Rusty replied. "Reckon he wouldn't know for certain until Abreu comes back with the horse but the man sounded pretty sure of himself." A look of apprehension crossed Rusty's face. "I ain't gonna have to ride back to Springer and ask him who brought the horse back, am I?"

I laughed in spite of myself. "One of us may have to follow up to get an answer but it don't have to be right now and you don't have to be the one to do it." I leaned my chair back and looked at Nathan. "I think we need a plan. Right now, we got a pretty good idea that Felipe Alvarado is behind all this and it looks like Jesus Abreu is in it with him somehow. What we don't have is any solid proof of that."

"The other thing we have is some murderous scoundrels tearin' around Colfax County killin' innocent folks," Nathan said.

"My idea would be for us to find 'em and stop 'em. Whether we bring 'em in to hang for their deeds or shoot 'em for resistin' arrest is pretty much up to them." He pushed his hat back on his head. "We should try to bring at least one in alive, though. As bad as I want those fellas, we need to take down the man or men that's givin' the orders. That means there's got to be one survivor left to question."

"I agree with all that," I said. "We know where they're likely gonna head at some point. When they hit a ranch, looks like they head back to their hideout in Compos Canyon to conceal the stock they've stolen until they can run 'em up to Colorado." I frowned. "Problem is, last time we looked, they weren't there. I'm afraid that means they may have to strike again before we can figure out when they're likely to be back there."

"Much as I hate it," Nathan said, "I'm afraid you're right. The only thing to do besides waitin' around for them to act is for one of us to hide and watch the place in Compos. If they show up, that fella needs to hustle back to town to fetch the rest of us so we can go after 'em."

Nathan and I both directed our gazes

toward Rusty. He turned a pale shade of green.

"Let me guess," he said, sounding like he might be sick to his stomach. "I'm the one who gets to hide and watch."

"Better you than me," Nathan said with a grin.

CHAPTER 30

The morning was calm with a slight chill in the fall air. Birds were chirping eagerly, greeting one another and passing on the news of the day. There was nothing in their tone to indicate that danger lurked nearby. Of course, birds don't know everything.

The splendor of the changing season did not touch Felipe Alvarado as he rode toward the line shack to meet Jesus Abreu. His mind was on other things, specifically, the telegram that the operator in Las Vegas brought to him from his cousin. The message was both brief and vague . . . *Felipe, meet me at the line shack.*

Although nothing else was mentioned in the telegram, Felipe had a bad feeling about it. There were rules they followed to keep their association in the shadows. One was that Jesus never contacted Felipe directly. Telegrams were always sent to Ramon, who would deliver them to the proper destination with a maximum of discretion. This time, Jesus had breached that protocol by sending the message directly to him.

Another important rule was that they rarely met. Since they'd only recently visited at the same line shack to where he was now headed, Felipe suspected something significant had occurred. He doubted it was something good. *What have you been up to, cousin?*

Shielded by the trees as he approached the cabin, Felipe saw his cousin pacing in front of the door. Even from a distance, his distress was evident. Felipe shook his head, feeling annoyed at the prospect of having to clean up whatever mess Jesus had created. His cousin was smart and manipulative. These were his greatest strengths as well as his greatest weaknesses. Unfortunately, he was not as clever as he liked to think.

As Felipe's horse stepped into the clearing in front of the line shack, Jesus Abreu looked up and greeted his cousin with enthusiasm that rang hollow.

"Cousin," he said with a strained smile. "Thank you for coming on such short notice."

Felipe shook his head, his disapproval obvious. "What choice did I have, Jesus? That you broke rules for contacting me that we have had in place for years tells me that something is very wrong." He stepped down from his horse and led him to the hitching rail in front of the cabin. "Tell me what you have done so I can attempt to fix it."

"Oh, it is only a minor hitch, Felipe," Abreu said as he waved his hand dismissively. The beads of sweat on his forehead belied his statement. "Deputy Stallings was in town asking questions. He seemed to know that we are cousins."

"It is not surprising that this would come to light, Jesus. It is common knowledge." Alvarado eyed his cousin with suspicion. "Something else happened."

A drop of sweat ran down Abreu's forehead. He wiped his eye with his coat sleeve and considered his options before speaking. Realizing that he would need help to fix this problem, he chose to share the truth, or at least a portion of it, with his cousin.

"Others who were questioned by Deputy Stallings may have seen Ramon in town," he said. "Stallings was asking which direction he rode when he left town. Apparently, he thought if he rode south, he would be heading back to Las Vegas. He seems to believe Ramon was in Springer conducting business on your behalf."

"I can hide Ramon if those *pendejos* come

around asking questions," Alvarado said. "As long as no one saw you talking with him, it is not a problem." As the words left his mouth, he saw his cousin flinch. "Do not tell me someone saw you."

Abreu began sweating profusely. "I doubt anyone did but I do not know for sure." He couldn't look his cousin in the eye. "I also told the deputy the stranger rode out of town to the north. It seems that others told him he rode out to the south. He may think I was lying."

Alvarado exploded. "You were lying!" He stepped up to his cousin and poked his finger in his chest forcefully. "Why did you even say anything at all about having seen a stranger? What were you thinking?"

Abreu was terrified by Alvarado's murderous rage. His face lost all its color and he was unable to speak for a moment. Then he found his voice. "Felipe, I was trying to appear obliging while at the same time throw the deputy off the trail. I did not think . . ."

"That is absolutely right," Alvarado hissed. "You did not think."

He moved the hand he'd been using to poke his cousin in the chest up to his throat and began to squeeze. Abreu turned red as his wind was cut off. He grabbed Alvarado's wrist with both hands but the man was unbelievably powerful and he was unable to dislodge it. Abreu tried to speak but could only make choking sounds. For a brief moment, Alvarado's eyes glazed over and it appeared he might strangle Abreu. Abruptly, he came to his senses and released his grip. Abreu sagged to his knees.

"We need to take action," Alvarado said in a calm voice as if he had not almost murdered his cousin. "We need to silence this deputy."

Abreu leaned over and was violently ill. Alvarado looked over, disgusted. "You need to gather your wits, cousin," he said in a voice laden with disdain. "This is no time for the weak."

Gasping for breath and rubbing his neck where red marks had appeared, Abreu struggled to regain his composure. When he found his feet, he said in a barely audible voice, "You are right, Felipe, I know. I am sorry for my mistake."

"Your apology means nothing unless we can correct this problem," Alvarado said in a cold voice. "You should have followed the deputy and left him in a shallow grave."

Given his close brush with mortality only a moment before, Abreu decided not to share with his cousin that he had, in fact, attempted to do that very thing and failed.

"I considered it, Felipe, but I am not the hunter that you are. I was afraid I would only make things worse if I followed the man." He shrugged. "You know my talents lie in other areas."

"That is true, cousin," Alvarado said in a reasonable tone that stood in stark contrast to his homicidal behavior only moments before. "You did come up with the plan to frame the young sheriff. That threw them off the trail for a while and gave my men some time to carry out another raid." He eyed Abreu thoughtfully. "I believe the White Caps's work in your part of the territory is almost done. I think we should shut down our operation."

"You are probably right, Felipe," Abreu said, the relief evident in his hoarse voice. "The situation has gotten too heated. We should let it cool down for a bit. When your gang delivers the last of the goods to Colorado and returns to Las Vegas, maybe they should stay in San Miguel County for some time."

"You do not understand my meaning, Jesus," Alvarado said.

Puzzled, Abreu asked, "What are you saying?"

"Right now, the only thing the lawmen have are their suspicions. Maybe they can connect us to each other but they have no way of tying us to the rustling and killing." Alvarado smiled without humor.

Abreu was still confused. "That is true unless, of course, they capture one of your men and he talks. Then they would . . ." He stopped in mid-sentence as the realization of what his cousin was implying sunk in.

"Exactly." Alvarado had no expression on his face. The image of that predatory bird, the paisano, flashed through Abreu's mind.

"So, when you say you want to shut down the operation, you mean . . ." Again, he stopped in mid-sentence, unable to put into words what his cousin was implying.

Alvarado nodded. "That is what I mean. We tie up the loose ends."

Chapter 31

"What's a potshot?"

The things that Mollie chooses to pay attention to never cease to amaze me. When I told her about the ambush attempt on Rusty as he headed back here from Springer, I used the word "potshot" to explain what had happened. I guess they don't take potshots at folks in Ireland since she didn't seem to know what it meant. Now that I think about it, I'm pretty sure they *do* take potshots at people in Ireland; they probably just call it something different. They got some strange expressions over there.

"It means somebody tried to bushwhack Rusty," I said.

"What's bushwhack?" Mollie seemed intrigued by these expressions, which to me were common.

"It means somebody hid out and tried to shoot him," I said with as much patience as I could muster.

"They tried to kill Rusty?" Mollie was horrified.

"Well, yeah," I said. "Reckon he got a little too close to the truth about someone when he was askin' questions in Springer. Who-ever it was didn't want him to make it back to pass on the information to me and Nathan so they tried to ambush him."

A tear trickled down Mollie's cheek. "I know some of those filthy gobshites have taken potshots at you," she said. "I just hadn't thought about them tryin' to kill Rusty, too."

Gobshite is one of those quaint Irish expressions. As best I can tell, it's not a compliment. As to why Mollie appeared so cavalier about people taking potshots at me but was upset about Rusty's personal safety, I was a bit confused.

"Wait a minute," I said. "Are you sayin' it don't bother you for folks to try to shoot me in the back but you don't like the idea of 'em blazin' away at Rusty?"

"Oh, Tommy, you just don't understand," Mollie said. Her tone indicated she knew she was dealing with a simpleton. Maybe she was. I didn't understand.

"Well, maybe if you explained what you said to me, I'd understand a little better." I tried to keep the irritation out of my voice but I don't think I succeeded. I didn't try all that hard.

"I've gotten used to the idea that outlaws shoot at you, Tommy," she said patiently. "I don't like it; it scares me; I hate it. At the same time, I know it's part of your job." She raised her eyebrow at me and said, "If you recall, you were shot when I first met you."

She was right. A back-shooter named Gentleman Curt Barwick . . . though in my humble opinion, he was no gentleman . . . shot me in the Colfax Tavern. On my behalf, I'll say that I shot him as well. Course I only got him in the leg whereas he dang near killed me. If Mollie hadn't been there to staunch the bleeding, I would have died right there on the floor.

"Thanks for remindin' me," I said, perhaps with a little less grace than I might have. Then I remembered her getting down on the floor with me and getting herself all bloody as she saved my life. Thinking about that made me change my tone. "Well, I do remember, Mollie. Reckon if I hadn't gotten shot, we might never have found each other and fallen in love." I grinned. "Does that mean I owe the late Mr. Barwick a debt of gratitude?"

She used another colorful Irish expression

that I can't repeat in polite company to refer to Barwick, which led me to believe she wasn't inclined to give him any kind of credit. She has a way with words, my Mollie. I sure do love my Irish colleen.

"Never mind about that," I said. "What I'm tryin' to tell you is that things are heatin' up. I think we're on the brink of findin' the rotten cull who are behind all this rustlin' and killin'. With a little bit of luck, we might be able to take 'em down."

"Oh, I hope so, Tommy," she said with a great deal of fervor. "I hate that you have to risk your life to stop these dreadful men." She took a deep breath. "I know it's part of the job. You don't need to say it."

"I wasn't gonna say that, Mollie." Well, maybe I would have but I sure wasn't going to after she said that. "I was gonna say it's the part of the job I hate. Well, it was the part of the job I hated most until they made me move to Springer. Now bein' away from you so much of the time is the part of the job I hate the most."

Her face fell. For a moment when I looked at her, I caught a glimpse of the forlorn child who lost her mother too soon and had to deal with her drunken father before leaving her home and traveling to a different country. She'd been through so much. I couldn't stand her suffering because of the job I'd chosen.

"I can't endure much more of this, Mollie," I said. "And I don't want you to have to bear any more, either." I threw up my hands. "I don't know what folks expect of me. They want me to do a job they'd never do themselves where people shoot at you or try to frame you. They move me away from my family and friends to another town just so's some small-time politician can feel more important. I'm about half a mind to quit right here and now."

"You'll do nothin' of the sort, Tommy Stallings," Mollie shouted with a fire that startled me. My wife is full of surprises. "I'll not have people sayin' my husband is a quitter."

I couldn't hide my confusion. "I thought you wanted me to quit, Mollie. I thought you wanted me to do some other kind of work so I could be here in Cimarrón with you."

"Of course I do," she said. "But you can't quit right in the middle of this thing with those terrible white hats." She shook her head emphatically. "Would you leave Nathan and Rusty hangin' out to dry while you took the easy way out?"

All right, she had a point. "Well, of course

not," I said. "And they're the White Caps."

She flashed her eyes at me. Maybe it would have been smarter to not have corrected her.

"White hats, white caps, what does it matter?" She was getting wound up now.

"It don't matter, Mollie," I said with as much contrition as I could muster. I didn't want us to get sidetracked from what was most important here.

"You know me, Mollie, better than anyone else in this world. You know I'd rather take a beatin' than quit anything. I dang sure wouldn't want to leave Nathan and Rusty in the lurch." In my mind, I went over all the events that had transpired in the past few weeks. "But I'll tell you this . . . I'd leave 'em both roastin' in hell if by doin' so, I could make you happy again."

She shook her head and sighed. "Don't you see, Tommy, that if you did that, I could never be happy about it. I don't like the way things are . . . that's not true, I *hate* the way things are! But I'm tough enough to hang on while you do what needs to be done. Once that's finished, we'll figure somethin' out."

She looked at me and I could see the trust in her eyes. She believed that I would see this hazardous job through and come back to her here in Cimarrón when it was done. And she was right, I would. The problem was that I'd made a promise to my cousin that I would return to Texas with him to help out my aunt and uncle. I didn't know how long that would take and more importantly, I didn't know how to tell her what I was planning.

I shook my head as I took her in my arms. "Ah, Mollie, we're sure a mess, ain't we?"

Pony Dolan watched as Pat Maes built a fire to heat up coffee. He noticed that John Dorsey was limping as he walked over from where he'd left his bedroll. Both he and Manuel appeared worn and haggard even after having slept for hours, which made Pony apprehensive about carrying out the proposed raid on the ranch. He was torn between postponing even longer or going ahead with it in order to get it behind them. Either way, he was beginning to think his time with the White Caps gang was growing short. Too much uncertainty about who was running the show, not enough men he could count on when things got rough.

"How's the leg, John?" Pony didn't care how Dorsey's leg was except in terms of how it affected his ability to ride and shoot. He was curious to hear how the man responded, though.

"Hurts like hell," Dorsey said in a flat voice. "I'll be fine." He waited for the coffee to heat up and didn't seem inclined to say anything more.

Dolan took it as a good sign that Dorsey didn't whine and complain about his injury but he was still concerned about how it would affect the raid. He decided to push for an additional day or even two of recovery time. His only hesitation was how hard he would press Maes to agree with him. He didn't know how much longer he could maintain this pretense that Maes was in charge.

"Pat, I'm thinkin' we might want to hold off stealin' them cows until tomorrow or even the next day," he said in an offhand manner. "What do you think?"

Maes appeared to be thrown off by his unexpected suggestion. "Well, Pony, I thought we was plannin' on doin' it today. Why would we want to wait?"

Dolan nodded toward the men by the fire. "These boys are tuckered out, Pat. Them cows'll still be there. I figure we'll all be in better shape to take 'em if we wait. That's all I'm sayin'."

Maes considered what Dolan had said. After a minute, he nodded and it appeared to Pony that he was about to agree with him. Manuel Maldonado, who'd been standing a little ways apart, walked over.

"He's right, Pat," Maldonado said. "A fool could see we need to put this off for a day."

Maes whirled on Maldonado. "Are you callin' me a fool, you sorry *pendejo*?"

Maldonado's hand reached across to where it hovered over his pistol. "Reckon I am, *cabrón*. You want to do somethin' about it?"

Maes took a step back and glared at Maldonado. Dorsey stepped away from the fire where he'd been standing to put some distance between himself and the gunfights that loomed. Pony Dolan stepped between Maes and Maldonado. No one saw him draw his gun but somehow, it appeared in his hand. He faced Maldonado.

"Manuel, I'm done with your belly-achin' and questionin' every decision. You ain't in charge and you ain't got nothin' to say about this."

Maldonado's face had turned white. He raised his hands shoulder high to show Dolan that he had no intention of drawing on him. "Hey, Pony, calm down, amigo," he said in a voice that trembled with fear. "I was just agreein' with you."

"No, you weren't, Manuel," Dolan said,

his voice as cold as a snow-fed stream. "You were tryin' to start trouble with Pat. You been tryin' to stir up trouble with him the whole time we been up here in Colfax County. It ain't helpin' things and it stops right now. You do it again and I'll kill you. *¿Comprendé, amigo?*" Dolan laced the word "amigo" with contempt. If Maldonado had harbored any illusions about their being friends, it was clear that this was not the case.

For a moment, Maldonado looked as if he might argue with Dolan. Realizing it would prove fatal if he did, he simply nodded. "Yeah, Pony," he said in a subdued voice, *"Yo comprendo."*

Dolan turned back to Maes and continued as if nothing had happened. "So, Pat, what do you think?"

Pat Maes's jaw had dropped when Pony stepped in between them. It took him a moment to close it. "Uh, I reckon I see it your way, Pony." He grinned sheepishly. "I'd be a fool not to."

You got that right. Pony kept that to himself. "All right, then, it's settled. We'll hang here and rest a bit more before we go steal us some cattle."

Chapter 32

"Have you been in contact with Sheriff Little down in San Miguel County since you last went down to see him?"

As he asked me the question, Nathan puttered around the former sheriff's office, placing a Winchester that was standing in the corner back on the new gun rack he'd installed on the wall. He took a step back and eyed his handiwork with satisfaction. It appeared he had chosen to pay no heed to this whole move to Springer. I reckon if anyone could get away with that, he could.

"No, I ain't been in touch with him since I last saw him," I replied. "Why do you ask?"

"I was wonderin' if he'd noticed anything suspicious goin' on with Felipe Alvarado."

"Suspicious how?" I wasn't sure what he was getting at but I respected him enough to want to know more.

Nathan stopped puttering and sat down in one of the three chairs that now occupied the office. He leaned back, crossed his legs, and said, "We're pretty sure Jesus Abreu took a ride out in the countryside two days ago, which, according to the liveryman, ain't somethin' he does every day. I'd be interested to know if Señor Alvarado happened to take a ride around the same time."

"You think they were meetin' up somewhere?" I felt a little guilty that I hadn't thought to check in with Todd Little on my own. Of course, I'd had a few other things on my mind, like attempting to clear my good name and stay out of jail myself.

"If they are workin' together, they got to talk from time to time," Nathan said. He pulled out a pipe and began stuffing it with tobacco from a pouch he took out of his vest pocket.

"When did you start smokin' a pipe?" I'd known Nathan for quite a few years. This was the first time I'd seen him do such a thing.

"I smoked one back in my younger days," he said. "It got to be too much trouble when I was workin' full-time as sheriff. Once I stepped down and Tomás took over, I had way too much time on my hands. I had to fill it up with somethin' so I took up the pipe again."

"I didn't know that." Here I was supposed

to be looking after all of Colfax County and I'd plum missed that our former sheriff was a pipe smoker. Some investigator I am.

"Well, it ain't that big a deal," he said. "And to answer your other question, yes, I do think maybe they met up and had a palaver. All these things that've been happenin' up here in Colfax County have the stamp of Felipe Alvarado. If Abreu is involved, I don't think he's operatin' independently."

"I think you're probably right," I said. I frowned as I contemplated the best way to get the information from Sheriff Little. "Seems like things are comin' to a head with all this. I don't think there's time for me to make another trip down to Las Vegas to talk with Todd."

Nathan nodded. "I would agree. My thought was that you send him a telegram askin' him if he noticed Alvarado bein' gone two days ago. Maybe he did, maybe he didn't. Even if he did, it don't necessarily mean the man was meetin' up with Abreu. What it might do, though, is strengthen the case that the two are workin' together."

"I see what you mean. We know they're cousins, which is one way they're connected." I ran my hand through my hair to get it out of my eyes. "If they'd ventured out and about at the same time, we'd know there was at least a chance they met up. Not that any of this would make a bit of difference in a courtroom if this ever came to trial."

Nathan shook his head vigorously. "Neither of those things would make a difference by themselves," he said. "Put 'em together and it creates suspicion. And we don't know what else we're gonna find out." He grinned at me. "This is what's called 'makin' a case,' if you was interested in learnin' to be a lawman."

I laughed at myself. "You know, I find myself less interested in bein' a lawman all the time. I see your point, though. I'll run down to the telegraph office and get Ben to send the message."

"Why don't you just write it down on a piece of paper and I'll take it down there. I need to send a telegram to Manuel Salazar."

As I wrote down a brief message to Todd Little, I thought about the cocky little mayor of Springer. I'd managed to put him out of my mind for the past several days. Now, at the mention of his name, I felt my resentment flare. "You gonna tell him that so far, you ain't been able to prove that I'm a crook?"

"No," he replied, "I'm gonna tell him he's got a traitor in his camp and he needs to be on the alert." He leaned forward in his chair and looked me in the eye. "Tommy, we'll get your name cleared. I give you my word on that."

I felt a swirl of emotions that almost knocked me out of my chair. I was angry and scared but, at the same time, grateful to Nathan for the faith he had in me. For a moment, I didn't trust myself to speak. Finally, I found the words I was looking for.

"Nathan, I can never thank you enough for standin' up for me like you have. I know I act like I don't take anything serious so I doubt anyone could tell that my good name means a lot to me." Once again, I had to pause to let my feelings calm down. "I've worked awful hard to earn the respect of men like you, Jared Delaney, maybe a few others. Bein' called a criminal like I was, that hurt me somethin' fierce."

"I expect it did," he said. He stood up and headed for the door on his way to the telegraph office. Turning back, he said, "For what it's worth, I never thought for a second you were a crook."

You know, that *is* worth a lot.

Jesus Abreu was writing out a message he

wanted telegraph operator Jim White to send to the president of the bank in Taos. He was almost finished when White spoke to him.

"Jesus, I just received this telegram for the mayor from old Nathan Averill over in Cimarrón. It looks kind of important. Would you mind takin' it to him as soon as we're done gettin' your message sent?"

Abreu felt a surge of panic, which he did his best to cover up. "Certainly, Jim, I would be happy to take it over to Manuel." In as casual a voice as he could manage, he asked, "What does it say?"

Briefly, a look of suspicion crossed the telegraph operator's face. He appeared to relax then and said, "I know y'all work together a lot. I suppose it's all right for me to let you see it."

"I appreciate your concern for the mayor's privacy, Jim," Abreu said in a smooth voice. "I assure you, though, Manuel would not mind in the slightest that I read this message. I am sure if it is important, he will discuss it with me, anyway."

Mollified, White handed over the message. Abreu looked down and quickly read the words on the telegram.

It said, *Manuel STOP Be careful STOP You have a snake in your camp STOP Someone close to you is a traitor STOP.*

It was all Jesus Abreu could do to keep his hand from trembling. That damned old sheriff was getting closer to the truth all the time. He couldn't let Salazar see this message. It was vital to get rid of it and get in touch with Felipe Alvarado as soon as possible. It was clear that they needed to speed up the timetable they had agreed upon for tying up the loose ends of the White Caps gang.

"I will take this right over to him," he said to the telegraph operator.

Abreu headed for the door. Jim White asked, "Don't you want to send your message?"

"Not now," Abreu said in an impatient voice. "I will tend to it later." As he walked out, he thought, *if I do not take care of this as soon as possible, nothing else that I am doing will matter, anyway.*

Chapter 33

I'm sitting by myself in my former office trying to enjoy the peace and quiet. Nathan went to the telegraph office to look after his business. Rusty is back at the house resting up before heading out to Compos Canyon to see if the White Caps gang are at their hideout. For maybe the hundredth time, I'm pondering whether or not all this trouble and danger is worth it. It seems like every time we stop one criminal, two more replace him. In the meantime, my marriage is suffering and my character is tarnished. Maybe it's time to let someone else step up and deal with the problems. Or maybe we should just give up and let the bad guys win.

The door opened, interrupting my reverie. I looked up and saw Tom Figgs standing there with his hat in his hands. I have to be honest . . . a spark of anger shot through me. I did my best to control it.

"Nathan ain't here right now, Tom," I said

in as polite a manner as I could manage under the circumstances. "He's sendin' some telegrams and talkin' with Ben Martinez. He should be back directly, though."

"That's all right, Sheriff," he said in a soft voice. "It ain't Nathan I wanted to talk to, anyway. It's you."

I could feel my stomach muscles tense up. With an effort, I replied in a civil tone. "What is it you want to talk about, Tom?"

He shifted from one foot to the other, clearly uncomfortable. "Do you mind if I come in and sit down?"

"That'd be fine, Tom," I said. Trying to lighten things up a bit, I said, "We only got three chairs these days and I'm usin' one of 'em. You can have your pick of the other two, though."

He didn't respond to my wit, he just walked straight to one of the chairs and sat down. Clearly, he had something to say and wasn't going to let anything distract him from getting it said. He set his hat on the floor next to the chair and looked at me for a moment before beginning.

"I let you down as a friend, Tommy." His voice sounded a little different to me, almost as if someone had their hand around his throat and was squeezing. "I've known you for a while now. I know you've always been aboveboard and honest." He looked away for a moment and then looked me square in the eye. "I should have trusted you and taken your word you hadn't accepted any bribe. I shoulda done that."

"Yeah, Tom, you should've," I said softly. He flinched a bit when I said that. "It wounded me pretty deep that you had so little faith in me."

He shook his head. "I got me some reasons why," he said, "but I got no excuses. All I can say now is I'm sorry and I'm behind you all the way. I know you didn't do nothin' wrong. I'll do whatever I need to do to try to make it up to you."

It was sort of funny to me. As hurt and angry as I'd been with this man, it was like all of that just blew away. Tom is a proud man and it must've cost him a lot to come to me, own up to being wrong and say he was sorry. A man doesn't do that if he doesn't mean it. And if his apology is sincere, what kind of man would refuse to accept it? I chuckled, which caused his eyes to widen a tad in surprise. I reckon he didn't yet see the humor in the situation.

"I've made more than my share of mistakes," I said. "Pretty much every time, I didn't realize I was makin' a mistake when I made it. It was only later I either figured it out on my own or more often, someone pointed my foolishness out to me." I laughed. Tom allowed himself a small grin. "People have forgiven me for a lot worse things than you done. I reckon I can put this behind me without too much trouble."

Tom looked at me with gratitude all over his face. "I appreciate that, Tommy. This has been eatin' at me ever since it happened. I'd like to do what I can to make it up to you."

"You've said you're sorry," I said. "I don't think there's much more you need to do." I thought about the impending showdown with the White Caps. "On second thought, we got us a hell of a mess here, though. We could use another man. If you was inclined to come along, it would help out a lot."

Tom took a deep breath. He knew enough about the state of affairs to be aware of the danger. I could see he was thinking through all the possible outcomes that could result from his throwing in with us. He let out the breath he'd been holding.

"I could do that," he said. "Let me know what you're doin' and when you need me to be there."

"I appreciate it, Tom," I said. "I know Nathan will, too. It's likely to be pretty soon. We won't get much advance warnin'.

We'll have to wait and see when those yellow dogs come back to their hideout in Compos Canyon. Soon as they do, we'll go after 'em."

Rusty perched behind some boulders looking down at the corral in Compos Canyon from a distance of a little over a hundred yards. He couldn't get comfortable because every way he turned, another sharp rock poked him in the behind. The sun was rising up over the canyon wall to the east but so far, he saw no movement.

He'd left Cimarrón a little after midnight. Fortunately, the moon was still nearly full and he'd been able to find his way without a great deal of difficulty. He was under strict instructions from Tommy and Nathan to only observe and not take action to engage the outlaws should he find them present at the hideout. Having narrowly escaped death from the recent ambush attempt on his way back from Springer, Rusty was in no hurry to be a hero. He'd tied his horse to a small aspen about a half mile back up the trail. As soon as he saw any evidence of the rustlers, he intended to sneak back, mount up, and make tracks for Cimarrón.

Shifting again to avoid yet another rock, Rusty glanced down at the tiny building that he assumed was probably a bunkhouse. A slight movement caught his eye. His heart beat faster and his palms immediately began to sweat. He stared intently, trying to discern what had grabbed his attention. He noticed the door to the little cabin was slightly ajar. As he continued to watch, he made out the figure of a man who lurched out the door, stumbling as he went. The man staggered over to a large cottonwood tree. He undid his pants and braced himself with one hand against the tree as he urinated on the trunk.

From inside the cabin, a voice called out, "Maldonado, you drunken skunk, you make enough noise to wake the dead."

Rusty listened carefully and could barely make out the coarse reply of the man called Maldonado. At this point, he knew at least two members of the gang were at the hideout. Even though he was hidden from view, he felt horribly exposed. His impulse was to creep back to his horse and head back to town with the news that some members of the White Caps were at the corral in Compos Canyon. He considered what Nathan Averill would want him to do. Most likely, the man would want him to remain there and gather as much information as he could before reporting back. It would not do for them to ride into a showdown expecting two men only to discover more.

How did that old rascal do this for so many years? I ain't been at it but a couple of weeks and I'm so scared, it's all I can do not to wet myself.

He tried taking deep breaths to calm himself down. It didn't help much. He settled in to wait a while longer to see who else might make an appearance. Soon, two men walked out of the bunkhouse. One went to another tree and relieved himself as Maldonado had. The other walked over to a firepit and began making a fire. When he had a blaze going, he grabbed a coffee pot that was set off to the side and filled it with water from a canteen lying nearby. Apparently, he decided to use the same grounds again as he set the pot on a pile of rocks that had been stacked over the fire.

That's three. Let's see what else crawls out from under the rocks.

He didn't have to wait long. In a matter of minutes, one more man walked out of the cabin, perhaps drawn by the smell of the coffee. Rusty noticed something that set him apart from the others. Whereas the other three staggered about as if in a fog, this man was alert and on the lookout. Rusty reflexively hunkered down a bit further behind the rock. There was something in the way the man carried himself that spoke of danger. If Rusty had spent more time around Mollie Stallings and thus improved his vocabulary like his cousin, he might have used the word "menacing."

Rusty felt a strong urge to get away from the scene. He forced himself to sit quietly and observe for a while longer. It felt like he'd waited another hour but in reality, it was probably closer to fifteen minutes before he figured he had a pretty good idea of how many men were at the hideout in Compos Canyon. Now he just needed to get back to Cimarrón alive so he could report in.

As he started to get up, Rusty felt a tingle in his left leg. Dang. His leg had gone to sleep. He carefully pushed himself up with his hands in order to take his weight off his backside and waited for the feeling to return. The last thing he needed was to trip over one of the rocks that'd been plaguing him for the past several hours and give away his position. After a few minutes, he was ready. He pulled his legs under him so he was in a crouch and started to ease away.

Glancing toward the corral, he saw something that made him freeze. The man with the menacing air was talking to one of the other outlaws and pointing up in his general direction. Rusty was sure he hadn't made any noise and had no idea what might've tipped off the man but it definitely looked like he suspected something. For an instant, he was paralyzed by indecision. He realized if he stayed where he was, he would most certainly be discovered. If he left quickly, they might hear him and pursue but at least he would be moving away from them.

Staying in his crouch, he began moving back down the path toward his horse. He was much more interested in speed than stealth at that point and he knew he was making too much racket. He figured it was better to mount up and ride out of the canyon as fast as he could than to tiptoe quietly while waiting for a bullet in the back. He'd almost reached his horse when he heard a shout. He didn't know if he'd been seen. He suspected the man who'd come looking for him had noticed the disturbance on the ground behind the rock where he'd hidden.

There was no time to wait around and find out if he'd been discovered. He untied his horse and threw his leg over the saddle. Spurring his mount, he pushed him into a fast lope. As soon as he could, he moved out into the middle of the canyon where the land was flatter and less rocky. Once there, he hit his horse with his spurs again and in seconds, he was galloping through yet another canyon. *I'm gettin' tired of this,* he decided as the wind whipped past him. *Too many more of these deals and they won't be callin' me Rusty, they'll be callin' me Old Gray cause my hair will have turned white.*

CHAPTER 34

Manuel Salazar fumed as he sat at his desk. He had read over the same set of papers three times and still didn't know what they said. He was too distracted by his exasperation with his friend, Nathan Averill. It wasn't that he didn't trust the old lawman, it was just that he felt disconnected and therefore out of control of the proceedings with Nathan remaining in Cimarrón. *This was the whole purpose of moving the sheriff's office to Springer, after all.*

While he didn't want to offend his friend and mentor, he felt he was within his rights as mayor to, at the very least, inquire about the progress he was making. He began composing a message for Jim White to send urging the sheriff to report in. It occurred to him that he might drop a subtle hint suggesting that the proper way to conduct the investigation would be to utilize the sheriff's office in Springer as the headquarters.

Salazar spent some time composing the message, even starting over twice because he didn't want to seem overbearing in his demands. Really, they were expectations or guidelines. As this idea crossed his mind, he felt a stab of resentment. What if he made demands? After all, he was the mayor. He was well within his rights to do so. He immediately felt ashamed as he remembered how his old friend had helped him out and stood by him through the years. Finally, he constructed a message he felt was balanced and clear. He took up the paper and walked over to the telegraph office.

Jim White looked up when the mayor entered his office. "Howdy, Mayor, how're you doin' this fine day?"

Salazar was in no mood for small talk. "I am exceedingly busy, Señor White. I need to send a message to Sheriff Averill over in Cimarrón right away."

White seemed oblivious to the mayor's sense of urgency. "Are you respondin' to the telegram he sent to you?"

Mayor Salazar was confused. "What telegram do you speak of?"

"Well, the one he sent earlier today where he warned you about somebody you couldn't trust." White frowned. "Made me curious to know what he was talkin' about but I figured it wasn't none of my business."

"I never got this telegram," Salazar said with impatience. "I do not know what you are talking about."

Now White seemed confused. "I gave it to Mister Abreu when he came in a while ago. He said he was gonna take it right over to you." White shrugged. "Maybe he had to run an errand before he brought it to you."

Salazar had an uneasy feeling about all this. He didn't want to jump to conclusions and yet he was uncertain. "You say the sheriff was warning me about someone that I could not trust?"

"As best I can recall, the telegram said somethin' about you havin' a snake in your camp. Said there was somebody close to you that you couldn't trust." White wrinkled his brow as he tried to remember any more details. "I think that was all it said. Seems like he coulda been a little clearer about who the snake was but that wasn't in the message."

The uneasy feeling in his gut became more intense. In light of this new information, there were interactions he'd had with Jesus Abreu that took on a different meaning. Times when he had not been entirely comfortable with the advice his counselor gave him. While these moments had left him feeling uneasy at the time, he'd dismissed them and trusted Abreu. Now, in retrospect, he could see where if a number of these incidents were taken together, they could look suspicious.

Salazar's first impulse was to confront Jesus and demand an explanation. He quickly decided this would lead to nothing but denials on Abreu's part. He had no solid proof the man had done anything wrong. He wanted to talk to Sheriff Nathan Averill in person. He wadded up the sheet of paper on which he had written his original message. He thought about the distance between Springer and Cimarrón, and what the quickest way to arrange a face-to-face meeting would be. For a moment, he was stumped. Then he decided what to do.

"Señor White, this is what I want sent to Sheriff Averill." White grabbed his pad and pencil. "Tell him I need to meet him tomorrow afternoon at the Romero place."

White looked up at him, his eyebrows cocked. "There's more than one Romero place, Mayor. Don't you want to be a little more specific?"

Manuel Salazar smiled. He was confident Nathan Averill would know the Romero place to which he referred. After all, it was almost the sight of his undoing back in the day when he was an impetuous youth. If not for Nathan Averill, he would have been hung for stealing a horse. The old sheriff would know where to meet him.

"No, Señor White, that is all you need to say."

Chapter 35

Ben Martinez walked into the former sheriff's office as Nathan, Tom, and I were discussing the best way to assail the outlaws' hideout in Compos Canyon. Nathan was concerned the canyon was pretty narrow at that point, which would make it difficult for us to spread out. He'd been suggesting that two of us sneak around on either side of the bunkhouse so that none of the men could slip out the back. I was just saying the risk was that one of us might slip on the rocks going up the side of the canyon and alert them to our presence.

"Afternoon, gentlemen," Ben said. "I got telegrams for both of you."

"Thanks for bringin' 'em to us, Ben," I said. "I appreciate it."

"Seemed to me like they were pretty important," he replied. "I figured you boys might need to do somethin' about 'em pretty quick. I didn't figure you'd want any time wasted."

He handed a telegram to me and one to Nathan, then stood there waiting for us to discuss the contents of the telegrams. I reckon there's just certain things you can depend on. The sun will rise in the east, and Ben Martinez will try to stick his nose into people's business.

"I think we got this now, Ben," I said, trying to be polite but clear. I appreciated that he brought us our messages personally but I didn't want our discussion about what was in them to be spread around town like wildfire. Apparently, I did all right with the polite part. I must not have done as well with being clear. Ben just stood there.

"Ben, get on out of here and go back to your office," Nathan said brusquely. "If there's anything you need to know, I'll tell you." Ben slunk out the door without a word, looking for all the world like an old dog that had been scolded. Nathan turned to me. "What does yours say?"

I finished perusing the telegram I received from Sheriff Todd Little and contemplated what he said. Like a lot of the information we had, it wasn't incriminating by itself but it certainly supported the pattern we'd been seeing.

"Todd says that he's noticed Alvarado

bein' gone more often than usual," I said. "He keeps close tabs on what's happenin' at the Imperial Saloon so he has a pretty good idea of when the man is there."

"Did you ask him about the day Rusty was bushwhacked comin' back from Springer?"

"I did. He said he was there at the saloon on that day."

Nathan shook his head in disappointment. "That don't help much," he said.

"This might, though," I said. "Todd remembers him bein' gone the next day. That makes me wonder if that was the day Jesus Abreu was out and about. You reckon that liveryman would recall if he took his horse out two days in a row?"

"I got a sneakin' suspicion that livery fella knows most of what goes on in the town of Springer." Nathan chuckled. "It's a possibility he's ever bit as nosy as our Ben Martinez."

I couldn't stop a grin. "I wouldn't have thought there was anyone who could compare to old Ben when it comes to snoopin' in folks' business. I reckon this fella might be the one, though."

Nathan's expression became grave. "I'd like to know the answer to that question. I believe Abreu's been parlayin' with Felipe Alvarado. If so, he's in this neck deep."

"We don't know when Rusty'll be back from Compos Canyon. I'd send him over to Springer to check it out but it seems to me things are heatin' up pretty quick," I said.

"That's all right," Nathan said. "I can find out by tomorrow."

"How you gonna do that?"

Nathan held up the telegram Ben Martinez had handed him. "I'll be meetin' with the mayor of Springer tomorrow afternoon. I'll ask him to find out."

"You're meetin' with Salazar tomorrow?" I wasn't sure what to make of that. "Does he have information that'll help us with the investigation?"

"I suspect he does," Nathan replied. "I sent him a message the other day warnin' him not to trust anyone. Now he's askin' to meet with me, which sounds to me like he's got some ideas that might be helpful."

I shook my head. "I'm still gettin' used to the notion that old Manuel is one of the good guys. He sure ain't done much of anything towards helpin' me out."

"Maybe he'll take a shine to you once all this is over," Nathan said with a chuckle. He got up and headed for the door. "I'll send him another telegram right away tellin' him to ask the livery fella if Abreu took his horse out two days in a row. With any luck,

I'll catch him before he leaves Springer to meet with me. Soon as that's done, I'll head out."

As he opened the door, I asked, "And what am I supposed to be doin' while you're out palaverin' with Mayor Salazar?"

"You wait," he said. "Wait for Rusty to get back and then no matter what news he brings, you wait for me to get back." He showed me that steely gaze that had helped make him famous. "These are dangerous *hombrés* we're goin' after. We're gonna need all the firepower we can get to take 'em."

As Nathan rode east towards Springer, his mind wandered back through the years. He remembered clearly the young man who had "borrowed" the horse from the Romero family. His initial reaction when Nathan confronted him was to bluster that he'd done nothing wrong. Once Nathan laid out the evidence and the potential consequences for him, the boy . . . and at that time, Manuel Salazar was only a boy . . . had become distraught. At first, Nathan hadn't had any sympathy for him. He should've thought of the consequences before he'd done the deed, simple as that. However, after his initial denial, Manuel had owned up to his crime and seemed genuinely remorseful. On a hunch, Nathan decided to give him a second chance. He had never regretted following his intuition.

It was midafternoon when he arrived at the old Romero place. The Romero family had been gone for years, packing up and moving to greener pastures in the southern part of the state. The house was in disrepair and some large animal had apparently knocked down one side of the corral fence. A horse was tied to the weathered hitching post out front. As Nathan dismounted, Manuel Salazar stepped out on what was left of the front porch.

Salazar nodded in acknowledgment and looked around. With a look that was both contemplative and perhaps a bit wistful, he said, "Many memories, amigo. If not for you, I would not be standing here today. You changed my life for the better."

"You changed your own life, Manuel," Nathan said. "I just gave you the chance. Everybody deserves a chance."

"I thank you for that, amigo," Salazar said. Nathan could see the corners of his mouth twitching. "It looks like I might need another second chance."

Nathan was puzzled. "What do you mean?"

Salazar spoke in a quiet voice. "I have

become full of myself, amigo; blinded by my ambitions." He took a deep breath. "When I first decided to run for public office, it was because I thought I could make a difference in the lives of people I cared about. Now I find myself more concerned with the power and prestige of the office. I want more of it and I have not been very concerned with who I step on as I seek it." He shook his head. "This is wrong."

"That's correct." The old sheriff nodded. "What do you propose to do about that?"

Salazar wore an amused look. "Just like that? No lecture, no recriminations?"

"Nope," Nathan said. "You're a grown man and a good one, too, in your heart. Anything I might say to you, you've already said to yourself."

Salazar nodded. "You are right." He squared his shoulders before continuing. "Here is what I came to tell you. The telegram you sent warning me that there was a traitor in my midst, Jesus Abreu intercepted it. Señor White, the telegraph operator, thought Abreu had given it to me. When I discovered he had not, I realized he was the traitor of whom you spoke."

"We'd begun to think the same thing, Manuel," Nathan replied. "There wasn't any one thing to confirm it but there were a number of times where he gave misleading information to someone. And, of course, there's his longtime connection to Felipe Alvarado."

Manuel Salazar stamped his foot and cursed in Spanish. "I trusted that *cabrón.* I have been a fool."

Nathan shrugged. "We've all been fools a time or two, Manuel. The trick is, once you figure it out, you stop bein' one and correct your mistakes."

"You are right, amigo. I will call out this snake and force him to confess to his deeds."

"Hang on there, pard," Nathan said. "You've done your job, which was to report this to a lawman. Me and Sheriff Stallings can take it from here."

"Perhaps you are right." Salazar's eyes narrowed. "And yet I may not be able to hold my tongue when I see Jesus."

"Well," Nathan said firmly, "give it your best shot. These are treacherous men we're dealin' with. I don't want you gettin' yourself shot." A smile creased his face. "Since you're rememberin' why you got into politics, I kinda like the idea of you puttin' yourself in a position to make a difference and help folks out. You can't do that if you're buried six feet under."

The mayor considered the old lawman's

words. He shrugged and said, "Perhaps you are right." He stepped down off the porch and walked over to his horse. "I will ride back to Springer now and leave you to do your job. Let me know if I can help in any way."

Nathan held up his hand. "There's one more thing. Did Abreu take his horse out two days in a row?"

"Ah, yes," Salazar said. "I had almost forgotten. I spoke with Arturo Garcia at the livery."

"What did he say?" Nathan placed his hand on his pistol as if he were preparing to draw on some foe.

"Arturo said that Jesus took his horse out twice in the past week, which is highly unusual. And yes, it was two days in a row."

"All right then." Nathan relaxed his hand. "Old Jesus is startin' to look guiltier by the minute."

"He certainly is," Salazar replied. He held out his hand to the old sheriff, who took it and grasped it firmly. "*Hasta luego,* Sheriff Nathan Averill. Until we meet again."

"Vaya con Dios, amigo," Nathan replied. "Be careful around Abreu. We don't want to tip him off."

Salazar nodded. "I will be careful," he said. He had a different thought as he rode away, however. *I will be careful but if I have an opportunity, I will confront this cabrón. No one makes a fool out of Manuel Salazar.*

Mayor Salazar stewed the entire way back to Springer. The more he thought about how Jesus Abreu had used him as a pawn, the angrier he became. Although Nathan Averill had been too polite to say so, Salazar was certain the old lawman's respect for him had dropped a notch. There was no man in the world whose opinion mattered more to him. He felt humiliated.

By the time he reached town, he'd worked himself up to a boil and was determined to confront Abreu with his double-dealing. He dropped his horse off at the livery and walked directly to the bank. Several citizens nodded to him as they passed on the boardwalk but he was so furious that he ignored them. Word spread quickly, as it tends to do in small towns. The mayor was on the warpath.

Jesus Abreu's personal secretary, who handled his appointments and correspondence, asked the mayor if he had an appointment. Salazar barely glanced at the sputtering man as he stalked into Abreu's office. To his dismay, he found the office empty.

The secretary had followed him into Abreu's sanctuary. Salazar turned to him and demanded, "Where is he?"

"That's what I was trying to tell you, Mayor," said the man, flinching as he saw the fire in the mayor's eyes. "He's not here. Hasn't been all day."

With great effort, Salazar controlled his temper. It was not this man's fault the deceitful *cabrón* was not in his office. "I can see that he is not here, sir," he said with as much patience as he could gather. "My question was where he is at this time."

The man began to perspire. His eyes darted from side to side as if he might find an answer on the desk or in a chair. "Um, I don't know, sir."

"You do not know?" Salazar tried without much success to keep the exasperation out of his voice. "You keep his schedule. How can you not know where he is?"

The secretary perspired more freely and wiped his sleeve across his brow. "Well, you're right, sir, I do generally keep his schedule. This time, all he told me was that he would be out for the day. He didn't say where he was going." With his index finger, he tugged at his collar. He shrugged feebly. "Sometimes he does that."

Manuel Salazar considered the situation.

As he reflected on it, he realized it was probably for the best that Abreu hadn't been there. Nathan had warned him about tipping the banker off and had he been present, that's just what Manuel would have done. He sighed deeply.

"As soon as he returns, I'll tell him you called on him," the secretary said, clearly hoping to get back in the mayor's good graces.

Manuel shook his head. "That will not be necessary. I will catch up with him soon enough." *You can bet on that,* he thought as he walked out of the bank.

"We have to do something quickly, paisano," Jesus Abreu said. "I am afraid these two lawmen are onto us."

"Do not call me that," Felipe Alvarado said. He did not speak in a loud voice but there was no mistaking the threat there.

"Sorry, amigo," Abreu said quickly. "It is an old habit."

"It is a habit you need to rid yourself of," replied Alvarado. "I do not like the name. I never have."

"As you wish," Abreu said deferentially. *You may not like it but it certainly fits.* "As I was saying, we need to take action fast. I had hoped we could put the young sheriff out of play by casting suspicion on him. I was not counting on the old lawman having so much influence on our good mayor."

"I already told you what needs to be done, *primo.* The loose ends must be tied up and all evidence erased." He stared at his cousin long enough that Jesus became ill at ease.

"What?" Abreu shifted uneasily in the hard chair on which he was sitting. Alvarado gave a snort of derision. "You say 'we' need to take action. I know what you really mean is that *I* need to take action. You are happy working behind the scenes like you are some puppet master at a county fair. When the time comes for the difficult task, that is when you turn to me."

Abreu shook his head and shrugged. "I do not know what to tell you, *primo.* What you say is true. I am better at pulling strings, you are better at taking lives. It has always been so."

Alvarado leaned forward in his chair. Abreu felt mesmerized by his gaze. Once again, he thought of the paisano bird, the one with the dead, cold eyes of a killer. He wisely chose not to share this thought with his cousin.

"That does not mean it always must be that way. We know what must be done. Someone must kill the members of my band of rustlers." He leaned back. "Perhaps it is time for you to get your hands soiled."

Abreu shook his head. "What matters now are results, Felipe. If you wish to teach me how to be a killer, perhaps we can begin the lesson another time."

Alvarado's eyes narrowed. "I have not yet decided about this. I will take more time to make up my mind."

As emphatically as he dared, Abreu said, "Time is the thing we do not have, *primo.* We need to take action right away."

Felipe Alvarado rose from his chair and took a step toward the door of the cabin, signaling that the meeting was over. At the door, he turned and said, "I will send you a telegram tomorrow. It will contain two words. If it says 'your turn,' that means I expect you to take care of the problem. If it says 'my turn,' that means I will do what I so often do, which is save you from the untidiness you have created."

Jesus started to protest but Alvarado raised his hand to silence him. "This is the way it will be, Jesus. Question me further at your own risk. I will decide and let you know."

Felipe Alvarado walked out, leaving Jesus Abreu wondering what tomorrow would bring.

Chapter 36

We gathered in my old office in Cimarrón a half hour after sunup. Nathan and Rusty were there, as was Tom Figgs. Nathan started.

"I spoke with Manuel Salazar. Like the rest of us, he believes Jesus Abreu is in this up to his hat. He may have even taken the shots at Rusty on the way back from Springer." Nathan paused. "Of course, it could have been Alvarado as well or one of his men."

"Any chance either of those sons of bitches will be at this hideout we're headed for?" Rusty's eyes were slits. Clearly, he had a score to settle.

"That ain't the way these fellas operate," I said. "They order their minions to do the dirty work."

"That's probably truer of Abreu than it is of Alvarado," Nathan said. "I get the sense he doesn't mind gettin' bloody."

"So, we don't know if he'll be there at the hideout," Tom Figgs said. "How many of 'em you reckon there'll be?"

I pondered the question. "Hard to say, Tom. From what the survivors of their attacks have told us, there's likely to be between four and six."

"Did you consider askin' Tomás to join us?" Although Tom posed the question in a casual manner, it was clear that he was very interested in my response.

"I gave it a lot of thought, Tom," I said. "I decided not to ask him. In fact, I didn't even mention to him what we were gonna do."

Tom nodded, a contemplative look on his face. "From what you've told me about these desperados, Tommy, we could use all the firepower we can get. Do you mind tellin' me why you decided against askin' Tomás to come along?"

"Not at all," I replied. "Tomás has risked his life over and over from the time he was a young pup. He's lost his father along the way. He's set to marry the love of his life soon and maybe find some happiness in this mean old world. I just figured he'd given enough."

"We've all given, Tommy," Tom said with just a trace of resentment in his voice. "We've all taken risks. Seems to me you could have at least asked him and let him make the call."

I did my best to hold my temper. Me and Tom had just been through a rough patch. I didn't want to risk losing his friendship again. "I reckon I could have, Tom, but it seemed pretty clear to me what the right thing to do was."

Tom turned to Nathan. "What do you think, Sheriff? Don't you think we should at least give Tomás a chance to say no?"

Nathan scratched his head and considered the question. "Tommy's the sheriff. It's his call." He paused for a moment. "I do think he's right. There's a time when a man has to put his family and his own wishes first. I'm afraid if Tommy had asked him, Tomás might have decided to ride along with us out of a sense of obligation. I believe he's earned the right to stay home this time."

"You could just as well say the same thing about Tommy and you, Sheriff . . . I mean, Deputy Sheriff. You could say it about me, too, though not nearly as much as the two of you. How many times must we risk our lives for the people that live in Cimarrón?" The edge of resentment in Tom's voice was stronger now. "Most of 'em don't seem to be grateful for what we do, anyhow."

I couldn't blame Tom for his resentment.

I turned to the old lawman. "Tom is askin' the same question I've asked myself a thousand times, Nathan. How many times have we been down this trail before, facin' off with some greedy, cruel villain who wants more than his share and tries to take it by force? Here we are again. When does this end?"

Nathan smiled but there was a hint of sadness in it. "Where'd you get the notion it'll end? This has been goin' on as long as people been walkin' upright on two legs. There's decent folks . . . Miguel Marés was one of 'em; Jared Delaney and his lovely wife, Eleanor, are a couple of more. They care about other people and only look to do what's right. Then there's men like Curt Barwick, that Bill Chapman fella from the Santa Fe Ring, and others we've faced. They're just plain wicked. They not only don't care who they hurt, they enjoy hurtin' 'em."

My frustration boiled over. "But *why* is it that way?"

"That's just the way it is," Nathan replied. "Always been that way, likely to be that way forever. You can either stand up to 'em or look the other way. Your choice." He smiled the wintry smile again. "And mine."

I wanted to argue with him. It *was* unfair.

The thing is, he was *more* right about what he'd said. This was the way things have always been and it was the way they always would be. There's evil in the world. We could waste a lot of time trying to figure out why or we could just get on to the business of taking care of the problem. Or we could decide to allow the evil ones to have their way without being challenged. I knew what my decision was. There was no point in talking any further about it.

"So, it looks to me like the four of us are all in." I knew if Jared Delaney had been at home while this was unfolding, he would be here with us. He was in Colorado, though, looking after his business. I looked at Nathan, Tom and Rusty in turn. "It comes down to us. Am I right?" They nodded. "Reckon we better come up with a plan then. We don't want to ride in willy-nilly and get killed for lack of thinkin' this through." Again, everyone nodded. "Nathan, you've got the most experience at this. I'd appreciate hearin' your thoughts first."

Nathan leaned forward in his chair. "A couple of things come to mind right away. First, we don't want to wind up shootin' each other."

Rusty chuckled, which came out as sort of a snort. "I dang sure agree with that,

Sheriff. How do we steer clear of it?"

The old lawman smiled patiently at Rusty. "One thing is that we don't start bangin' away like a bunch of wild men. If you can't clearly make out your target, don't shoot. Another is we plan ahead of time where each of us will be and we stick to it."

Tom Figgs took off his hat and held it in both hands, examining the hat band as if it held the secrets of life. "What exactly are you thinkin'?"

"I been up in Compos Canyon," Nathan said, "as have all of you. It's pretty narrow where that hideout is located. Two of us need to be on either side of the canyon, even with each other. Use the brush and trees for cover. The other two should climb up either side of the canyon about fifty feet or so. That way they can be lookin' down at the outlaws."

"Climbin' up the canyon walls is risky," I said. "If either man slips or knocks some rocks down the hill, that'll give us away."

"You're right," Nathan replied. "That's why you can't slip. The two of us in the canyon ought to have rifles but the two goin' up the sides should just carry pistols. That way you got both hands free. It ain't ideal but we got to spread out. If we all congregate across that narrow canyon floor, we'll make too big of a target." He cleared his throat. "The other thing the two up the walls got to remember is to stay even with the two in the canyon and not go past the hideout. You do that and you'll wind up shootin' directly across the canyon or even backwards. That could lead to catchin' yourselves or the boys in the canyon in a crossfire. We want to be shootin' out in front of where we are."

"Sounds like you think it's pretty likely it'll come down to gun play," Rusty said.

Nathan shrugged. "Can't say for sure. If I had to bet, I'd say the odds are pretty good."

I'd given this part quite a bit of thought. "I think Nathan's right. Here's what I propose. We try to get as close as we can without bein' seen. Within fifty yards would be best but we only got so much control over that. If we make it that far, I'll holler out that we're the law and they are to give it up."

"You don't really think they'll just surrender," Tom Figgs said. "These fellas have been killin' folks all over Colfax County. They don't seem like the type to give up without a fight."

"I wouldn't argue with you, Tom," I said. "But we're on the side of the law. That means we got rules that must be followed.

Givin' 'em fair warnin' would be one of 'em."

I heard Rusty's snort of laughter again. "So, you'll give 'em fair warnin' and they'll put a bullet in you?"

I rolled my eyes and shook my head. "I plan to be standin' behind a rock or a tree when I give 'em the warnin', cousin. I try to follow the rules but I ain't dim-witted." He laughed some more. I ignored him.

"I agree with Sheriff Stallings," Nathan said. "We got to do this the proper way. That includes bein' prepared to blaze away at them if they start shootin'."

"So, what you're both sayin' is they get to make the call about how this all goes down," Tom Figgs said. He didn't look too pleased.

"I'm afraid that's the way it's got to be," I said. "We all knew this would be dangerous. No one would hold it against you for havin' second thoughts. You ain't been deputized yet. If you've changed your mind about goin', it's all right."

"I didn't say I'd changed my mind," Figgs said hotly. "I'm just askin' questions. I want to make sure we've thought this through all the way."

I held out my hands in a gesture of appeasement. "I understand, Tom. You got a right to do that. We need to be sure we've thought of everything we can ahead of time."

"None of which will matter if the shootin' starts," Nathan said. "Things tend to go to hell in a bucket pretty quick in deals like this." No one argued with him. "There's one more thing we should keep in mind."

We all looked at him. Rusty asked the question. "What's that, sir?"

"If there's any way to take one of these hombres alive, we need to do it."

"I guess you're right," Rusty said, "though it wouldn't break my heart if we wound up shootin' all of 'em. These are some venomous snakes."

"Ordinarily, I'd agree with you," Nathan said. "There's an important reason to keep one alive, though."

"And that would be?" I asked.

"For your sake," Nathan said as he looked me squarely in the eyes. "We have to take one of 'em alive to tell us who planned all this and most especially, whose idea it was to frame you. I don't want there to be any doubt left over that you played this on the up-and-up all the way."

I took a deep breath and let it out slowly. "I hadn't been thinkin' about that, as crazy as that seems. I reckon I would like to clear my name." My lips twisted. "Funny, we're riskin' our lives to catch these murderin' thieves and I got to worry about clearin' my own name in the process."

In a quiet but firm voice, Tom Figgs said, "As far as I'm concerned, your name is clear. Any doubts I had were on account of my own shortcomin's and none of yours."

"Thanks Tom, I appreciate that," I said. I meant it, too. Having him doubt me had been one of the most hurtful things I'd been through in a long time.

Rusty spoke up. "I guess it'd be a good thing for Mayor Salazar to come to that conclusion, too. He might take a bit more convincin'."

"That's why we want to keep one of these filthy polecats alive, Rusty," Nathan said. He looked around at us and turned to me. "Anything else we need to discuss, Sheriff?"

"Not that I can think of," I said. "We'll have time ridin' out there to converse some more and make sure we're clear on what we're doin'." I stood up. "Everybody get the guns you're takin' and plenty of bullets. We'll leave in an hour."

Nathan stood up. "I may stroll over to the school and spend a couple of minutes with my wife." He shrugged. "Not that I don't expect to come back but you never know."

I nodded. "You're probably right about

that. Think I'll head over that way myself and take a moment with Mollie."

As I started out the door, Rusty grabbed my sleeve. He whispered, "Can you give me just a minute, cousin?"

I turned to Nathan and said, "You go on, I'll be right behind you." Rusty and I stepped outside. "What's on your mind, cousin?"

Rusty appeared nervous. Under the circumstances, I figured that made good sense. After all, we were leaving in an hour to undertake a task that could leave some or all of us dead. I thought he might have some more questions for me about our plan and his role in it. It turned out that wasn't what he wanted to discuss with me.

"I just wanted to tell you that if I make it through this thing, I'll be headin' back to Texas pretty quick," he said. "Mama and Pa need me. I feel bad for stayin' away so long." He scratched his bushy red beard. "I think I'll shave this dang thing off before I go. I had no idea how much food could collect in one of these things. It's sorta disgustin'."

I laughed at him. "I didn't want to say anything about it to you but I've noticed some strange things lookin' like they were takin' up residence in there. Shavin' it ain't a bad idea." I reached out and poked him on the shoulder. "You sound like you're sayin' goodbye to me, cousin. If you'll recall, I'm gonna be goin' with you."

"That's what I wanted to talk to you about." He shuffled his feet nervously. "I think maybe it'd be better if you didn't do that."

"What are you talkin' about? I told you I'd go and I meant it."

"I know you did," he said, "and I appreciate it. I been givin' it a lot of thought, though. I just think it'd be best if you stayed here . . . with Mollie."

"Well, I fully intend to come back to Mollie as soon as we wrap up this business back in Texas," I replied. "She and I've been apart for a while now. It ain't been a lot of fun but it ain't killed either one of us yet. I reckon we can stand to be apart a little bit longer."

He took a deep breath. "Maybe it ain't killed you but it seems to me it's driven a wedge between the two of you. I worry about what'll happen if you stay away even longer." He cocked his head and looked at me. "What did she say when you told her I'd asked you to go?"

It was my turn to shuffle my feet nervously. "Well, that's kinda hard to answer."

He stared at me incredulously. "You ain't told her, have you?"

"Not in so many words," I said. I realized how lame that sounded as soon as the statement came out of my mouth. "Well, all right, I ain't told her anything about it yet."

He shook his head. "How could you not say anything to her?"

I shrugged. "Hell, Rusty, I may not make it back alive from this little foray we're about to go on. If I tell her now, she's gonna be awful upset, which I hate to see. Why in the world would I want to go through a hailstorm of harsh words from my wife, only to get killed before I had a chance to do the thing she would be upset about?"

Rusty looked at me, confusion written all over his face. "I ain't sure I understand. Are you sayin' you don't want to tell her 'cause you might get killed and you don't want to get a tongue-lashin' from her unless you have to?"

I had to laugh in spite of myself. "When you put it like that, it don't sound very noble, does it? I'd prefer to think I was helpin' her avoid feelin' guilty for dressin' me down and then havin' me get killed."

Rusty started to chuckle as well. "So, you can go out and face murderin' thieves without flinchin' but you'll do almost anything to avoid your wife scoldin' you. Am I right?"

"That pretty much sums it up," I said. My smile faded. "The thing is, though, if we do make it through this deal today, I will tell her when we get back. I gave you my word I'd come back to Texas with you and I meant it. I know Mollie won't be happy about it but deep down, she'll understand. She'll have to."

Rusty looked off in the distance. Maybe he was looking towards Texas. I'm not sure. He turned back to me and said, "It means more to me and my folks than I can ever say, Tommy. I hate to see you and Mollie go through all this because of us but we need your help."

I nodded. "You got it, cousin." I reached out my hand and he took it. We held firm for a moment, conveying more in the handshake than we could have with words. Then I let go of his hand and said, "Speakin' of Mollie, I need to go tell her I'm headin' out after these outlaws in a little while. I want to give her a hug before I go."

"Give her a hug for me, too," Rusty said. "I'll go gather my guns and ammo."

"I'll do it," I said. "She'll appreciate it. She's become right fond of you in a fairly short time. Seems like she finds us Stallings boys hard to resist."

Rusty didn't smile at my attempt at humor. He said, "I don't know how much she's gonna like either one of us when she finds out I'm takin' you off to Texas . . . that's assumin' we both survive this little dustup we're fixin' to have."

"Quien sabé," I said, quoting my good friend Tomás Marés. "With any luck, we'll both get shot out in Compos Canyon and we won't have to face her."

Again, he didn't respond to my attempt to lighten the mood. He looked at me for a moment and then said, "There's nothin' funny about any of this, cousin." He turned and walked off to collect his weapons.

He was right; I just didn't know what to say about it, so as usual, I tried to laugh it off. Unfortunately, that wasn't making me feel any better about the situation. For some reason, I thought about my pal Jared Delaney. Other than Nathan Averill, there's no one I respect more than Jared. I thought about how he would handle a challenge like this one, searching for some direction that would help me make it through. I remembered him telling me once that all you can do is take one task on at a time and get it done before you go on to the next one. My next task was to walk over to the school and tell my wife I loved her. I headed that way.

I was about a block away from the school when I heard a merry and boisterous din, the sound that children make when they receive an unexpected windfall. As I walked into the yard beside the school, I saw youngsters running around like wild savages, playing games and yelling at the tops of their lungs. Nathan and Miss Christy were under the cottonwood tree deep in a discussion. Mollie waited for me over to the side of the back door to the schoolhouse.

"Nathan told us you were right behind him," she said. "Christy decided to give the urchins an extra recess." She smiled. "As you can see for yourself, they're pretty pleased."

Although she smiled as she watched the children play, Mollie seemed subdued. Under the circumstances, I couldn't say I blamed her. She knew we were about to ride into an extremely hazardous encounter from which some of us might not return. Beyond that, there was a sea of uncertainty awaiting us if I lived through the day.

I had considered telling her about my plan to accompany Rusty back to Texas to help out my family but now, it seemed to me that this would be too much information to dump on her all at once. I'd kept it from her this long, so I decided to spare her the burden. Maybe I was sparing myself, I don't know. There's a lot I don't know. I do know I love my wife more than life itself. I figured I could at least tell her that much.

I reached out and took her hands. Some of the children glanced over at us and giggled. I didn't care. "Mollie, there's so much I want to say yet I can't find the words." My voice sounded tight to my ears. I kind of choked up a bit. Must be from all the dust those children were kicking up. "I want you to know how much I love you. I don't know what's gonna happen but whatever it is, I want you to know you're my girl. You always will be."

She squeezed my hands and smiled at me. "Sure and I know that, Tommy Stallings," she said in her lilting and adorable Irish brogue. "You've won me heart forever. We'll find a way to get through all this, you wait and see."

The dang dust was so bad my eyes watered. I let go of one of her hands so I could wipe it away. "I know we will, my love. We'll live through it. Things will be better, I swear it."

Just then, I heard Christy raise her voice over by the cottonwood. I couldn't hear what she said but she looked upset. Nathan reached out to comfort her but she turned away from him.

"Is Miss Christy mad at Nathan?" I figured if anyone would know the inside story, it would be my wife.

Mollie sighed. "She was not happy when he decided to step up and help you out by bein' your deputy. She thought the times she sat wonderin' if her husband would live through the day were behind her." She shook her head. "It's not that she's mad so much, it's that she's scared."

As usual, I didn't know what to say. "Oh," I said. Nothing else occurred to me to say after that but it seemed like I should say more. "I'm sorry," I said, realizing how feeble that sounded.

"It's not your fault and there's nothin' you can do about it," Mollie replied in a matter-of-fact manner. "They'll have to work it out."

She was right. As much as I wished I could solve their problems, I couldn't even figure out my own most of the time. Better to not fret about something I had no control over. It was time for me to head back to my old office and get my rifle. I reached out and wrapped my wife in my arms.

"I love you, Mollie Stallings."

"I love you, too, Tommy," she whispered

in my ear. She squeezed me tighter and said, "You know what I always tell you. When you come ridin' back this evenin' and look down into the valley, you'll see the lights of Cimarrón. There'll always be a light burnin' for you."

I hugged her a little longer, then let go and turned away. I hesitated but I couldn't think of anything more to say. I walked back up the street to get my guns.

In Springer, Jesus Abreu walked back to the bank, a telegram in his hand. He was afraid to look at it. He walked into his office, shut the door, and sat down behind his desk. His hands trembled as he took a deep breath and stared at the two words on the paper. *My turn.* He exhaled a sigh of relief.

CHAPTER 37

It was midmorning and John Dorsey was still in his bedroll. He was on fire with fever. Pony Dolan was thinking that this whole cattle rustling business was going south. Of the four members of the gang, he had one man who was too sick to get out of bed and two who were ready to go at each other with hammer and tongs. The notion of their being able to successfully steal fifty head of cattle and dispatch the three cowboys who were checking them was pretty far-fetched in his mind.

He considered his options. They could delay another day or two to give Dorsey time to heal up but there was no guarantee that he wouldn't get worse rather than better. They'd lost Espinosa, and Pony knew there was no healing the rift between Pat Maes and Manuel Maldonado. Things were likely to get even edgier in the next couple of days. He was starting to think the best course of action would be to take the horses they had on up to Trinidad and head back to Las Vegas. The Boss would not be pleased but at this point, Pony Dolan didn't much care. He just wanted to survive and move on as soon as possible.

Pat Maes sauntered over to the log where Pony was sitting drinking coffee. "So, what do you think, compadre? Do we go steal us some cows today?"

"I ain't inclined to do that," Pony replied. "Not today and maybe not at all."

"What do you mean?" Maes's brow was furrowed. "I thought we was supposed to get them cattle and head up to Trinidad with 'em. The Boss ain't gonna be happy if we don't take care of business."

Dolan stared at Maes until the man began to shift nervously from one foot to the other. "Well, *I* ain't gonna be happy if we get killed tryin' to pilfer a few more head of cattle with a gang that's more interested in shootin' each other than the cowboys guardin' the cows." He snorted. "Not to mention that Dorsey can't even walk, much less ride."

Pat Maes struggled with whether he was more afraid of the Boss, who was back in Las Vegas, or Pony Dolan, who was standing in front of him. Both were violent and sadistic killers. Since Dolan was right here in front of him and thus presented a more immediate danger, he decided it would be safer to go along with him now and figure out a way to lay the blame at his feet once they got back to Las Vegas. Maybe he could even implicate Manuel Maldonado as a partner to Pony Dolan. He liked that idea.

"I see your point," he said. "Reckon we should head on up to Colorado with the horses today?"

Dolan considered the question. "Nah, let's give Dorsey one more day to mend. If he ain't better tomorrow, we can just shoot him."

He smiled but his eyes held a cruel glint. Maes wasn't sure if he was joking or not. Looked like he'd made the right call in going along with Pony Dolan's recommendation.

"Yeah, you're right. We been pushin' pretty hard for a while now. We can stand to hang around here one more day and rest up a bit more."

We hit a long trot out of Cimarrón and made it to Templeton Canyon in about an hour. I was riding in front with Nathan next to me, and Rusty and Tom were riding just a tad behind us. I looked ahead and saw where the canyon twisted around to the northwest into Chase Canyon. I slowed down and eased old Rusty . . . my horse, not my cousin . . . over to the side of the trail.

"Let's review the plan one more time, make sure we're all thinkin' the same way," I said. "If it comes to shootin', things will get confusin' enough. We don't want to have four different ideas about what we're supposed to be doin'."

Rusty and Tom had pulled up even with us. Rusty said, "I know I'll be crawlin' up the right side of the canyon up into the trees. I hate not havin' my Winchester but I think you're prob'ly right that we'll need both hands free to keep from trippin' up in the rocks." He took a deep breath to calm himself. "I'll try to keep an eye on you and Nathan so we don't get out ahead of you. We'll wait for your sign."

Tom Figgs asked, "Do you think we should dismount and hide the horses before we get to the entrance of Compos Canyon? They might have a lookout."

Nathan responded to this question. "That's a judgment call, Tom. From what Rusty told us, it's about a mile into the canyon where their hideout is located. If it was me, I wouldn't want my lookout a mile away from my hideout. I'd want him close enough that he could get back and alert me as soon as possible if there was trouble."

"That makes sense," he said. He shrugged. "I ain't done this sort of thing much. I don't know a lot about how to do it."

I noticed that Tom was clenching his saddle horn so tight that his knuckles were white. I understood the reaction but I also knew frayed nerves made for tight muscles, which resulted in lousy marksmanship. I searched to find a way to help Tom calm down a bit.

"Keep this in mind, Tom," I said. "Your job is to provide cover fire for me and Nathan if we need it. As we get close to the hideout, be lookin' for a rock or a tree to get down behind, somethin' you can rest your gun hand on and steady your aim. You'll be up in the trees where they can't see you very well." I laughed, trying to ease the tension. "If the shootin' starts, the main thing is to try *not* to shoot me and Nathan. If you hit one or two of them, that's gravy."

Tom smiled at my joke and loosened his grip on his saddle horn. "I'd hate to think if we survive this to tell the tale, my only contribution to the battle would be that I didn't shoot the sheriff and his deputy."

"Believe me, son, if you don't shoot me,

I'll consider it a major contribution," Nathan said with a laugh.

I figured we were about as loose as we were going to get. It would be slow going from here on out. We needed to get moving.

"Boys, we won't get any readier lollygaggin' around here. Let's head on up the trail. We'll keep to the sides of the canyon, move slow and careful. I'll give the sign when it's time for the two of you to head up into the trees. No talkin' from here on out."

Manuel Maldonado was in a foul humor. Unlike Pat Maes, he was more afraid of the Boss than he was of Pony Dolan. He knew when they got back to Las Vegas, there would be hell to pay. Pat was supposed to be in charge of this outfit but he'd let Dolan take over without so much as a whimper. Maldonado was fed up with his spineless ways. He strode over to where Maes was standing with Dolan.

"Hey, *cabrón,* I thought you were running this outfit, not Pony," he said. The challenge in his voice was unmistakable. "The Boss wants us to hit this last ranch before we head up to Colorado. Now you lose your nerve, go riding back to Vegas with your tail between your legs, like some whipped pup." Maldonado stepped up to Maes nose to nose, chin to chin. "I said it before, you are a *cobarde.*"

"You calling me a coward again, *perro sarnoso?*" Maes glared back at Maldonado. "I let you slide before. That won't happen again."

"You talk, Pat," Maldonado said, scorn dripping from his voice. "You talk all the time but you don't do *nada.* I think *you* are the mangy dog."

With no warning, Maes punched Maldonado in the jaw. The man staggered back a couple of feet, shook his head, and smiled at Maes.

"You hit like a girl, Pat."

With a snarl, he charged Maes and grabbed him in a bear hug. The two wrestled for a moment, losing their balance and falling to the ground. John Dorsey, too weak to get up, turned over in his bedroll to watch the scuffle. "I been waiting to see this for a while," he said to Pony Dolan. "I thought they were just going to talk each other to death."

Dolan shrugged as the men rolled around on the ground, trading ineffectual blows, and he considered shooting both of them. Neither man was much of a brawler so there was little risk of their hurting each other. He decided he couldn't watch this poor excuse for a fight so he walked over to the fire and bent over to get another cup of coffee. His mind was made up. He was done with this outfit as soon as they got back to Las Vegas from running the stolen horses up to Colorado.

A little way inside the entrance to Compos Canyon, I directed old Rusty up into the trees on the southwest side of the canyon. I dismounted and motioned to the others to do the same. I tied Rusty to a low-hanging branch and drew my Winchester. Nathan was more adept with a pistol than I was and I figured he'd start out using it. Since I wasn't sure how close we might approach before the shooting started . . . and I was pretty confident the shooting would start . . . I decided I would be better off with my rifle.

I waved to Rusty . . . my cousin, not my horse . . . and pointed towards the right side of the canyon. He nodded and walked up the incline into the trees. I turned and saw Tom Figgs had seen my signal to Rusty and taken the cue. He picked his way carefully up the left side of the canyon. Nathan nodded to me and walked over to the right edge of the canyon where he was partially concealed by the trees. I did the same on the left side. On my signal, we began walking slowly toward the outlaws' hideout.

My senses were on high alert as we moved up the canyon. I smelled the strong scent of the pine trees and heard the birds chirping. I listened closely for the sound of Rusty or Tom stumbling on the rocks but so far, they were moving stealthily. It took us the better part of an hour to get close to the hideout, caution being more important than speed. The sun was directly overhead as we drew near.

The canyon made a gentle bend to the left. I was pretty certain the corrals were right around that bend. I was starting to feel that mishmash of fear and excitement that precedes a gun battle; my nerves were stretched taut. As a result, I nearly jumped out of my skin when I heard what sounded like a snarl and then loud voices cursing. I looked over at Nathan and he responded with a puzzled shrug. He motioned for us to move ahead and twirled his finger to signal that we should speed up our pace.

We walked rapidly up to the bend in the canyon and eased around the turn. The sight we beheld was baffling. Only fifty yards or so ahead of us, two of the outlaws were grappling in the dirt, engaged in a fistfight. A third man was seated on a log by the fire drinking coffee and ignoring the brawlers.

Behind him, a fourth man was lying in his bedroll propped up on one elbow. Again, I looked at Nathan. He nodded vigorously at me, which I took to mean it was time to announce our presence.

I walked rapidly forward and in a loud and what I hoped was a commanding voice, hollered, "It's the sheriff, put your hands up."

The two men who were fighting ignored my command. I don't know if that was because they couldn't hear me for all the noise they were making or if they were so intent on doing damage to each other that they didn't care. The man in the bedroll sat up and pulled a pistol from inside his bedroll. He was just starting to aim it when I heard a shot off to my right. I glanced over to see that Nathan had whipped out his pistol and shot the man where he lay.

Off to his right, the man who'd been drinking coffee disappeared behind a large rock nearby. I couldn't see him so I didn't know if he had drawn a weapon. This was a bit nerve-racking but there wasn't much I could do about it. I hoped that with the angle Rusty had from the canyon incline, he might be able to see the man and have a clear shot.

Belatedly, the two men who were fighting

seemed to become aware that there was a gun battle raging around them. One of them shoved the other off and staggered to his feet, drawing his pistol as he got up. He got off a wild shot and was about to let loose with another when Tom Figgs shot him twice from his vantage point on the left side of the canyon. By that time, the other man had risen and drawn his gun. He didn't get off a shot before Nathan gunned him down. The entire gunfight probably lasted less than a minute although it seemed longer. Gunsmoke hung in the air and the smell of gunpowder filled our nostrils.

We all turned to look for the fourth man hidden behind the rock. I crouched down, trying to make a smaller target as I aimed my Winchester at the rock. Like much of what happens in a gunfight, I hadn't been consciously aware of the sequence of events. It was just something that I did instinctively. Nothing happened for possibly ten seconds, although ten seconds seems endless when you don't know if someone is getting ready to come out blazing away at you with a pistol.

"I'm done." A voice carried strong and clear from behind the rock. "I'll come out with my hands in the air but I need to know y'all ain't gonna gun me down when I do."

We had just shot and killed three men in less than a minute. When I considered the brutality they'd perpetrated on the good people of Colfax County, I couldn't say I felt bad about it. In fact, I probably wouldn't have felt bad about killing the man behind the rock if he chose to come out shooting. The difference between us and them, though, was that we lived by rules. Shooting an unarmed man is murder. Doesn't matter if he deserves it.

"Come out real slow," I said, raising my voice a bit to make sure he heard me clearly. "You better have those hands raised high above your head. Any hint you're reachin' for your gun, you'll be a dead man."

Another moment passed and then the man stepped out from behind the rock. He did indeed have his arms extended almost straight up above his head. He walked very cautiously towards me.

"That's far enough," I said. Turning, I saw Nathan moving deliberately in his direction. "You got him covered, Nathan?"

"Yep," he answered.

"All right," I responded.

I turned to my right and hollered up to Rusty to come on down. I did the same on my left to Tom Figgs. They both half-walked, half-slid down their respective sides of the canyon and trotted over to where we stood. When they reached me, I turned and approached Nathan and our prisoner. He looked familiar.

"I know you," I said. "Seen your picture on a wanted poster. More than one."

He nodded. "In that case, I might as well tell you I'm Pony Dolan. You'll figure it out soon enough."

"Pony Dolan, huh," I said. "I thought you were makin' trouble in the Arizona Territory these days, runnin' with Curly Bill and them boys."

He grinned and shrugged. "I was out that way a while back. Things weren't goin' so well so I decided to come back to the New Mexico Territory."

I grinned back at him. "Looks like things ain't goin' that well for you here in the territory, either. You got a lot to answer for."

"Maybe I do," he replied in what struck me as an oddly confident manner for a man with four guns trained on him. "There's them that are a whole lot guiltier than me, though. For the right deal, I might be willin' to tell you all about 'em."

I'd forgotten we intended to capture at least one of the outlaws alive. That's a bit peculiar since I'm the one who needed at least one live witness from this lawless bunch to confirm that I hadn't accepted a bribe to look the other way.

"I won't promise you any deal," I said, "but you might avoid swingin' from a rope if you name names and fill in some gaps we have in our knowledge of who runs this outfit."

"I don't know if that's good enough," Dolan said in the same confident manner. "With the things I know, I ought to get more than just avoidin' a necktie party. I'm thinkin' I should get a pretty light jail term as well."

"That ain't likely," I said. I was bluffing at this point because I didn't have much say about what kind of deal he cut with the prosecuting attorney. "Maybe if we start your time in jail right away, you might reconsider after you've cooled your heels for a while."

"Tell you what," he said, as if he held a full house in a poker game, "let's both think on it while we ride back to Cimarrón." He smiled broadly. "I reckon that's where y'all are takin' me since there ain't much of a jail in Springer."

Clearly, he knew a considerable amount about the situation in Colfax County. That made me suspect that he was likely pretty well-informed about what had gone on behind the scenes and who was pulling what strings. I hoped with time and the right forms of persuasion, we might be able to pin this wave of murder and rustling where it belonged . . . on Felipe Alvarado and Jesus Abreu.

"Yes, sir," I said, "we'll be haulin' you back to Cimarrón." I turned to Rusty and said, "Get your catch twine and tie his hands behind his back." As an afterthought, I said, "Make sure you take off his gun belt first."

Rusty gave me a look of disapproval. "I ain't no idiot," he said haughtily. "I know to take his gun from him."

"Course you do," I said. "I'm just tryin' to be thorough."

Speaking of being thorough, Tom Figgs had alertly decided to check the other three outlaws to make sure they were no longer among the living. He apparently found no signs of life and walked over to me.

"They're all dead," he said in a matter-of-fact voice. If he was upset about this, it wasn't obvious.

"Thanks for takin' care of that *hombre* in the fancy vest," I said. "That was a tough shot with a pistol."

"I found a rock I could steady my hand on," he said. He hesitated. "When we were walkin' in, I was so scared I was shakin'. I was worried I wouldn't be able to hit the side of a mountain if I had to shoot." He shrugged. "It was strange. When it all went down, I didn't have time to think so I didn't have time to be scared."

"Lucky for me," I said. "Not everyone reacts like that. Some freeze right up. That fella had a pretty good bead on me. It coulda been sticky if you hadn't taken him down." I reached out and clapped him on the shoulder. "I owe you one."

"You don't owe me nothin', Tommy," he said. "After the way I doubted you, I ain't sure we're square yet." He turned and looked back at the dead men. "You want me and Rusty to start diggin' graves?"

I thought about it for a minute. "I don't think so. We're gonna have to take the bodies back to town so we can identify 'em. I want to confirm that they're part of that White Caps gang if I can." I paused to think about our situation. "We need to get them horses back to their rightful owner, too. Reckon you and Rusty are gonna have to make two trips."

"What am I gonna have to do?" Rusty had just walked up when I told Tom what I wanted him to do.

"We're gonna load them bodies up on

some horses and pack 'em into town," Tom told him. He pointed to the horses in the corral. "Then we got to come back and take this bunch to the livery in town. If there's anyone left alive at the Morgan place, I reckon they'll be glad to come get 'em back."

"Nathan and I will escort Mister Pony Dolan to his accommodations in Cimarrón," I said. "Maybe we'll be able to get to the bottom of this mess and find out who's behind all of it."

Rusty and Tom nodded and went over to start the grisly process of tying the bodies to their horses. I walked over to where Nathan was standing guard over Pony Dolan.

"Let's load up this filthy bugger and head back to town with him," I said to Nathan. "We'll have to get his horse." I looked at Dolan and asked, "Which one of them nags is yours?"

"That sorrel paint gelding over there," he said. "Been ridin' that horse for a bunch of years now."

I turned and hollered to Rusty to bring the paint over. Turning back to Nathan, I said, "We'll have to walk back to where we left the horses. Tie a lead rope to that paint. You hang on to that and lead the way. Once we get our mounts, Dolan can ride in the middle and I'll bring up the rear." I looked at Dolan. "I'll have my gun aimed right in the middle of your back, pard. You try any funny stuff and you won't live to make any deals."

Dolan nodded nonchalantly. He didn't seem intimidated by my threat. Rusty came up leading the gelding and Nathan tied a lead rope on the horse.

"You walk in front of me, Dolan," I said. "Keep in mind that I'm right behind you. You try to make a break for it, I'll put a bullet in you."

He smirked. "I already got the message, Sheriff; you don't have to keep tellin' me."

I walked a few feet behind him and Nathan brought up the rear leading Dolan's horse. It took a lot less time to cover the ground to the entrance of the canyon where our horses were tied. Of course, we weren't tippy-toeing on the way out like we had been coming in. When we got to the spot where we'd tied them, we found all four horses grazing and waiting patiently.

"Why don't you mount up first," I said to Nathan. "That way if this desperado decides to make a break for it, you can catch up with him and shoot him."

"I told you I ain't gonna run off," Dolan

said with an edge that reflected he was running short of patience with my dwelling on the possibility of shooting him. That was okay by me. It showed that he was getting the point.

"Good to know," I said. "We got a lot to talk about. I'd hate to shoot you before we had a chance to have a conversation."

I helped Dolan mount his horse, which was a bit tricky with his hands tied behind him. We got it done, though, and I handed Nathan the lead rope. Then I went over and untied Rusty and walked him over to take up the rear position in our little procession. Nathan was watching me and once I was situated, he headed back down the canyon trail. We hadn't gone very far when Dolan spoke up.

"I'm guessin' you want to know who the brains is behind this operation, right, Sheriff?"

Here we go. The dealin' begins. "I'd like to arrest everyone who was involved in all this murderin' and rustlin'," I replied. "How do I know you weren't the one who planned it all?"

Dolan laughed. "Reckon you don't . . . yet." He didn't speak for a moment, then he continued. "There's a real bad *hombre* behind all this, Sheriff. It ain't me. I'm just a hired hand. For the right deal, I can give you a name and offer proof that what I say is true."

Since I already figured Felipe Alvarado was the leader of the gang, I was pretty sure Pony Dolan was telling the truth when he said he wasn't the mastermind behind this scheme. I also thought it was likely he could identify Alvarado as the boss. He was probably right that the prosecutor would offer him some sort of bargain in exchange for testifying against Alvarado if all of this came to trial. The other thing I was interested in, though, was whether or not there was someone else involved in planning this lawlessness. In particular, I was hoping he might identify Jesus Abreu as a cohort.

"Maybe you can do that," I said nonchalantly. "Course, maybe we got enough proof to put away your boss without your testimony. Why should we make a deal with you?"

Dolan laughed. "I don't think you got that kind of proof, Sheriff. Even if you do, though, there's some other stuff you got to be curious about. I got the answers you need to wrap this whole thing up and put a nice bow on."

I had no real authority to make any kind of pact and Dolan had been around long enough to know that. I didn't see any point in continuing the conversation when it was clear to me that he was just planting seeds to strengthen his position. In fact, he was probably right that the prosecutor would cut him a nice deal with no hanging and a reduced jail term. As badly as I wanted the men at the top, that didn't go down easy with me.

"I'm tired of listenin' to you yap," I said. "I'm ready to get back to town and stick you in jail."

Dolan shrugged. "Won't be the first time I been in jail," he said. "With all I know, though, it might be the last."

I didn't bother to respond. I kept my eye on Dolan but part of my mind began pondering the next steps in trying to get the goods on Alvarado and Abreu. Out of the blue, Nathan stopped in his tracks. He sat up in the saddle, his body taut and alert as he scanned the sides of the canyon. I noticed that his hand drifted down beside his pistol.

"What is it?" I kept my voice low. "You see somebody?"

"Don't know," he said in a terse tone. "I heard somethin'."

No sooner had those words came out of his mouth than pandemonium ensued. I heard a series of shots fired, most likely a rifle from the sound. The first shot or two took Pony Dolan clean out of the saddle. Up ahead, Nathan had drawn his pistol and was looking around rapidly. Within seconds, he located the source of the shots and fired off several of his own.

I decided I'd present less of a target if I dismounted. I hopped off Rusty and moved around on the opposite side of where the shots seemed to be coming from. I hated to use my horse for cover but that's what the situation called for so that's what I did. I drew my pistol as I jumped off and came up shooting in the direction I thought the bushwhacker was hidden. I fired three times and stopped. Since I couldn't see my target, I didn't want to waste my ammunition.

I looked over at Nathan, who was still in the saddle firing up the side of the canyon. I wondered if he had a bead on the bad guy. Wherever he was hiding, he continued to rain bullets down on us. All of a sudden, Nathan lurched in his saddle. He slowly lowered his hand that held his pistol. It seemed to me that he had a confused expression on his face. Very gradually, he slumped over and almost casually toppled out of his saddle.

I dropped Rusty's reins and ran to his side. I stayed low in order to make a smaller target, but I wasn't thinking about getting shot. All I could think of was that this man who was my hero had been shot out of the saddle. I had no idea if he was alive or dead. I reached his side and crouched down beside him. His eyes were open and he was looking at me.

In a weak but resolute voice, he said, "Get behind cover, Tommy. He's got a rifle."

I didn't care. I could see the wound in his chest and it was leaking blood at an alarming rate. I pulled off my wild rag and placed it firmly on the opening. Nathan winced as I did it but it seemed to me that the blood flow slowed a bit. It took a moment for me to become aware that no more shots were being fired. My ears still rang from the fusillade.

Nathan raised his head a tiny bit and looked around. "Dolan?"

He didn't have enough strength to put all the words to the question together but I got his meaning. I didn't want to take any pressure off his wound but I needed to know if Pony Dolan was still alive.

"I'll be right back," I said. "Hang on."

I jumped up and scooted over to where the outlaw lay. Before I even checked his pulse, I knew he was no longer among the living. There was a bullet hole right smack in the middle of his chest. Someone was either awful lucky or a hell of a good shot. Clearly, there was nothing I could do for the man. So much for our star witness. I had more important things on my mind, though. I hurried back to Nathan's side and resumed my attempt to staunch the bleeding.

This was a terrible mess. I didn't want to leave Nathan unattended but I knew I would need Rusty and Tom to help me out. I was thinking about how to strap a belt around my wild rag to keep pressure on the wound when I heard the sound of hoofbeats approaching. I glanced back up the canyon and saw my compadres come flying around the bend. They galloped up and dismounted with guns drawn.

"What happened?" Rusty fairly screamed at me.

"We got ambushed," I said. "The lowdown back-shootin' son of a whore that did it took off a few minutes ago, I think." I nodded back over my shoulder. "He was in the trees up yonder. How 'bout y'all takin' a hike up there and makin' sure he ain't reloadin'."

Rusty looked at Nathan's motionless body with horror. "Is he gonna make it?"

I was losing patience with my cousin and my efforts to remain calm vanished. "If you don't get up the hill and make sure that gunman ain't there anymore, none of us is gonna make it!"

For a second, I thought he was going to argue with me. Instead, he nodded, drew his pistol, and headed up the side of the canyon. I turned my attention back to trying to contain the bleeding from Nathan's wound. When I did, I saw the smallest hint of a grin on his lips.

"A little rough on him, weren't you? You know he means well." His voice was weak and I could barely hear him. Still, I figured if he was cracking jokes, there was hope.

"He's kinda like his namesake, my horse," I said with a snicker. "Sometimes you just got to get his attention." I turned serious. "Hang in there, pard. As soon as we know the coast is clear, we'll get you loaded up and back to town where the doc can fix you up."

Unfortunately, I'd had more experience than I would have preferred with transporting a critically wounded man from the wilderness back to town. It was only a few months ago that we'd had to do the same thing with Tomás Marés's father, Miguel. Thinking about that caused a chill to run down my spine. It hadn't turned out well.

In a couple of minutes, Tom and Rusty

returned. “Nobody up there,” Tom said. “There was a bunch of shell casings, though. I didn’t look too close at ’em but I’d guess they were likely from a Winchester.” Tom looked down at Nathan and then back at me. “Do you want us to follow his tracks?”

His question put me in a dilemma. Now that I’d had a moment to think about what had happened, I figured it was no coincidence the first man killed had been Pony Dolan. To me, that meant the likeliest choices for our shooter were either Felipe Alvarado or Jesus Abreu. They had the most to lose if the man started spilling his guts. I leaned towards it being Alvarado. He struck me as the more bloodthirsty of the two. Anyway, based on Abreu’s poor performance in what I was pretty sure was his attempt to ambush Rusty a short while ago, I couldn’t see him making the kind of difficult shot it had taken to hit Dolan right square in the heart.

“I hate to let him go,” I said, “but we got to get Nathan back to Cimarrón pronto.” I didn’t add that if we didn’t, he’d likely die. Hell, he’d most likely die, anyway. “It’s gonna take all three of us to get him and Dolan back to town.”

“We’re takin’ Dolan’s body back?” Rusty frowned.

"I think we better," I said. "We may have some explainin' to do to higher authorities about what happened out here. We'd better have some proof that we tangled with the outlaws."

"You don't think that preenin' little rooster Salazar would question us, do you?" Rusty seemed to be on the edge of losing his composure completely. It reminded me of the high regard he held for Nathan Averill.

"No need to go off on the mayor, cousin," I said gently. "I'm just tryin' to be careful is all." I cast my eyes around. "We better start lookin' for some suitable poles for a travois. We got to get a move on if Nathan is to have any chance."

"What about the others?" Tom probably already knew the answer to his question. I think he just wanted to be thorough . . . and have me make the decision.

"We'll leave 'em where they lay until we get Nathan back," I said. "I'm afraid you boys'll have to make a couple of trips out here tomorrow to collect them and the horses. I know it's a pain but there ain't no gettin' around it."

"Fair enough," Tom said. He turned and walked over toward the side of the canyon where he had spied a straight piñon pole that could be used to make a travois.

While he did that, Rusty set about getting the body of Pony Dolan flung over the saddle of his horse and tied on so he wouldn't slide off. I'd been watching Nathan's face close so I wasn't sure how Rusty got the man on the horse all by himself. Dolan wasn't a big fella but he was most certainly dead weight in every sense of the word. Somehow, he got the job done.

Once Tom had put the travois together, we moved Nathan onto it. We tried to be as gentle as we could but he still groaned in pain when we lifted him up and put him down on the blanket that was stretched between the two poles.

Rusty looked over at Tom Figgs and said, "You lead Dolan's horse and mine, too."

"What are you talkin' about?" I wasn't sure what my cousin had in mind.

"Draggin' him behind a horse over this rough ground is gonna be too rough," he said. "I'll take ahold of the other end, smooth out the ride."

"It's an awful long way back to town, cousin," I said. "You sure you're up for the task?"

Rusty locked gazes with me for a moment. I waited but he didn't say anything. Then he turned and went to the back of the stretcher. He picked it up and waited. I shrugged and mounted up. Tom did the same, grabbed the reins of the two horses, and we headed down out of the canyon. My heart was in my throat the whole way.

CHAPTER 38

It's been two days and nothing has changed. Nathan was still breathing when we got him to Cimarrón but he'd been out cold from the time we loaded him on the stretcher. Rusty had carried the end of the stretcher the whole way, stopping to rest only when I insisted on it. I don't know how he did it. I reckon it was a measure of the respect he had for the man. I don't think I could have managed it.

It was early in the evening when we arrived at Doc Adams's place. He took one look at Nathan and told us to get him inside. We carried him in and transferred him as gently as we could to the bed in Doc's examining room. He groaned once but didn't wake up. Doc shooed us out of the room while he examined him.

When he came out a few minutes later, his face was grim. He said it was a miracle he was alive, seeing how much blood he'd lost. He said all he could do at this point was keep the wound clean to guard against infection and hope Nathan had the strength to recover. He didn't say it out loud but it sounded to me like he didn't think the odds were any too good.

Once Doc had given us his bleak report, I sent Rusty and Tom out to inform folks of what had happened. Tom rode out to let the Delaneys know. Rusty went over to tell Tomás and Maria. Immediately after that, and upon my instructions, he went to the telegraph office and had Ben Martinez sent a telegram to Mayor Salazar letting him know what had transpired. I knew that would serve a dual purpose. Mayor Salazar would get the news and right after that, Ben would make sure everyone in the village of Cimarrón would find out the tragic occurrence that had befallen their former sheriff.

As soon as Tom and Rusty left my office, I left to head over to the rooms behind the schoolhouse that Nathan Averill shared with his wife. It was all I could do to keep myself from seeking out my Mollie and getting lost in her arms. I couldn't waste any time, though, because I knew Ben would spread the word swiftly. I didn't want Miss Christy to hear it from anyone other than me.

I can't recall a time when I dreaded sharing terrible news more. I couldn't believe so much had happened in the course of one day. I thought back to the schoolyard earlier in the day when Miss Christy got upset with Nathan. I hated to think the last words that passed between them might have been harsh ones. I also feared she would blame me. The only reason Nathan came out of retirement was that he saw I was in way over my head as sheriff. He could have stayed out of it and let me flounder along as best I could but he didn't. As a result, he was lying in a bed barely clinging to life.

I underestimated this fine woman. She spent not a single moment on recriminations, instead asking me for Doc's report. I had very little information to share with her and almost immediately, she left to go over to Doc's to wait by Nathan's side. I was relieved that she didn't blame me but nevertheless, I felt like it was my fault.

The next morning, Eleanor Delaney came into town with her two young children in tow. She reported that Jared was still up in Colorado on a cattle drive and she expected him home in a few days. Tom's wife, Annie, volunteered to watch over the Delaney children so Eleanor could join Miss Christy in her vigil. I knew from things Tomás had told me in the past that when Eleanor lost her parents as a young lady, Nathan had stepped in and filled the role of a second father. I knew the loss would hit her hard if he didn't make it. I didn't even want to think about Jared's reaction.

Tomás and Maria alternated back and forth between the café and Doc's office, spelling Eleanor so she could take a break and eat a bite. Christy refused to leave Nathan's side so Tomás brought food over to her. He also served as a buffer between Doc and the citizens of the village, most of whom were extremely curious about how Nathan was doing. I lost count of how many times he passed along the news that there was *no* news.

Late in the afternoon the next day after we brought Nathan in, Mayor Salazar showed up. He had ridden all day to get to Cimarrón from Springer and was exhausted. In spite of that, he rushed immediately to Nathan's side, brushing off my attempts to fill him in on what had taken place in Compos Canyon. All he said was that I could tell him later. I have to say, my respect for the man went up a couple of notches when I saw how dedicated he was to his former mentor. I don't know how long he stayed at Nathan's bedside or even where he slept when he finally left Doc's office for the night.

Now, like I said, it's been two days and nothing has changed with Nathan's condition. In the meantime, I've had very little conversation with my wife. Other than falling into an exhausted but restless sleep by her side the past two nights, there hasn't been much opportunity to talk. Truth be told, I've been willing to put off the discussion I know we need to have about my plan to accompany Rusty back to Texas. Until I know whether or not Nathan is going to make it, I just don't have the wherewithal to take on any more challenges.

I accompanied Rusty and Tom back out to Compos Canyon where we loaded up the bodies of the three outlaws and rounded up the horses to return them to their rightful owner. Sure enough, once we got the bodies back to Cimarrón, I was able to identify them from the wanted posters Todd Little had sent me from down Las Vegas way. They were Pat Maes, Manuel Maldonado, and John Dorsey, all suspected members of the White Caps gang. A fourth man on the poster, Rafael Espinosa, hadn't been at the hideaway.

I sent Sheriff Little a telegram telling him what had happened. He responded with a telegram asking if I expected to make other arrests any time soon. We both knew he was referring to Felipe Alvarado. I responded that I needed more information before I could make any more arrests.

Mayor Salazar approached me just as I was leaving Ben Martinez's office. As he walked up the boardwalk, I noticed he lacked that cocky spring in his step I was accustomed to seeing.

"Howdy, Mayor," I said, keeping my voice neutral. "How's Nathan?" I didn't know what kind of reaction to expect and I didn't want a confrontation. My fears were unfounded.

"Good morning, Sheriff Stallings," he said. He had dark circles under his eyes and appeared to be worn out. "Nothing has changed since last night. Sheriff Averill is still hanging on by a thread." He paused for a moment and I could have sworn he choked up a bit. When he continued, I could see the sorrow in his eyes. "It does not look good."

"I'm afraid you're right, Mayor." I tried to think of something else meaningful to say but couldn't.

He stared at me for a moment and then motioned to a wooden bench over to the side of the telegraph office porch. "Can we talk?"

I had no idea what to expect but there didn't seem to be any point to putting off the conversation any longer. "Yes, sir," I said, "we prob'ly need to. Are you sure you don't want to go back to my office?"

"No," he said, "I would prefer sitting out here in the fresh air if you don't mind. It has been a long night."

Once we were seated, he turned to me and said, "Perhaps you could fill me in on what happened in the canyon. Take your time. I will not interrupt."

I filled him in as best I could, giving him the bad news that we'd failed to get any solid information out of Pony Dolan before he was killed. I could see he wanted to ask more about this but he kept his word and didn't speak until I'd told the entire tale. I brought him up to the time when the shooting stopped and Rusty and Tom arrived on the scene.

"I want you to know it was my decision alone not to try to follow the man who did the shootin'." If he disagreed with my call, I didn't want Rusty or Tom Figgs getting any blowback. "Right or wrong, I decided tryin' to get Nathan back to town alive was more important than chasin' that damn bushwhacker."

He waved his hand in dismissal. "That is

exactly what I would have wanted you to do, Sheriff. You have no need to be concerned that I question your judgment."

I was a little surprised. "I appreciate that, Mayor. I hated to let the son of a bitch get away but lookin' after Nathan first just seemed to be the right thing to do."

"I agree," he said. He sat back for a moment, his brow furrowed. "So this Dolan *cabrón* gave you no hint about who was in charge?"

"No," I replied. "He played his cards pretty close. He was hopin' to cut a deal with the prosecutor. Reckon that ain't gonna happen now." I shook my head. "One thing for sure though, he was clear that there was a boss and it wasn't him."

"Did he say anything about there being more than one man in charge?" Mayor Salazar held his breath and waited for my answer.

"I'm afraid not, Mayor," I said. "We all got our suspicions about that, I know, but he didn't say nothin' about it one way or the other."

The mayor cursed softly in Spanish under his breath. "I was hoping we would get information that might lead to an arrest of these filthy murderers." He cursed again, this time out loud. "I know that *pendejo*

Jesus Abreu is a part of this. I will prove that and see that he is brought to justice."

"For what it's worth, Mayor, I think you're right about Abreu bein' in this up to his ears. Him and Felipe Alvarado down in Las Vegas. I'd like to see 'em both brought to justice." I paused for a moment, unsure of what to say next. This was rocky territory I was about to tread upon. Finally, I just busted on ahead. "I'd like to help with that, Mayor, but there's some complications."

Before I could go any further, he nodded vigorously. "If you are referring to the charges that you accepted a bribe, Sheriff, you need not worry." He took a deep breath. "I have had a chance to reflect on all of that. What I have concluded is that if Nathan Averill believed you did nothing wrong, that is good enough for me. Those charges will be dismissed as soon as I get back to my office."

"That's a relief, Mayor," I said. It was, too. With the only witness who might have cleared me dead from the ambush, I'd been a bit worried I wouldn't be able to prove my innocence. "There's more to it than that, though." Again, there was no way to sugarcoat what I had to tell him. "The thing is, I'm gonna have to resign as sheriff."

Salazar looked at me as if I were speaking

in an unfamiliar tongue. "What do you mean, Sheriff? I just told you that you were cleared of any allegations of wrongdoing."

"I know it, Mayor, and I sure do appreciate it. But that don't change the fact I'm gonna have to quit the job."

"I do not understand," he said, his confusion apparent. "We are not done with this. The head of the snake is still out there. If we do not kill it, it will grow another body." He slammed his hand down on the seat of the bench. "If Nathan Averill dies, his death must be avenged. You must be a part of that."

I understood his need for vengeance and his passion for justice. Nathan Averill was like family to him. But Rusty Stallings wasn't *like* family to me, he *was* my family. Of all the things that are important in this world, nothing is more important to me than family. I didn't know if Mayor Salazar would appreciate and value that but it didn't really matter. I knew in my heart what I had to do.

"Mayor, I got a family matter that's gonna take me away from the New Mexico Territory for a spell. It ain't nothin' I can shirk and it ain't up for discussion. I'm not askin' your permission, I'm informin' you of my decision."

"But who will serve in your place?" Mayor Salazar sputtered, clearly indignant at the manner in which I had shared this information with him.

"I don't know, sir," I said. I kept my tone respectful. I've gradually changed my opinion of this man and I knew I was putting him in a tough spot. "The thing is, that ain't my problem. If I had a good answer for you, I'd give it but the fact is, I don't."

"Would Tomás Marés take the office back?" I could see why he might think that but I knew Tomás would not be interested.

"I kinda doubt it, Mayor, but you'd have to ask him yourself," I said. As bad as I felt about letting the mayor down, I figured I'd said my piece about the topic. Now I wanted to check on Nathan and then speak with my wife. "I wish you the best, sir. I believe you want to do what's right. I think, in the long run, you'll get it done."

I got up and started to walk in the direction of Doc Adams's office. Mayor Salazar stood up as if to follow and perhaps protest further. We both heard a noise and looked up the street to see Tomás Marés walking in our direction. The sound we'd heard was his weeping. I ran to his side. I wasn't able to ask the question out loud but he answered the question he saw in my eyes.

"He's gone."

Chapter 39

"You're doing what?"

The thing that struck me was that there was no outraged or indignant tone in Mollie's voice. It was more like she wasn't sure she'd heard me correctly and needed clarification.

"I'm goin' to Texas with Rusty." I said the words slowly and plainly to make sure she understood. Well, maybe "understand" is the wrong word. I didn't know if she would understand what I was doing or why.

"And why would you be doin' such a thing?"

Again, I was surprised by the lack of emotion in Mollie's voice. I'd anticipated an angry outburst and had steeled myself for it. I wasn't prepared for this matter-of-fact reaction.

"Rusty's folks . . . my aunt and uncle . . . have been gettin' harassed by some thievin' sidewinders. Stealin' stock, foulin' their wells, things like that," I replied. "They ain't even sure why they're doin' all this. It ain't just them, either. Their neighbors have been dealt the same kind of treatment."

She gave me a suspicious look. "How long have you known about this?"

"I've known about it for a while." I was having trouble meeting her gaze.

"And you couldn't see your way clear to tell me?"

I could hear an undercurrent of hurt and anger in her voice now. In some ways, it was reassuring. "I could give you all kinds of reasons for why I didn't tell you, Mollie. I was confused, I was desperate for you to be with me, I was afraid you wouldn't understand."

"Well, you'd be right," she said. "I don't understand how you could ask me to move with you to Springer when you intended to follow your cousin to Texas once you got these outlaws rounded up."

"I told you I had my reasons," I said. "That doesn't make what I did right."

"No," she said in a quiet voice, "it doesn't."

I took a deep breath. "You know how I always make a big deal out of havin' people call me Tom 'cause it's a grown-up name? I reckon that I've had it all wrong. Your name ain't what makes you a grown-up, it's how you act, how you treat people. Not tellin' you what I had in mind was wrong. It was flat-out wrong."

"Yes, it was," she said.

"Mollie, I know I still got a lot of growin' up to do. I make mistakes and this one was a big one." My voice caught and it took me a minute to regain my composure. "But I love you more than life itself. I'm so sorry that I hurt you. If you never want to see me again, I'll try to understand but I wish you would give me another chance."

She looked at me for a long moment. "I know you're not perfect, Tommy. Neither am I. I'll do my best to forgive you but it may take some time for me to trust you again."

I felt a surge of relief. "I know that, Mollie. I'll just have to earn that trust back."

"Does this mean you won't be goin' to Texas?"

It felt like my heart dropped into my stomach. "Mollie, that's somethin' I got to do. I intend to come back to you as soon as I can but I've got to go."

"Rusty and his folks need your help so you're gonna drop everything and go gallivantin' off to Texas," she said.

"Rusty and his folks are family, Mollie.

They need my help," I said. "And I ain't 'gallivantin'.' You make it sound like I'm goin' on a holiday."

"I know it's no holiday, Tommy," she said in a tired voice. "I know they're your family, too." I could see tears beginning to form and pool up in her eyes. "Am I not your family?" One teardrop traced a path down her cheek. She brushed it away quickly.

"How can you ask me that, Mollie? Of course you are!" In spite of myself, I responded with a passion that was out of line with her question. It was a fair question. I had no right to be angry with her for asking it. I tried to calm down. "You're my wife, I love you. You'll always be my family. I'll write to you every day. When we get this business taken care of, I'll come back to you and we'll build a better life than we've had."

"Sure and we will," she said, her tone skeptical. "That is, if you don't get yourself killed by some Texas outlaw. Or worse yet, find some Texas floozy and take up with her."

My jaw dropped. "Texas floozy?" I was dumbfounded. "You think I'm goin' to Texas so I can take up with some other woman?"

"It could happen," she responded in a

small voice. She sounded like a little girl.

"Oh, Mollie, that'll never happen in a hundred years." I reached out and took her in my arms. She resisted briefly, then folded herself into me, clinging ferociously. She sobbed. I held her. It went on for a time and slowly subsided. I heard her sniff, then she gently pulled back and studied my face.

"No floozies. You've got to promise me that." I almost laughed but she seemed so serious, I figured that would be a big mistake.

"You've got my word," I said. "No floozies. I won't look at any other women while I'm there. Well, maybe my aunt but it won't be *that* kind of lookin'."

She smiled. "You can look at your auntie all you wish, you eejit. I ain't that unreasonable."

I smiled back at her. "Of course not," I said. "You're never unreasonable."

She burst into laughter at that. So did I. I held her hands and we laughed. Finally, I asked, "So this is all right with you?"

She shook her head vigorously. "No, it's *not* all right with me, Tommy Stallings. I hate it. I'll miss you every day." She shrugged. "But it's what you need to do. Rusty stayed here and risked his life helping you out when you needed him. He's family.

You go do the same for him."

I have to confess I got a bit choked up. When I could finally speak, I said, "It ain't just that Rusty helped me out, Mollie. My aunt and uncle took me in after my folks and sister got killed. They were kind to me." I stopped for a moment, overcome by the memories that came flooding back. "I repaid their kindness with anger and resentment. None of it belonged to them. I got to make amends. They deserved better."

"And better is what they'll get," she said. "You're a good man, Tommy. They'll be proud to know you and proud of what you've become."

"I hope so," I said. "I try to do what's right."

A worried look passed over her face. "What about Nathan? The filthy devil who shot him is still out there."

"I know it. Part of me feels like I need to stay here and track the bastard down. But I can't be two places at once." My head drooped. "Someone else will have to do it."

"I suppose you're right," she said. "Nathan didn't deserve to have it end this way." She squeezed my hands. "Neither did Miss Christy. Someone needs to avenge his death for both their sakes."

"I can only think of one man who could

do it," I said, "and I don't know if he's willin' to pay the price it would cost."

For a moment, she appeared puzzled but then a look of understanding appeared on her face. "Jared Delaney."

"That's the way I see it," I replied. "He doesn't know yet what happened. I don't know how he'll react." I let go of her hands and stepped back. "I don't reckon I'll have a chance to find out. I told Rusty we could leave at first light in the mornin'."

There was a sad smile on her face. She said, "You tell that Rusty Stallings if he lets you get killed in Texas, I'll be comin' after him with a shotgun." She chuckled. "You can tell him I love him, too. Tell him he's my family as well."

"I'll tell him. That'll mean the world to him," I said. I looked around our little house. I wasn't sure when I would see it again after tomorrow morning. I turned back to Mollie. "I'll talk to Bill Wallace before I go, tell him you're gonna stay here until I get back from Texas. I don't think he'll like it, but I guarantee he'll go along with it. He owes me."

"Thank you," she said. "It'll be hard enough with you goin' off to Texas without me havin' to give up me home as well."

She came over and embraced me, gently

this time, resting her head on my shoulder. We stood that way for a long time. Finally, I pulled away.

"Well, Mrs. Stallings, I need to pack up some things. Once I'm done, we should make the most of the time we have remainin'." I wiggled my eyebrows at her to make sure she understood my meaning.

She gave me a sharp look. "You silly gobshite, you make it sound like we'll never see each other again."

Gobshite? I'm leaving for Texas and my wife calls me a gobshite. The Irish are so romantic. "I'll miss you, Mollie."

RIP Sheriff Nathan Averill
May 9, 1829–October 12, 1886

ABOUT THE AUTHOR

Jim Jones is the author of four novels set in northern New Mexico in the late 1800s: *The Big Empty* and the Jared Delaney series, which includes *Rustler's Moon, Colorado Moon,* and *Waning Moon.* He was the Western Music Association 2014 Male Performer of the Year and performs across the Western United States. He sings songs about the West . . . cowboys, horses, cattle rustlers, and the coming of the train, as well as songs about the people and the land, the beauty of the Western sky, and small-town America. His most recent album, "Headin' Home," released in January of 2018, has met with critical and popular acclaim. He lives in Albuquerque, New Mexico. Visit his website at www.jimjoneswestern.com.

The employees of Thorndike Press hope you have enjoyed this Large Print book. All our Thorndike, Wheeler, and Kennebec Large Print titles are designed for easy reading, and all our books are made to last. Other Thorndike Press Large Print books are available at your library, through selected bookstores, or directly from us.

For information about titles, please call:

(800) 223-1244

or visit our Web site at:

http://gale.com/thorndike

To share your comments, please write:

Publisher
Thorndike Press
10 Water St., Suite 310
Waterville, ME 04901